The Eyes of Destiny
The Chasm

By S. Roach Seymour

Dedication

This book is for my children, Sydney, SaNia & Sheldon. I hope they recognize that you can always achieve your goals, no matter how long it takes.

This book is also for every young woman who feels like her dream has been deferred. Time is a social construct. Remember it will happen when it's supposed to happen.

Acknowledgment

To God:

Thank you.

To My Parents:

Thank you for instilling the confidence in me needed to not just survive but to succeed. Thank you for exposing hard truths about life to prepare me to be my own person in this world.

To My Household:

Thank you for the space to create and the conversations to help me get through my writer's block, but especially to my husband who always wants me to succeed.

To My Family and Friends:

Who have always believed in my craft – Thank you! Your encouragement is priceless.

Prologue

The sound of his heartbeat echoed in his ears. It was like a base drum, reverberating throughout his entity. The moment felt surreal yet familiar. Jasiah found himself at the wrong end of a gun—again. The dark barrel instantly sent him into a state of shock, confusion, regret, and pain as the night air kicked up dry leaves around them. But this time, he knew he couldn't remain silent. He couldn't just freeze.

As Jasiah peered into his girlfriend's hazel eyes, brimming with fear and anger, he felt his chest tightening. Fighting against his own fear, he decided to find his voice quickly as he knew it wasn't just his life at stake.

He quickly rationalized that whatever he did or said, his actions wouldn't be enough. He couldn't go back in time, just by ten minutes, and chose to just get in his car and leave instead of savoring in last-minute kisses from his girlfriend. He never had any intentions of taking heed of his mother's warnings about staying out in the city. He was only equipped to hand over one of his most prized possessions.

Stepping away from his Chevy Caprice on the dimly lit street, Jasiah yelled, "Here!" as he threw his car keys at the gunman.

Chapter 1: Strictly Business

Hypnotized by the alluring beauty of her eyes, Jasiah couldn't resist the urge to call out to her.

"Aye, girl!" he shouted from the window of his dark-tinted Bubble Chevy Caprice.

Startled, Destiny looked over her shoulder but realized his catcalling couldn't be aimed at her. Her mind swiveled with the thought of why someone like him would call her. He looked like a drug dealer from his car to his haircut and the herringbone gold chain dangling around his neck. Her intuition sparked, and she knew it would be a bad idea to engage.

Striding down the street, she crossed New Jersey Avenue, her eyes sunk into the cracks of the street, her mind lost in the fog of thoughts – suddenly, she felt a strong grip on her shoulder. She quickly twisted the wrist attached to the hand holding her shoulder. Her self-defense classes were paying off. As she turned back, she came face to face with the man from the car.

"God damn, girl," Jasiah grunted, stunned by her actions.

As her eyes lay on his face, she loosened her grip and backed away.

"Sorry," Destiny mumbled as she averted her eyes towards the bus arriving at a distance.

Jasiah massaged his wrist, needles of pain piercing through it. His pain soothed as he gazed into Destiny's hazel eyes, sparkling under the warmth of sunlight.

Destiny glanced at him. A large diamond earring, sparkling; a chain with an oversized diamond medallion was the cherry on top of his Solbiato shirt and baggy jeans. In one glance, she captured the entirety of Jasiah – to her, he was a carbon copy of the corner boys and her older brothers.

She imagined her boyfriend, Eric, beside this stranger. Eric, barely 5'10", stocky in frame with shoulder-length braids, was drastically different from the tall, muscular figure standing before her. But the thought that someone like Jasiah was interested in her flattered her.

"I'm Jasiah," Jasiah introduced himself with a smile etched on his face.

"Destiny," she replied.

"I can give you a ride if you want," Jasiah offered hastily.

"Thanks, but I'm good," Destiny declined, "Plus, I'm not what you want," she concluded for him as she looked down at her baggy Levi's 501s and an oversized Warner Brothers embroidered T-shirt.

"You gonna try to tell me what I want after I ran across the street to get assaulted by you, and I'm still standing here?" Jasiah laughed. "I always know what I want."

Destiny bit her bottom lip. It was something she did when she was lost in the plane of thoughts. But to Jasiah, it was sexy, blooming the flowers of hope in his heart.

"I have a boyfriend," Destiny informed him as she turned to enter the Metro bus once it pulled up.

"I didn't ask you all that, beautiful," Jasiah responded. Lost in the realms of his own determination, he boarded the bus behind Destiny before he knew it.

"I want your number," Jasiah declared.

Destiny turned back around, surprised to see Jasiah behind her, her hazel eyes widening.

"Token!" the bus driver yelled.

"Boy, you better get off this bus," Destiny laughed.

"You, pay or exit," the bus driver blared.

"Pipe down," Jasiah dismissed the bus driver's demands as he continued to look at Destiny. "Girl, give me your number."

"I have a boyfriend," Destiny repeated.

"Fuck him."

"Now, is that the kind of girlfriend you want me to be to you?" Destiny asked with her head tilted to the side and her hand on her hip.

Jasiah laughed. Not because it was funny but because he was entertained by her spunk. "I'll see you around, Destiny," he concluded before exiting the bus from the rear door.

****

Jasiah was contemplating how he could pick up his little cousin, Lafayette, from school the next day to avail himself of another chance to see Destiny.

Lafayette had attested to the fact that Destiny was pretty, but she was still in her tomboy phase – which was a turn-off to him. Her style and demeanor pushed one to use their imagination as if her beauty was dependent on it, and Lafayette couldn't believe his cousin wanted to pursue her.

"When we get to the crib, just figure out how you gonna get me her number," Jasiah instructed his little cousin, his eyes focused on the road.

"What, Nigga?!" Lafayette could only imagine how many phone calls he would have to make to get her number.

As a last-ditch effort to avoid the task, Lafayette started to explain to Jasiah about Destiny's family. "Teachers swear her older brothers and cousins ruined so many lives in the late '80s and early '90s. They were known throughout Dunbar as pushers. You don't want to get caught up in that."

"La, stop the bullshit and get the number," was Jasiah's response, his gaze piercing through Lafayette.

Eventually, Lafayette figured out a way to get Destiny's number. Instead of the barriers he had anticipated, he got lucky, as getting her private line number only took three calls.

"See, I knew you were resourceful," Jasiah commended his cousin as he stared at the number on a post-it while he twirled in his desk chair.

***

Destiny was seated at her stationary desk chair when the telephone rang. "It's about time you called," Destiny beamed into her cordless phone as she left her computer's keyboard and flopped down on her bed.

"Oh? You been waiting?" The voice on the other line questioned, shocking Destiny. The voice, the accent – it was familiar to her, but she couldn't immediately place the gentleman's voice.

"Who is this?" Destiny questioned quickly, realizing her error.

"Jasiah," he answered plainly. He was nervous and didn't want to play many games on the phone, unwilling to take the risk of her hanging up on him and, even worse, blocking his number.

"How did you get my number?" Destiny grilled as she figured quickly that this would be a short conversation.

"A little determination will get you anything you want in life," Jasiah stated, his voice wavering but reflecting confidence.

Quietness took over Destiny as she bit her bottom lip, trying to figure out how not to be rude.

"You still there?" Jasiah whispered amusingly.

"I'm here," Destiny admitted.

"Evidently, you were waiting for someone else to call," Jasiah tried to figure out some small talk, though he was drawing a blank on what to talk about.

"Evidently," Destiny traced her initials on her desk. "Who gave you my number?"

"I'm resourceful," Jasiah answered.

"I already told you. I'm not what you want," Destiny sighed. "I'm not that type of girl."

"Are you really trying to tell me I'm not what you want?" Jasiah questioned.

"I didn't say that," Destiny quickly responded but regretted it as uncertainty plagued her mind. "I told you I have a boyfriend."

"I'm not trying to get to know him. I'm trying to get to know you," Jasiah affirmed.

Caught by surprise, Destiny blushed and giggled.

"Why would you think I wouldn't want to get to know you?" he questioned.

"You ever heard of the Peay family?" Destiny deflected.

"Naw," Jasiah replied, even though his cousin had briefly warned him about her family's reputation earlier.

Destiny was surprised. Most people in the area knew one of her family members – especially a cousin or uncle since they were scattered around the city.

"Where are you from?" she questioned.

"I'm from uptown."

"Can't be," Destiny shook her head as if he could see her. "Everybody from uptown knows a Peay," she stated. "What school did you go to?"

"I'm telling the truth. I'm from uptown. I know you know my cousin Lafayette," Jasiah replied in haste as if he were in the interrogation room with Destiny asking the questions.

"That means nothing," Destiny retorted. "Are you still in school?" she asked, trying to gauge how old Jasiah was.

"I go to Sidwell Friends," Jasiah answered.

Destiny laughed, thinking he must be a dropout from Wilson who is trying to perpetrate and impress her.

"What's so funny?" Jasiah asked, confused by Destiny's sudden laughter.

"So, your drug dealer-looking ass went to school with Chelsea Clinton?" Destiny blurted out, "You know the president's daughter?" sarcasm oozing out each word.

"I do," Jasiah answered honestly. "And what about me says that I'm a drug dealer?"

"The chain, the car... *you*," Destiny tapped her fingers on her desk as she became irritated. "I can't play these games with you. I already told you I have a boyfriend."

"Destiny, you're not attracted to me?" A hint of loss and sadness lingered in Jasiah's question.

"Boy, I don't know you."

"Well, get to know me."

"A nigga from Sidwell Friends wants to get to know me," she laughed. "I'm really not what you want."

Jasiah became a little frustrated. "You think I had my cousin track your number down so that I can—"

"Run game on me," Destiny finished his statement. "I know I looked real green when you saw me and all, but I'm not clueless."

"I could tell that by the way you twisted my damn wrist," Jasiah sneered. "Getting to know one another doesn't have to be that difficult, Destiny," he added.

"It doesn't," she agreed. "It's just that... that..." Destiny stuttered as she didn't want to be honest about her insecurities to a person whom she just met.

"Destiny, I just want to get to know you," Jasiah stated plainly and truthfully once again.

Destiny stood up and looked at the small mirror over her desk. *What did he see?* she thought as she ran her fingers over her ponytail, swirling her hair around her fingers.

"Don't think you can sweet talk me out of my drawers," Destiny stated firmly.

A hearty laugh echoed from the other side of the phone.

"Oh, you think it's funny?"

"I'm not worried about your drawers right now. I'm just hoping to say something that will keep you on the phone," Jasiah explained.

"That's gonna be impossible," Destiny responded as she looked at her incomplete paper due the next morning.

"How come?"

"Hamlet," she retorted, and quickly Jasiah understood.

Jasiah took a deep breath. "Listen to many, speak to few," he quoted Polonius, as he had done one in an adaptation of the play in his junior year.

"Now that quote has me a little more convinced that you go to Sidwell Friends... 'cause a regular nigga wouldn't have that memorized," Destiny laughed.

"I'm telling you the truth," Jasiah laughed with her. "I'm no drug dealer. I'm just a kid imitating the rappers I see on TV, not the drug dealers in the street," he admitted.

"Is that so?"

"It's terrible you stereotyped me like that. I'm just a fly-ass nigga," Jasiah self-proclaimed. "But I guess where you're from, I could fit that typecast."

"It is the norm," Destiny admitted.

An awkward silence cultivated on the phone between the two of them. A seed of interest was sowed into Destiny's heart – the desire to know the truth sparked within her to confirm what Jasiah claimed to be.

"My family is legit," Jasiah blurted out.

"Do you have a circular driveway?" Destiny questioned with a keen interest; her tone filled with intrigue.

"I do," Jasiah admitted. "In Potomac, Maryland… it's more like a semicircle. But who cares?" he replied.

A surge of emotions whirled within Destiny as she told him to call her back in an hour. The spirit of curiosity flourished within her, and she was eager to find out how a young man imitating the hip-hop culture, dwelling in Potomac, ended up in the heart of the city that afternoon.

***

The sun shimmered brightly, illuminating the blank canvas of sky painted in azure; the wind breezed lightly, causing the newly fallen leaves to dance in waves as Destiny exited Dunbar High School. She was dressed professionally in fitted black slacks, a white collared blouse adorned with one of her father's black ties, and a cardigan, ready for her internship interview that she hoped would open doors for her in the future.

Jasiah watched her walk toward his car from the rearview window of his black Bubble Chevy Caprice and thought it was nice to see her in an outfit that complimented her petite frame. He sat inside his car, waiting nervously, wondering at what point he should go out to greet her.

Destiny's mind was captivated by nervousness, enchained in shackles of reasons.

First, there was her new friend, Jasiah, who was parked on the corner waiting for her. Second was Eric, her boyfriend. Though he was home with a stomach bug, she still feared getting into another boy's car. Lastly, her mind was drowning in nervousness because she remembered her parents' teachings; she knew better than to get into a car with a stranger.

Destiny held her breath, second-guessing herself, as she moved closer to the vehicle. She was liberated by the thought of Jasiah last night as she talked to him until the sun imbued the sky with its golden aura. A thread of trust had linked Destiny to Jasiah during their all-nighter. She tried to embrace that trust as she walked toward his car, each step brewing up a storm of doubts and questions in her mind. Manipulated by the strings of doubts, she stopped in stride, marking the beginning of a beeline.

Just as Destiny turned to ditch the ride and find her own way to downtown DC, her hazel eyes fixated on Jasiah's cousin, Lafayette, walking toward her.

"You walking sorta slow for a girl with a job interview downtown," he spoke, his tone sarcastic.

Glaring at him, Destiny quickly blurted, "Tell your cousin...never mind."

She turned her gaze toward the street, hope flickering in her eyes as she thought about whether it would be better to catch two buses or walk to the nearest train station.

"This boy cut his last two classes to be your chauffeur, and I cut mine to wait with him. You better bring your ass on," Lafayette erupted at Destiny's reluctance.

"Nigga, who the fuck you think you talking to?" Destiny replied quickly, her body now fuming with irritation as she continued, "I ain't ask you or your cousin for shit."

Surprise took over Lafayette's face; he hadn't imagined Destiny could be this blunt. Tension grew between them as Jasiah's footsteps oscillated as he approached them.

"Aye, what's the holdup?" Jasiah intervened, breaking the threads of tension.

The grip of doubt grew stronger around Destiny's heart as her eyes lay upon Jasiah, dressed in regular street attire. She instantly felt that she was being bamboozled. Seeing specks of doubt flickering in Destiny's eyes, Jasiah trod closer to her.

"What's wrong?" he asked, affection mingling in his voice.

"I thought you would be in uniform," Destiny admitted, meeting his gaze.

During their phone conversation, he told her he went to Sidwell Friends. Considering it was the most prestigious private school she had heard of, she imagined Jasiah would arrive in a uniform similar to what Will Smith wore in the *Fresh Prince of Bel Air*.

"They did away with uniforms a long time ago," Jasiah replied, unveiling a warm smile. "I can show you my school ID," he suggested, but figured there was something more, "What's the problem?"

Destiny took a deep breath; she couldn't express the thought to his face—she thought he might be a rapist. Manifesting resolve within her heart, unshackling her mind from the prison of presumptions, she whispered. "I just don't know if this is a good idea."

"Come on. I won't bite," Jasiah assured her, his voice soothing away her fears. His wide smile amplified his dimples, making Destiny smile as it embodied an aura of kindness. At that moment, Destiny admitted to herself that Jasiah was indeed handsome. But the weight of her doubts had her feet cemented to the pavement. She couldn't budge.

"I promise...La won't bite either," Jasiah pleaded as he looked back at his cousin, who now stood beside the passenger door in the distance. "Get your scrawny ass in the back!" he yelled as he simultaneously held out his hand to Destiny.

"Nigga..." Lafayette grunted as he moved to the back door.

Taking a deep breath, drowning her doubts in the pool of trust, Destiny took Jasiah's hand and allowed him to lead her to his car against her better judgment. Like a gentleman, he opened the passenger door for her, slightly bowing, inducing a sense of respect in her heart.

"Aye, Destiny, don't think you can keep talking to me like you did earlier either," Lafayette muttered from the backseat once they all were in the car.

"Whatever," Destiny shunned his remarks as she gazed at him through the side mirror while they made their way toward downtown.

Seeing the strings of tension entangling between Lafayette and Destiny, Jasiah intervened.

"You nervous about the interview?" he asked.

"I'm more nervous about being in the car with two boys I barely know," Destiny answered, imbuing honesty in her words.

"You don't have to worry about me," Lafayette interjected from the backseat. "I get mine. I don't have to take nothing by force."

"Excuse my cousin," Jasiah stated.

A blanket of silence cloaked the car until Lafayette asked, "Aye, Destiny, is what they say true?"

Destiny rolled her eyes; she knew what Lafayette was referring to but decided to play dumb to avoid the topic. "What they say about what?" she asked.

"That your brother killed a teacher at Cardoza."

"That was my cousin," Destiny corrected, "And it was a janitor who owed him some money."

"So, is your brother the one that robbed the Safeway at Hechinger Mall?"

"I don't know what you're talking about," Destiny dissuaded hastily, even though she did know. Her brother had gotten away with the crime, and his deeds were now a tale for the streets. "But I do have a brother locked up for distro," she acknowledged. "A few cousins in for larceny and other nefarious crimes, if you must know."

"Nefarious? Oh, you two might be made for one another with these damn SAT words," Lafayette stated, impressed but somehow not embarrassed for his own lack of knowledge.

Both Jasiah and Destiny just shook their heads in unison.

"So, what they say is true?" Lafayette continued with his questions, "Your family the mob?"

Sighing at the unending streak of questions, she replied, "I just come from a big family." She looked over at Jasiah as she rubbed her fingers against her forehead.

"I ain't worried about none of that shit," Jasiah responded.

"I bet your stepdad represented somebody in her family," Lafayette continued, oddly interested in uncovering the mysteries of Destiny's family. "You heard of his stepdad? Roy Netaspend Esquire? He represents all the uptown dope boys. Ain't that where your family is from?"

"Your stepdad a criminal defense attorney?" Destiny looked over at Jasiah, her eyes now sparkling with the specks of interest as she ignored Lafayette's nagging comments.

Jasiah simply nodded in reply.

"So, is this a conflict of interest?" Lafayette laughed, mockery dripping from his tone.

"I never heard of him," Destiny stated as she turned her attention toward the window. She stared at the worksites with cranes they passed as Jasiah drove deeper into the downtown area. Destiny could see change coming to her city and secretly hoped she wouldn't be around long enough to see it.

"Then how do you know he's a criminal defense attorney?"

"What other type of lawyer would represent someone in my family, considering you assume they are all criminals?" Destiny retorted frustratedly. "Ain't like you talking about tax fraud offenses."

"Like I said, I'm not worried about none of that," Jasiah interjected as he pulled up in front of a tall building of glass. "Every family has its own problems. Don't mind, La, he's just curious."

Jasiah's gaze landed on Destiny again, swimming through her hair, noticing how long her hair was since she had half of it out.

"I'll be right here when you finish. Break a leg," he said, winking at her.

Bathing in the kindness emitting from Jasiah's words, his gestures, and his smile, tranquility swarmed her heart as she smiled and exited the car.

"I don't know why you want to fuck with her," Lafayette muttered as he got into the passenger seat. "She crazy just like the rest of her damn family. You got the baddest and richest bitches up Sidwell, and you worried about Destiny's ass? The best thing about that bitch is her eyes."

"She feisty," Jasiah shrugged, "I like it."

"Her family is like the mob, and she is a little princess," Lafayette warned.

"One minute you tell me she is a plain Jane at school, and now you're saying she's a mob princess," Jasiah laughed.

"She all of that!" Lafayette exclaimed, shaking his head. "I'm trying to tell you to stick with those snotty bitches at your school or from the country club or wherever you normally get them from."

Jasiah didn't respond. His mind lingered through the chasm of the past as he remembered what happened to him over the summer. Caged in that feeling, he wanted to stay clear of any girl from either of those places.

"Can we at least get something to drink while we wait?" Lafayette asked. "Might as well get some snacks from the hot dog stand since I know there won't be even a bag of chips back at the crib."

"When y'all going home?" Jasiah responded, reminding his cousin that he was a guest.

Lafayette stopped talking and shrugged his shoulders while Jasiah relished the moment of silence.

Three nights before, Lafayette decided he was old enough to defend his mother against his father's constant abuse. He had watched his father periodically manhandle his mother throughout his entire life from inside their LeDroit Park home. Sometimes, it was as minor as a shove aside. Other times, it was a slap in the face. The older Lafayette got, the more he tried to help defuse the situation and shield his mother, as he couldn't bear to see her being ridiculed like that.

But on a random Monday night, he mustered up enough courage to shove his father into a wall, building rage in his father as he threatened to kill him and his mother while waving his service revolver in the air. Scared, finding himself in a bind, he called Jasiah for help, and at 1 a.m., Jasiah and his mother picked Lafayette and his mother up to find refuge in their Potomac home. Since that night, Lafayette had been camping out in his big cousin Jasiah's room while his mother was trying to figure out her next move.

"I'ma walk to the stand on the corner. You want something?" Lafayette asked as he opened the car door.

"Naw, I'm good," Jasiah looked around for a legitimate parking space in the immediate area. He knew sooner or later he would have to move from the loading zone in front of the building. "I'ma buck a U and park over there," he pointed in the direction of a car moving from a metered parking space.

Lafayette had a bottle of water in his hand for Jasiah when they met up again. Lafayette always wondered why Jasiah never played music despite having an Alpine sound system with double din installed. He was always weirded out about it as he occasionally thought- *Who drives without music when they got such a cool system?*

"You mind?" Lafayette asked before he touched the radio, his mind craving a distraction from thinking about his home life.

"Go ahead," Jasiah replied as he pulled his notebook from the backseat and started to work on his chemistry homework. Time slipped by as he scribbled on his notebook; he had just finished the assignment when he averted his gaze toward the building and spotted Destiny standing in front of it. "I'll be back."

Jaywalking through traffic, Jasiah joined Destiny in front of the building and asked. "So, how did it go?"

"I think I did well," she smiled, "There weren't any Black people on the panel, which kind of made me nervous."

"Don't let that spook you," Jasiah uttered, emitting confidence. "I'm sure they were captivated by you the same way I am."

Destiny looked away with her eyes lowered as she wasn't prepared for Jasiah to compliment her out of nowhere.

"I'm starting to think you are a Casanova," she joked.

Jasiah just smiled in return and asked, "You want to take a walk? We have a little time before my meter is up."

"Sure," Destiny wasn't eager to enter the vehicle with Lafayette again. His presence aggravated her. She couldn't believe his audacity in questioning her about her family. They had not said more than ten words to one another in the three years they were in school together. She grew even more infuriated to know that people were gossiping about her family in the school.

At Dunbar, the teachers were continuously referring to the Rayful Edmond era, when a crack kingpin terrorized the community. Their stories of Rayful and his crew depicted teenage pregnancy, deaths, disfigurements, and imprisonment in an attempt to deter students away from crime. She wondered if they referred to the Peay Family in the same cautionary tale fashion when she was not around.

Jasiah stated, "Don't worry about my cousin. He's going through a tough time right now and is just trying to avoid talking about himself."

Destiny looked at Jasiah and, with a smirk, replied, "I thought he was just an asshole."

"Well...that too," Jasiah affirmed as he laughed. "I just want to tell you that you look cute...a little businesswoman-like or whatever," he molded his feelings into words as he bumped into her intentionally, wanting to be as close to her as possible.

A smile blossomed on Destiny's face as she thanked him. Just in that instance of closeness, she could smell his cologne—a masquerade of scents: Citrus, mixed with sandalwood and musk, hypnotized her mind, blooming the emotions of intrigue in her while evaporating the beads of her anxiety.

Looking up at Jasiah, Destiny noticed little waves in his hair. She reached up to touch the top of his head without hesitation. When the white girls did it at his school, he was offended, feeling like a spectacle in front of them. But right now, it was soothing, instilling tranquility in him, the way he felt when his mother used to rub the top of his head as a young child – pure affection. As Jasiah relished in her touch, Destiny savored touching him. When their eyes met, she stopped abruptly, like a kid with their hand caught in the cookie jar. As Destiny retreated, she picked up the faint smell of Kemi oil from her hand. Jasiah secretly wished that she had not stopped. Gazing into Destiny's honeycomb eyes, he felt like Destiny was finally seeing him for who he was. In the moment, he felt seen.

"What do you know about Kemi oil?" she questioned, rubbing her hands together to diminish some of the oil in her palm.

"I am still Black, you know."

"I know, but are there beauty supply stores in Potomac?"

Jasiah erupted in laughter as he answered, "They sell it at CVS."

Destiny shook her head at her own ignorance, still intrigued about the neat set of waves on top of his head.

"How often do you brush your hair?" Destiny questioned as she ran her fingers across the length of his head one more time.

"A lot," Jasiah responded. "I had to restrain myself from doing it while I drove you here so you wouldn't think I was conceited."

Destiny laughed. "Thank you for that."

As they turned the corner on 16th Street, Jasiah pointed out that his stepfather's law firm was just a few blocks away. Destiny smiled as he spoke of his summer internship there, which he hated, even though traces of envy sprouted in her hearing of his circumstances. He was given an opportunity just like the one she had just interviewed for.

"So, when you gonna let me really take you out?" Jasiah asked, his emotions leaking out the more he spent time with her.

Destiny shook her head, avoiding the question, and answered vaguely, "I really think you're nice and nothing like I expected."

"Is that good or bad?" Jasiah asked impatiently.

"Good," Destiny smiled at him. "I'm just talking about my very first impression…. Who knew they made spoiled rich kids like you?"

Jasiah shrugged. "Well, circumstances are just in my favor."

"Just because you're not a drug dealer doesn't mean I don't have a boyfriend," Destiny reminded him of her original hesitancy in giving him the time of day the previous day when they met.

"Just because you have a boyfriend, it doesn't mean we can't get to know one another," Jasiah pointed out. "I wouldn't have had Lafayette hunt your number down for me if I wasn't serious about getting to know you."

Destiny was flattered by his tenacity, but she didn't want to show it. "Why don't you have a girlfriend?" Destiny bluntly questioned.

"Cause it's over," Jasiah stated simply.

"Cause it's over?" Destiny repeated after him, unsatisfied by his answer. "So, it's just that simple?"

"My mother told me to always give the abbreviated version," Jasiah shrugged.

"My mother told me," Destiny playfully imitated his proper English.

"What you want me to say? My muhva?" Jasiah immediately knew what she was doing because he had listened to his cousin make fun of him for the majority of his life for how he spoke. Though Jasiah felt like he was a chameleon in verbiage, sometimes his prep-school voice did shine through.

"Yes," she nodded. "You over here sounding like Waymon Tinsdale III," Destiny gave him a *Strictly Business* movie reference that made Jasiah burst into laughter.

"I'm not that bad now," Jasiah rejected the notion.

"It's okay, I'll be your Natalie," she winked at him, feeling relieved that the boy she had rejected at a bus stop the previous day had a sense of humor.

"That's what I'm looking forward to," Jasiah admitted with a smile.

Chapter 2: Invitations

Faint sounds of various televisions playing around the overcrowded house reverberated in the room as Destiny brushed her fingers against the dent in the wall of Eric's room – right above his bed. She could hear the sound of Jeopardy from the downstairs television and cartoons playing from Eric's sisters' room as she fell into a light trance.

Subconsciously, Destiny recalled the day she and Eric were on the verge of a breakup when she had popped up unannounced and caught a girl at his house. Tracing the fist-sized hole with her fingers, she remembered Eric, in frustration, punching the wall as he insisted that he couldn't lose her.

Entangled in the mess of the past, her mind couldn't focus on the scholarship essay about laws affecting her community. The words weren't flowing as the distractions around her grew louder with the off-beat music coming from Eric's headphones. Frustrated and annoyed that she couldn't make progress with her essay, she started doodling on her paper.

Bang! Bang! Bang!

The sound of three slow gunshots from what she gathered as a revolver broke her out of her trance as she thought, *who's shooting this early?*

Sighing to alleviate some of the agitation growing within her, she averted her eyes to the back of Eric's head as he penned something in a journal while sitting on the floor. A surge of emotions whirled within her.

For some reason, the sight of Eric started to sprout disappointment in her heart. Destiny frowned as her gaze landed on his bushy cornrows, her ears trying to catch what song he was listening to, but to no avail.

Frustratedly, she knocked his headphones off his ear.

"Did you hear those gunshots?" she questioned.

"Naw…" Eric stared back at her, and the signs of irritation were clear on his face. "What's up?"

"You don't have any homework you could be doing instead of this?" Destiny asked, subconsciously pouring the frustration she felt into her words.

"This is homework," Eric responded in a firm tone. "Mr. Kofi challenged us to present on the African diaspora in a creative way, so I'm preparing for that."

"Oh," Destiny responded just as her pager went off. It was Jasiah.

"Who that?" Eric asked as he climbed on the bed with Destiny.

"My cousin," she lied quickly as she threw her pager to the side and felt Eric climbing on top of her. He lightly brushed his lips against hers and darted his tongue in briefly.

"How was work today?" Eric asked as he rubbed his nose against hers. Destiny smiled as they shared an Eskimo kiss.

"It was fine," Destiny answered as she felt Eric's broad shoulders and gazed into his eyes. "Just some filing and doing my homework."

She reached up for another kiss, shrugging away the shreds of doubts that had begun to bloom in her heart recently.

Slowly, their bodies became entangled, lost in the moment between one another just as sirens entered the symphony of sounds permeating the wall of Eric's room. The possibility of someone being harmed from the gunshots Destiny heard before never crossed either of their minds as Eric nestled between Destiny's legs and started to dry hump her.

The friction between them aroused Eric, and he groped Destiny's breast from under her shirt. He reached under her bra and teased her nipples. Destiny moaned lightly at the sensation, only arousing Eric further.

Suddenly, a loud knock on the bedroom door untangled them from each other. The knock was like a bell telling two fighters to go to their respective corners. Both Destiny and Eric looked at the clock. It was 8 p.m., which meant Eric's older brother, who happened to be his roommate, was home from work.

"Is that Dex?" Destiny asked, specks of irritation lingering in her voice.

"Yeahhh…probably," Eric assumed, with frustration evident on his face.

"Well, that's my cue to get out of here," Destiny said as she sat up and began to gather her things. Eric jumped up from the bed to adjust himself before he opened the bedroom door.

"What's up!" Dex spoke nonchalantly, addressing both Destiny and his brother at the same time as he entered, filling up the room with the smell of motor oil.

"What's up!" they responded in unison.

"You ain't gotta leave because of me. I'm headed right back out," Dex stated as he started to strip from his Metro uniform.

"Naw, it's a weeknight. I gotta get home anyway," Destiny replied as she closed her book bag, feeling relieved that she didn't have to hear Eric eventually plead for her virginity. Destiny repeatedly had made it clear that she wouldn't allow him to take her virginity in the twin-size bed that he slept in head-to-toe with his nephew most nights. But that didn't stop him from trying.

She slipped into her Nike Air Force Ones and stood to leave.

"A'ight, but you coming to the block party this weekend?" Dex inquired.

"I guess," Destiny looked at Eric, her gaze emotionless as it was the first she had heard about a block party.

Averting his eyes from Destiny's stare, Eric grabbed her backpack and carried it without saying a word. Destiny grabbed her pager and followed Eric toward the front door, saying goodbye to his family members, even though tension was building between them with each step.

"Block party, huh? Were you even planning on telling me about it?" Destiny interrogated but suppressed her emotions, keeping her tone breezy.

Caught off-guard, Eric turned his attention toward Destiny, nervously skimming his hands through his cornrows. His lips opened to speak, but the words betrayed him. After being in the relationship for almost a year, Destiny could read through Eric's body language like an open book.

Is he secretly seeing that other girl again? Why can't he tell me if there's someone else? - Thoughts flooded Destiny's mind as she sighed defeatedly, unwilling to entertain the pressure of such thought while she had her own discretions with Jasiah.

"Look, Eric, I ain't in the habit of being where I'm not welcome," Destiny uttered, her eyes averting from Eric toward the red and blue lights at a distance, confirming that she had indeed heard gunshots moments earlier. The sight of the parked police car and ambulance at a distance also confirmed that danger was always near. Destiny silently prayed that she would soon find her way out of the city alive as she looked back at Eric.

"It's not like that, Destiny. I just planned on kicking it with my boys. We were gonna chill at the block party for a while, then hit Pentagon City for a movie," Eric claimed as he opened the car door for Destiny.

"So, basically, you had no plans to see me this weekend?" Destiny replied as she sat in Eric's mother's 1996 Nissan 300ZX hatchback, which felt like a shield on the breezy September evening.

"Come on, Destiny, don't do this. We going to the mall tomorrow, right? Don't Friday count as the weekend?" Eric shut the door behind Destiny and began to tread toward the driver's side. "It shouldn't be a problem that I want to spend a day with my boys," Eric continued when he entered on the driver's side, pleading his case.

"It's whatever," Destiny sat back, unfazed by his excuses, and cracked her window to allow the cool night breeze to brush against her face.

"I know you don't have an attitude." Eric reached over to try to tickle Destiny, trying to distract her mind from the sudden tension before he pulled off.

"Stop," Destiny whined. "Stop it." She moved away. "Stop now, Eric," Destiny popped his hand. "I gotta get home, so just drive."

Amidst Eric's little games, Destiny's pager went off again. She ignored it, figuring it was either her father or Jasiah.

"That's probably your dad," Eric assumed as he pulled off.

"Yep," Destiny readily agreed as she turned the radio up, unwilling to listen to Eric's probable lies further.

They drove off, but anxiety built up in Destiny as they grew closer to the emergency lights. The yellow and black crime scene tape blocked their normal route to her house. Still, both Eric and Destiny could see the devastation behind the tape before being directed by the police to turn right. The blood-stained porch steps on a row house, the crying family members, the handcuffed young man in the back of a squad car. The scene was too familiar and made Destiny's heart long for a change of scenery.

"Damn," was the only word that escaped Eric's mouth as he drove away. Destiny continued looking out the window as the peace-inducing light of the moon flickered in her eyes. Her thoughts wandered to how Jasiah might be able to look at the same sky as her, but their surroundings were totally different. A smile crept across Destiny's face as she thought of Jasiah and their late-night conversations about their futures. Compared to her new friend, Eric had no aspirations of going to college or leaving their hometown. Her mind was still strangled by Jasiah's fleeting memories, and she realized how she craved to see him, considering it had been a month since they had seen one another when he drove her to the interview. For the past month, he had become a reliable friend who lived in her phone.

Destiny exited the car without saying goodbye to Eric, distracted by thoughts of Jasiah. Eric watched her walk away, silently not wanting their evening to end on such a bad note.

"Damn, it's like that?" Eric called out from the car window.

Destiny didn't turn around to acknowledge him. She wanted him to feel the disconnection she was feeling between the two of them.

"Really, Destiny... you're that mad?"

Destiny took a deep breath as she placed her key into the security screen door, then turned to say, "Thanks for the ride, Eric... I'll talk to you later."

Eric drove off.

Destiny rolled her eyes as she turned around to enter her home. She was greeted by a house full of relatives for a Thursday night football game. The roars and cheers erupted from the living room. It wasn't uncommon to see her father surrounded by his son and nephews. Their home was always lively during football season. Destiny glanced at the big screen television to see what opponent of the Redskins made it worthy of people coming out on a weekday – it was the Cowboys.

"Ahh, where you been?" one of her cousins, Ron, quickly inquired as Destiny dropped her bookbag at the door and quickly started to greet everyone with a kiss on the cheek and a half hug.

"With that lil' nigga, where else," her father grumbled.

Faint chuckles emerged from the crowd. Destiny rolled her eyes as she traveled upstairs.

"I thought you got off work at 6?" her mother, Gail Peay, stated from her perch on her king-size four-poster bed. She looked regal in her robe and turban as she combed through one of her latest home décor magazines.

"I did," Destiny sighed. "I just hung out with Eric for a little while afterward," she admitted.

"You better not fall behind messing with that nappy-headed boy," Mrs. Peay stared at her daughter in the eyes. "You know you have three choices coming up, so use yo' time wisely," her mother's southern accent rearing its head as she spoke.

"Ma, we're focused, don't worry," Destiny assured her mother.

"I'm telling you, Destiny. You're going to college, in the military, or you gonna get a little poo putt job. But you're *not* going to sit around here after graduation while I go to work every day," Mrs. Peay continued with her lecture.

"Ma, I'm focused," Destiny tried to sway her mother's worries.

Destiny sat on the rug and started playing with her twin nephews, who lived with them, unfazed by her mother's comments as she felt confident that she was doing everything needed to attend college in the Fall of 2000.

"Your phone been ringing while you were out," Mrs. Peay informed her daughter after a few moments of silence between them.

Immediately, Destiny thought of Jasiah's pages. "A'ight, Ma," Destiny kissed her nephews on the cheeks. "I have a scholarship packet due tomorrow." She got up and made a beeline toward her room to see what Jasiah wanted so badly.

"Damn, Girl, you tough to get ahold of today. I thought something happened to you," a playful yet soothing voice resonated from the other side of the phone.

"Boy, what is the matter?" Destiny questioned as she sat at the desk.

"Straight to the point as usual, huh?... I wanted to ask if you wanna go to dance with me?" he asked.

"A dance?" Destiny questioned with a hint of disbelief in her voice.

"Come on, I'll have you home before curfew. I promise."

"When is this dance?"

"Saturday."

"Ha!" Destiny laughed. "Who turned down the handsome Jasiah Sheffield?"

"I wasn't gonna go," he admitted. "But I got crowned homecoming king at tonight's game, and I can't go to the dance alone. A king needs his queen."

Destiny wondered if he realized what he had said, but at that moment, she didn't want to remind him that she was not *his.*

"Is that right?" Destiny blushed, "I know there is an ex-girlfriend waiting in the wing for you to ask her out," Destiny continued as she moved to her bed, astonished that he had just asked her out again.

"Destiny, no one can compare to you."

"And yet, you haven't seen me in a month," Destiny pointed out.

"I have been respecting your wishes," he reminded her. "And I know it's a lot handling school, applying to colleges, scholarships, and a job."

"You're just waiting in the wing?" Destiny shook her head.

"The wait is over," Jasiah stated loudly as if he were making an announcement.

"I did not say 'Yes'."

"You know you want to see me as much as I want to see you," Jasiah responded confidently, his voice carrying the scent of affection.

"Jasiah, you know I have a boyfriend," as Destiny gave her a common statement, Jasiah said the words with her in a mocking tone.

They both laughed.

"Destiny, come on. I'll pick you up. We will have dinner and go to the dance. That's it," Jasiah pressed on.

"Jasiah, this is late notice, and I don't have anything to wear. My hair's a mess, too."

"You look beautiful as you are. But you still do have a day," he insisted. "Look, ditch work tomorrow. I'll pick you up, take you to the mall, get you straight."

"Jasiah…" Destiny whined, her voice fading out as the barriers of restraint began to shatter within her.

"Destiny, please?" Jasiah was determined to spend time with her in person. He had been patient about seeing Destiny face-to-face because they talked almost daily over the phone.

"Jasiah, my father is gonna—"

"Your father will love me," Jasiah cut her off. "Leave that part to me."

Destiny had always wondered how people on the other side of the spectrum lived. She pondered a strategy. She could ditch work, go shopping with Jasiah, and make it home in time for Eric to pick her up to hang out at the mall that evening.

"Destiny, my mom is so excited for me to get homecoming king. This would be epic. Just come," Jasiah tried to convince Destiny, flourishing the emotions he felt for her.

"Hold on," Destiny told Jasiah.

"Don't leave me on hold forever," Jasiah warned. "You know you get distracted."

Destiny laughed. "Boy, put me on speaker phone and don't hang up. I'll be back."

Destiny left her cordless in her room and walked toward her mother's room to talk to her.

"Ma, can I go out this weekend?" Destiny asked.

Her mother looked up from her *House Beautiful* magazine and asked, "What you mean go out?"

"To a dance," Destiny answered honestly.

"Girl, give up the details. With whom and where? How much is this going to cost me?" her mother looked at her.

Destiny bit her bottom lip, realizing that, apparently, she hadn't gathered enough details from Jasiah. "Hold on."

Destiny strolled back to the phone hurriedly, emotions of excitement and curiosity broiling up in her with each step she took. Hastily, she reached for the phone to ask Jasiah for the details.

"Jasiah!" Destiny yelled as she could hear him playing what she assumed was *Mortal Combat* on his Nintendo 360.

Simultaneously, as if on cue, her father walked up the steps and asked, "Who the hell is Jasiah?"

"My friend," Destiny replied.

Her father stared at Destiny like she was crazy, "Another lil' nigga? Really, Destiny?"

"Daddy," Destiny whined and decided this was it – the moment when she disclosed the friend who had lived in her phone for nearly a month. "Jasiah goes to Sidwell Friends and just asked me to join him for his homecoming dance."

Her father just stared at her silently, waiting for her to spill more information.

"It's on this Saturday. Can I go?" Destiny pressed on.

"He on the phone?" Mr. Peay asked.

"Yes."

"Hang up the goddamn phone, Destiny, and explain." Mr. Peay demanded, traces of anger swelling up in his demeanor.

Destiny hung up abruptly without uttering another word.

"I know you ain't on no hoe shit," Mr. Peay stated without blinking an eye.

"What?" Destiny looked at her father like he was crazy.

"Didn't you just have one muthafuckah drop you off? What's the deal with this other Jesse or whatever?" He came closer to his daughter.

"Jasiah, dad—" Destiny corrected in a hushed voice, her fingers dwindling with each other.

Footsteps echoed through the small hall, and suddenly, Destiny's mother appeared in the doorway as well. "What's going on here, Ray?"

"Destiny got another lil' nigga," Mr. Peay answered his wife. Directing his eyes back at Destiny, he continued, "I thought your boyfriend's name was Eric."

Destiny took a deep breath, realizing it was now or never, and tried to figure out how to tell her father that Jasiah was just a friend and make it sound believable.

"Destiny, do you hear your father talking to you?" Mrs. Peay chimed in, slamming her hands on her hips.

"Ma, Jasiah is just a friend. He won homecoming king and asked me to join him on his homecoming dance with him," Destiny responded, "He goes to Sidwell Friends. I was about to ask him the details of the location when Daddy interrupted."

"But I thought your boyfriend was named Eric!" Mr. Peay repeated.

"Yes, that's my *boyfriend's* name. Jasiah is just a *friend*," Destiny tried explaining but couldn't find the convincing words.

"Destiny, what are you doing?" Mrs. Peay inquired.

"Daddy told me he wanted me to drop Eric because there would be some guy for me whose parents would have a circular driveway… And Jasiah has a circular driveway in Potomac."

Mrs. Peay looked at her husband in disbelief, "Ray!"

"I-I-I was talking about in college," Mr. Peay shrugged. "I didn't think she would take me so literally so quickly."

"Can I go?" Destiny asked.

"This is a school-organized event?" Mrs. Peay asked.

"Yes, you both can meet him when he picks me up."

"Naw, I need to make sure he isn't blowing smoke…. We'll bring you to his house and meet his parents," Mr. Peay demanded.

"You're gonna take me to Potomac, Maryland?" Destiny questioned, worried that this was going in the wrong direction.

Her parents looked at one another and answered in unison, "Yes." Then Mrs. Peay added, "Get the details… I'll call your aunt to do your hair."

Destiny waited until her parents left the doorway before picking up the phone to call Jasiah back; her heart was fluttering, thumping wildly, thinking how Jasiah would take it. Taking a deep breath to calm her wavering voice, she dialed, but there was no ringing.

"Hello?" she inquired.

"Hey, Destiny, who were you trying to call?" Eric asked, surprised. "The phone didn't get to ring."

Destiny cursed to herself; she had picked up the phone before it could ring with Eric on the line. Gathering her scattered senses, she lied, "You." An unwelcome taste occupied her tongue after she did it.

"Look, I know I said I was hanging out with my boys this Saturday, but why don't you and Bria come to the block party?" Eric invited Destiny and her best friend.

Usually, Destiny would have happily complied, but now, the circumstances were different.

"It's fine. I'ma hang out with my family," Destiny said, discarding the notion of them seeing one another on Saturday. "I might go to North Carolina on Saturday with my mother," the story to cover her tracks rolled off Destiny's tongue so quickly that it even surprised her.

"Oh," disappointment oozed out of Eric's voice.

"I was just calling to make sure you got home safely. I'm going to finish up this essay for the scholarship packet. I'll call you back before I go to bed," Destiny continued, barricading the room for further conversation.

"A'ight, cool," Eric hung up.

Breathing out the distasteful emotions, Destiny instantly dialed Jasiah's number to ask for the details.

"Man, your daddy doesn't play," Jasiah affirmed Destiny's suspicions that he heard the conversation.

"So, you were listening," Destiny was slightly embarrassed but pushed forward to warn Jasiah, "And he wants to drop me off at your house to meet you and your parents."

"I don't know if my stepfather will be around, but that's cool... at least I'll save some gas."

Destiny rolled her eyes at Jasiah's reaction and responded, "You sure that's cool with your mother?"

"My mother is always ready to meet anybody. And she will get the chance to show off her home – it's a win-win, for sure," Jasiah stated confidently, "She is so excited I got homecoming king that she told me to get a new fit from Georgetown."

"You're not going to Solbiato, are you?" Destiny referred to an exclusive Georgetown DC brand.

"Naw, flier than that," Jasiah laughed.

Destiny had never purchased clothing from Georgetown other than at the GAP. The prices of brands located there were sky-high; she couldn't fathom shopping there. Sometimes, her brothers would allow her to tag along when they took a girl out, so she was fully aware of the cost and expectations that came along with shopping on M Street or Wisconsin Avenue in Georgetown.

"I guess I'll catch the train to Pentagon City," Destiny mentioned, liberating herself from the idea of shopping with him.

She was quite confident that she could find a cocktail dress in Express or The Limited within her price range. If push came to shove, she could use her mother's credit card at Macy's.

"You are hanging with me tomorrow," Jasiah stated confidently. "I got you, so let's shop together."

"Jasiah, I know how to dress myself," Destiny replied as she sat at her desk and switched on her computer.

"I know, but I want to see you."

"Jasiah, I already have plans tomorrow evening," Destiny informed him, hinting that Eric was taking her out. "I'm already skipping work to find a dress."

"Oh, so you have plans with Eric on Friday night, and you making plans with me for Saturday... player, player," Jasiah teased Destiny. "Yeah, go ahead. Get ready to say your final goodbyes to him."

Destiny burst into laughter, sensing the confidence imbued in Jasiah's words. She thought to herself that there could be no *final goodbye* between her and Eric, considering they went to the same school.

"What you eat for dinner?" Destiny asked, trying to sway the direction of conversation from Eric while she noticed that she left her bookbag downstairs. Stepping down the stairs playfully, her feet galloping like a horse with the cordless phone stuck to her ear, she trod toward the door. She bypassed her cousins' game of Craps in front of the big-screen television to get her bag as she intently listened to Jasiah's afternoon with his old tennis team members at a neighborhood deli. A rush of gleeful emotions swept through Destiny at the thought of everyone Jasiah had ever mentioned being in awe of them together.

Returning to her room, she looked at herself in the mirror over her desk as she thought-- *Why not? Why not seize the opportunity while I have it?*

Finishing his story, Jasiah went back to convincing Destiny to join him on the shopping date. He craved to gaze upon her hazel eyes. Laying across his bed, Jasiah recalled the way he felt when she rubbed the top of his head and the sweet scent of honeydew and vanilla on Destiny's skin that enveloped his car while she was in it.

Still, there were some specks of anxiousness tainting his thoughts. He wanted to make sure that Destiny fit the bill when he introduced her to his friends. He hadn't talked about her to anyone, as his associates would make assumptions about Destiny based on where she lived.

Chapter 3: Popeyes

Jasiah and Destiny giggled on the phone all night, sparking a flame of nervousness and excitement within them as they both craved to see one another.

That morning, Destiny stood in front of the full-length mirror in her parents' room, dressed in blue stretch jeans and a fitted white shirt, with a pair of Jordan 7s on her feet. Looking down at the sneakers, she remembered the day she bought them with her first paycheck because Jasiah couldn't stop talking about them. She smiled, knowing it was the perfect day to debut them at school.

When Eric saw Destiny walking down the hall with her best friend and his cousin Bria during the first period, flickers of adoration sparkled in his eyes. He silently admired her and threw his arm around her shoulder.

Destiny removed his arm with a scowl on her face.

"What's going on with you two?" Bria asked, sensing the unsettling energy revolving around Destiny.

"She tripping because I wanted to go the block party with Jacob and them," Eric quickly responded.

"I'm tripping because he didn't even mention there was a block party," Destiny insisted.

"I'ma stay out of it," Bria held her hands up. "Let me get to class."

As soon as his cousin stepped off, Eric asked, "Who got you those?" he motioned toward her shoes with a nod.

"These are things you can do for yourself when you have a job," Destiny responded in a matter-of-fact connotation, her tone stern.

"You don't look like you're going to work today," he questioned as his gaze lingered on Destiny's fit.

"It's casual Fridays," Destiny retorted, averting her eyes as the falsehood escaped her lips.

"We still on for this evening?" Eric inquired as the bell rang for their next period.

"You sure you don't want to hang out with your boys?" Destiny responded sarcastically.

"Come on now, Destiny. I told you that with you is where I want to be," Eric licked his lips as he looked at Destiny seductively.

Destiny blushed. "Boy, bye!" She strolled toward her next class, waving goodbye to him.

Destiny's heart thumped once she left school as if she were going to work, knowing she had called in sick that morning. Jasiah was parked exactly where he had when he picked her up previously. The possibility of being caught mixed with the allure of seeing Jasiah face to face excited her a little this time. Jasiah stepped out of his Caprice as she grew closer.

To her surprise, he was dressed in the exact fit, just his white T-shirt was from Hugo Boss. Casually, he strode toward her and suddenly stretched his arms wide out to give her a hug as if two long-lost friends were reuniting.

Nervousness gripped Destiny's heart when she thought of hugging Jasiah back in a similar way. Walking forward, Jasiah enveloped Destiny in his arms; the fresh scent of citrus, leather, and musk entangled Destiny's senses. She inhaled deeply, hypnotized by Jasiah's aura when he suddenly squeezed her harder.

"Boy!" Destiny playfully punched him on the side.

"Girl, you better hug me back. I know you are happy to see me." Jasiah's gaze focused on her, his arms still holding her tight.

Destiny sensed Jasiah's gaze as she stared back at him. For a moment, both were lost in the eyes of one another, connected by the threads of longing and affection. Jasiah craved to kiss

Destiny as their breaths danced in unison, mingling between their faces.

"Hi," Destiny broke the moment of silence.

"Hi," Jasiah replied in a hushed voice, his fresh minty breath carrying notes of warmth on it as he winked at her.

Destiny embraced Jasiah back, laying her head on his broad chest as the feelings of peacefulness settled within her. Jasiah caressed her back; the sweet scent he craved – honeydew and vanilla – was there again, filling his nostrils and making him smile.

Snuggling, he whiffed her hair; the familiar sweet smell of Kemi oil pierced through his barriers of restraint as he unconsciously squeezed her even tighter.

"You are suffocating me now, Jasiah," Destiny said playfully to tease him as she patted his hip and attempted to back away.

"I'm not letting you go," Jasiah exclaimed.

"I don't belong to you," Destiny reminded him.

"But I belong to you," Jasiah whispered without thinking.

Destiny could feel the sincerity lingering in his velvety voice as she felt his heartbeat quicken. A warm, affectionate smile curled up the edges of her lips as she held him until his heartbeat simmered down.

Seconds passed by; their breaths became one, both hearing the melodies of their hearts, disconnected from the world. A thought sparked within Destiny—a thought with Jasiah is where she should be. Slowly, they pulled away from one another, brushing away their hands from each other's waists, only for Jasiah to hold her hand until he opened the car door for her.

Destiny sat in the car and took a deep breath as she came to her senses. Just the previous evening, she had been intertwined in Eric's arms, and now, here she was, openly sharing another intimate moment with someone else. Taking a deep sigh, exhaling any thought about Eric, Destiny checked herself out in the visor mirror. This wasn't like her at all, she thought.

"Jasiah," Destiny sighed his name aloud before he entered the car as if she was taking it all in.

Jasiah was well-read. He had collegiate aspirations just like her. When she was stumped on calculus homework, he could walk her through it over the phone. Jasiah was what she would call a charming gentleman and scholar.

"What are you thinking about?" Jasiah asked, noticing the tinge of worry on Destiny's face as he cruised through the city.

"You," Destiny replied casually as she looked over at him. "You sure you want to take me around your friends?"

"The question should be, am I sure I want to bring my friends around you," Jasiah smiled, his dimples vivid on his vibrant face.

Destiny shrugged. "Well...I think I'm nice."

"I think you're nice to me, but the way you bite off Lafayette's head when he speaks is crazy," Jasiah said with a mischievous smirk plastered on his face.

"He always talking crazy in front of you. In school, he only acknowledges me with a head nod. But when you're around, he suddenly has so much to say."

Jasiah laughed, "Maybe he doesn't want Eric to get suspicious."

Destiny sighed, "Maybe."

"After this weekend, Eric's gonna be a sad puppy," Jasiah stated confidently.

"Yeah, sure," Destiny agreed sarcastically as she turned to Jasiah. "So, tell me, am I gonna get evil stares at this dance?"

"Of course," Jasiah glanced over at Destiny. "Everyone will wonder where I got a beauty like you from," he reached over and grabbed her hand.

Jasiah held her hand gently, and Destiny didn't pull away as she sat there, hazed by the sparking emotions within her.

"Let's start with some lunch," Jasiah suggested to Destiny once they parked at Georgetown Park Mall.

"We have time for that?" Destiny asked, looking at her watch.

"I got all the time in the world for you, girl," Jasiah winked and got out of the car.

He escorted her to Beni Hana's Japanese Restaurant with his arm around her shoulders. Destiny had only been there with her brothers and cousins.

"You ever been here?" Jasiah asked once they sat in front of the hibachi grill.

Destiny nodded, looking at the menu. "What you think about starting with a shrimp tempura roll?"

Jasiah was surprised. He thought he was taking her somewhere new.

"Jasiah," Destiny waved her hand in front of him. "Wake up. Do you eat sushi?"

"Oh, I'm awake, beautiful, but I'm surprised you eat this stuff," Jasiah stated honestly. "You're always talking about getting Wendy's or Popeyes."

Destiny shook her head. "We go to restaurants, Jasiah," she said, not knowing whether to laugh at the dumb look on his face or be insulted.

Jasiah turned and stared at his menu for a second.

Destiny threw her menu down and sat back. She knew she was ordering the teriyaki shrimp.

Jasiah stared aimlessly at the menu, not knowing what to say.

For a moment, Destiny became agitated with his silence, but when she saw him bite on his bottom lip, she thought maybe he was nervous too. After all, this was their first time alone.

"You never answered me," Destiny spoke, breaking the uncomfortable silence that swirled between them. "Do you eat sushi?"

"No," he mumbled.

"Just try this one, it's cooked," she encouraged.

Jasiah nodded.

Destiny placed her hand on his knee when she noticed his leg jumping. "You okay?"

Jasiah looked over at Destiny and smiled, but specks of worry remained on his face. He was trying to restrain himself from kissing her.

Destiny smiled back, imbuing the emotions of comfort in her expression, "I'm the one risking a relationship to hang out with you," Destiny reminded him. "I should be the one nervous."

"I know, but I just want to impress you," Jasiah admitted, looking at his hand instead of Destiny.

"Just be yourself," Destiny touched him on the shoulder. "You impress me every time you recite Shakespeare or walk me through a calculus problem on the phone."

Jasiah got a bit shy at the compliment and smiled nervously. "You sure it's not these muscles?" he flexed his arm playfully.

Destiny caressed his bicep with her hand gently. On the inside, she felt like his physique was titillating, but on the outside, she mockingly said, "Naw, these little arms don't do it for me. Remind me of chicken legs from Popeyes."

"Now, you are tripping," Jasiah retorted, snatching his arm away, slowly drenching in embarrassment.

Witnessing his reaction, Destiny couldn't hold herself back as she broke into laughter.

Silence engulfed them again as they waited on a server. Destiny looked around, watching the intentional flames spewing at another table. Then, she looked down and noticed Jasiah's leg start to jump again.

"Sooo, what impresses you about me?" Destiny asked as she placed her hand on his knee in an attempt to help calm his nerves.

"Your confidence, your drive, your beauty," he answered honestly. "And those eyes are mesmerizing."

Destiny didn't expect him to answer like that; caught off guard, a flush crept across her cheeks.

"Can I kiss you?" Jasiah asked suddenly.

Destiny nodded without a second thought.

Jasiah liberated himself from the chains of restraint as he leaned in closer for the kiss, the warmth of his hefty breath spread across Destiny's face. Her eyes fixated on Jasiah's plump, fresh lips, beguiled by the intensity of Jasiah's breath as she grew anxious. Before Jasiah could lean in for a kiss, a group of people dressed in suits came over with the waitress to fill up the table and take their orders. Both leaned back to their spots, the moment of affection quickly evaporating.

"Goddamn," Jasiah whispered in Destiny's ear.

She turned quickly and pecked him on the cheek before whispering in a lusty tone, "Patience is a virtue."

Jasiah was amused by the tingling sensation her lips left on his face, but he simply nodded in return.

"Something wrong?" Destiny asked.

"I don't know whether something is wrong or ever so right," he smiled at her.

"We're gonna figure out if this sushi is right for you when it comes," Destiny sipped her water. "You know I can't wait to see where you live," she admitted out of the blue as if the water was a truth serum.

"Is that so?" Jasiah's eyes widened. "You want to know where I lay my head?"

"If you're talking about your house – yes – if you're talking about your bedroom – no," Destiny made it clear.

"I'ma change that," Jasiah stated confidently.

"We'll see," Destiny looked at Jasiah in the eyes as she smiled merrily.

Jasiah could have kissed her right then and there – his whole existence screamed to touch her, but he knew he had to restrain himself at a table full of strangers. As time flew by, during the meal, they made small talk about Destiny's upcoming road test in a few weeks and pranks that she played with her nephews around the house. Jasiah felt like he would love to be around Destiny's family.

Though his cousin had pegged them all as misfits, Destiny painted a different picture of her family. The stories she told of dinner time, Football Sunday, weekend trips to North Carolina, and even repast only displayed camaraderie that he had never experienced. Drowning himself in Destiny's bewitching voice, he felt like he could listen to her stories for hours.

On the other hand, Destiny was dreaming about how extravagant Jasiah's life seemed to be. He was always eating out or having something delivered. She knew that he didn't have to worry about leaving out of the house smelling like fried chicken. He was always at the mall buying something new or hanging out with his friends instead of working like she did. He didn't have to worry about helping his little brother with his homework, unlike Destiny, who was responsible for her nephews' homework most nights. He didn't have to worry about the expense of his own gas, even though Destiny had to ensure she had bought enough Metro tokens and train fare cards weekly.

To each, the grass was greener on the other side of the fence. Their craving to be part of the other side magnetized their emotions, attracting them slowly yet steadily toward each other.

Soon, they were out in the street, strolling hand in hand as the dazzling light of the sun shimmered across their faces. Jasiah let his thriving, unquenched emotions take over him as he grabbed Destiny, pulled her closer, and planted a sloppy, wet kiss on her in the middle of the sidewalk.

He could feel the softness of her lips, his heart unwilling to pull away from this tender feeling. The firmness of Jasiah's touch was stimulating for Destiny as she gave in and drowned herself in the intimate moment. When Jasiah noticed that Destiny didn't pull away, he darted his tongue into her mouth, tasting the sweetness and saltiness of their meal.

The heat between the two flourished as Jasiah wrapped his tongue around Destiny's. The world around them vanished as they stood on M Street with their lips locked. Their souls were isolated from the prying eyes and street noises around them as if the earth and the skies were enjoying the moment alongside them.

Suddenly, a screeching voice pierced through the haze, "Get a room!" making them instantly separate in laughter.

Destiny walked alongside Jasiah, her heart a captive of the blossoming emotions. There was a tingling sensation growing inside of her that she could not shake as Jasiah took her to the nearby boutiques. She had never been kissed like that. But the sensual sensation quickly vanished as nervousness grew within Destiny. Her mother had given her a hundred dollars for a dress, shoes, and accessories. But when she saw the prices in the boutiques, she knew she didn't have enough money. She fumbled through a rack of bejeweled clutches as if she didn't like anything, but the truth was, she couldn't afford anything.

"I think this was a bad idea," Destiny stated honestly after walking out of the second store.

"Let me pick something out for you," Jasiah suggested, grabbing Destiny around the waist.

Destiny bit her bottom lip, nervous about whether she should tell Jasiah it wasn't that she didn't like anything – it was just that the price was too much.

"I got you," Jasiah kissed her on the cheek as if he was reading her mind. "You trust me?"

Destiny nodded. She was shocked when Jasiah picked out a black Iceberg dress to match the outfit that he was purchasing. "Sir, I still have a prom to think about," Destiny said, looking at the price tag and shaking her head.

"I got this," he dismissed her as he pulled out a credit card.

"Your parents are going to kill you," Destiny murmured in his ear, her teeth clenched.

Jasiah laughed, knowing he had spent more on the double din in his Caprice, and no one had mentioned anything about the charge on his credit card bill.

"This is nothing. I still gotta get you some shoes," he winked at her.

"Jasiah, you can't spend this much money on me," she whispered. "It just...it makes me nervous."

"You don't owe me anything but a good time this weekend," Jasiah assured her. "I'll be a perfect gentleman, and you'll be my lady."

Destiny bit her bottom lip and looked at Jasiah. *Could he like me this much? What does he want in return?* she wondered.

Jasiah leaned down and planted a kiss on her forehead. "I got you. Stop looking scared," he reassured Destiny, a gentle smile on his face, carving dimples in it.

"I just don't want to feel like I owe you something," Destiny admitted. "I cannot afford to return the favor," she whispered.

Jasiah shook his head and waited until they were outside of the store before stopping Destiny in her tracks. "I can be this nice to you without wanting anything in return but your time," he informed her.

"Where I'm from, only drug dealers drop money like that, and they always want something in return."

"I just told you I want your time," Jasiah replied. "I have patience. If you can't tell," he grabbed her hand, "just let me spoil you."

"Jasiah, you hardly know me," Destiny reminded him. She didn't want to remind him again about her boyfriend after he dropped nearly $200 on a dress for her.

"Let's not make this so difficult," Jasiah caressed the side of Destiny's face. He wanted to kiss her again, but this time he held himself back, not letting her think he was just some horny boy looking for any opportunity to fondle her.

Destiny closed her eyes for a split second, his touch inducing the emotions of calmness and assurance within her. When she opened her eyes, she wondered if she was looking at the young man she was supposed to be with because Eric had never made her feel this special. But she knew he didn't have the means to do so, which wasn't a fair comparison. However, it was still a fact that Destiny couldn't ignore.

"Okay, I won't make this difficult," Destiny replied, vowing to herself that she would simply enjoy the moment.

After rummaging through several shops, Jasiah bought her everything he had promised. Destiny couldn't help but feel excited; her heart was thrilled seeing how Jasiah cared for her. Soon, they were driving back home, and Destiny noticed that her home was now only a few blocks away.

"You can drop me off here," Destiny said.

"Let me drop you off at home," Jasiah insisted when Destiny told him to drop her off two blocks down from her house after their afternoon together.

"Naw, Eric's been blowing my pager up, and he might already be in front of my house. Let's just play it safe," Destiny said as she looked down the street, trying to figure out if she could see any vehicle that Eric would have access to.

"You better tell that nigga what's up," Jasiah stated confidently, some part of him annoyed at the mention of Eric.

Destiny just looked at Jasiah, noticing tinges of jealousy on his face.

"It ain't no competition, Destiny," he continued.

Jasiah was right, but Destiny didn't like his sudden cockiness. It was a turn-off for her since she thought he looked down on others so casually.

"Let me find out you arrogant on the low," Destiny stared into Jasiah's eyes. "You a narcissist?" she quizzed.

Jasiah broke into laughter, a bit surprised by Destiny's unexpected question.

"What is so funny?" The roots of agitation started to grow in Destiny.

"It's just that Lafayette would say that's an SAT word," Jasiah answered, still chuckling.

Destiny couldn't help but chuckle, knowing well that he would.

"I don't know what to do with you, Destiny. I play it cool; you keep me as your homework buddy – friend-zoned. I finally get to see you, and you let me treat you like you're my girl all day. And now I'm back in the friend zone, just that fast? It feels like I'm in a circus ring or something."

Jasiah shook his head, shackles of disappointment binding his heart as he poured his distress into his words.

"Jasiah, you asked me out – knowing that I already have a boyfriend."

"You're letting me take you out – knowing you have a boyfriend."

Destiny shook her head. She didn't like the pressure. "Jasiah, just let me figure this out, please," she touched him on the shoulder, "I promise I'm not trying to lead you on or hurt anyone's feelings."

"Feelings will be hurt, Destiny."

"Okay, well, let me not get *my* feelings hurt." She was honest. "You live a world away from me."

"Forty minutes," Jasiah corrected her.

"Jasiah," Destiny rolled her eyes. "Sometimes I can't believe you're this into me."

"Why wouldn't I be?"

"I can't say it out loud. I can't let my insecurities get the best of me."

"Then don't." Jasiah grabbed her hands. "Destiny, you're beautiful and smart as hell, and did I mention sexy?"

Destiny rolled her eyes.

"I wish you could have seen yourself from my eyes when you put on that dress," he winked at her.

"Jasiah, I don't want to be anyone's charity case, pet project, or *side piece* on the other side of town."

Jasiah laughed. "You are literally sitting in my car, two blocks from your house, because *your* boyfriend might be lurking around, and you're worried about being *my* side piece."

"No, for real, Jasiah." She punched him in the shoulder.

"I'm homecoming king. Taking you to the dance. If that's not being on display, I don't know what is," Jasiah continued to laugh.

Destiny took a deep breath, letting out the growing agitation from the sudden pressure, and looked at Jasiah. Her mind still couldn't wrap around the fact that someone like him was into her, and she couldn't believe that she was going to break it off with Eric.

She thought she loved Eric. He wasn't the first boy to take interest in her, but he was always the sincerest. He was patient and kind. They rarely got into arguments even though she knew that her disappearing for the whole afternoon would be a big disagreement. She was stuck in this chasm; she wanted Jasiah, but the thought of hurting Eric strangled her mind from making a decision.

To Jasiah, Destiny's silence spoke volumes. The day had started light and fun; he thought the flowers of love had bloomed, but now, facing this gutting silence, they slowly began to wilt. He had been anxious to see Destiny after a long time. He thought he was prepared to continue to take things slow with her, and he was confident he could win her heart. But as the day passed, he realized he didn't want to play in the background anymore.

"You don't feel the same way about me as I do about you," Jasiah murmured as he leaned his head on the steering wheel — suddenly feeling like he was a fool for believing this could work.

"I do," Destiny responded. "It's just that I've known you for a month, and I've been with Eric way longer," she reminded him. "Jasiah, I really like you, and I had a good time with you today. Hopefully, we will still have a good time tomorrow, but I just need some time to figure this out, okay?" She explained as she pulled Jasiah by the shoulder so that he had to sit up. "I know you're a spoiled kid who is used to getting whatever he wants whenever he wants it, but you're going to have to be patient. Okay?"

"Okay," Jasiah pouted.

"You look so cute with your lips poked out," Destiny smiled as she plucked Jasiah's lips in her fingers. "Come here, let me kiss 'em."

Jasiah leaned in eagerly for their lips to meet. He still had his lips puckered playfully when Destiny pulled away.

She giggled and gave him one small peck. "Playing it cool has gotten you this far with me," Destiny reminded him. She wanted to tell him to play his role, the line she heard her brothers telling females too often, but she decided against it. "Page me when you get home, okay?" she told him.

Jasiah nodded. "I just need a hug," he opened his car door.

Destiny became nervous that someone would see them but didn't want Jasiah to feel any more defeated at the moment. He opened her side of the car door while she was contemplating her next move. When she got out of the car, he had her pinned against the car.

"Jasiah," she tried pushing him back as a reflex.

"Naw, you can't run from this," he scooped her up by the waist, bringing her eye to eye with him. "You call me when you get settled later tonight, okay?"

Destiny nodded as she secretly enjoyed that he could easily pick her up like plucking a flower from the garden. "But you know this is not how people hug, right?" she reminded him.

"I just wanted to show off these muscles you called Popeye's chicken legs earlier," Jasiah stated as he placed Destiny back on her feet.

"Umm hmm," Destiny took a deep breath, and her pager went off again. This time, it was her house number. "Boy, let me go. I was supposed to be home thirty minutes ago."

"It's barely seven o'clock."

"But I told my mom I would be back by six, six thirty," she reminded him. "One thing about my parents is they are sticklers for time."

"A'ight. I will not hold you," Jasiah hugged her and planted a kiss on her forehead.

Jasiah stood away from his car, his eyes fixated on Destiny, dazed with affection as he watched her stroll down the sidewalk with shopping bags in hand. He couldn't take his eyes off her; no matter how much he looked, it wasn't enough. To him, she had disappeared from his sight too quickly. He wanted her to turn around, to catch a glimpse of her hazel eyes, and come back to him to enjoy the evening, but she didn't.

For Destiny, it was the longest walk of two blocks of her life. Her mind was circling in an overflow of thoughts. She desperately tried to think of an excuse to tell Eric why she had ignored his pages. She lied to him about going to work. What if he tried to surprise her and pick her up there even though she told him not to bother because she wanted to come home and change her clothes first? Struggling through her thoughts, she entered her house to see her mother and father sitting alone at the dining room table.

"Where are the boys?" Destiny questioned as she tried to head upstairs with her bags.

"First, let me see what you got," her mother yelled after her. "And the boys are with your brother."

"That lil' nigga been calling here for you," her father stated flatly as he turned the page of the Metro section from *The Washington Post.*

Destiny reluctantly retraced her steps back down the stairs with her bags still in her hand.

Letting out a deep sigh, she dangled the dress Jasiah bought her in front of her parents. Upon the reveal of the dress, seeing its exquisiteness, her father got up and trod into the kitchen. Her mother almost choked on the water she was sipping.

"Mr. Peay, I guess your daughter is over her tomboy phase," her mother touched the material and secretly admired her daughter's taste. It was a world away from what she would normally wear at a dance.

Destiny shrugged at her mother's remark. "I gotta go call Eric back."

"Mr. Peay, your daughter gonna have two dates in one day," her mother stated, looking at her daughter in the eyes. "Destiny, do you know what you're doing?"

"Shittt!" Mr. Peay chimed in from the kitchen, displaying his disdain in the matter.

"I'm trying to figure it out," Destiny answered honestly.

"May the best boy win," Mrs. Peay mumbled as she went back to turning the page of *House Beautiful*.

Mr. Peay cursed again from the kitchen while Destiny sprinted upstairs, her mind swirling in the torrent of the lies she would tell Eric. She sat down on the bed and took a deep breath, gathering her senses before calling her boyfriend. Swirling in the conflict of emotions, she dialed Eric.

"What's up?" she stated nonchalantly.

"What's up!?" Eric retorted in an angry tone. "You been missing all fucking day, and you call me with a *what's up* like nothing happened?"

Sensing the anger in Eric's voice, Destiny stayed quiet, biding her time to figure out the best way to reply.

"Why haven't you responded to my pages all day?" Eric questioned.

"I was working… I left my pager in my book bag," Destiny shocked herself with how easily the fib rolled off her tongue.

"Destiny, you didn't think to call me all afternoon?"

"I have a lot on my mind, goddamn it!" Destiny knew she needed to get loud and frustrated to redirect the energy of the conversation, imitating how she had seen her brother Jax cover his tracks from his wife. "I have A/P classes… I'm working…. Getting ready to submit my college applications and scholarship packages," she rambled off, trying to justify her tone by explaining her daily to-do list. "I was tryna get shit done so I don't have to worry about it all weekend."

"You could have called," Eric replied flatly.

"My bad, but I'm calling now," Destiny apologized for her lack of communication, so that didn't become an issue later. "Are we still going to the mall?"

"I'll be there in twenty minutes," Eric answered before hanging up.

Destiny hung up the phone as she exhaled, the restlessness spreading its roots deep within her. She hoped her lies worked so she could enjoy the evening with her boyfriend without a hitch. Jumping up from the bed, she quickly changed into a sweatshirt to combat the cool night air and brushed her teeth, ensuring that none of Jasiah's scent lingered on her skin. She had just freshened up her ponytail when the doorbell rang.

"I'll get it!" Destiny yelled as she grabbed her denim jacket and purse. She hopped down the stairs just as her father was headed to the foyer. "I got it, Daddy."

"Bring your ass home by eleven," Mr. Peay reminded his daughter of her curfew.

"Aye, aye, captain," Destiny gave her father a fake salute as she opened the door for Eric. A wave of shock jolted her soul as her eyes lay upon Eric, holding a small bouquet of wildflowers in his hands. Guilt flickered in her eyes as she sighed and thanked him for the flowers.

"You sounded a little stressed when I was talking to you," Eric kissed her on the cheek. "I know you have a lot going on. Hearing how you feel, I thought to myself, I better get as focused on college as she is."

Destiny clamped her lips shut for a second before saying, "Let me put these in some water. I'll meet you in the car."

She laid the bouquet on the table under the prying gaze of her parents.

"Let's see how long this shit last," Mr. Peay commented.

"She is mimicking the bad behavior that you and your sons have set as an example," Mrs. Peay reminded her husband, shoving him into the pits of silence.

Mr. Peay just took a deep breath and slumped down in his seat as a response. It was rare that Destiny's father didn't get the last word. Destiny was grateful that her mother had shut him up, but she didn't like being reminded of her father's infidelities either.

Destiny really couldn't figure out why her mother didn't ever permanently leave him. They had packed up and moved out two times as far as Destiny could remember.

"Can you put these in some water, Ma?" Destiny requested as she shook off the memories of her parents' tumultuous marriage.

"Sure, have fun," Mrs. Peay said as she stood up to get a vase.

Destiny quickly left the house before her father could think of something else to say, meeting Eric as he patiently waited outside his car so that he could open the door for her. At that moment, she decided she didn't want to run a game on him. But she had to be sure that Jasiah was worth giving up everything she had with Eric.

"You okay?" Eric asked as he reached over to hold Destiny's hand as he drove.

With guilt still looming heavily over her head, Destiny wanted to spill everything about Jasiah to Eric. She wanted to tell him that she wasn't at work and that she had a fantastic day with another guy. She wanted to show him the little black dress that he could never afford to buy her. She wanted to tell him that within twenty-four hours, she would be rubbing elbows with the heirs of the most powerful people in DC. But holding the reigns of her emotions, she bit her bottom lip and thought about something else to talk about.

"Are you still thinking about going to Maryland Eastern Shore?" she quizzed.

"I'll probably end up at UDC," Eric looked over at Destiny. "But don't worry, I'll visit you wherever you are."

Destiny smiled. "You should start applying for scholarships," she rubbed his hand. "I can help you put your packet together."

Eric just nodded, "That would be cool."

Instantly, Destiny started to feel even more guilty. *Why am I making plans with him?* She asked herself.

"Man, let me tell you about Jacob," Eric started. "This why I've been blowing your phone up," Eric continued, telling Destiny about how his best friend had gotten a girl pregnant. "He's telling me that she must have roofied him."

Eric shook his head. Destiny laughed.

"When his grandmother finds out, she gonna flip," Eric said.

Destiny couldn't imagine being so comfortable with any boy that she wanted to take the condom off. Not with the way her father talked about the girls that came into his weekend security job at Planned Parenthood. Mr. Peay's cautionary tales of teenage pregnancy and the emotional anguish he saw after an abortion ensured that Destiny took sex seriously.

Peering into Destiny's eyes, Eric noticed that she was lost somewhere far away. As an attempt to unshackle Destiny's silence, he changed the subject.

"You hungry? Want to go to Popeyes?" He asked.

The mention of Popeyes made Destiny's mind plunge into thoughts of Jasiah and his muscular arms. A smile crept across her face.

"Sure," she replied, twirling the strands of her hair in her fingers.

Chapter 4: Homecoming

The landscape blurred as the Peays' Pontiac revved through narrow roads, headed toward Potomac, MD. Destiny sat in the backseat of her parents' car, dressed as Jasiah had styled her, hoping that the evening would go well. She could not take her eyes off the houses, which seemed to get larger and larger under the serene and peaceful canvas of the blue sky.

Her gaze fixated on the landscape, the vibrance of the sky flickered in her eyes as her mind wandered into the events of last night – she had a great night with Eric, yet here she was, riding with her parents to the house of another boy.

Averting her focus from the hypnotizing scenery outside, she focused her mind on her parents. They weren't dressed in their Sunday best, but they were elegant enough to enter any type of cabaret and fit right in. She wondered if they would be underdressed or overdressed for the suburbanites they were about to meet.

Lowering her gaze to her bare legs, she couldn't believe that she was wearing a tight-fitted dress to a party. Usually, she wore pants or a maxi dress to shroud the insecurity her mind developed about her thin, slender legs that her family often teased her about. But this time, Jasiah's enchanting words convinced her that her slim frame would look exquisite in a mini dress.

Slowly, the sight of the Netaspends' luxurious house came into view. Destiny's eyes widened, sprouting a tinge of insecurity within her. As they pulled up to the house on River View Drive, Destiny and her parents' eyes sparkled in awe after taking in the landscaping and architecture.

The driveway was shadowed by a line of mature oak trees planted on either side. Gradually, they drove into the circular driveway, blossoming with a garden of roses in the middle.

The trio felt the difference between them and the rich society as they lay their eyes upon four luxury cars parked in the driveway – making their Pontiac stick out like a sore thumb. Cloaked by the insecurities, at that moment, Destiny wished that she never got to witness how Jasiah lived as nervousness gripped her heart.

"The choices we make in life," Mrs. Peay scoffed defeatedly as she felt like she was staring at a real-life version of the front page of *House Beautiful*.

"We're certainly not in Kansas anymore," Destiny joked with her parents, easing the strings of uneasiness that had entangled their minds.

Hearing her comment, they laughed.

"My man Roy lives somewhere around here," Mr. Peay conjectured as he parked. "Gail, you know Roy, right?"

"Considering how many times I had to write a check for Junior's defense? I definitely know Roy," Mrs. Peay mumbled, referring to her oldest son, who was imprisoned. "Let's see the inside of this mansion," Mrs. Peay coaxed as she was the first to open her car door.

"The niggas might not let us in," Mr. Peay mumbled as he exited the car as well. "But I bet Roy knows these folks."

Destiny followed suit with her parents, enchained in the pits of her own thoughts about her inadequacy. They slowly walked up the travertine walkway – its sides embroidered with the fully bloomed purple mums extended all the way to the front door. She took a deep breath, hoping they wouldn't look too out of place. As they grew nearer to the front door, TLC's "Ain't 2 Proud 2 Beg" could be heard blaring from the speakers inside.

"Is the party here?" Mrs. Peay whispered as she straightened the Coach belt on her slacks.

"We shall see," Mr. Peay rang the doorbell.

Within moments, a woman dressed in a tight fire-red minidress opened the door, revealing that there, indeed, was a party going on inside.

Embracing a smile on her face, she welcomed the Peay family, but her eyes looked past the adults as she stated, "You must be Destiny."

Destiny nodded. "And these are my parents, Mr. and Mrs. Peay."

"Ray," her father extended his hand.

"Gail," her mother introduced herself next.

"Well, y'all come on in. I'm Faye – Jasiah's mom," she extended her hand, reaching past the Peays and grabbing Destiny's hand. "I've been waiting to meet you, young lady."

Destiny smiled and scanned Faye in a quick glance. She reminded her of Halle Berry with a short haircut and evenly toned chestnut skin. She was young – a lot younger than Destiny's mother and beautiful, she thought.

"You're having a party?" Destiny looked around at the cocktail tables filled with well-dressed teenagers like herself while some adults dressed plainly lingered around who seemed to be the parents of the young ones.

"Just celebrating the homecoming king," Faye smiled as she looked back at Destiny's parents. "Make yourselves at home, please. There is a raw bar to the left and a fully stocked bar over there, too."

Mrs. Peay was lost in the moment, her gaze admiring the marble floors in the foyer and the large crystal vase filled with dozens of red roses.

"That mother looks familiar," Mr. Peay whispered to his wife as he squinted at Faye.

"She can't be no older than Junior," Mrs. Peay commented.

"Well, let's have shrimp," Mr. Peay suggested once he couldn't place Faye.

"Don't mind if I do," Mrs. Peay smiled at her husband as she continued to survey the house while simultaneously trying to keep an eye on her daughter.

Destiny tried to hold back her anxiety as Faye pulled her around the formal living room to show off a few of Jasiah's photos. Destiny took note of the many stages of his life, including the herringbone chain he sported daily. She realized that Jasiah had been rocking that chain since he was around four years old. A faint thought birthed in her mind as she assumed it might once belong to his dad.

"My son speaks very highly of you, Destiny," Faye remarked, glancing at her as they circled around the formal living room where no one was.

"Where is your son?" Destiny quizzed as the absence of Jasiah made her concerned.

"He'll be down shortly," Faye uttered as she took a seat and passed a piercing gaze at Destiny. "This good girl act you have going on isn't fooling me," Faye commented as she sparked a cigarette. "I'm from the city; I know your family and their deeds."

Startled by the sudden change in the mood, Destiny felt a tinge of embarrassment. She had underestimated the reputation of her family and didn't expect Jasiah's mom to be familiar with the Peay family at all. But the irritation in Destiny overshadowed the humiliation.

Anger boiled up inside her as she nearly cursed out loud – frustrated that she had thought things would be different in suburbia. Destiny wanted to tell Jasiah's mother that being a Peay didn't define her and that she tried all her life to clean herself from the stains of the family. She wanted to inform Faye that she was at the top of her class with a job and that, unlike most of her kin, she would be going to college.

But instead, gulping the blazing anger inside her, Destiny opted to disengage.

"I probably should see about my parents," Destiny replied, her voice wavering from the concealed anger as she figured avoidance was her best tactic. After all, she was here on Jasiah's invitation to spend an evening with him – untainted by the grimes of anger and arguments. She instantly retreated from the room, not allowing Faye to say another word.

Just as Destiny spotted her parents with mini plates full of shrimp and cubed cheeses, her eyes revolved back to the curved staircase, unveiling Jasiah, twirling a crown around his index finger as he descended the steps.

A photographer snapped pictures, and a wave of applause echoed over the beat of the music. Destiny was conflicted, thinking about whether to keep walking to her parents or wait for Jasiah to recognize her. Before she could weigh the pros and cons, Faye walked up behind her.

"Don't think you can trap my son," Faye whispered in Destiny's ear.

Amused by Faye's bold comment, Destiny burst into laughter; her cackles reverberated through the house, bringing all the attention to her.

A tinge of confusion erupted on Jasiah's face as he looked at her, puzzled.

"Are you laughing at me?" he questioned as he came closer.

"Your mom is funny," Destiny smiled at Jasiah and ignored Faye, indicating that Faye wasn't as important as she thought to Destiny.

Breaking out of the net of Faye's insinuations, Destiny relished in Jasiah's handsomeness. Dressed in his all-black Iceberg outfit, topped off with frameless personality glasses, he looked dashing to Destiny. Instead of the bold diamond jewelry Jasiah usually sported, he had a thin silver chain around his neck and an understated onyx stud earring.

"Look at you, looking like a young Denzel Washington," Destiny poured the ecstatic emotions she felt into her words.

"What can your boy say?" Jasiah pimped over to Destiny. "I clean up nice, but you are the showstopper here. You look beautiful," Jasiah didn't hesitate to compliment Destiny as he walked closer to her, smiling – wanting to hug her the same way he did in front of her high school, but instead opted to wink at her. "Ma, I'm glad you got to meet Destiny," he said to his mother.

Faye nodded, looking at the two of them together.

"Come, let me introduce you to my parents," Destiny said excitedly as she took Jasiah's free hand to guide him over to her parents. However, she quickly let it go when she saw her father frown.

"Daddy, Ma – this is Jasiah. Jasiah – my parents."

"He's tall," her mother recognized straight off, eyeing Jasiah from top to bottom.

"Ma!" Destiny rolled her eyes as specks of mortification revealed on her face.

"Nice to meet you, Jasiah," Mrs. Peay smiled.

"I don't know if it's nice to meet him just yet," Mr. Peay stated firmly. "What made you want to take my daughter out?"

"She's beautiful," Jasiah looked at Destiny, "I'm just happy she said yes to me."

Faye strolled forward and joined the conversation but opted to stay silent.

"You have a lovely home," Mrs. Peay complimented Faye as she noticed her standing silently.

"Thank you," Faye gave a half smile, part of her disappointed that Ray Peay didn't recognize her.

"Come on, Destiny, let's take some pictures," Jasiah took Destiny's hand and whisked her away before any adults could say a word.

"I could call your father Dapper Dan in those crocodile loafers," Jasiah snickered as soon as he figured they were out of earshot.

"If you mention anything about those shoes, he'll go into how much they cost and not how much he paid for them," Destiny laughed. "These shoes cost fit'teen hun'net dollas!" she imitated her father.

Jasiah laughed with her.

"But your mom is a piece of work herself," Destiny wanted to tell Jasiah what she said to her but held her intrusive thoughts back, realizing she didn't want to ruin their playful mood.

"Don't I know it," Jasiah uttered. "But enough about them... Look at you," he twirled Destiny around to get a 360-degree view, "the hair and the dress... you look stunning. I like it."

"You clean up nice yourself," Destiny playfully bumped into him.

"I want to kiss you so bad right now," Jasiah whispered in her ear, his warm breath raising goosebumps on Destiny's neck.

"Uhm, let's just take these pictures," Destiny suggested, paddling away from the sudden excitement she felt.

"Yes, so I can have a reason to hug you nicely," Jasiah pulled Destiny closer to the photographer, "I can't believe you're here with me and in that dress. No matter how much I look, these eyes still want more."

"All in good time, boy...all in good time," Destiny smirked at Jasiah.

They snapped pictures like they were a couple. Jasiah introduced Destiny as "his girl," and she didn't object. She was silently in awe of the way he lived. It was like Black folks took over a house from *Dynasty* or *Knots Landing*.

All the crystal and custom drapery was something right out of her mother's coveted magazines. She couldn't wait to discuss everything with her mother at the end of the evening. She was even more shocked when a stretch Hummer Limo pulled up. As they all ushered outside to leave, Destiny saw the distaste on her father's face.

Destiny strolled toward her parents to say goodbye and tell her father not to worry.

"Let me talk to that young man," Mr. Peay stated. "Tell him to come over here."

Destiny recognized that her father didn't call him a lil' nigga, so she thought it was a good thing. She motioned for Jasiah to come closer to them.

"It is a pleasure meeting you, Mr. and Mrs. Peay," Jasiah stated quickly. "Thank you for allowing me to take Destiny to the dance," he extended his hand to her father.

"She means the world to us, son," Destiny's father stated sternly as he held onto Jasiah's hand. "We expect her to come back the way we dropped her off. You understand?"

"Yes, sir," Jasiah nodded.

"No later than midnight," Mr. Peay added.

"Yes, sir," Jasiah agreed.

Mr. Peay released Jasiah's hand.

"Have a good evening, Mr. and Mrs. Peay. Destiny is in good hands," Jasiah assured her parents as he took her hand to assist her into the limo.

Destiny took in the sounds of teenage laughter instead of tires skidding and cars honking. To be in the serene setting so close to home felt surreal as she had only experienced it while visiting family In North Carolina. Suddenly, the blossoming peace started to wilt in Destiny's heart as she saw miniature liquor bottles coming out of pockets and purses. And then a little baggie.

"What the fuck?" Destiny whispered to Jasiah, shocked by the barrage of drugs being displayed.

"That's them," Jasiah assured her. "Just chill."

When one boy tried to pass the tightly rolled twenty-dollar bill to Jasiah, Destiny thought that she didn't know Jasiah at all.

"Naw, Bryce. I'm good," Jasiah dismissed the offer. "You know I don't do that shit."

"More for us," Bryce laughed.

At that moment, entangled in the crowd of strangers and drugs, Destiny wished the limo was a Metro Bus so she could ring the driver to let her off at the next stop. Discomfort swarmed over her once gleeful face, and she didn't hide her disdain for what was going on around her.

The other girls in the limo started to whisper, and Jasiah realized the nonverbal communication going on. He turned his body toward Destiny, but she never turned to look at him.

"Hey, you," Jasiah tapped her on the knee.

"This what you into?" Destiny asked, feeling like she had been bamboozled.

"Naw," Jasiah shook his head. "I've definitely had some drinks before, but that is their thing."

"Takes the edge off," another boy, Jason, commented, letting it be known that he was listening to their conversation. "By the looks of things, you could use some."

Many people giggled, but Destiny narrowed her eyes on Jason and started rubbing her hands together as she tried to figure out her next move. Her body language made everyone uneasy.

"Get your girl," Bryce whispered to Jasiah.

"She good," Jasiah responded. "Just keep your shit over there."

By the time they got to the school campus, Destiny was ready to find a pay phone to call someone to pick her up.

"You okay?" Jasiah asked Destiny as he felt her tense up every time he tried to touch her.

"No," Destiny answered honestly. Disgusted by the unfolding events around her, she stayed in the limo and let everyone exit the vehicle when they parked in front of the gymnasium.

"Destiny," Jasiah called her name affectionately as he stood outside. "What are you waiting on?"

"Debating if I need to find my way back home," she cut her eyes at Jasiah. "These motherfuckers were way too comfortable pulling that shit out, so I'm left to assume that all of you do it."

Jasiah took a deep breath as he tried to figure out a way to reply to Destiny.

"I don't fuck with drugs, let alone cocaine," Destiny looked at Jasiah in the eyes. "Or people that do."

"Destiny, I don't do drugs," Jasiah responded as he climbed back into the limo and shut the door behind him. "Half of them aren't my friends... It's just that my mother is cool with their parents."

"Jasiah, somehow, your mother is under the impression that I want to trap you." Upon the mention of Faye, Destiny brought up the thing that had been irking her since Faye attempted to humiliate her. "What did you tell her about me to give her that impression?"

"I just told her you went to school with La," Jasiah responded. "Now, what did my mother say to you?"

"Don't think you can trap my son."

"My mother said that?" Jasiah was shocked.

"Verbatim," Destiny responded. "And told me don't think I was fooling anyone with a good girl routine because she knows my family."

Jasiah burst into laughter, surprised since he didn't know his mother would behave that way. He believed that his mother didn't care, considering she was always so nonchalant about any girl he dated.

"It's not funny, Jasiah," Destiny frowned.

"I'm sorry," Jasiah reached out to touch her hand. "Come on, let's just have a good time."

"Jasiah, I've seen what those drugs do to people. I don't get down like that, and I don't fuck with nobody who does," Destiny stated sternly as she peered into his eyes.

"Destiny, I don't do drugs," he affirmed again. "I lost my father because of drugs," Jasiah decided to confide in Destiny, but some part of him immediately regretted it. He had never mentioned anything about his father and drugs before.

Destiny rubbed Jasiah's hand; sympathy flickered in her eyes as she recognized the sincerity and sadness in his voice.

For a moment, he became lost in the world of emotions Destiny's hazel eyes transported him to. He tried to shake off the buried sadness of being fatherless and put on a smile.

"I just want to make sure I'm getting to know the real you," Destiny squeezed Jasiah's hand.

"You are," he reached over and kissed her on the cheek. "Now, come on. Everyone awaits the king and his queen."

A smile appeared on Destiny's face again. Being called *his queen* brought her immediate gratification. She walked with Jasiah, hand in hand, across the freshly paved parking lot as the sun disappeared. Strands of her hair danced in the flurry of air, captivating Jasiah's attention as he gazed at her. He smiled to himself, confident that she was the perfect accessory on his arm.

As soon as they entered thru the double doors of the gymnasium, Jasiah placed his crown on his head, continuing to hold Destiny's hand tightly. Fascinated, Destiny silently took in her surroundings. She paid close attention to the amenities in the gym as well as the different ethnicities of the students. At every one of the schools Destiny had attended, African Americans were the majority, but at Sidwell, they were clearly the minority. Destiny looked at Jasiah with admiration as he slapped hands with nearly everyone, no matter who they were, while never letting her hand go.

"So, you're the man?" Destiny asked jokingly.

"I've just gone to school with most of these people since first grade," he replied. "I'm like the longest-running Black kid," he kissed Destiny on the cheek again and whispered, allowing his lips to gently graze her ear as he spoke. "Girl, I knew you were hiding this body in those straight-legged jeans."

A sudden ripple of arousal swept through her as she blushed.

"You thirsty? You want to dance? What do you want to do?" Jasiah asked as he looked into her eyes.

"Can you get me something to drink while I go to the bathroom?"

"Sure, I can walk over there with you."

"I can manage the bathroom by myself," Destiny assured him as she started to walk away but got jolted as he refused to let her hand go. "Jasiah, I'm good."

Apprehension guided his actions as he dwelled on the thought of what could go wrong if she walked alone. Would someone try to holler? Would she run into one of his ex-girlfriends? Would she catch someone else getting high and want to leave? There were so many variables, and he couldn't control the narrative if he weren't there.

"I really have to use the bathroom," Destiny informed him. "You have to let my hand go."

Sighing out the shreds of fear, strengthening his resolve, Jasiah pulled Destiny to him in one swift motion and kissed her on her lips. The softness of her lips, the warmth of her breath – his fears melted under the passion between them.

Destiny's heart fluttered as she slowly opened her eyes, affection dripping through her gaze as she relished in his touch. Biting her lips, she remained close to him.

"I will come back," she assured him as her hand grazed his chest.

"I'll be right by the door," he responded, slowly letting go of her hand.

She strolled quickly toward the restroom, not paying attention to anyone around her. She didn't want to make eye contact with anyone. She feared that everyone could see through her expensive clothing, that she couldn't afford it, and that she didn't belong there. Hastily, she entered the restroom, escaping the weight of prying gazes.

Once in the stall, Destiny leaned her back against the door and took a deep breath, exhaling the insecurities rising within her. Locked in her trance, she replayed various moments that had transpired over the past two hours. Jasiah's house, his mother, his friends. As she used the bathroom, she questioned herself on why she would ever think she could fit into Jasiah's world.

While washing her hands, she gazed at her reflection – admiring how she looked. She had never taken such care to make sure her hair stayed bone-straight after her aunt did it as she did today. She never even sported the tinted lip gloss that she was reapplying. But a part of her was excited at this version of herself. Maybe being with Jasiah would bring out the best in her, she thought to herself.

Just as she convinced herself she could manage a relationship with Jasiah, a girl walked in.

"Jasiah's date, right?" the girl stated as she flung her honey-blonde hair off her shoulder.

Destiny looked over to see a tall, slender White girl standing before her.

"Yessss?" Destiny responded in a slow drawl.

"Nobody has heard of you before. Where did you come from?" she questioned.

Destiny's nostrils flared as she held back her normally quick-witted tongue. She knew she had to keep her composure.

"You're not his normal type. You do know that, right?" she continued.

Destiny took a deep breath and simply responded, "Excuse me," as she reached for the door handle.

The young lady flinched at Destiny's movement as if she feared being hit by her. Destiny shook her head as she moved out of the bathroom.

"Ask him what happened to Lauren," the blonde yelled after Destiny.

She cringed as she stepped into the hallway. A hundred terrible scenarios went through her mind quickly. A bad breakup? A car accident? An overdose? Her thoughts left an unpleasant taste in her mouth as Jasiah met her in the hallway with a smile on his face. "I was getting worried."

"*I'm* getting worried," Destiny responded. "Jasiah, who is Lauren? And who is this bitch trying me in the bathroom?" she questioned, using her thumb to point over her shoulder at the bathroom door behind her.

His eyes widened. "Destiny, calm down."

"Oh, I'm calm," she responded. "I just can't stand rude people, and I'm encountering a lot of them this evening."

"Want to step outside for a second?" he suggested.

"Sure."

Once they were outside, Destiny noticed that the temperature had dropped with the disappearance of the sun.

"Who is Lauren?" she questioned again. "Why is she approaching me?"

Jasiah's demeanor changed quickly, his smile vanishing, taking his dimples away with it. "What did she say to you?"

"Ask you about Lauren. Well, she said to ask you what happened to Lauren," Destiny stated as she silently admired the immaculate greenery surrounding the building and compared it to the overgrown landscaping at her school.

"Lauren is just a crazy bitch," Jasiah concluded as he looked down at his feet.

"That's it?" Destiny looked back at Jasiah, recognizing that he was hiding something because of his lack of eye contact.

He shrugged. "Lauren is nobody to talk about. Nobody for you to worry about."

"I have to start asking you more questions about your past," she concluded as her instincts told her there was more to the story.

"Lauren is someone I never want to talk about," Jasiah grunted. "Especially not tonight. I'm homecoming king, and I have the prettiest and sexiest girl on my arm tonight," he smiled at Destiny. "Fuck her."

"How many girls in that gym have you slept with?" she inquired.

Jasiah laughed. "You don't want to know."

"It's been that many?"

"We are a curious set of kids… left unsupervised quite often," he answered vaguely, realizing how unsettling it could be for Destiny. "Look, everyone I've slept with has been protected and consensual."

Destiny suddenly felt the cold breeze brushing against her as her irritation started to subside. But she couldn't shake the feeling of being a fish out of water.

Seeing her start to shiver, Jasiah suggested that they go back inside.

He wanted to wrap his arms around her but didn't want to push it. Instead, he just rubbed her shoulders.

"Look, Destiny, I really like you. We don't spend our time gossiping about people. We talk about us, and current events and finding the flop of a function and whatever else comes to mind."

"You're the only person I know that finds Calculus fun," Destiny sneered at him.

Jasiah sputtered into laughter. "It is to your benefit," he shrugged. "But I guess we should spend some time really talking about the events in our life that make us who we are."

"I think that's a great idea," she smiled back at him.

Jasiah felt relieved to see her smile. "So, we can do whatever you want to do. We can go back inside, we can leave. I can take you home. Just tell me what you want to do," he sighed. "I just don't want this to be the last time we see one another."

"Well, we're definitely going back inside because I'm cold. And maybe we should head out," she suggested.

"Cool. If that's what you want," Jasiah looked her in the eyes, loving the way her long, straight hair framed her face under the moonlight. "Did I tell you how beautiful you look?"

"You always do, Jasiah," she blushed.

"And I've been dying to kiss you," he moved even closer to her.

"You may be pushing it now," Destiny stopped him as she took his crown from his fingertips.

"Destiny," he whined.

"Jasiahhh," she whined back as she placed it back on his head. Then she took his hand and led them back into the gym.

"Girl, that must be jelly because jam don't shake like that," Jasiah commented about her butt as he watched her walk slightly ahead of him.

Destiny pulled his hand so that they were side by side.

"You are aggressive," he squeezed her hand back.

"You like it," she implied.

"I do," Jasiah opened the door for them.

When they stepped back inside, the "Macarena" was playing. Destiny released Jasiah's hand and quickly went to the dance floor. Jasiah was amazed at how she jumped in, not caring about the onlookers at all. Jasiah admired her change in disposition – from the shy girl tightly holding his hand to the vibrant version of herself that he always favored.

He stood on the sidelines, watching her move around as if the world around him had slowed down; only Destiny remained vivid in his eyes as he saw her laugh with people in her immediate area. She moved her hips with much more rhythm than half the people on the dance floor.

"Where did you find her again?" Jason, Jasiah's friend, asked.

"Walking across the street," Jasiah answered truthfully.

"You had us looking crazy in the limo, bro... why didn't you tell us she wasn't cool like that?" Jason asked as he punched Jasiah playfully on the shoulder.

"How would I know Bryce would bring that shit out?" Jasiah looked at Jason. "Y'all got me answering questions that shouldn't even be asked."

"She can't be that green, bro."

Jasiah shook his head. He didn't feel like explaining to Jason that coke wasn't a recreational drug for inner-city kids.

Instead, he opted to say, "I'ma check you later," as Next's "Too Close" started to play. With his hands in his pockets, he strode toward Destiny and joined her on the dance floor, thinking his presence would prompt her to leave. But she felt like it was her chance to be herself. She grabbed at Jasiah's clothing, bringing him closer to her.

"I love it when you shake it like that," Jasiah sang along with the song in Destiny's ear as he quickly caught on and began to dance with her.

"I see that you like it like that," Destiny sang back as she rubbed her body against his.

Before they both knew it, many songs had gone by. Somewhere in between, he had tossed his crown to a chair, so he didn't have to worry about it falling off his head. The pair created an atmosphere around them where no one could deny their connection. Between the music, the laughter, and the delicate touches, Jasiah and Destiny became infatuated with one another.

On the dance floor, it was as if all of the hiccups of the evening had never happened, causing them not to want to part once it was all over.

"How about some steak and eggs?" Jasiah suggested once he escorted her through the crowd in the parking lot toward an old school cherry red Mercedes Benz S Class.

"Your muhva let you drive this?" Destiny inquired as she slid onto the peanut butter leather seat.

"She taught me how to drive in it," Jasiah answered, closing her door.

While he lingered outside the car, saying goodbye to those around him, Destiny admired the interior of the classic vehicle. She remembered when her older brother Junior had one similar.

Once Jasiah entered the car, he went back to his original question, "You hungry, right?"

"It's whatever," Destiny agreed.

"That's what I like to hear," Jasiah beamed as he pulled off campus and headed for Steak and Egg Diner on Wisconsin Avenue.

As they zipped through the streets, Destiny's fingers traced the edge of the armrest, suddenly feeling nostalgic. "My brother used to have a car like this."

"My father gave it to my mother when she was pregnant with me," Jasiah informed Destiny as he kept his eyes on the road.

"Your dad had good taste," Destiny recognized.

"Seems that way, but I don't even remember him," Jasiah admitted. "I don't know anything about him but his name and date of birth."

"You don't remember his funeral?"

"I was a toddler," Jasiah shrugged. "He's probably in some unmarked grave at Harmony Cemetery."

Destiny placed her hand on Jasiah's arm, which was resting on the armrest. She couldn't imagine never knowing her dad.

Jasiah turned to her with a smile on his face. "It was nice of you to try to teach some of my classmates the electric slide."

Destiny giggled and thought Jasiah's change in subject was a sign to stop talking about his father. "Somebody has to," she smiled back. "I told you I am your Natalie."

After a pleasant dinner, Jasiah was disappointed when she reminded him she was nearing her curfew. He thought they solidified their connection throughout the evening; therefore, Destiny would be willing to break curfew and fool around with him in the backseat. However, he quickly realized that Destiny did not disobey her parents the way he had seen other girls do.

"You want to see me again. Don't you?" she politely turned down Jasiah as she exited the car.

"I just don't want it to be another month before I see you again," he admitted through the car window.

She giggled as she ascended the steps to her rowhome. "Thanks for a great evening, Jasiah! Call me when you get home!" she waved behind her. "Pull off, don't be a sitting duck in that pretty car."

She heard the tires screech as she placed her key in the door. Relishing in how their evening ended, Destiny strode into the house, wishing Jasiah had kissed her as fervently as he had done in Georgetown at the end of the evening.

A tinge of surprise came over her once she entered the house; she wasn't expecting her mother to be the one to greet her. Usually, it was her father sitting in his recliner, awaiting Destiny to return home safely.

"Ma, what are you doing up? Where's Daddy?" Destiny asked, searching for the traces of her father.

"That shrimp did a number on your father's stomach," Mrs. Peay sighed. "So, I figured I would wait up and see how things went for you."

"It certainly didn't start off magical," she admitted.

"How so?" Mrs. Peay inquired. "Certainly, it looked magical to me. The house was so festive; everyone seemed nice. You and Jasiah certainly hit it off."

"He's not the problem, Ma. It's everybody else," Destiny said as she sat on the sofa and began to spill the unpleasantness that weighed heavy on her heart in front of her mother. "Miss Faye thinks I'm not good enough to date her son."

"She needs to know her son is pursuing you and not the other way around," Mrs. Peay rolled her eyes.

"Ma, I'm tired of this family's actions dictating how people treat me," Destiny blurted out. "She said she's from the city and knows the Peays."

"Oh, Destiny," her mother took a deep sigh, "all families have their faults… Being a Peay has its advantages, too."

"I'm certainly not experiencing them lately," she kicked off her shoes, "I just want people to not make assumptions about me."

"People will do that your entire life," Mrs. Peay consoled as she lectured in a soothing tone. "It's your job never to change your character to fit those expectations."

"Easier said than done," Destiny muttered.

"Well, did you say anything to Faye to help ease her worries?"

"I laughed at her," Destiny responded. "I was thinking of telling her that your son pressed me out and bought me these clothes to be here."

Mrs. Peay smiled at her daughter's confidence. "Like I said, don't change your character to fit those expectations."

"Speaking of expectations… I didn't expect that house to be *that* nice. Ma, where did y'all go wrong in life? Why aren't we living in Potomac somewhere?" Destiny asked, half joking and half serious. "Since people think we're the mob and all."

"I got to peek in their kitchen, girl. Your father would have a good time cooking in there," Mrs. Peay ignored the sarcasm from her daughter. "And I swear everything in that dining room was Baccarat crystal."

"No, Ma, did you get a view of the backyard?" Destiny chimed in.

"The pool has to be heated for them to have it open this far into the season," Mrs. Peay nodded. "You sure have upgraded from that, Eric," her mother added with a slight giggle.

Destiny rolled her eyes, "Ma, I'm not in a relationship with Jasiah," she informed her mother. "Not after Miss Faye told me I was trying to trap her son."

Mrs. Peay shook her head. "Doesn't she know that you are the prize?"

"That's what I'm saying," Destiny smiled.

"You just don't forget it, Destiny Penelope Peay. You are the prize."

"I will never forget it, Ma," Destiny affirmed as she stood up and hugged her mother.

Chapter 5: Profiled

The sun painted strokes of gold on the cobalt sky as Destiny sat by the window in her room with her phone glued to her ear.

She was trying her best to plead the case of her absence without hinting at Jasiah's existence to her best friend, Bria. Her conscience wanted to spill all the feelings and experiences she shared with Jasiah to Bria. She wanted her friend to be a part of the hectic and serene moments she daydreamed about during her classes, at work, and when she was alone.

She wanted to take Bria into that abyss but couldn't – Bria was Eric's cousin. The urge to share her story with Bria chipped away at Destiny's conscience, but she knew she needed to break up with Eric first. Even though the threads of sisterhood between them were strong enough to hold the weight of countless secrets, this time, Destiny knew that she had to stay an enigma for the time being.

Three days had passed since Destiny lived through one of the most cherished moments of her life – the homecoming dance with Jasiah. The evening had been pivotal for both of them. Together, they weaved threads of adoration as they shared more of their life experiences in order to find out what they had in common instead of comparing the differences.

During her conversation with Bria, Destiny's sight caught a pigeon landing on the air conditioning unit that hung out of her only window. She tapped the glass to scare the pigeon away as her mind drowned in the thoughts comparing Eric and Jasiah.

'Should I stay with Eric? Or go with Jasiah?' The thought occupied her mind daily. In her heart, she knew she couldn't keep up the charade for long – sometime soon, she'd have to decide.

"Is something going on with your family?" Bria questioned as she noticed the silence from Destiny's side. With years of friendship behind them, Bria began to connect her own dots.

"Last time you got like this, Junior was going to trial," Bria continued.

Hearing the mention of her brother, Destiny was transported to the disturbing memory of when the DEA raided her eldest brother's apartment.

The unforgettable event crossed her mind as she remembered how she was babysitting her nephews when the officers barged in with their guns out. Destiny could still see their masked faces, the epitome of hatred in their eyes, with faint emotion of fear etched in them. She remembered peering down the barrel of the assault rifle pointed at her as the cop screamed, "Don't move!!"

Even a flash of that memory buried the claws of dread in her heart as she hoped never to experience that traumatic moment again.

"I...it's nothing like that..." Destiny stumbled across her words as she dismissed the idea. "I'm just helping out with the boys and working. I'm just trying to stay focused," she continued as she moved to her desk.

"I get it," Bria sympathized, sensing a tinge of tiredness in Destiny's voice. "Eric's worried about you, and so am I," Bria confessed to her best friend since seventh grade.

Destiny sat in her chair, unfazed, as she silently doodled Jasiah's name on a piece of paper, his warm smile suddenly at the forefront of her mind instead of her trauma. It took a moment for her to notice the silence between her and her best friend widening. Destiny thought about changing the subject to ease the lingering discomfort.

"What's going on with you and Carl?" She inquired as she stenciled designs in Jasiah's name.

"Girl, don't mention him. I caught that nigga all up in Angela's face during the fourth period the other day," Bria's infuriated voice echoed from the other side of the phone.

Destiny's brows raised in concern. She listened intently to Bria explain how she couldn't trust Carl and was thinking of letting him go so at least she could pursue someone else before Christmas time came along. Destiny agreed with her.

Carl was a popular guy in school. He played varsity football and thrived in a bunch of different clubs in school. He hung in a large crowd, which Bria didn't fit into. In terms of socializing, she resembled Destiny – astute and quiet. So often, the couple went their separate ways in school, leading people to think they weren't together.

"I'm just so close to giving it up to him," Bria admitted. "I tell you, that boy has a way with his tongue."

"Where has he been putting his tongue?" Destiny playfully asked as she stopped doodling, interest flaring in her voice. "Girl, spill it!"

Just as Bria started blabbering about the details of their sexual exploration, Destiny's other line beeped; Destiny cursed as she told Bria to hold on, only to find Eric on the other line.

"What's up, boo?" Eric's energetic voice pierced through Destiny's ears.

"Damn, you're interrupting a good-ass story from Bria," she blurted out.

"Call me on three-way," Eric suggested, curious to hear Bria's story.

"Naw, this is girl talk," Destiny rejected bluntly. "Hold on for two minutes," she said as she clicked back over to hear the sultry details of Bria and Carl skipping school to explore one another in his mother's bed.

"Girl, you have more heart than me," Destiny snickered, though the details of their foreplay intrigued Destiny. She had never been touched in a way that Bria described.

"Her room was nice," Bria confessed in a mischievous tone. "I felt a little bad, but it was way better than his twin-size bunk bed."

"I know about fooling around in a twin-size bed," Destiny mumbled.

"You been with Eric this long, and you still holding out," Bria mentioned.

"Speaking of which, he is still on the other line."

"That boy is patient."

"Someone is always home at his house. You know that!" Destiny blurted as expressions of frustration freckled on her face. "I'm not about to get the side eye by your aunt and uncle when I need to wash up."

"I hear that," Bria agreed. "I'm glad Carl doesn't have those problems."

"Girl, let me go," Destiny stopped the conversation. "I will talk to you later," she clicked on the other line. "What's up?" she stated to Eric.

"You are what's up," Eric replied. "Why have I only seen you in school this week?"

Destiny took a deep breath. She wanted to tell him the truth – confess the growing guilt in her. Instead, she decided to place the onus on him.

"You haven't invited me anywhere."

"So, now you need an invitation?" Surprise lingered in Eric's voice.

Destiny has always been the one to make plans for them during the week since she had a job and responsibilities in her home.

"Maybe," Destiny balled up the paper she had been doodling on and opened her science textbook. "Did you get through Mr. Abdul's homework?" Destiny questioned.

"I want to see you tomorrow," Eric exclaimed.

"You know Wednesdays are no good for me," Destiny sighed. "That's when my mother works her part-time job."

"I'll pick you up from work and bring you home," he suggested.

"Are you sure you can get someone's car?" Destiny quizzed as she flipped through the pages of her textbook for the homework assignment. Part of her mind was thinking of how she didn't even have to worry about these things with Jasiah.

"I think so," Eric confirmed.

"I was having a problem with number 8 on the homework," Destiny changed the subject. "Did you find that answer?"

"Destiny, I don't want to talk about homework. I want to talk about us," this time, Eric didn't seem to play Destiny's deflection game. Destiny threw down her pencil and tried to figure out if this was the moment she had been dreading.

"You went missing over the weekend. You haven't been talking to me or Bria. What's going on?"

"I didn't go missing. I told you I might visit Goldsboro with my mother to see my grandparents. And I went. I know you weren't expecting me to call you long distance," Destiny continued to tell her falsehood.

"Man, I wish I could afford to get us some cell phones," Eric said in a wishful manner.

"Get a job!" Destiny blurted out irritated.

"I've been trying," Eric retorted. "Nobody's buying me any new shoes until Christmas. I gotta get some new kicks."

Disappointment swirled in Destiny's heart. All she could think was that she would never be able to have sex with Eric or even do the non-penetration things that Bria had just described to her because of not only the thin walls in his house but also the risk that his brother needing access to their bedroom in the middle of things. He would never have money for a hotel room, and she wasn't eager to spend her money to give away what her mother called her "prized possession."

"You gonna buy me some shoes for Christmas?" Eric asked, pulling Destiny out of her thoughts.

Startled by Eric's shamelessness, Destiny laughed. "Eric, stop playing," she said as she started to search for keywords in her textbook to answer the missing question on her homework.

"Dex said since you're not giving up the goods, you might as well buy some."

Destiny looked at the phone, thinking she must be getting pranked since Eric couldn't be this brazen.

"Hello?" Eric said when Destiny didn't respond immediately.

Annoyed by Eric's absurdity, Destiny debated about hanging up on him. At that moment, she understood why her father continued to refer to him as *that lil' nigga*.

"Hello?" Eric stated again.

"Put Eric on the phone," Destiny's stern voice reverberated through the phone. Some part of her heart suspected her boyfriend had lost himself during the one Saturday evening they had not talked.

"I am on the phone."

"Man, put Eric on the phone and stop playing," Destiny continued, hoping Eric would come to his senses.

Eric laughed. His blatant laughter spiked her anger.

"I don't have time for this," Destiny yelled as she hung up the phone roughly.

Immediately, the phone rang back. Destiny stared at it indifferently and decided to focus on her homework instead of catering to Eric's neediness. Eradicating thoughts of Eric from her mind, she finished her work and got through a load of laundry.

As she prepared herself to iron her nephews' uniforms, the line in her room rang again. With each ring, her face grew sour.

'Buy him some kicks!?' She murmured to herself infuriatedly as she pressed on the iron with more pressure. She couldn't believe *that lil' nigga.*

She started to look at Eric as a pestering child, craving attention when he should be developing into a man like Jasiah. The bond she thought she had with Eric began to unravel with her unsettling emotions. Until Jasiah came along, she thought that Eric was *the one*. But now, she thought that maybe her lack of interest in him over the last few weeks revealed more about him than she realized.

With a defeated sigh, she sprawled across her bed, trying to figure out what she really wanted to do. Did she wish to attempt to get back on track with Eric or just let him go? With the growing irritation for his lack of intrinsic motivation, there was suddenly no light at the end of the tunnel of their relationship.

***

As Destiny lay in her bed trying to figure out how to tell Eric she needed space, Jasiah lay across his bed thinking of Destiny. He felt relief in sharing his secret about his father without fear of judgment. But Destiny's questions on Saturday night shattered through his shell, and a floodgate of emotions opened that he didn't even know was there about the loss of his father.

Agitation strangled Jasiah's heart as he started to contemplate talking to his mother about his emotions several times but never felt like it was the right time. Whenever he mustered up the courage to ask, she was either on the phone, fussing over his little brother, hosting someone, or tending to her husband.

The void of distance began to grow between them as Jasiah felt he could never catch her alone in the past three days, nor did she approach him, which frustrated him. Through the day, the tiny moments he got, he thought of opening up to her but couldn't muster the courage to ask – ask about his father's death or where he was buried. Jasiah remembered questioning her as an adolescent, but he never got a solid answer to extinguish the consuming fire of finding the truth in his heart. All he heard in response was, "He's gone. And I'm doing the best I can."

"Siah, wanna play the game?" Jasiah's younger brother RJ asked from the doorway. "I got the new Mario Cart."

"I didn't think you could play the game on a school night," Jasiah sat up.

"Well, I can't play my game, but nobody said I can't play your game," RJ revealed a Nintendo game cartridge from behind his back as he snickered.

"Where is Mommy?" Jasiah questioned before agreeing.

"Dad called a car for her to meet him somewhere."

Jasiah shook his head defeatedly, thinking- *It would have been nice to tell me I was left to babysit.*

"Did she say something about dinner?" Jasiah questioned as he watched his little brother fly over to the television, landing on his knees before his Nintendo 64.

"Pizza on the stove," RJ turned on the television.

Jasiah fell back on his bed. "You have thirty minutes, and then you need to go take a shower."

"Ughh," RJ whined.

Jasiah ignored his brother and stared at the ceiling, his mind slowly drifting away into the thoughts of calling over his neighbor, Tangey. Though she once broke is heart, they have been able to remain intimate friends.

"You showed off your new girlfriend to the whole school… but now you're calling me," Tangey huffed.

Jasiah smiled as he could imagine Tangey twisting her neck around and swinging her loose, curly ponytail as she talked.

"Goddamn, word travels fast," Jasiah mumbled.

"What's up, Jasiah?" she questioned curtly.

"I'm trying to see if you want to come over?" Jasiah got straight to the point.

"Mommy said no company," RJ mentioned without looking up from his game.

"Stay out of my business," Jasiah yelled at his little brother as he got up from his bed and went over to the reading nook in his window. He looked across the yard, searching through the trees, hoping he could see Tangey's bedroom light.

As mischievous adolescents, they used to send signals by flickering their flashlights from their bedroom windows to meet in their backyard or an empty pool house. But now, the elm trees had grown tall enough to block the view until they shed their leaves in the breeze of autumn.

Jasiah could hear Tangey's faint laughter.

"You know you miss me," Jasiah teased Tangey.

"Maybe a little," Tangey playfully admitted. "But back to this new girlfriend of yours."

"You don't need to worry about her," Jasiah sighed. "Come on, meet me in the pool house," he suggested.

"It sounds like you're babysitting," Tangey guessed.

Jasiah peered over at RJ, thought for a while, and said, "He's about to go to bed."

"You said thirty minutes," RJ interjected again, his eyes still focused on the television screen.

"It's about to be ten minutes if you don't stay out of my conversation," Jasiah warned his brother.

"Maybe another night," Tangey suggested.

"Don't shut me down so quickly," Jasiah refused to let her go. "At least humor me a little."

"How can I humor you?" she inquired.

"What do you have on?" Jasiah whispered into the phone.

"Boy, if you have to whisper like that, we can't even have the conversation," Tangey sucked her teeth. "Put your brother to bed and call me back," she insisted before hanging up.

Jasiah leaned back against the cold windowpane and heard his stomach growl. He was vexed by the thought of eating pizza for the third night in a row. He strolled downstairs to heat up a few slices in the microwave when he heard the giggles erupting from the backdoor – it was his mother and stepfather. Listening to their slurred voices, Jasiah instantly knew the pair was wired.

Faye sported a red, off-the-shoulder satin dress that seemed to be stained by red wine. Roy had removed his tie and unbuttoned the collar of his starched blue shirt, but he was still sporting his suit jacket.

"Siah!" his mother called out. "My handsome son."

"Hi, Ma," Jasiah opened the cardboard pizza box to see a plain cheese pizza – his little brother's favorite. "Ma, could you think of me just once when ordering pizza?"

Faye rolled her eyes and didn't respond.

"It's time for you to submit your college applications," Jasiah's stepfather, Roy, stated as he reached into the cabinet for two champagne glasses.

"Hello to you too," Jasiah mumbled.

"Jasiah has his recommendations from his teachers. He has a decent SAT score. I don't see any problems with him getting into Harvard with your alumni connections," Faye interjected.

Roy walked over to the small beverage fridge by the wine rack to get a chilled bottle of Moët Impérial without saying another word.

"Can you stock the regular fridge as often as you two stock liquor cabinets?" Jasiah spouted with annoyance evident in his voice.

"Good night, Jasiah," Faye sang in a fake opera tone as if she didn't even hear her son as she followed her husband toward his study, leaving Jasiah alone in the kitchen.

Without a second thought, his entity growling from anger, Jasiah grabbed his car keys from the island and ferociously slammed the backdoor as he exited. His first intention was to get something from McDonald's, but the more he drove, the angrier he became with his "parents."

The fire of anger blazed brightly in him as he thought about how his mother was more concerned with appearances than his actual well-being. He cringed at the memory of how initially when Lauren, his pompous self-entitled classmate, screamed rape, his mother's only concern was how she looked as a mother.

Jasiah's anger trickled from his eyes as he raced through the dark roads of Potomac, pain imbued in each tear as he recounted his mother yelling at him in front of the arresting officers, "What did you do? What did you do!?"

At that moment, hopelessness swallowed his existence. He still struggled with the reality that his own mother could think that he could stoop that low – to think that he could be a rapist. He had spent years at Sidwell Friends, feeling he didn't belong there, among the children of corporation presidents and dignitaries. He was the son of a dead drug dealer and gold digger. He was the burden of a ruthless lawyer.

He gripped his steering wheel tightly as his mind flashed to the lonesome feeling associated with being guilty until proven innocent. It didn't matter that he had no disciplinary actions in his academic file. It didn't matter that he was class president and the tennis team captain. When Lauren screamed rape, regardless if she pursued him for consensual sex, he felt like public enemy number one. Though the experience was behind him, Jasiah felt as alone at that moment, driving down Seven Locks Road, as he had been when a target was on his back at school for weeks until finally, Lauren's story unraveled.

As the painful memories reeled through his mind, Jasiah banged on his steering wheel, grunting in pain as the demon of sorrow rested on his shoulders. He turned up his radio, trying to diminish the memory of the stares, statements, accusations, and private meetings he sat outside as his fate was being determined.

Shaking off his mental anguish, he wiped away his tears, realizing he had driven too far from the familiar territory, and made a U-turn in the middle of the street. He hadn't driven a third of a mile back toward McDonald's before the sirens blared behind him, the red and blue lights reflecting in his rearview mirror as the police car closed the distance between them.

As if on cue, seeing the approaching officer, the instructions of his stepfather about situations like this shuffled through Jasiah's mind. He mumbled to himself as he pulled over, "Have your license and registration ready. Don't have an attitude. Keep your hands on the steering wheel. Answer the questions asked. Don't agree to a search. Don't resist."

"Do you know why I pulled you over?" the officer asked bluntly from the driver's side window.

"No," Jasiah stated as he tried to hand the officer his information through the open window.

"I've been following you for a ways. Did you do that U-turn to avoid me?" the officer interrogated; his brows knitted together tightly in suspicion.

"No, sir, I just missed my turn for the McDonald's," Jasiah answered plainly as he handed over his documents to the officer.

"You from around here, boy?" the officer asked as he scrambled through Jasiah's license and registration.

"Yes, sir," Jasiah answered.

"This car registered to you?" the officer asked. "You have insurance?"

"I do," Jasiah turned to get it from the glove box.

"Keep your hands on the wheel!" the officer screamed as he jumped back a few steps, his face now brimming with anger and fear.

Jasiah quickly turned forward, noticing the officer had drawn his service weapon and pointed it at him.

"Keep your hands on the wheel!" he shouted again, removing the safety lock from his gun.

Jasiah's heart dropped, and fear blanketed his face as he gripped the steering wheel tightly, unable to stop his legs from shaking. He swallowed the last bit of saliva in his mouth and stared straight down the barrel of the gun.

"Don't you move!" the officer yelled as he switched on his radio, still aiming at Jasiah.

"I was just trying to retrieve my insurance card, sir," Jasiah tried to clarify, but his voice wavered, seeing the gun still aimed at him.

"Get out of the car!" the officer shouted.

"Sir, why do I need to—"

"Get out of the car! Now!!" the officer continued to scream as if he was dealing with an assailant.

Under the immense pressure of the officer, Jasiah froze. He was like a deer caught in the headlights as he stared down the gun barrel. His mind went numb; his heart shivered with fear. He could no longer see the cars zipping past them. He felt paralyzed as his eyes focused on the darkness lingering in the barrel of the gun. Jasiah feared that if he blinked, the darkness would consume him.

In the face of Jasiah's noncompliance, agitation took over the officer. He lunged over and pulled open the door. The obscurity of fright covered Jasiah's face as he gasped for breath. The officer tried to yank Jasiah out of the seat but only made him dangle as if Jasiah was a rag doll by the seatbelt. Vexed, the officer thrust the back of his gun into Jasiah's temple.

At that moment, Jasiah managed to blink as his eyes lingered toward the beat-red face of the officer – terror, mixed with throbbing on the entire left side of his face, swarmed over him as he lost control over his consciousness. For the millisecond, his eyes closed, his surroundings went dark, and with the sound of another passing car, his mind warped – Jasiah was back in the interrogation room refuting Lauren's accusations. His stepfather was there, instructing him not to say anything.

When Jasiah realized his surroundings again, his face was against the pavement. He opened his eyes as drops of blood trickled from the side of his head, the voice of his stepfather echoed in his mind as he instructed him time and time again. *If you comply, you'll get your citation, if warranted, and be on your way.*

Tears of helplessness dropped from Jasiah's eyes as he felt the unfortunately familiar cold feeling of handcuffs against his wrist, his back heavy under the weight of the officer's knee. Jasiah could feel every pebble on the ground scraping against his face when he moved, so he stayed still and tried not to whimper in pain. He watched the blurry red and white lights reflect off of everything around him as more police cars joined the scene. He didn't know what to do, what to say, or how he had gotten into this situation.

"This thug done went mute," he could finally hear the officer stating as he removed his weight from Jasiah's back.

Jasiah thought to himself, *Thug? How did I get to be a thug?*

"You run his license?" another officer asked.

Jasiah lay there on the pavement, handcuffed, with a growing migraine until he heard someone say, "Get him up."

Two officers assisted Jasiah in sitting up on his knees.

"Hey, hey, hey!" a faceless officer started to snap his fingers in front of Jasiah, "what are you doing around here?"

Jasiah took a deep breath and figured he had better find his voice. "I live on River View," Jasiah stated as he found it hard to focus.

The police officers looked at one another.

"What did he do?" one officer asked the arresting officer.

Silence sealed the arresting officer's mouth.

"Run his tags," another officer stated.

"Come on, you can have a seat on the curb," the officer, who was snapping his fingers, stated.

Jasiah sat on the curb with his head down as the officers huddled. Helplessly, he stared at the pavement, wet from his tears, for a moment. The voice of his stepfather oscillated through his mind again - *That car is gonna get you robbed or arrested*, when his mother purchased it for him.

At that moment, Jasiah retraced his steps to see where he made an error. He looked out into the street to see that he had not crossed a double line when he made a U-turn, confirming that he had done nothing wrong. He tried to dry his face with his sleeve as his fear started to transform into anger. His vision returned as the heat from his fury dried his tears.

"I was complying when he pulled me out of the car!" Jasiah yelled as the tight handcuffed pinched his skin. "All I did was make a U-turn!"

The officers looked over at him. The anger blazed within Jasiah ferociously as he read the lips of the other police officer saying, "Let him go."

"This is police brutality!" Jasiah yelled in a firm tone.

"Shut up! You thugs don't belong around here!" the arresting officer screamed abrasively as he marched closer to Jasiah and raised his fist as if he were going to hit him. An officer on the side placed his hand out and stopped him from moving closer to Jasiah.

During the moment of anger and pain, things suddenly changed. A car pulled up, and a voice resonated as the driver rolled his window down, "Jasiah!!??"

Jasiah looked up to see his stepfather's partner, Chad, at the law firm, peering out his car's window. Chad immediately stepped out of his Porsche Carrera, leaving it in the middle of the road, and treaded toward the hoard of officers.

"What's the meaning of this?" Chad inquired with the officers in a firm, authoritative tone.

"Sir, I'm going to ask that you get back into the car," a female officer stated as she walked up to the scene.

"I suggest you tell me what is the meaning of this!" Chad spoke louder, undermining the female officer's voice in his sharp, hoarse voice. "I'm his lawyer. Let me get your badge number while I get your captain on the line," he pulled out a flip phone and went through his speed dial.

The officer who helped Jasiah to sit on the curb came over and uncuffed him. "You just sit right here," he instructed as he patted Jasiah's shoulder.

Jasiah didn't say anything as he started to rub his wrist, feeling little relief from the removed constraints.

"It's going to be okay, Jasiah," Chad assured Jasiah, looking at him in the eyes. "You hear me?"

Jasiah nodded before covering his face with his hands. He took a deep breath. He couldn't believe this was happening to him.

"This is the worst night ever," he mumbled to himself as he rubbed his head to keep his composure. He felt the gash on the side of his face and hoped he didn't need stitches. When he looked up, the arresting officer was striding toward him. Remnants of the fear that the officer imbued in his heart tangled Jasiah's consciousness. He jumped back.

"I want to apologize for the misunderstanding," he held out Jasiah's license and registration. "You are free to go."

Jasiah realized that his hand was shaking when he reached for his documents. He quickly snatched it and stood up.

"You okay to drive?" Chad asked as he came to Jasiah's side and gave him a pat on the back.

Jasiah nodded.

"Well, you get home. Your parents are waiting for you," Chad instructed Jasiah as he started to walk him to his car. He looked at the cut along the side of Jasiah's hairline, "That officer will pay for this," Chad assured him.

Once Jasiah got behind the wheel, he felt as nervous as he had been in the driver's seat for the first time. When he touched the steering wheel, his hands feverously shook, so he immediately removed them and rubbed them together, trying to gain composure. The darkness in that barrel of the officer's gun flashed before his eyes as he took a deep breath, pulled on his seatbelt, and started up the car, with his feet still trembling.

He looked up and felt like all eyes were on him, reminding him of the time when he was called a rapist. Sighing out the distasteful emotions, he pulled out onto the road slowly, only to drive far enough so that none of the police car lights were in sight. He pulled into a parking space and leaned back on the headrest. Jasiah sat there in his seat, organizing his scrambled thoughts to gather himself before making it home. Every time he closed his eyes, he could see himself being swallowed by the darkness of the gun barrel.

"Just make it home," Jasiah murmured to himself as he pulled off again and drove home, maintaining a speed under the speed limit. His mother and stepfather stood in the driveway when he pulled up, talking to Chad. He expected his stepfather to chastise him about the car and tell him *I told you so!*

"What took you so long?" his mother questioned.

"Faye, be easy on the boy," Roy stated. "You okay, son?"

Jasiah tried to mask his emotions as he nodded his head, but the overwhelming emotions grappled his heart, and he immediately shook his head sideways. His face manifested the feelings of agony as tears sparkled in his eyes, and he wiped his nose with his sleeve. Roy rushed forward, grabbed him, and embraced him tight.

"It's okay," he whispered to him. "You're okay," he continued.

It was the first time Roy had embraced Jasiah in a strong, genuine hug; therefore, it was the first time that Jasiah had ever felt the warmth of a fatherly embrace that he could remember. It was the hug that he didn't know he needed; however, it was still uncomfortable for him to accept it from Roy.

"I'm good," Jasiah whispered as he pushed away. "I'm good," he tried to convince those around him as well as himself.

"Jasiah, we know being racially profiled isn't an easy pill to swallow," Chad chimed in. "We can talk about what happened if you need to."

"I don't want to talk about it. I just want to take a shower and go to bed," Jasiah stated.

Faye lit a cigarette and blew smoke into the cool night air. "Should have just eaten the damn pizza," she mumbled.

"Faye, now ain't the time," Roy stated as he tried to reach out for Jasiah again.

Jasiah moved away quickly. "I'm good."

"Son, I remember the first time I got racially profiled by the police," Chad began.

"It's part of the reason why we started our practice," Roy added.

"You need to talk about what happened before I got there? How about that cut on the side of your head?" Chad stated.

"I... I.... I... can't," his voice cracked when he spoke as he relived the brutality of that officer in his mind.

"What do you mean you can't," Faye said. "We're going to sue the whole force."

"It's cold out here. And it's getting late," Chad interrupted. "Let's table this for a statement in the morning. But I need to get photos of your wrist and face."

"Okay," Jasiah agreed on the plan of action.

As soon as Jasiah was alone, he felt sick. Hastily, he ran upstairs to his bathroom. It felt like the fear and anxiety were tearing his insides apart, and now were hurling out of him. Gasping for breath, clutching at his stomach, Jasiah grunted in agony. The moment the sick feeling stopped, he turned on the shower but found himself staring at his reflection in the mirror.

Usually, he reveled in the idea that people thought he was into illegal money-making activities. But at that moment, he wanted no part of anything that made him look like a drug dealer.

Is this how Destiny saw me? He asked himself as the pain from his excruciating headache trickling through his body.

He bellowed out his agony, allowing the pain of the evening to engulf him. As he attempted to wash away the discomfort, he promised himself that he wouldn't be a statistic no matter how people saw him.

Chapter 6: Mercy Me

Hues of magenta settled into the sky as Destiny stood on the sidewalk, waiting for Jasiah after work. She was excited to see him, feeling like the emotions being cultivated between them made her feelings toward Eric fade into nothingness. When a 1997 Camry pulled up in front of her, Destiny didn't give the car a second glance until Jasiah rolled down the passenger side window, revealing it was him inside.

As she opened the passenger car door, she quickly surveyed his obviously different look. There were no signs of a sparkling diamond earring or branded clothes on him. The boy in front of her looked like a shell of the Jasiah she had known for the past few months. Caressing Jasiah's weary face with her eyes, a thought spiraled in Destiny's mind. *He must be on some kind of punishment.*

"You sick?" Destiny poured her worries into her words as she felt his forehead.

"Nah, I'm not sick. I just... haven't been myself for the last few days," Jasiah explained as he gently held her hand.

"You sure? You look a little pale," she voiced her concern.

"I'm more than fine now that you're by my side," he smirked, merging into traffic.

"Jasiah, if you don't feel good, you didn't have to come get me," Destiny assured him.

"I wanted to see you," Jasiah exclaimed as he averted his eyes from the road to her while they waited at a red light.

His words instilled a flurry of emotions within her as if her heart had received validation and freedom to adore the man beside her.

"I wanted to see you too," she whispered in an affectionate tone as her gaze met Jasiah's.

They smiled at one another, relishing the moment of honesty between them.

"What's your curfew?" Jasiah quizzed, trying to gauge what they could do in their time together.

"Midnight," Destiny responded, knowing that her parents were going to enjoy a night of hand-dancing at the Chateau while the twins were at Jax's.

"Do you want to go back to my house?" Jasiah quickly suggested when he learned they could have nearly six hours together.

"I thought we were going out to eat," Destiny reminded him.

"We will eat," Jasiah smiled, flashing his dimples at Destiny.

"Is your muhva home?" Destiny queried. Her mind instantly warped to the thought of how Faye had treated her the last time she had been there.

"It doesn't matter."

"Your muhva doesn't like me," Destiny reminded Jasiah.

"I like you. That's all that matters," he intertwined his fingers with hers.

Destiny tried to detangle her mixed emotions. She would love to be at Jasiah's home, but then again she didn't want to go where she was not welcome.

"Whatever you want to do," she responded, giving in to lust buried within her. She peered at the city lights, flickering with a variety of hues as they headed for Whitehurst Freeway, trying to avoid staring at her love interest.

"Where is your car?" Destiny questioned suddenly to break the silence between them.

"It's at home," Jasiah informed her as he focused on driving.

"How many cars do you guys have?" she asked as she turned back to him. She couldn't help but admire how handsome he looked. Though their hands were locked together, she wanted to touch him in other ways.

"A few," Jasiah answered as he tried his utmost not to reveal the truth behind the pain on his face, even though every fiber within him wanted to tell the details of his trauma. Nevertheless, he felt like his truth was a burden and didn't think telling her would give him the relief he needed.

"Where is your earring?" Destiny flicked Jasiah's earlobe daintily, sending quivers of tickles through his body as he retracted himself away.

"What's the matter? You don't think I look good without it?" Jasiah retorted.

"Boy, you know you are fine without it," Destiny touched his face with the back of her hand.

In that moment, Jasiah's silent suffering started to dissipate. He basked in the soothing feeling of Destiny's touch. Instinctively, guided by his emotions, Jasiah kissed the palm he had been holding. The feeling of his tender lips against her palm sent a tingly sensation through Destiny. But she noticed how he avoided eye contact with her, even when they were still in traffic.

"Are you alright?" she asked as she couldn't shake the feeling that something had happened to him since they had last seen one another.

In the face of Destiny's questions, Jasiah sighed deeply as he couldn't bring himself to answer her earnestly, not at that moment. "I'm fine," he lied with a smile.

Burying her worries, she turned up the radio and leaned back into the seat. Destiny's mind started to spiral in the silence between them with thoughts of school, home, work, and her last conversation with Eric.

She had spent the prior night explaining to Eric why she couldn't fit him into her life anymore. For hours, they took turns saying something hurtful, the other person hanging up, and then the insulting person would call the insulted one back. It was a horrible game of phone tag that left her trying to conceal puffy eyelids in the morning.

She could feel the emotions that had vanished from her relationship with Eric creeping into her relationship with Jasiah. They were so intense that she could not shake them off. As she sat in the car listening to Whitney Houston croon, Destiny enjoyed the sense of tranquility and warmth she felt in the moment.

Destiny exhaled loudly.

Jasiah heard it. He felt the relief associated with the sound and wished he could exhale away his stress. He looked over at her as she aimlessly stared out the window.

"You're deep in thought over there," Jasiah broke the silence as he pulled up to a small pub.

Destiny slowly turned her head and looked at Jasiah as she embraced a smile on her face. "I have some things on my mind."

"So do I," he leaned over and kissed her. She didn't resist- she found herself moving forward, plunging deeper into the moment as she kissed him back — their breaths intermingled, forming, strengthening, and flaming a spark within each of them.

"Girl, you're gonna get yourself into trouble tasting that sweet," Jasiah stated playfully.

"Whatever," she rolled her eyes and turned to get out of the car.

They ordered food to go and got back in the car to wait. Destiny transitioned into the role of a DJ as she fumbled through his catalog of CDs, creating a carefree vibe between them with every song she selected.

"You had all of these CDs in the Bubble?" Destiny inquired as she inserted Janet Jackson's "That's the Way Love Goes" disc into the player.

Jasiah nodded as he ran his fingers through her hair; the feeling of her long, straight hair between his fingers pacified him somehow.

"We gotta take this one in the house," Destiny confirmed as she bobbed her head to the intro.

Jasiah watched her in amusement and started to mimic her car dance moves. For a moment, the car served as their capsule, protecting them from outside influences as they laughed at one another. Suddenly, during his seated dance moves, Jasiah's eyes lay upon a Montgomery County squad car pulling into the parking space next to them. Suddenly, anxiety shackled his entity as he dreaded getting out of the vehicle to get the food.

"You think the food is ready?" Destiny posed the question as she stared at her watch.

"Ugh, yeah," Jasiah nodded as he rubbed his temple. "Can you get the food? I'ma run across the street and get us something to drink from the quickie mart."

"Well, give me the keys so I don't look stupid waiting out here for you," Destiny suggested.

Hastily, Jasiah threw her the keys and strode out of the car in the opposite direction as Destiny. His eyes were drenched with disgust as he kept staring at the cop car from a distance – his heart screaming at him to stay across the street until the police cruiser left, but he knew he couldn't leave Destiny stranded like that. To calm his anxiety, Jasiah chanted a quick prayer, wishing that he could get home without crossing paths with any police officers – especially not the one who assaulted him.

Before he could move, memories of that dreaded night and the events after that flashed through his mind. He could still feel the officer's weight on his back, the tight handcuffs pinching his wrists, and the throbbing pain on his face.

Sweat trickled down Jasiah's chiseled jaw as the camera flash went off in his mind's eye – Roy taking pictures of his bruised wrist and face to file a formal complaint against the officer for assault and the entire police department for perpetuating the behavior of the officer. When Jasiah finally blinked, he could vividly hear the large oak door closing behind him after he testified before the grand jury trying to get charges brought against the offending police officer. Clenching his fists, Jasiah focused on present day and saw a silhouette of Destiny's figure through the pub window with a bag in her hand.

He thought he was in the clear and jogged back across the street. Just as he grabbed the door handle, he could see an officer holding the door open for Destiny. She smiled and said thank you, but when Destiny looked at Jasiah, she could see the look of worry on his face.

"You okay?" she lipped to him.

Jasiah averted his eyes to avoid making eye contact with the officer.

Destiny used the remote key fob to open the car door, and Jasiah quickly slid into driver's seat.

"Boy, why are you acting so hot?" Destiny interrogated him as soon as she got into the car, her heart thumping with worry as she knew something was awry.

Jasiah just stared at the woodgrain steering wheel; his eyes widened in distress as he couldn't carve himself out of the nightmare he was still living.

"Jasiah!" Destiny waved her hand in front of his face. "Jasiah!"

"I'm fine," Jasiah started the car. "I'm fine."

Destiny placed her hand over Jasiah's on the steering wheel. "You're shaking," she said as her eyes soaked with concern. "You're not about to drive us off a cliff, are you?"

Destiny's joke lifted the fog of trauma from his heart for a moment. He leaned back into the seat and took a deep breath, exhaling away the heaviness strangling him. He could hear his stepfather's words the morning after the assault resounding in his mind: *You can't live in fear.*

"Girl, you will always be safe with me," Jasiah smirked, replenishing his composure as he tried to mask his anxiety with his charm.

"That's what I like to hear," Destiny grinned. "Come on before this food gets cold. How far in the boonies do we have to ride?"

"I do not live in the boonies. It's the suburbs."

"Suburbs, my ass, this is the boonies," Destiny pulled on her seatbelt. "The air is different around here. It has a different smell."

"This air has a different smell?" Jasiah laughed and pulled off like he usually would. "It's clean, that's why."

"It's almost as fresh as the air in Goldsboro," Destiny referred to her mother's hometown in North Carolina as she continued bask in the surrounding landscape. She felt like she was in a different world where there were pubs and quickie marts instead of liquor stores and carry-outs. "I feel like I'm out of town," she admitted to Jasiah.

"That's how I feel every time I take you home," Jasiah confirmed.

Nervousness arose within Destiny as Jasiah pulled up to his home. The feeling of how unwelcomed she was by Faye the last time she visited suddenly warped back.

"Now I have to ask you, are you okay?" Jasiah looked at Destiny.

"Just thinking about how your muhva doesn't care to get to know me," Destiny riposted earnestly.

"I don't know what to say about that, to be honest," Jasiah placed his arm around Destiny's shoulder. "But I like you."

"Oh, yeah?"

"Oh, yeah," he kissed her on top of the head, inducing peace in her tensed nerves as her heart thumped ferociously under the breeze of his mesmerizing cologne.

As they entered the house, the fresh scent suddenly shifted into a pungent, heavy smell of cigarettes. Destiny was startled as she didn't remember the smell being so intense the last time she had been there. Though she saw his mother smoking, she didn't remember the lingering odor.

"Can we open a window?" Destiny requested as she covered her nose.

"We're going down to the basement," Jasiah mentioned as he guided her. "She just smokes in the kitchen and her bedroom."

Surprise swarmed over her eyes as she peered at the fireplace in the kitchen, and she recognized how there were no newspapers, outdated magazines, or mail randomly thrown on the kitchen table, island, or foyer table. No shoes by the door or jackets were thrown casually over the banister. In her mind, she compared the tidiness of Jasiah's house to hers as she concluded that she would never invite Jasiah into her home.

Destiny followed Jasiah to the basement. He flicked on the gold-plated light switches in every space they entered, unveiling how dynamic the house design was. As Destiny followed him, she submerged herself in the luxuries of the house, judging how it looked without the crowd, balloons, and backdrops.

Jasiah revealed a basement that reminded Destiny of a five-star hotel lobby with a bar. The lighting was elegant yet bright; the creamy beige furnishing made her think she might stain them if she touched it. However, the chill in the air down there made Destiny shiver and instantly uncomfortable.

"I'll turn on the heat down here. It's on a separate thermostat, so it might take a minute," Jasiah stated, seeing Destiny shiver as he placed the food on the bar.

"I think I'ma need a blanket or an extra sweatshirt in order to come out of my jacket," Destiny reasoned as she stood in the middle of the room, rubbing her biceps.

"I got you," Jasiah assured Destiny, "Sit down, take your shoes off, and relax," he coaxed as he marched over to the 10-disc CD changer.

Destiny took a seat on one of the high-back bar stools. She skimmed her hand over the quartz countertop and remembered her mother saying - *The choices we make.* Suddenly, Destiny wanted to know Faye's story beyond what little Jasiah told her. Destiny wanted to know if Faye's father had told her to date a boy whose parents have a circular driveway, too.

Jasiah played "The Miseducation of Lauryn Hill," turned the thermostat up to seventy-three, and joined her at the bar.

"Are you sure it's cool for me to be here?" Destiny questioned as she slowly took in the well-stocked bar before her.

"It's a little late for you to ask me that," Jasiah bit into his sandwich as a trickle of mayonnaise splotched around the corner of his lips. "Eat."

"What happened to a blanket?" Destiny inquired as she wiped the mayonnaise from Jasiah's lips with her thumb.

"Are you that cold?" Jasiah quizzed with a twisted brow in disbelief.

Destiny nodded.

"A'ight," Jasiah jumped out of his seat and vanished upstairs quickly.

Destiny began to eat her club sandwich, relishing the taste of every bite as she sang along with Lauren Hill. A wave of relief swept across her when she heard movement on the steps; she assumed it was Jasiah. But the shock consumed her when she stared at one of her father's oldest friends dressed in his gym attire descend the stairs.

"Mr. Roy!" she recalled quickly.

Roy stopped in his tracks and squinted his eyes at Destiny, trying to recognize her.

"Hello," he spoke, but confusion was evident in his eyes as he tried to recall how this teenage girl knew him. As he surveyed her face, the color of her eyes reminded him of his high school classmate, Ray Peay. Then, it dawned on him that it was his daughter. He looked at her bewildered.

Destiny assumed her looks had changed since they had last seen one another. She was no longer the twelve-year-old little girl being coaxed by Mr. Roy on how she should speak when she got on the stand at her brother's trial. Prompted by the sight of Mr. Roy's tall stature, a flood of memories gushed over her, including the days she spent waiting outside the courtroom to be called to testify. In a split second, she relived the most detestable moments of her life thus far – the time when police raided her brother's apartment up until her brother was sentenced two years later.

Roy and Destiny were in a stare-off until she broke the strings of silence, "I'm Destiny, Ray Peay's daughter. And you represented my brother, Ray Junior."

"Oh," Roy smiled. "Look at you, all grown up," he came closer and leaned on one of the bar stools. "How did you get mixed up with my son?"

"I still ask myself that," Destiny replied as she started to open her bottled Pepsi.

"I see," Roy nodded his head. "Your brother should be coming home soon, correct?"

"I think he up for parole in a month or so," Destiny answered. "I'm sure you'll be at the parole hearing with him."

"Of course, of course," Roy agreed. "And how are your parents?" Roy inquired as he stood up straight.

Destiny could see how uneasy he was with her presence in his home, which started to make her feel nervous. She answered, "They are fine," as a sinking feeling came over her as she thought she would soon be barred from the residence if both Jasiah's mother and stepfather didn't want her there.

Roy simply nodded in response.

"Well, it was nice to see you," Destiny turned forward without attempting to continue a conversation.

"Well, I'm glad to see you, Destiny, under different circumstances," Roy responded as he stepped back. "Tell your dad I said hello," Roy added with a wave as he continued to his home gym on the other side of the basement.

Suddenly, the clopping of footsteps erupted again from the staircase – this time, it was Jasiah. He noticed the light on in the gym and asked if his stepfather had come downstairs.

"I know your stepdad," Destiny admitted quickly. "He went to high school with my dad."

Startled by the sudden revelation, Jasiah stood motionless for a moment and finally aimed a question from the top of his head. "Really? When Lafayette mentioned him to you, you acted like you hadn't heard of him."

"I was twelve or thirteen the last time I saw him. And he has always been Mr. Roy. I didn't recall his last name. It was really his face that made me place the name just now."

"I don't know if this is a good or bad thing," Jasiah murmured to himself.

"I don't think it's a good thing, to be honest," Destiny pushed her food away from her as her stomach started to turn.

"Well, I definitely don't care what he thinks," Jasiah assured her as he draped a blanket over her shoulders.

"Thank you," she smiled at him.

"What are you staring at?" Jasiah asked as he sat back down.

"You," Destiny stood and started to squeeze Jasiah's cheeks like he was a little kid. "Show me those cute little dimples," she joked.

Jasiah beamed as he held her around the waist, giving her what she asked for.

"I could just kiss you," Destiny warned him as she started to lean into him.

"Then do it," Jasiah coaxed.

Destiny leaned in even closer, locked her lips with his, and both lost themselves in the haze of lust. They shared a long, deep kiss that flared exciting emotions in both of them. When Destiny pulled away, Jasiah still had his lips puckered.

"Boy, eat," she laughed.

"Girl, you know you do something to me," he started to shake as if he was having a seizure.

Destiny laughed as she leaned against him, not wanting to be without his touch, and stuck a fry in her mouth.

After eating, Jasiah and Destiny plunged onto the couch and began chattering about what they thought college life would be like if they went to the same college, though they both had two different ideas of where to go to college. Jasiah seemed to only think about attending Harvard, while Destiny opted for historically Black colleges and state schools.

"Okay, let's make a pact," Destiny suggested. "We'll both apply to Duke and North Carolina A&T."

"You can get into Harvard, Destiny," Jasiah encouraged her as he embraced her waist.

"It's not about what I'm going to get into. It's about having the money to pay for it," she reminded him, suddenly feeling the brisk air leave the room. She dropped the blanket off from her shoulders.

Just as they were making a pinky promise, Jasiah's stepfather strolled out of the gym. He caught a glimpse of Jasiah smiling at Destiny and said, "It's good to see you smiling, son."

Jasiah's facial expression immediately changed; his brows knitted together, and his eyes were void of emotions.

"I have that effect on him," Destiny grabbed Jasiah's hands and squeezed them when she noticed his shift in mood. She looked over at Roy, "My dad won't believe it when I tell him I saw you."

Roy replied with a smile and headed upstairs.

Once Destiny heard the basement door shut, she made Jasiah look at her in the eyes. "Tell me what's going on."

"Destiny, it's difficult to talk about," Jasiah shunned the uncomfortable topic.

Destiny could feel Jasiah was in pain but decided not to push. Jumping up from the couch, she marched over to the CD player and started to search through the CD collection for something upbeat. Jasiah crept up from behind her and wrapped his arms around her as he sniffed at her neck – his consciousness drowned in the hypnotizing and exciting scent of vanilla lingering around her body. Destiny turned around and hugged him back. It was the type of hug that he wished his mother had given him days ago when he was deep in physical pain and mental anguish. But as Destiny wrapped her slender arms around him, caressing the back of his neck, his worries started to melt away under the security of her embrace. He held onto her and contemplated what he wanted to tell her.

"Jasiah," Destiny called out his name softly as she rubbed his back.

"Destiny," he sang back as he pulled away slightly.

Lost in the melodies of the song, the beat of each other's hearts, both gazed into each other's eyes as their silent, hefty breaths conveyed the emotions on its waves. Liberating themselves from worldly affairs, they found comfort in each other's lips as they kissed and snuggled back onto the couch. Jasiah skimmed his firm hands over her body as she ruffled her hands over his broad shoulders, their hearts colliding with each other – singing the same beat. Grabbing Destiny by her hips, Jasiah rolled her on top of him as he stared into her hazel eyes sparkling with vibrant emotions.

"Jasiah!" Destiny let out a muffled scream as she was startled by the sudden shift.

"Shhh!" Jasiah warned her not to be too loud.

The emotions of ecstasy sparkled between the two as Jasiah brushed his hands against Destiny's waist and started to pull up her shirt as he planted kisses around her neckline. Instincts took over Destiny as she suddenly pulled away from Jasiah, confused by yearning growing within her.

"Hey, you cool?" Jasiah asked as he clasped his lips, savoring the taste Destiny's lips left on them.

"Y-y-yes, I don't know why I did that," she stuttered as she pulled down her shirt.

"Hey, it's okay; I'm ready when you're ready," Jasiah said, a hint of sadness flickering in his eyes as he tried his utmost to bury the arousing emotions.

"I'm sorry, Jasiah, it's just..." Destiny stared at him worriedly.

"It's fine." Jasiah consoled her as he embraced her in his arms. "I promise."

The music reverberated through the room faintly as they cuddled again and continued singing along with Lauren Hill. The music swayed around them as Destiny and Jasiah relished each other's embrace, feeling the synchronized beat of their hearts. Destiny gently caressed Jasiah's chest as he kissed her forehead, blanketing her in his arms even more. Just as serenity shrouded their existences with their eyes closed, a loud thud from the basement door opening carved them out of each other's grip.

Quickly moving to the opposite end of the sofa, Destiny ran her fingers through her hair and pulled up the blanket over her feet.

"I didn't know you had company this evening," Faye's playful voice vibrated through the basement.

"Ma, you remember Destiny," Jasiah announced, rubbing the back of his head as he understood that he hadn't given any heads up to his mother about Destiny's arrival.

"I'm back," a faint sarcastic statement escaped Destiny's mouth that she tried to mask with a smile.

"I see," Faye glanced at Destiny as she flipped the lighter between her fingers – agitation sparking in her as Destiny's taunts submerged in her mind.

"You're dressed like you have a job," Faye continued.

"Ma, I told you Destiny has an internship at MCI," Jasiah reminded his mother.

"Ohhh! So, she's that one?" Faye returned Destiny's taunt with sarcasm as the corners of her mouth curled up.

"That one?" Destiny repeated as she squinted at Jasiah.

Sensing the nature of Destiny's question, Jasiah shook his head and peered back at his mother.

"What's up, Ma? If you were coming to say hello, you still haven't done it yet," he continued as flickers of irritation painted vivid on his face.

"Hi," Faye uttered as she lit up the cigarette she held delicately in her fingers and walked further into the room.

"Hell...o," Destiny greeted back, coughing as the smoke from the cigarette suffocated her.

"Ma, could you put that out? Or just go back upstairs?" Jasiah pleaded as he fanned the swirling smoke away with his hands.

"What do you mean? This my house," Faye shunned off her son's pleas as she puffed out a ball of smoke into the air.

"Come on, we can just hang in my room," Jasiah gestured to Destiny.

"Oh, no, no, no," Faye flailed her hands in objection as she puffed up another stream of smoke.

"Really, Ma?" Jasiah wailed - frustrated. His mother had never objected and acted like this when he had company before.

"We don't need another Lauren incident," Faye muttered sloppily as she revolved her indifferent gaze between Jasiah and Destiny.

Jasiah's heart sank in embarrassment. Part of his soul was bruised with the blades of betrayal – he couldn't believe his own mother would casually bring up the horror. The barriers of patience shattered within him as frustration and pain imbued his tongue.

"What the hell, Ma?" Jasiah yelled as he threw his hands in the air. The veins in his neck and forehead started to protrude as anger filled his veins.

From the sidelines, Destiny noticed the pain reflected in Jasiah's eyes and the change in his demeanor. She wanted to quickly defuse the situation, though she pondered what exactly was a "Lauren situation."

"Jasiah's been nothing but a perfect gentleman," Destiny interjected as she placed her hand on Jasiah's leg, which was the closest thing to her. Her firm hold was an assurance to say *I got you.*

"That's how I raised him," Faye stated as her gaze scrolled over Destiny. "Roy heard y'all talk about college. Destiny, you do know that Jasiah's going to Harvard, right?"

Destiny felt the arrogance in Faye's tone. Shrouding herself in the shield she had created for demeaning comments, Destiny simply shook her head as she waved away the cigarette smoke.

"Is she deaf?" Faye inquired, looking at her son.

"My parents taught me that if you don't have anything nice to say, you shouldn't say anything at all," Destiny retorted, peering straight into Faye's stare. "Jasiah, I think I should leave," Destiny added as she stood.

Uneased by the unfolding situation, Jasiah checked the time on his watch – it was only 9 p.m.

"Ma, could you please go upstairs?" Jasiah pleaded, his voice stern as he spoke through clenched teeth.

"Faye!!" Roy's voice thundered from upstairs. "Faye, leave those kids alone and come upstairs!" Roy called after her.

Faye shook her head in disapproval as she headed upstairs upon her husband's request.

Breathing out a sigh of relief, Jasiah got up to change the CD and played Puff Daddy's "Satisfy You." A smile played on his face as he listened to the starting beat of the song. But it vanished as he turned toward Destiny. She had her shoes on and stood ready to leave.

"Hold up, Destiny," he uttered, holding his arm forward.

"Where I'm from, when a muhva acts like that, you leave," Destiny responded as she put on her backpack.

"Well, that's not how it works here," Jasiah said as he approached Destiny and removed her backpack. "Come on, I have been wanting you to listen to this song with me."

Destiny glanced at Jasiah, revolting at the idea of staying under the same roof as Faye anymore.

"Come on, Destiny. You see, she went upstairs. We are good," Jasiah persuaded her as he held her hands.

She wanted to stay. She was having such a pleasant time with Jasiah – the peacefulness of his embrace numbed her senses, but part of her knew she couldn't be in the house where she wasn't welcome, especially as she started to question why she was hearing about "Lauren" again.

"Come onnnnn," Jasiah grabbed both her hands and urged her to stay. "Just stay until ten."

Destiny couldn't resist asking, "Who is this Lauren?"

Jasiah felt like he was being tortured at that moment. He sat back on the sofa and tried to figure out if he could trust Destiny with his darkest of secrets, the most vulnerable parts of himself. At that moment, Destiny had no idea what the load of mental anguish Jasiah was carrying.

"Jasiah, who is Lauren?" Destiny was relentless in her interrogation. "What the fuck is going on?"

"I fucked her at a party," Jasiah immediately admitted. "But she claimed I raped her after I told her I wasn't interested in a relationship with her or even doing it again."

Breath betrayed Destiny as she gasped and grabbed her chest in disbelief.

"The only thing that saved me was our conversation through our two-way pagers."

Destiny felt immediate relief and couldn't help but ask, "Why would she bring it up to me? Why would your mother bring that up around me?"

"She's fucking crazy," Jasiah shook his head. "But when it comes to Lauren, my stepfather made her sign something to say she can't keep spreading the rumor, or we would sue her or press charges or something."

"And y'all still go to school together?" Destiny asked as she stared at Jasiah – puzzled about how anyone would try to label him as a rapist.

"My mother wanted her arrested for making a false police report or at least expelled, but you know how it is. Her father is a judge in Montgomery County Circuit court," Jasiah took a deep breath, "I never thought she would be so crazy to say something to you personally."

"That's what you get for messing with those White girls," Destiny uttered as she walked over to the CD player.

Jasiah was relieved that Destiny didn't pry anymore. He joined her at the CD player and started to fumble through CDs.

"Start the song again," Destiny suggested as she took her jacket and shoes off as she felt a tinge of sympathy for Jasiah.

When Puff Daddy's "Satisfy You" faded in from the beginning, Jasiah started mimicking Puffy Daddy's dance moves and rapping the lyrics in sync with the song.

"I can promise everything that I do is to satisfy you," he sang along with R. Kelly, making Destiny smile.

"You need your chain on for this performance," Destiny chuckled as she bopped her head to the song.

Jasiah ignored her joke. He leaned in closer and planted a kiss on her lips, feeling relief as they touched. As she tasted Jasiah's lips, Destiny wondered if he really meant what he was saying to her.

"I'm telling you, Destiny, me and you would be a good thing," Jasiah mumbled as he pulled away from her.

"How did we get to this moment?" Destiny asked as she flung her arms around Jasiah's neck and stared into his enchanting brown eyes.

"Destiny, I know you want me the way you want me... what are you scared of?"

"I'm scared that I'm committing myself to someone I don't know," she admitted. "I'm really trying to process this Lauren shit."

"I'm not lying about that."

"You're standing here with me and still a student at Sidwell Friends instead of in prison, so I believe you," Destiny assured him.

"I've told you some of my deepest thoughts," Jasiah whispered affectionately as he embraced her waist and started to dance.

"But I don't know what is happening to you right now, and I know it has nothing to do with false accusations of last spring," Destiny removed her hands from around his neck and lightly touched the scar on his temple. Jasiah winced, even at her faint touch.

Seeing her worry-drenched eyes, Jasiah's heart screamed to spill everything before her. Sighing out his soaring emotions, he stood quiet as he lowered his gaze to the carpet.

"Jasiah, I thought we promised to share the events in our life that make us who we are."

"We did."

"And I know something happened to you in the last few days," she stared at Jasiah, awaiting his explanation.

He peered into her eyes, conversing inaudibly yet loud enough that Destiny could hear the wails of pain behind Jasiah's glare.

"If you don't trust me like that, I can respect it," Destiny murmured. "As your friend," she added as she moved out of his grasp and started to fumble through the CDs.

Jasiah rubbed his head as he strolled away, trying to figure out where he wanted to start the story. Did he want to go into how he felt leaving the house? How does he still have unaddressed questions about his father?

The pent-up emotions surged into the tip of his tongue as he opened his mouth to reveal that he got harassed by the police, but he ended up starting with, "I hate it here. I can't wait to get out of here and go to college... To be honest, I don't care where I go."

Destiny almost wanted to laugh at Jasiah. "Boy, you're so dependent on your muhva," she shook her head. "You're not ready to leave this plush life."

"You don't understand, Destiny."

"Make me understand, Jasiah."

"It's so frustrating when people think this empty ass house is so wonderful. It's just a reflection of my shallow ass mother."

"Jasiah," shock warped through Destiny's veins at Jasiah's statement.

Jasiah couldn't hold his emotions back anymore as he began to disclose the events of the traumatizing night he had a few days ago.

"I got harassed by the police the other night, and all she was worried about was who saw her son on the ground. Not because I was racially profiled, hit in the head, and thrown out of the car. But because her friends would think they couldn't trust me in their house or around their children."

Jasiah's quivering voice sent jolts of worry through Destiny as she covered her mouth in shock to contain herself.

"Are you okay?" she asked Jasiah as she sat him down on the sofa. She was shocked when he instantly laid his head in her lap.

"No," he answered honestly. "I can't even face a police officer without thinking that I will be violated again."

The memory of being in front of the pub flashed through Destiny's eyes as she understood why Jasiah clammed up when leaving the pub. She leaned down and kissed the side of his face. She held him and rubbed the top of his head, trying to comfort him as he revealed the intricacies of the incident.

"The racist cop pulled a gun on me because I was getting my insurance card," Jasiah recalled as he hid his face in his hands. He curled up into the fetal position as his stomach cramped from the unpleasant memory.

Destiny gently stroked his back as she closed her eyes, picturing the horrific scene as Jasiah recounted the police officer abusing his power. She held her breath as her mind warped into her own traumatizing encounter with the police.

***

On a bright summer afternoon, eleven-year-old Destiny was at her brother Junior's house with his wife Sarah and their twin boys. Sarah had just returned from the carryout with lunch when a loud knock erupted from the door. Destiny strode toward the door to answer it but saw no one through the peephole. She tried listening for a voice from the other side as she yelled, "Who is it?" but the noises around her muffled into the cartoons playing on TV.

"Somebody playing at the door," Destiny told her sister-in-law as she strolled toward the kitchen to fill the twins' sippy cups.

Within moments, a loud thundering bang at the door shackled everyone in their spots – fear rendered them motionless. Gasping from the sudden shock, Destiny gazed at the police officers and DEA agents pouring in, covered in full riot gear, with their guns drawn. Fear pierced through her innocence as she froze in place, dropping the toddler cup and bottle of Twister juice on the vinyl floor.

Sarah grabbed for her children, but a police officer hollered, "Don't move!"

"How old are you?" a female officer asked Destiny as she took off her face shield and lowered her gun, which she had aimed at Destiny until an officer yelled, "All clear!"

"E-e-eleven," Destiny sputtered.

***

Before the terror clawed at her consciousness, Destiny broke out of her trance and confessed to Jasiah, "I know how you feel," in a hushed voice.

"How you know how I feel, Destiny?" Jasiah asked as he quickly sat up and gazed into her pain-drenched eyes.

"Because I've had guns pointed at me before," Destiny affirmed. "I know about the fear, I know about the confusion, I know how it feels to be unprotected."

Empathy swarmed over Jasiah's entity as he hugged her tightly, not wanting to let her go. A breeze of relief and peace swirled within them as they snugged their heads into each other's shoulders – sharing the weight of pain that burdened their innocence.

"But you're here," Destiny assured Jasiah once she regained her composure. "You're not the next Rodney King or Rafael Briscoe."

"Briscoe?" Jasiah asked, raising his eyebrows as he didn't know that person.

"A teen from Southeast the DC MDP killed for having a cell phone," Destiny revealed as she stood up and stretched. She felt like she needed to move around to help dissipate the heartache growing within her. "Let's see if we can find an N.W.A. CD around here," she suggested.

"There is nothing like that in this house... Roy feels like those lyrics incite hate."

"Fuck the police.... Fuck... Fuck... Fuck... the police!" Destiny rapped the lyrics of a NWA classic until she came across a Marvin Gaye CD. "This right here gets the same job done, though," Destiny placed the CD in rotation.

"You sure know your way around music," Jasiah recognized.

"We all have our own personal soundtrack," Destiny responded as she hit play.

As the congas came in on the beat of "Inner City Blues," she turned up the music and started to do a two-step on the floor. She had heard this song so many times before, and it hit home every time. She took Jasiah's hand and lifted him up from his seat to dance. In the past, the song had just been in the background on some evenings during Jasiah's childhood, but as Destiny swayed in front of him, the words took on a new meaning.

She fixed her palm on his and coaxed him to move with her.

"Come on, don't you bop your head to this with the old heads at the cookout?"

"They are not playing this at our social gatherings," Jasiah responded as he started to sway his body to the rhythm.

"Well, as you can see, you're not above this," Destiny continued to dance with Jasiah. He was memorized as she moved effortlessly to the beat. The way she sang along to the song helped him hear every word of the song, especially the line, "Trigger happy… policing, panic is spreading, God knows where we're heading. Ohhhhh."

Jasiah pulled her close to him and pressed his waist against hers as they swayed in place. The snap of the snare drum dictated the beat and their movements. As "Mercy Me" began to play, Destiny snapped her fingers and sang the chorus to him with affection.

He swooped his arms around her shoulders and said, "Girl, you are something else."

"I listen to this, and I see myself playing with cousins while my uncles and father play cards. I see smoke in the air from the grill. I see laughter," Destiny recalled as she looked into his eyes. "Close your eyes and tell me what you see."

"I can only see us in this very moment," he replied as he leaned down and brushed his lips against hers.

She fondled her nose with his as she enjoyed the soft brush of his lips; her consciousness drowned at that moment until they heard footsteps. They quickly pulled away from one another, but the scent of affection hovered close to their bodies. Destiny grabbed one of the CD catalogs and pretended to search through it as Jasiah took a seat on the floor facing the CD player – his focus solely dedicated to trying to hide his arousal.

"I heard the Prince of Soul playing and thought I would see what was going on down here," Roy's voice swirled in the basement, originating from the bottom step. He was now sporting a pair of slacks and a Coogi sweater.

"I just thought it was fitting for how Jasiah has been feeling," Destiny spoke as she found Aaliyah's "One in a Million" disc. "I mean, considering you don't have any N.W.A. in the house."

Laughter erupted from Roy – instinctively knowing what song Destiny was referring to.

"You're definitely Ray's daughter," Roy chuckled.

"No denying that," Destiny glanced at Roy. "I'm sure he would have been excited to see you at the homecoming dance send-off."

"I'll catch up with him later in the week."

"I've been wondering what his response would be to Jasiah being your stepson."

"Well, at least he will know you're in good hands in our home," Roy mentioned as his gaze went over to Jasiah. "I know how you're his 'pumpkin,'" he continued as he averted his eyes back to Destiny.

Specks of embarrassment flourished on Destiny's face – she blushed at the mention of her nickname.

"I think it's time for me to get out of here... I know Miss Faye is ready for me to go."

"Don't mind her. You should D.J. for this house more often," Roy commented as he started walking back up the stairs.

Once the door closed, Destiny turned to Jasiah, "He's not that bad."

"I don't want to talk about him," Jasiah held out his hand. "Come down here with me."

"You cool?" she asked as she kneeled before him.

"Yeah, I'm cool." Jasiah lay on his back and stared up at the ceiling. For the first time, he didn't feel like *why me*; he felt relieved that someone could honestly relate to what he was dealing with.

"Are we hanging out tomorrow?" Jasiah asked as Destiny intertwined her fingers with his and crawled on top of him.

"I might have plans, sir," Destiny joked as she smirked at him, resting her chin on his chest so she could look at him.

"Well, make me a part of your plans," Jasiah insisted as he pulled her up to be at eye level with him. "I don't want you to go."

"I live far away, and you still have to make it back home safely," she reminded him as she poked his nose. "And if I don't get home before my parents, my ass won't be seeing you for a while."

"Well, let's get your ass home then," he tapped her on the butt.

But once Destiny strolled through the front door of her empty home, she suddenly took notice to how disheveled their home looked with things scattered around – shoes left at the foot of the stairs, coats stacked on the banister instead of the coat rack, a weeks' worth of newspapers on the dining room table, and disheveled pillows on the sofa. After being in Jasiah's home, where there seemed to be no sign of clutter, a tinge of shame motivated her to start putting away things constantly thrown about in her house. She placed the random shoes and jackets around the house in everyone's room where they belonged. She cleared the catch-all dining room table from newspapers, mail, and books and recentered her mother's large porcelain vase. She fluffed and lined up the throw pillows on the sofa before dusting off the built-ins.

Once Destiny was finished, her mind wondered if she would ever invite Jasiah into her home. Visitors often complimented her mother on her décor, but none of those guests lived in mansions. Nothing in the Peay's humble abode seemed to compare to the style at the Netaspend's residence.

Letting out a heavy breath as Destiny wiped the beads of sweat from her forehead, she decided to go upstairs to take a shower. As if on cue, her parents walked through the door just as the thought crossed her mind.

"Ray, I think we've been robbed," Mrs. Peay joked as she wandered her eyes through the house, noticing Destiny's housework. Instantly, she looked at her daughter, who had specks of dust on her clothes and a sweaty forehead. "They stole our child and replaced it with a robot for sure," Mrs. Peay continued in jest.

"You been home all evening?" Mr. Peay questioned his daughter.

"No, I just thought I would tidy up a bit," she responded as she ran her fingers through her hair.

"She must want that boy to come over here tomorrow," Mrs. Peay took off her jacket and threw it over the end of the banister.

Destiny rolled her eyes as she cringed at her mother's compulsive action.

"What's wrong with you?" Mrs. Peay inquired, looking at her daughter.

"I just hung up twelve jackets in everybody's closets," Destiny admitted.

"Thanks for straightening up," Mrs. Peay declared as she picked up her coat.

"Daddy, guess who I saw today," excitement oozed from Destiny's voice as she stood on the steps.

Mr. Peay had unbuttoned his shirt, flopped in his oversized recliner, and switched on his big screen television.

"Ray, I know you're not about to sit down here and watch TV at this hour?" Mrs. Peay scoffed.

"I'm just going to catch some highlights," he answered.

"Daddy, guess who I saw today," Destiny repeated.

"Who did you see, Pumpkin?"

"Mr. Roy."

"I knew that was his goddamn house," Mr. Peay jumped out of his chair. "I told you, Gail."

Before his wife could respond, loud shots echoed through the neighborhood. Silence engulfed the trio until the shooting stopped.

"That was a nine," Destiny guessed.

"Maybe a glock," Mr. Peay shrugged.

"Well, where was he when we were there?" Mrs. Peay asked, ignoring her husband and daughter's guessing game about what type of gun was being fired.

"Seems like he's too busy for his stepson," Destiny shrugged.

"I'ma call that nigga tomorrow," her father said. "I knew it... I know that mother too... what's her name?"

"Faye," Destiny and her mother answered simultaneously.

"It's coming back to me. She used to run with these niggas off Kennedy Street uptown. Real young, but she liked to run with some heavy hitters."

"You think you knew Jasiah's real dad?" Destiny asked.

"My brother, Harvey, would probably know more about her… They were kids to me back then."

"Jasiah doesn't know what happened to his real dad," Destiny informed her parents.

"That's sad," Mrs. Peay added as she started to ascend the steps, brushing pass her daughter. "Ray, make some calls and figure it out for him."

"There's a reason why that boy's momma hasn't told him about his daddy. It ain't my business," Mr. Peay recognized with a yawn.

"Now, Mr. Peay, you know you want to crack the case," his wife pressured as she knew her husband could get answers. "I'ma get in the shower and hit the bed."

"I'll be up in a few," Mr. Peay uttered.

"Daddy, can you make some calls, please?" Destiny requested, thinking how she could help Jasiah get some closure.

"How long Roy been in that boy's life?" Mr. Peay inquired as he rocked in his recliner.

"Since he was four or five," Destiny voiced.

"Roy is that boy's daddy… Don't you get into that," Mr. Peay warned without turning away from his television screen. "That's his daddy."

"That's his stepfather. He wants to know what happened to his daddy," Destiny declared.

Mr. Peay equipped silence in response.

"Daddy," Destiny whined.

"Good night, Pumpkin."

"His name is Jasiah Sheffield," Destiny blurted as she walked upstairs, knowing that between her father's curious nature and contacts in the streets, he wouldn't be able to resist investigating.

Chapter 7: Cautionary Tales

Destiny looked up at the bright sun rays stretched across the sky, blanketing the docile sidewalks of downtown DC on a Saturday afternoon after her mother dropped her off at Martin Luther King Jr. Memorial Library. Mrs. Peay was under the impression that Destiny was there to do some research on scholarships. However, Destiny had ulterior motives. She thought it was a good area for her and Jasiah to spend time together without worrying about their parents' prying eyes and comments.

Though Destiny planned on being productive, she also looked forward to being with Jasiah. She immediately immersed herself in browsing through the scholarships in *The Scholarship Book 1998- 1999*. Flipping page after page, she penned down fifteen possible scholarships to apply for before Jasiah arrived. By the time she looked at the clock, she noticed that Jasiah was thirty minutes late, which was unusual since he was usually relatively on time.

Destiny picked up a random book on preparing for college and skimmed through it to avoid overthinking Jasiah's tardiness. Soon, she was immersed in an interesting section about housing but got distracted by her pager going off. She assumed it was Jasiah canceling, but as she peered at the phone number, she recognized it was Eric. Curious about what Eric wanted, she decided to call him back from a pay phone.

"What's up?" Destiny asked.

"Where are you?" Eric inquired. "I want to see you."

"Eric, I'm doing me, so you can do you," she retorted.

"Destiny, stop it," Eric demanded.

"Eric, no," she protested. "I told you I need space."

"Who is he?" Eric interrogated. "There must be someone else the way you're icing me out."

"I just don't like all of the pressure you're putting on me," Destiny whispered into the phone, covering her mouth so that her voice wouldn't echo in the empty library corridor.

"I thought you loved me…. You know that I love you," Eric whined.

"Eric, this is not how I pictured things going," Destiny voiced her honest feelings.

"Nothing is picture perfect," he took a deep breath, "I know we can work this out."

Silence echoed through the telephone line as Destiny pondered how to discourage Eric from pressuring her.

"Hello?" he questioned.

"I'm here," Destiny leaned against the wall as she mustered up the courage to reveal her honest feelings to Eric. "Eric, I don't want to do this anymore," Destiny confessed so many truths in that one statement. She didn't want to lie to him anymore. She didn't want to sneak around with Jasiah anymore. She didn't want to be with Eric anymore.

"We're coming up on our one-year anniversary soon," Eric mumbled from the other side of the phone. Destiny cringed since she knew that they wouldn't make it another month to celebrate. "I've been patient, and I can continue to be patient," he added. "Sometimes I just get caught up in what everyone else has going on and forget that I have a good thing with you."

"You've said some mean things that I haven't forgiven or forgotten," Destiny admitted.

"Where are you?" he asked again trying to avoid apologies. "We can spend the day getting back to us. I miss you."

"Are you hearing what I'm saying?" Destiny questioned as she saw a glimpse of Jasiah searching for her. Immediately, she surveyed Jasiah's entire being – noticing that he was still without his chain from his open The North Face jacket, but he was now sporting a diamond earring again.

"Destiny, don't do this," Eric pleaded. "I'm telling you... I can wait."

Wandering his gaze through the crowd, Jasiah located Destiny peering at him with the pay phone stuck to her ear. As their eyes met, a smirk appeared on Jasiah's face. Destiny turned her back toward him to show him that his tardiness wasn't cool. Hastily, he made his way to her. Sensing his nearing footsteps, she quickly hung up the phone right before Jasiah suddenly picked her off her feet, making her squeal.

"Shhh!" Jasiah covered her mouth with his free hand as her voice carried through the hall.

"You're late," she stated from beneath his hand as she elbowed him.

"I am late," he admitted as he sat her on her feet. "And I apologize for that, but I was trying to find parking, and then I wasn't sure if I was in the right place because I'm thinking there is no way Destiny wants to come into this library with all of these homeless people hanging around."

"They are just trying to stay warm," Destiny replied as she brushed her hand against his chest. "I thought you stood me up."

"Were you on the phone calling in an option?" Jasiah questioned.

"Maybe," she crossed her arms across her chest, with a smirk on her face.

"Yeah, whatever," Jasiah dismissed her statement.

She averted her eyes from him as she stared down the hall. An awkward silence hung between them as Destiny wondered if Eric was sincere or not. Being in a relationship with Eric was a lot easier on some fronts. They went to the same school, and they lived fairly close to one another. His family loved her. And most importantly, she never felt inadequate around him.

But then there was Jasiah. He was extremely handsome– an embodiment of a gentleman. He was thoughtful and extremely smart. They had a lot of common interests and goals. The icing on the cake was that Jasiah served as a window for Destiny to realize how the privileged lived.

Jasiah could see Destiny was lost in thought, but he craved her attention.

"Hey!" he tilted her face toward him with his index finger. "What's up?"

"What's up?" Destiny repeated the question back, finally staring at him.

Witnessing the innocence dripping from her tone and demeanor, he couldn't resist bending down and kissing her softly on the lips. "I thought about you all night."

"Thought about me how?" she questioned with a grin playing on her face.

"Just how beautiful and smart you are," he wrapped his arm around her waist and kissed her again. "I had a good time yesterday just hanging out."

"I did too, except for your muhva tryna carry me."

Hearing her frustration, Jasiah laughed carelessly as he replied, "I had a talk with her, and it won't happen again."

"Boy, your muhva doesn't care what you say to her."

"You're right," Jasiah grinned. "But Roy backed me up, so that makes a difference."

"We'll see," Destiny commented as she stood on her tippy toes and kissed him.

They only separated when someone cleared their throat and asked, "Can I get this pay phone?"

With giggles, they walked off hand in hand and decided to look for a foreign movie to watch in the viewing room. As they stood by the card catalog, Destiny's pager went off with her house number, signaling her to call home.

"You find us a movie, and I'm going to call home," she uttered to Jasiah, ready to leave him at the card catalog.

"Okay, cool," he nodded as he thought about a French movie that would help him get extra credit in his French class.

Destiny strolled back to the pay phones, nervously calling home.

"Yes?" Destiny asked once her father answered the phone.

"You still at the library?" Mr. Peay questioned.

"Yes."

"You know that boy's father locked up. Look up the newspaper while you're there."

"Locked up since when?" she questioned in shock.

"Since maybe '86, '87… His arrest and sentencing made the papers. Look it up," Mr. Peay's affirmed.

"Okay, thanks, Daddy," she murmured, unsure how to share the news she had just received.

"You make sure you home at a decent hour."

"Yes, sir."

They both hung up. Destiny knew that if she disclosed this information to Jasiah, it would jeopardize her day with him. When she got back, he had two VHS tapes in his hand.

"Everything okay?" he asked.

She nodded.

"So, we have *Louise* or *Nikita*," he gave her the options. "We might have to strain our eyes to read the subtitles, but at least I'll get my grade up in French class."

"Doesn't matter to me… I'll work on my scholarship essay," Destiny replied as she felt like she was drowning in conflicted emotions.

"And I'll steal a few kisses and feels in between," he kissed her on the neck.

After walking around for a few minutes, they found a viewing room. While Destiny scribbled down her thoughts on the need for historically Black colleges, her mind wondered if Jasiah's father was still alive and well. Jasiah watched the movie intently, writing down notes with his arm wrapped around her shoulders – oblivious to her internal conflict.

Just for a moment, she put her thoughts aside and enjoyed Jasiah's presence beside her. But her mind could not find that escape so easily. She kept mulling over the information her father had just shared with her. She wondered if she could find the answers that Jasiah longed for.

"I'ma go try to find a book about Cheyney University," she said.

"I'll go with you," Jasiah offered.

"No," she protested. "I shouldn't be long." She kissed him and slowly pulled away. "The librarian can point me in the right direction if I can't find it in the card catalog."

"Okay, I'll be right here," he assured her as he averted his focus back to his notes.

Destiny made a beeline for the microfiche area that housed the archived newspapers. She first looked up Cheyney University, the oldest historically black university, and found an article to quote in her essay. As she got that printed, she looked up the film that housed a story about Jasiah Sheffield Sr. It was easier than expected for her to find the "Drug 'Kingpin' Pleads Guilty" in a 1985 article in *The Washington Post*.

Her heart raced as she skimmed through the article to find that he pled guilty to avoid charges against his girlfriend, mother, and brother. She read through the rest of the dates on the index card from the card catalog to find the article where Jasiah Sheffield Sr. was sentenced to fourteen years in prison. She printed that article as well. Her hand shook as she folded the pages and stashed them in a book.

Standing in front of the viewing room's door, she took a few deep breaths to get herself together. Peaking in through the glass, she saw Jasiah typing on his two-way pager. She squished her face up against the glass and made a funny face attempting to cover her anxiousness with humor. When he looked up and laughed, she tapped her watch, indicating it was time to go.

"So, do you have any plans this evening, or are you free to spend the entire day with me?" Jasiah asked once they hit the street.

"I don't have any other plans," Destiny informed him as she stuffed her hands in her Avirex jacket.

"So, we can chill to like midnight?"

"Maybe," she shrugged. "I don't know if we will get on one another's nerves for like eight more hours."

"You could never get on my nerves," he assured her. "Let's get something to eat and see where the day takes us," he held out his arm for Destiny to take it.

Under the eye of the fading sun, they strolled down the street arm in arm toward Jasiah's car. Midst the breezy weather, Destiny's heart weighed heavy with the secret that held now. She didn't know if she could go the entire day without telling Jasiah she knew exactly what happened to his father.

Jasiah noticed how quiet she was once they were seated at Hard Rock Café.

"You okay?" he asked from behind his menu. "You haven't said much since we left the library."

"I was just thinking about how I ended up here with you," she replied.

"You know how you ended up with me," he winked at her. He then moved over to sit beside her. Destiny found relief in his presence and leaned into him as he wrapped his arm around her.

"You are awfully comfortable with me in these streets," he recognized.

"I've covered all of my bases," she retorted as she pondered if she should treat him to lunch, as she wanted to show him that she has a giving spirit too.

"So, you decided to drop that zero and get with this hero, eh?" Jasiah smirked as he let out a muffled laugh because of his own cheesiness.

She equipped silence in response as she peered at the menu.

"Don't have me get all attached to you and then break my heart," he whispered into her ear as he gently bit her earlobe.

Destiny shivered under the warmth of his breath against her face and the sensation his nibble sent through her nervous system. She gripped his thigh and bit her bottom lip to stop the moan from escaping.

"You like that?" Jasiah continued to whisper; his lips so close that they grazed against her skin – igniting a sensation within her that she didn't want to have in public.

She faked a cough and tried to gain her composure as she turned to him to figure out if he was a player saying all the right words or if he was actually sincere.

"I'm serious, Destiny," he looked at her in the eyes, "Don't play me."

"Jasiah, we've only seen one another a handful of times. You could be putting on an act for all I know."

"You think me being balled up on your lap last night was an act?" He shook his head. "Damn, I thought this was getting real." He retreated his arm from around her.

When Jasiah started to go back to his seat, taking his warmth with him, Destiny found herself grabbing him by the jacket to keep him right next to her.

"I don't doubt any of that was real," she assured him. "I just want to make sure we don't get into something we regret."

He pulled her close to him with a playful tug. "You know you like it here."

"I do like it here," she admitted as she got comfortable in his embrace.

"Then what's up? I'm not gonna beg you."

"I'm not asking you to beg me," she caressed his arm with her fingertips.

Her touch sent a tremor of chill down his spine. He was infatuated with her but didn't want to show her the depths of it. He realized the restaurant wasn't a place for their conversation, so he dropped the topic. After a waitress came and took their orders, the two forgot about the world around them and got lost in each other's arms and thoughts. Destiny told more stories of her country cousins in North Carolina to how her father would be preparing their Thanksgiving dinner. Jasiah listened intently as he drew a contrast with his own life. He didn't have any extended family to speak of besides his aunt and Lafayette. He didn't know what Thanksgiving dinner felt like outside a prix fixe menu at an exquisite restaurant.

"You and Lafayette seem tight… Y'all don't spend the holidays together?" Destiny inquired.

"Maybe at Christmas back in the day, I guess," Jasiah shrugged. "But now we go to Roy's partner's house for Christmas dinner."

"Really?" Destiny was shocked.

"Things been a little strained between my family and my aunt's husband for years… plus I'm tight with Chad's son, CJ… I'm sure you'll meet him one day."

Destiny smiled. She liked the idea of being intertwined in Jasiah's friendships.

"But this year, I'm coming over to the Peay's house for some of that home cooking," Jasiah predicted.

"Oh yeah?" Destiny laughed. "Boy, my family would eat you alive."

"I ain't no sucka," he assured her.

"But you a bamma."

Jasiah burst into laughter at her banter. "Now, you know you need to take that back. I'll outdress anybody."

Destiny didn't respond but simply stared at him with amusement flickering in her eyes.

"You better give me my props, girl."

"Okay, okay…. You fly," she admitted with a smile.

Once they hit the street after having a nice meal together, Jasiah realized that he didn't want their day together to end.

"Let's ride around a little while," he suggested, once they were in the car

"Where are we going?" she inquired bulking her seatbelt.

"Just sit back and relax… you're in good hands," he winked at her.

Destiny was relieved when Jasiah parked the car at a small park just off the George Washington Parkway to watch airplane arrival and departures at Ronald Reagan Washington National Airport. As the sun traveled from east to west, drowning the sky in the hues of ombre blues – they spent the evening trading stories about trips they had taken by airplane.

All the while, Destiny was still trying to figure out how to inform Jasiah that she had information that would change his outlook on life forever.

Chapter 8: Invisible Man

Darkness veiled the skies as Jasiah sat in his car holding the newspaper articles in his hand in front of Destiny's house. The sound of the city bustling around him was like white noise as chaos roared in his mind. Under the flickering lamp post, his eyes whizzed from line to line of the printed article. The hollowness in him now began to fill in with disbelief as he learned that he wasn't the son of a dead man. Jasiah had to put the article down once as his mind grappled with the fact that his father could still be alive.

He wanted to cry, he wanted to scream, he wanted to unleash the storm of emotions brewing in him in some way, but instead, he sat there in silence, trying to contain himself. His entire life, he was made to believe his father was dead, but the truth was he was imprisoned in a federal correctional institute. Questions flooded through his mind as he revved his car and headed straight to his house. He wanted answers; he needed to confront his mother immediately.

Once home, he bolted straight to Roy and Faye's bedroom. He stood there, clenching his fists- trying to calm himself. After several moments, he mustered up the courage to knock on the door.

"RJ, go to bed!" Faye yelled from the other side of the door.

"It's Siah," Jasiah announced. "I need to ask you something."

"And it can't wait until morning?" Faye's frothy voice resounded with tinges of frustration lingering in it.

"Ma!!!" Jasiah yelled as the burst of emotions he tried to hold back consumed him as his fist hit the door again.

The echo from the last bang hadn't faded away when Roy – shirtless with his pants belt buckle undone, suddenly opened the door.

"What's so urgent, Jasiah!?" Roy stated with a puzzled look swirling in his eyes, whereas Faye sat on the bed casually painting her toenails. Jasiah darted his gaze between the two as he tried to determine who was the villain.

Aiming his gaze at his mother, Jasiah asked, "Where is my father?"

"Siah, what are you talking about?" Faye spoke without looking up. "I have told you countless times your father is gone."

"You made it seem like he was dead… the whole time he's been in prison!" Jasiah roared. Averting his eyes from Faye, he looked into Roy's still-confused glance and assumed, "I know you know where he is."

Grasping hold of the tension-filled aura emitting from Jasiah's being, Roy maintained his composure as he firmly stated, "You need to calm down. This discussion might be better for the morning."

"For the morning?" Anger fumed in Jasiah's words as he looked at his stepfather as if he were crazy. "I have been lied to my entire life about my father, and you want me to wait until the morning!!???"

A tinge of pity crossed through Roy's eyes as he opened his mouth to say something but got interrupted by Faye's indifferent voice.

"I didn't lie to you. I just never told you the whole story." Faye casually twisted the top onto her nail polish bottle and looked at Jasiah as she continued. "It was for your own good."

"Leading me to believe that my real father was dead was for my own good?" Jasiah sneered at his mother's words.

"What kind of father do you think he would be to you from behind bars? He still would not have been at your little tennis matches or back-to-school nights or helped you with your homework… Might as well be dead."

"Faye! That's a bit harsh," Roy interjected as he peered at his wife.

"It's the truth. I married a good man who takes care of us. And you come in here after midnight yelling about the muthafuckah that left me to raise you on my own!" Faye's yelling made the room vibrate.

"How could you sit there and act like you lying to me all my life is right?" Jasiah questioned as he stood there in disbelief at how unapologetic his mother stayed.

"The only thing your father left behind besides you is that chain that you think the world of and that damn car... He is dead to me."

"Faye!!" Roy yelped, hinting at his wife to ease up.

"What!?" Faye snapped at her husband, darting her eyes in his direction.

Roy stood there in silence, unwilling to take on Jasiah's fight.

"Go to your room, Siah," Faye demanded as she stood up from the bed. "Go to your room before you make me say things I can't take back."

"Too late for that," Jasiah groaned and exited their bedroom.

Hatred for his mother began to stew within Jasiah. With each step to his room, a range of emotions burned through him. Entering his room, he attempted to slam the door behind him, but he didn't hear the satisfying sound. He turned back to see Roy standing with his hand on the door.

"Can we talk?" he asked as he folded his arms and leaned against the door frame.

"Talk about what? You want to talk about how you were his lawyer and how you have been hiding the truth alongside my mother for the past fourteen years?" Jasiah answered bitterly as he collapsed on his bed.

"It wasn't my idea to act like your father has been dead for the past thirteen years that I have been with your mother," Roy explained the situation to his stepson. "By the time she and I became serious, she had already started lying to you."

"And you just went with it?"

"Jasiah, I think we can talk about this more rationally in the morning. It's pretty late, and there is a lot to explain. With your emotions raging, I don't even think you would hear me right now."

"In the morning? So, you and my mother can get your story straight?" Jasiah presumed as he shook his head. "No thanks... I'll pass."

Roy let out a sigh, moved into Jasiah's room, and closed the door behind him. Sitting on the bed beside him, he peered at the boy, who had grown into a young man before his eyes.

As Roy looked around Jasiah's room, noticing the medals and trophies for various events, he started to ponder how his absence had affected his stepson. He hadn't been to his sporting events throughout his primary years, even though he always cut the check for all the fees and trips, thinking that an active boy would stay out of the court system. He had paid for tutors, thinking he couldn't have his stepson left behind in the school system, but he never helped with his homework. He had never been to a back-to-school night at the place he paid extravagant tuition for.

Guilt soared through Roy's mind as he counted everything he had failed Jasiah at as the male role model he prided himself to be. His consciousness acknowledged that all this time, he had just taken Jasiah as a package deal for a woman whom he lusted after.

The initial idea of responsibility had dawned on Roy during Jasiah's ordeal with the police. When he saw the familiar pain and confusion on his stepson's face, he remembered how his father had been there for him through the years as counsel, mentor, and confidant. He knew he couldn't just sow those things into his son, RJ, but he should have been giving it to Jasiah all along. For years, all he did was criticize and provide, but as Roy gulped through his guilt, he knew he had to take the opportunity to change the tide.

"Jasiah, you know your mother was young when she had you," Roy explained. "She didn't have good parents. She was just a teenager trying to survive."

"Is that what she told you?" Jasiah retorted as he sat up.

"This is what I know. If a girl had some sensible, caring parents, she wouldn't be having a baby at the age of sixteen with a twenty-four-year-old."

Jasiah just looked at Roy. His mind was conflicted over what to believe and what not to believe anymore.

"By the time I met your mother during the trial, she was twenty. I couldn't figure out how someone so beautiful and young got caught up in all of the bullshit your father had going on. But it was my job to represent him. I got him the best deal I could for all the evidence the feds had against him, and that took a lot of money. I'm not going to lie. I took it all. That red Benz was signed over to me as payment. I gave it back to your mother after I saw the two of you at a bus stop outside of DC Jail in the winter, visiting your father while I was seeing another client."

"So, in that deal, you told her to never return to jail?" Jasiah questioned, leading Roy to deviate from the story and reveal to him the mastermind of this plan.

"Once Big Siah found out we were serious, it was his idea," Roy shook his head in defeat as he realized there was no other way out other than to tell the truth. Taking a deep breath of courage, he continued. "He felt like you would do better in life with him out of the picture."

Confusion swarmed over Jasiah. He didn't want to believe the words coming out of the person who had lied to him for his entire life. But some part of Jasiah understood that it could be the truth.

"Don't take it like he didn't love you or didn't want you. He initially took the plea deal, hoping he could get out to be a part of your life in your teenage years… However, nearly 77% of incarcerated parents are children of incarcerated dads. Your grandfather died in prison, and hopefully, the generational curse will stop with you."

"And no one thought I deserved to know this family history?" Jasiah inquired while pain flickered in his eyes.

"Everyone thought that we were acting in your best interest."

"I've been walking around here feeling so empty at times. Missing a connection with family that I actually could have. How is it in my best interest when I felt so forgotten when there were dads cheering on their sons, and I had no one? I feel like I don't even know a part of myself!!"

"Jasiah, you don't know those people, the Sheffields, for a reason."

In that lingering tense moment, Jasiah's door swung open, revealing his mother. Wrapped in a robe, she began yelling, "Look, Siah, I did what I had to do. I do not regret acting in our best interest. You might feel like it's a mistake, but when you have children of your own, you will understand."

"Faye, you are not helping the situation," Roy exclaimed as he stood up.

"Helping? I'm trying to–"

"I want to meet him," Jasiah interrupted his mother as his gaze filled with determination. "I want to know how he felt about this."

Upon hearing Jasiah's words, Faye threw her hands in the air in defeat. "I guess I should blame myself that this boy feels so entitled," she said as she shook her head. "You're eighteen, so figure this shit out on your own."

She turned around and marched back to her bedroom.

"We can talk about it more in the morning," Roy stated as he followed his wife's footsteps and closed the door behind him.

Jasiah's ears followed their footsteps as he fell back on the bed, fighting the battle of emotions that were within him. His eyes focused on a minuscule blot on the ceiling while his mind hovered over the thoughts of his father.

Why didn't Roy just adopt me? Is what Roy told me even the truth? What is my father like? Will I turn out like him?

Countless questions circulated his mind as he found himself shackled into a spot – a spot where he was a captive of hearsays.

The ringing of his telephone broke Jasiah out of his trance – it was Destiny. He picked up the phone but didn't say anything.

"Jasiah…" Destiny sang into the phone as she heard him breathing.

He smiled, her voice soothing him.

"How do you feel? Are you okay?" her empathic voice danced in Jasiah's ear. He realized that those questions were what he needed to hear. He needed someone to care about his well-being.

"I'm not okay, Destiny," he answered honestly. He then sighed in relief of being able to be honest with how he felt with someone.

Destiny's heart sank as she felt the pain in his voice… his words. The energy, the hope, the spark from his voice had vanished as a tinge of guilt spiraled through her. She had wrestled with herself that entire evening over whether to reveal this information to Jasiah or not… and if so, then how?

Destiny realized that he deserved to know the truth – it was the least she could do for him at the moment, and she didn't want to be like Faye and keep secrets from him. After struggling to find the words in which she could reveal this information to him, she decided to leave the newspaper articles she printed out in the car like a forgotten note.

"I'm sorry, Jasiah, but I thought you should know," her apologetic voice whispered through the phone.

"It's fine, Destiny. You're not to blame," he sighed again as he rolled over on his bed and looked at a picture of them on his nightstand. He smiled, thinking that she was the best thing to come into his life in a long time. "How did you know?" he questioned. "What made you look up my dad while we were at the library?"

"My dad... I asked him to look into it for you," she confessed honestly.

"Your dad connected like that?"

"Well, my dad is my dad," she replied as she sighed. "But, Jasiah, I want you to be okay."

"I know, but I have a lot on my mind right now," he stated as he rubbed his forehead.

"If you want to get off the phone, I'll—"

"No, no, no... I feel like you are the only person who keeps it real with me," Jasiah inserted before she could suggest hanging up.

For some time, they conversed about the what-ifs. He talked about what life would have been like if he knew his father was alive. And that he could visit him in prison and talk about his experiences, studies, and progress. While Destiny listened to him intently, she interjected her experience with a loved one in prison to keep Jasiah from diving into wishful thinking.

She revealed to him things she knew he wasn't aware of about prison visits – the system of being pat down every time you visit, clothing restrictions, and the struggle she witnessed with her family in trying to beat the rules. She understood that if Jasiah knew his father was in prison, his life wouldn't have been as blissful as he imagined it to be right now.

"Jasiah, you don't really want to know that side of life. You have spent your Saturdays in better ways," she told him affectionately.

"Maybe he could have been a cautionary tale," he concluded.

"This is a cautionary tale," she steered his mind into reality as she corrected him. "That's how I feel about people in my family – so many cautionary tales. My cousin was shot in the head, execution style, with her mother for some shit she did for her drug-dealing baby father," Destiny revealed the dark truths about this side of life. "That's why I don't mess with dudes that have anything to do with drugs."

"I just wish I knew sooner," he muttered as he sighed.

"Imagine you being at Sidwell Friends telling everybody your dad is locked up," she said as she tried to make him see how different his life would have been.

"A lot of kids say their dad is away at camp or on an extended business trip," he laughed and explained, "I used to hear my mother gossiping about how they were really in jail for tax evasion or a DUI."

"See? You are laughing at them, too. Your mom just didn't want anyone laughing at you."

"Or her," he added, knowing that perception is everything to his mother.

"Be that as it may...Jasiah, I watch my dad and brothers take my nephews to see my brother in prison. I have seen the happiness on their faces turn into cries when the time to leave comes."

As she explained some brutal truths Jasiah didn't consider, he began to empathize and understand his mother's point of view. Yet he still felt betrayed by every adult in his life. His mind still pondered over how he would find out which prison his father was being held captive in until he drifted off to sleep.

The next morning, Destiny woke up and still pondered if she had done the right thing as she lay in bed, listening to ESPN highlights playing on the downstairs television envelope her space. She lay there and collected her thoughts, hoping Jasiah would not reveal to his mother that she was the source of uncovering the truth. Yawning away her sleepiness, she got up and strolled downstairs as she saw her house bustling with activity.

"Good morning," Destiny greeted her father as laziness dripped from her tone.

"Morning's gone, Pumpkin," Mr. Peay pointed out in a sarcastic manner as he eyed his daughter, "Get these pans cleaned up so I can start with macaroni and cheese."

"Who's coming over?" Destiny inquired as she grabbed the last two pieces of cold turkey bacon from a plate on the stove.

"Shit, I don't know," her father hunched his shoulders. "I'm just getting this shit out of the way so I can sit down."

"Who playing?" she asked as she strolled away with her breakfast and focused on the NFL highlights playing on TV.

"Redskins versus Giants at 4," he explained.

She rolled her eyes in agitation as she instinctively knew they would have a house full of people all day. As she bit through the turkey bacon, she planned to lock herself in her room and compile what was needed to send off her scholarship packets on Monday. After eating, she cleaned the kitchen as instructed and attempted to retreat to her room with a cup of iced tea and a few chips.

"Did you look it up?" Mr. Peay asked his daughter just as she hit the stairs.

"Huh?" she stopped in her tracks as she didn't understand the nature of her father's question.

"Did you look up that boy's father?" he repeated.

"Serving fourteen years for dealing," she clarified.

"It's a small world."

"Why you say that?"

"He's in the same dorm with Junior in Morgantown."

Destiny took a deep breath and shook her head as she knew what was coming. "His momma ain't never gonna like me," She uttered.

"Where is the lil' nigga at, anyway?"

"Who? Eric?" she instinctively knew his father was trying to change the subject. "I don't know, Daddy, and I don't care."

"Oh... so you've moved on?" he questioned with a playful glee plastered on his face.

"Something like that."

Before long, the blaring of the big screen television with football commentators' predictions about certain players noised Destiny's room with cheers and murmurs of the spectators arriving in her home. Having her peace disrupted, she was about to put on her headphones to muffle out the noise when suddenly her telephone rang.

"Hey, beautiful," Jasiah's voice echoed from the phone receiver.

"Hey, handsome," she blushed as the specks of frustration faded. "How are you feeling today?"

"Hmm, a hug from you would make me feel better," he whispered into the phone affectionately.

"Awwww," a warm, vibrant smile appeared on her face, "I wish I could hug you too."

"Do you want to go with me to the Redskin game this afternoon?" he inquired. "My mom said I could bring you."

"Your mom said you can bring me? Destiny Peay?" Destiny quizzed as she peered at her alarm clock. It was already 1:30 p.m.

"Yeah," Jasiah laughed.

Destiny wanted to question how Jasiah could want to participate in a family outing when just twelve hours he felt so betrayed, deceived – hurt. She swallowed her real questions and simple asked, "How is that gonna work?"

"We will pick you up in an hour."

"Jasiah, I don't think it's a good idea."

"Come on, it will be fun."

Destiny pondered for a second. *Would it be fun?* Though she would love to spend time with Jasiah, she didn't know how the turmoil had defused so quickly in their household.

"Destiny, what's the problem?" Jasiah could feel her apprehension through the phone.

"There's a lot of people here... not the best time," she covered her true thoughts. "You don't know about the chaos that could happen here."

"Well, I can just skip out of the game with my parents and watch it at your house," he suggested, as he was eager to experience the camaraderie Destiny described to him within her family.

"Boy, you need to slow your roll," she chuckled as she couldn't imagine Jasiah adjusting to her home environment.

"Eric coming over there or something?"

"No, of course not," she clarified. "I told you I just feel like—"

"Baby, stop worrying," Jasiah cut her off.

The way he said 'baby' gave Destiny pause. If anyone else called her 'baby' she would insist that she was no one's *baby*. Her name was Destiny. But she recognized that she liked it coming from him.

"Destiny, we're going to see each other today. One way or another," he spoke firmly.

She peered at the phone, slightly taken back by his assertiveness, as she was still not used to following anyone else's lead. But some part of her liked Jasiah's insistence. "Let me talk to my dad. I'll call you back in five minutes."

"Call me back, Destiny."

"I will."

Immediately, she hung up the phone, and as excitement powered her footsteps, she jolted into her parents' room to see if her mother had returned from service at New Bethel Baptist Church. But the room was empty.

Hoping that her father would be amenable, Destiny headed downstairs. She was greeted by her brother, Jax, and two cousins, Ron and Kita, sitting in front of the television with red cups in their hands. The cold breeze swirled through the house as she noticed the front door was wide open – she figured her nephews might be playing outside with Jax's children.

"Where's Daddy?" Destiny questioned when she couldn't find him in the kitchen.

"With Freddie Bush outside," Jax answered as he leaned back in Mr. Peay's recliner.

Without bothering to converse with Jax further, she stepped outside and saw her father standing with one of his oldest friends in the world, Freddie Bush. As she looked outdoors from the doorway, she saw her nephews playing with chalk on the sidewalk before recognizing the frustration swarming her father's face. Freddie Bush was already sloppy drunk before 2 p.m.

"I told you that you can't come around here like this with my grandkids here." Destiny heard her father state firmly.

"Come on, Ray, it's game day," Freddie Bush replied as he belched through his words.

"Daddy," she called out as she marched toward them.

"Help me get this muthafuckah in the house," Mr. Peay demanded.

A tinge of frustration ignited in her, wondering why she had to help with all the men in the house.

"Freddie Bush, you think I'm supposed to carry you in the house?" she yelled at the drunken man.

"Awww, Ray, why you call her out here?" he covered his face. "I don't want no problems, Destiny."

"Then get up and walk in the house like you got some sense," she riposted sternly, grabbing him by the arm as the cold air wrapped around her.

This scene was much too familiar to her. Freddie Bush had been a permanent fixture in their family for as long as she could remember. When Destiny was younger, Freddie Bush and Ray Peay ran the streets together. By the time she was in junior high school, the pair's schemes had started to dwindle, but now, his addictions were getting the best of him – especially alcohol.

Mr. Peay's sons questioned why their father would continue to let Freddie Bush come around after his addictions could no longer be hidden. But Mr. Peay refused to give up on his friend. Freddie Bush knew that he could count on Ray Peay's house for a sense of normalcy.

Destiny saw Freddie Bush more often than the rest of her brothers. She had become accustomed to assisting her father with handling him, especially on what she described as his "fall down drunk days." But now, she didn't want Jasiah and his parents to witness the commotion that Freddie Bush could cause.

"I'ma get-up, I'ma get-up," he jumbled through his words as he held on to the rail. "I can do it," he protested his friend's help.

"Then do it, goddamn it!" Mr. Peay yelled as he stood to the side, watching Freddie Bush stumble over his own steps.

"Shit," Freddie Bush pulled himself up to stand. He turned to Destiny to see disappointment evident on her face. "I don't want no problems, Destiny," he repeated faintly.

"Then you go in and have a seat. I'll fix you a plate when it's ready," she said as she held the door open wide.

Carefully walking inside, Freddie Bush saluted Destiny as if he would have done a superior while in the Army. She turned to enter the house and searched for a chair for him to sit in. She pulled a dining room chair with arms out and placed it against the wall.

"Here," she stated as she watched him stumble over toward her like an infant taking its first steps.

After Freddie Bush sat, she followed her father into the kitchen.

"Daddy, I wanna go out for a while," she told her father as she readied a cup of iced water for Freddie Bush.

"Go where?" Mr. Peay inquired.

"To the game with Jasiah and his parents."

"How you getting to the field?"

"They are coming to get me."

"You talk to your mother?"

"She's not home," Destiny answered. "Daddy, can I go?"

Her father looked at her. "Come straight home after the game."

A surge of excitement flooded through her as she gave her father a hug from the back and quickly left the kitchen, handed Freddie Bush the large cup of water, and ran up the stairs. Immediately, she called Jasiah and began to wait as she tapped her foot and simultaneously looked for something to wear.

"Girl, we were headed out the door," Jasiah stated when he finally answered.

"Is it too late?" she asked.

"We were on the way anyway," he told her. "Dress warm."

With a large grin splattered on her face, she grabbed her towel and hit the shower for a quick washup. As she was strolling out of the shower, she noticed her mother coming upstairs.

"To the game, Destiny?" she questioned. "You don't know the first thing about football."

"Well, maybe I can learn something," she shrugged as she hurriedly ran into her room to layer up in tight jeans, a long-sleeved shirt, and a black hoodie under her black Avirex jacket. Destiny started to rap "Crush on You" by Lil' Kim as it played on her stereo while she moved around her room until she found an old Redskins skull cap.

Twirling in the mist of the Vanilla body spray Jasiah loved, she glided downstairs and noticed the crowd had tripled in size, crammed into their small living room and stairs. Her brother, Jax, told her to double up on the socks because her tan Timberland boots wouldn't keep her feet warm out there. Pondering over his advice, she ran back upstairs to do as suggested when suddenly the doorbell chimed. Hastily, she reversed her footsteps and nearly jumped down all the steps in one leap to stop anyone else from answering the door.

"Naw, sis, I got this," Jax confirmed as he pushed his little sister to the side.

"What do you mean? I got it," she tugged on her brother. "You can't embarrass me."

"Easy! Let your brother get the door," Mr. Peay inserted.

Her cousin Ron snickered from the couch. "This might be good," he whispered to no one in particular.

"Destiny, control yourself," her mother's voice halted her movement.

She looked around and dreaded that she agreed for Jasiah to come there. She had been in his home with tables and backdrops, hosting at least thirty people. But she suddenly feared that the number of tatted grown men crowded around the television would be jarring to a newcomer. Her heart raced, but under the pressure from her family, she took a deep breath and let her brother go.

"Daddy, don't let them embarrass me," she whined as she sat on the arm of his recliner.

"Are you embarrassed by us?" her father stated, looking at his daughter over his glasses.

"This is a lot," Destiny admitted.

"I'ma stay right here," Freddie Bush jokingly whispered loudly as he raised his hand from his seat. "I won't say a word, Destiny."

"Ahh, Dad, is that Junior's lawyer out there?" Jax yelled.

Mr. Peay stood up quickly and started walking toward the door upon the mention of Roy.

"You make sure that boy come in and speak to your mother," Freddie Bush interjected from the side.

"I thought you just said you wouldn't say a word," Destiny glanced at Freddie Bush, hinting for him to shut up.

Holding his laughter, he motioned like he zipped his lips.

"He might as well come and say hello to everyone," her cousin Kita mentioned.

"Where you going, Aunt Dee?" Jax's son, Julio, asked, holding on to Destiny's leg.

"I'm going to watch the game. Maybe you can see me on TV," she told him as she patted his head just as Jasiah entered.

Silence thrived in the room as it seemed like even the TV paused. Destiny's heart thumped wildly as it would break through her ribcage any moment — with rosy cheeks from bashfulness in front of her cousins, she stood to her feet.

"Hello, Mrs. Peay," Jasiah waved to Destiny's mother, who was standing by the dining room table.

"Hello, Jasiah," she smiled at him.

"You ready, little boy?" Jasiah joked as he looked over at Destiny, who he was surprised to see in tan double sole Timberland boots.

A wave of laughter warped through the room as Destiny rolled her eyes.

"Don't be rude. Introduce your friend," Ron interposed.

"Everybody, this is Jasiah, Jasiah, this is everyone," she rushed through her words as she pushed him toward the door. "Bye Ma!" Destiny yelled behind her.

"Nobody has a name?" Jasiah asked.

Destiny ignored Jasiah's question as she tried to move past her brother. "Excuse us," Destiny told her brother, Jax, who was still in the doorway.

Sensing seriousness lingering in her voice, he moved out of the way. When Destiny and Jasiah hit the street, a sight sent shivers of anger through her spine. As Jasiah was busy trying to say goodbye to her father with a handshake, he didn't notice Jax slip Mr. Roy a little baggie with their firm handshake on the stoop.

Quickly, she grabbed her father for a hug and whispered, "Really, Daddy?" as she pulled away, she gave her family members a disapproving look.

"Have fun, Pumpkin," her father bid goodbye with a wink.

Destiny shook her head, relieved that Jasiah hadn't seen the transaction. She climbed into the backseat of the Black Lincoln Navigator with Jasiah. She looked over at him and wondered if he was hiding drug use from her.

"I thought your mom was coming?" she asked as she noticed the empty passenger seat. Destiny started to wonder how well they were actually getting along after last night's revelation.

"She rode with some friends; we will see her there," Roy affirmed as he sat in the driver's seat.

"Hey, Mr. Roy," she greeted him.

"Hello, Destiny," he looked at her through the rearview mirror, greeting her with his eyes. "Y'all buckled in and ready to roll?"

Awkwardness swirled in Destiny as she felt like they were being chauffeured. "You don't want to sit up front?" Destiny asked Jasiah, who was sitting beside her.

"No, I want to be beside you," he rested his hand on her thigh. "If that's cool with you?"

Embracing a warm smile, dissuading the dwindling thoughts, she nodded as she locked her fingers in his hand.

They didn't talk much on their way to Jack Kent Cooke Stadium.

But her consciousness hovered over Jasiah, calling her a *little boy*. Her confidence started to dwindle when she looked down at her clothing, hoping the way she was dressed wasn't an embarrassment to him.

As they pulled into the parking lot, Destiny released Jasiah's hand, and he shook his hand as if his hand was in pain.

"Girl, the way you were squeezing my hand...I thought you were trying to cut off my blood circulation," he joked as he massaged his hand.

She rolled her eyes and turned to get out of the car.

"Hold up," he pulled her by her arm, catching her in his arms.

Destiny looked at him confusedly, as a part of her relished the snugness of being enveloped in his arms.

"Hey, beautiful," he winked at her.

She blushed as she sat on the seat motionless.

"Let's go, let's go," Roy yelled excitedly from outside the truck. "I don't want to miss the kickoff."

Ruffling out of Jasiah's arms, Destiny got out of the car. Both, with their arms entangled in each other's, walked up to the stadium, where both Roy and Destiny ran into people they knew. Destiny was greeted by many "Hey, Baby sis" or "Hey, cuz" while Roy received firm handshakes and head nods.

In that instance, Jasiah felt invisible as neither of them introduced him, nor did anyone recognize him – a familiar feeling that had haunted him whenever people greeted Roy and his mother, and no one introduced him. When people asked Destiny who she was with, a spark of excitement ignited in him but vanished quickly as Destiny evaded the question.

"I can't be proud to call you my girl, and you act like I don't exist," Jasiah whispered in her ear as they ascended the escalator.

Destiny was taken aback by his statement as she didn't realize that he cared about it this much.

"I'm serious, Destiny," he spoke, embedding seriousness in his words.

"Can we talk about this in private?" she whispered back as she looked around. "Not on a crowded escalator."

The air turned heavy as the fog of tension clouded their senses until they got to the suite. Arriving at the suite door, he asked her if he could speak with her before they entered.

"Jasiah, we don't really have a title," she responded as she touched the lapel of his Redskins Varsity Jacket.

"I tried talking to you about it yesterday," he reminded her.

Destiny looked at him in the eyes and smiled, attempting to be coy. "Don't you just want to kiss me?"

Jasiah smiled back as he tapped into his emotions. "I do want to kiss you, but I can't keep going like this. I've been the invisible child behind Roy and my mom, and I don't want to be the invisible person in your life."

"You're not the main character in Ralph Ellison's novel," she tried to assure him.

"I am invisible, understand, simply because people refuse to see me," Jasiah quoted the line from the novel that had resonated with him since he had read it over the summer.

"I see you, Jasiah," she touched his face and looked at him with longing, "I promise I see you."

"Do you see us together?" he asked as he held her hand against his face.

Destiny bit her bottom lip and looked around at the hustle and bustle around the suite's entrance. People were laughing and joking while she was shackled in a serious conversation. Cutting herself off from her surroundings, she peered back at Jasiah and decided to turn the question on him, "Jasiah, can you see us together?"

"Don't ask me dumb questions."

"I'm serious," she exclaimed. "You come from a different side of town. You see how I live versus you. I dress like a boy. My head is always in a book..."

"Stop, stop, stop," he shook his head. "I never told you any of that stuff bothers me."

"You were just talking about my clothes," she reminded him.

"Did I hurt your feelings by making one joke?" he looked at her intently. "Come on now, Destiny. You crack on me all the time. You can't take what you dish out?"

Destiny started to shift in place, and she looked down at her feet. "You make me nervous, Jasiah."

"You make me nervous, Destiny," he retorted.

Destiny shook her head as she rubbed her temple. "It's no way… No way you could understand—"

She got interrupted when the door to their suite suddenly opened, with Faye peeking her head outside. "What are y'all doing?" she questioned.

"We are coming," Jasiah said sternly without taking his eyes off Destiny.

"Hello, Miss Faye," Destiny greeted Faye. "Thank you for allowing me to join you at the game."

"Yes, at the game… not at the door," Faye pulled her inside by the arm. "Come on, take your coat off… get something to eat."

"Give us a minute," Jasiah firmly placed his hand over his mother's as he stopped her from dragging Destiny.

Destiny could feel the pressure of his hand on her arm as she looked at Jasiah alongside Faye in surprise. The grimness in his eyes sent shudders down her spine as he didn't even look at his mother.

"We will be there in a moment," he released his hold.

Retracting her hand, Faye strolled into the suite without another word.

"Jasiah, I don't want to be rude," she figured that it was better for her to be brave whatever Faye would dish out than continue this conversation that was instilling a taste of awkwardness and unease in her.

"No, Destiny, you've danced around these questions long enough."

"Jasiah, calm down." She reached out for his hands, but he snatched them away as threads of anger in his actions.

It was evident to her that she had triggered something within him. "Jasiah, please. Don't make a scene."

"I'm sick of this shit," he uttered, looking down at his feet. "I can't do it."

"Jasiah, I didn't mean to hurt your feelings," she reached out again and grabbed Jasiah's face so he could look at her. "I come from a place where the less people know, the better," she looked him in the eyes. "That's all it is."

He took a deep breath and covered her hands with his. He slowly pulled her hands off of him, rejecting her excuse. As she stared into his eyes, she felt like she was looking into the eyes of a different person. "It won't happen again, okay?" Destiny reasoned.

"Thank you." Feeling relieved as the uneasiness in him faded under Destiny's reassuring words.

Destiny stood on her tippy toes and planted a kiss on his lips, slowly sliding her tongue into his mouth to remind him of their connection. Jasiah wrapped his arms around her as he enjoyed the sensation of their closeness. As their scents intermingled, the tension that lingered around them dissipated as he found comfort in her touch.

"We cool?" she asked once she came back up for air.

Jasiah nodded as he planted a kiss on her forehead. "Now let's get you a fitted long sleeve so you look like a little boy with earrings."

Destiny just rolled her eyes as Jasiah guided her by the hand toward the concession stands.

She wasn't worried about what she was wearing as much as she worried about how Jasiah's mother would act toward her. Once in the suite, Destiny spoke to everyone she passed and tried her best to avoid Faye. It seemed like Faye was avoiding her as well, despite her eagerness for Destiny to come into the suite earlier. It wasn't until Jasiah went to the bathroom that Faye slipped into his seat next to her.

"You're more dangerous than I thought," Faye muttered into Destiny's ear.

Destiny was stunned by her statement, so she kept her gaze locked on the field and kept quiet. In her silence she was trying to prepare herself for Jasiah's mother to tell her to stay out *their family business.*

"My son likes you more than you like him," Faye stated.

Faye's words meant nothing in Destiny's mind, and she could hear her mother saying, '*You are the prize.*'

"And you're resourceful," Faye continued.

"I like Jasiah," Destiny admitted, feeling like she had to say something reassuring. "His friendship means a lot to me," Destiny admitted.

"You know this won't work out long term for you two, right? All I have to do is take his car and credit card and you two are done."

Destiny shook her head as she looked Faye in the eyes. Seeing a mother trying to protect her son, Destiny knew that she shouldn't engage. "Excuse me," Destiny stood as she sensed Faye would only keep going. "You have something on your nose," she added as she moved over to Jasiah, who she spotted making another plate. Walking toward him, she placed her hand on his back and rubbed it. "Put a wing or two on there for me, please."

"I got you," he winked at her.

Smiling coyly, Destiny looked back at Faye, who was staring into a compact mirror and checking out her nose from different angles while repeatedly sniffing and wiping. Once Faye finally looked up in the direction of the pair, Destiny's smile faded, and she slowly turned back to Jasiah.

Chapter 9: Oprah Said

Enveloped in the gust of emotions that suffocated her conscience, Destiny realized that she had to face Eric in school and that avoidance would not help bring peace to their situation. Treading through the hallway toward her locker, Destiny questioned her own resolve to break up with Eric.

Am I doing the right thing? Will Eric overreact? If I do this, how will it affect my relationship with Bria?

Distracted by her thoughts, she didn't notice Eric until he was standing right before her. She scanned him from head to toe and quickly became irritated looking at his matted bush, lack of a shape up, and wrinkled baggy clothes on his stocky build. Even the Joop! The cologne that he wore smelled stale to her.

"Eric, not now," Destiny blurted out as she realized she didn't have enough courage to hurt his feelings in person.

"Well, hello to you too," Eric greeted her with an unexpected hug.

Destiny froze, not hugging him back or pushing him away either. "Hey," she mumbled as she took a deep breath to muster enough strength to tell him it was over.

Feeling the tension between them, Eric squeezed her tighter before pulling away.

"What's up with you?" Eric murmured as he put his hand in his pocket. "How did we get here? What did I even do to you, Destiny?"

"You told me the least I could do is buy you some shit since I'm not putting out. You told me something must be wrong with my pussy the way I'm holding on to it. You told me you felt like a fool being my boyfriend," she reminded him.

As she recalled the insults aloud, she questioned herself on why she was trying to spare his feelings.

"I apologized for that. I said those things out of anger," Eric responded through clenched teeth. "You said some hurtful things, too."

"That was only after you insulted me," she sighed. "Eric, you just let me know how you truly feel about me… and it wasn't love."

"People say hurtful things out of anger, Destiny. It happens between couples, for god's sake."

"Eric, I don't want to be late for class, and I need to get into my locker," she dismissed his justification by not acknowledging it. "I told you I didn't want to do this anymore."

As the dagger of humiliation pierced into Eric, clenching his fists, he observed the whispering students who were passing by; he stepped to the side.

"I just want what we used to have back," Eric whispered to her. "I've been thinking about you all weekend."

Destiny, again, looked at him from head to toe. Looking at him assured her that she had made the right choice, as he did not compare to Jasiah. He looked like he had just rolled out of bed, whereas Jasiah would never leave the house without looking pristine. Eric needed his hair done, and Jasiah never went without a haircut.

She knew it was time for her to officially let go of her relationship with Eric. Some part of her soul still doubted her decision as she stood there for a minute amidst the murmurs of the passing crowd around them. Letting out a sigh, she kissed Eric gently on the lips to test her emotions, to see if there was a spark, but she felt nothing.

"Goodbye, Eric."

"This ain't goodbye," he grabbed her around the waist as his face softened with the surge of emotions. "I'm not letting you go that easy."

The bell for class rang, and Destiny stated firmly, "I have to go!" while pushing him off.

"I'll walk you to the train to go to work," Eric pleaded as he regained his balance.

"You have class."

"So?" Eric stated, but his voice came out squeaky. "This is important."

"What's important is that you take care of yourself," Destiny replied. "Start figuring your life out," Destiny encouraged Eric as she felt a tinge of pity seeing him desperately trying to cling to her.

"You're not better than me," Eric spewed.

Destiny shook her head in disappointment and began walking toward her class. The halls had already cleared after the bell rang, so she knew she was late. Eric continued following her, unwilling to accept his reality as his pleas became hatred.

"I noticed you are dressing different… what? You think you're better than me now?" Eric taunted.

Destiny shook her head.

"That's the problem. You get a little bit of money in your pocket and think—"

"Don't get it twisted. Before I had a job, I had money in my pocket," hastily turning on her feet, Destiny cut him off. "But if you even tried to apply yourself at anything other than playing video games, hanging out with your boys, and bothering me, you wouldn't be worried about my pockets."

"I'm straight," Eric retorted confidently. "I get mine out here."

Destiny knew right then and there that Eric wouldn't get it, no matter how much she explained. "A'ight, you got it."

"What is that supposed to mean?"

"Find you somebody that's gonna lay on their back and spread their legs while your nephew is at the door because it's his bedtime," Destiny suggested without looking back at Eric on her way into the classroom.

She took her seat and tried to calm herself. She could feel the weight of her best friend Bria's gaze on her back. After a few moments, a note was passed to Destiny: *I saw you on TV yesterday.*

A wave of realization swept through her heart as she crumbled the paper up and decided to try to explain things to Bria after class.

As the teacher's voice reverberated through the room, Destiny picked up her Trapper Keeper, which felt heavier than normal. When she opened it, there was a two-way pager sitting inside. Jasiah's face flashed through her mind as she thought he must have put it there while they were in the library. A smile bloomed on her face as she flipped it open to read its only message: *So I can tell U how much I miss U all day.*

Her heart skipped a beat as she hid the device under her desk and responded with vibrant emotions fluttering inside her. *U R something else.*

She slid the device into her backpack just as the beeping sound began to echo through the room and turned everyone's attention away from the teacher.

Submerged in confusion and anxiety, she reached into her bag to figure out how to silence the device as quickly as possible.

"I'll take that," her teacher, Mrs. Bowen, ordered with her hand out as she stood beside Destiny's desk.

"Naw, I'm turning it off," Destiny assured as she slipped the device into the front pocket of her backpack.

"You can give it to me or get out of my class, Miss Peay," Mrs. Bowen demanded with her palm in front of her face.

"I said I'ma turn it off. I apologize for disturbing the class," Destiny retorted as she opened her notebook to turn in her homework.

"Get out, Miss Peay," the middle-aged woman instructed her sternly. "Leave my class."

Momentarily, shock blanketed Destiny's mind as she had never been put out of class before. Anxiousness torrented inside her as she really didn't know what to do.

"Do I need to call security?" Mrs. Bowen warned.

"Just give it to her," Bria poked Destiny as she tried to convince her in a hushed voice.

Destiny passed her homework to the person in front of her and stood to leave. She gathered her things in silence and began to stride out of the classroom. As she reached the parameter of the class, she could hear the teacher saying, "I used to teach her brother. He had the same shenanigans going on in his senior year."

"Now you know I'm nothing like my brother," Destiny mentioned as she got closer to the door.

"Leave, Miss Peay," the teacher demanded.

Seeing the teacher compare her to her brother, whether it be Junior or Jax, Destiny wanted to say *Fuck You*. But instead, she walked out of the class and headed to Mrs. Watkins, her guidance counselor, who greeted Destiny with a smile.

"I was just coming to your class, Destiny. I have a great scholarship opportunity for you," she spoke as she revealed a piece of paper in her hand.

"I have some scholarship packets that need my official transcript attached," Destiny replied.

"This is perfect timing," Mrs. Watkins smiled. "How are your college applications coming along?"

Destiny was relieved to use her time with the counselor instead of finding a bathroom to hide in until the bell rang. While she conversed with Mrs. Watkins, she was able to read Jasiah's message without a problem,

Have a good day, beautiful. Hit me when U leave school.

Moments later, the bell rang, and Destiny made her way toward the next class. A gentle breeze swept through the halls, making her hair dance and putting a smile on her face as her consciousness drowned in Jasiah's texts.

"What has you smiling so hard?" Eric inquired when he met her in the hall with Bria in tow.

Averting her eyes from her new pager, Destiny looked at Eric standing in her way. She shook her head, not bothering to reply.

"When did you get a two-way pager?" Bria asked.

"She has a two-way?" Eric looked on, puzzled.

"Yeah, it got her kicked out of Mrs. Bowen's class this morning," Bria added.

Destiny rolled her eyes and walked around the pair. She wasn't going to have them double-team her – to let them suck out the breath of happiness her heart finally felt. Bria grabbed her by the arm. "Destiny, what's up?"

"I can talk to you by yourself, but I'm done talking to Eric," Destiny answered.

"You can't be serious," Eric looked shocked.

"I'm very serious," she stared at him authoritatively as she was firm in her resolve. "We're done."

Cursing, he walked away – a loud thud oscillated through the halls as he punched a locker on his way down the hall.

"Oprah said if he punches a wall, he will punch you," Bria uttered as she stared at her cousin's back disapprovingly. "I told you that when he punched the wall of his room, and he was dead ass wrong."

"Your cousin tripping," Destiny exclaimed as she tilted her head towards Bria. "He can't talk all that shit to me and think I'm just supposed to be like, okay, it's cool."

"Destiny, you called him a broke ass nigga."

"After he called me a stuck-up bitch," she retorted. "I told him I needed a break. Between him, work, and school, it's been a lot."

"Well, you haven't been home on the weekends," Bria mentioned as she leaned in closer to Destiny. "Where you been, girl? Or should I ask who you been with? Did Poppa Peay move football Sunday to a skybox at the stadium?" Bria shot a myriad of questions to her best friend.

Once again, Destiny found herself stuck between truth and lies as she bit her bottom lip, trying to figure out if she could trust Bria with the truth.

"You not getting into no shit. Are you?" Bria questioned.

"Fuck no," she instantly rejected the idea of her participating in anything illegal. "You know I'm not interested in no shit like that."

"Then what the fuck is it? I know Mr. Peay ain't the one texting you at 9 in the morning."

"I'm just figuring some stuff out. And it's nothing illegal."

"How you get in that suite at the game yesterday? I know that was you. I saw for a split second on the screen," Bria wouldn't let up on the question Destiny avoided.

"An old friend of my father," she responded, trying to avoid lying.

"You don't even like football."

Destiny shrugged. "That's not important," she replied as she looked at her best friend. "I just hope our friendship doesn't change because I'm no longer with Eric."

"After that crazy display of anger? You're better off without him," Bria affirmed as she gestured towards the locker Eric had punched. "Oprah just talked about the signs of domestic violence again."

Liberation wrapped Destiny's heart – at least she was now being truthful to her feelings and didn't lose her best friend in the process.

"Call me later, okay?" Bria stated as the next class bell rang.

Destiny nodded with a smile on her face. She was able to breathe a sigh of relief as she no longer had to play the game of being divided by two.

But as she fiddled with the two-way pager in her hand, her insecurities rendered their ugly heads. *Is this what I want*? – Destiny questioned herself.

***

Jasiah was contemplating his choices just as Destiny was from the edge of his bed, his lower body wrapped in a black flat sheet as the sun kissed his naked skin. He checked his pager and wondered why Destiny had not texted him yet.

"Everything okay?" Tangey asked as she traced imaginary circles on Jasiah's lower back. "You think your mom is gonna come home early from shopping?"

"No," Jasiah looked back at his ex-girlfriend. For a second, he imagined Destiny laying there in place of Tangey – her breast barely exposed while the sun shone at just the right angle through the window to make her eyes glow. He smiled at the thought and turned back to his pager to send Destiny a message: *Everything okay?*

"Come back to bed," Tangey insisted in a lusty tone as she wrapped her arms around his waist and pulled him toward her. "We don't have much time."

Lured by Tangey's seductive voice and her soft skin, Jasiah moved, laying on top of her gently. A giggle escaped her gasping mouth as Jasiah brushed his fingers between her thighs. They shared wild, untamed kisses and touches until Jasiah snatched the condom from the nightstand. He eagerly thrust inside Tangey making them both moan in pleasure. But the intimate moment between them went quickly. With his eyes closed, Jasiah imagined himself with Destiny. He exploded at the thought of being one with her. But when he opened his eyes, the dark eyes of his ex-girlfriend stared back at him. He got up as quickly, shaking off his fantasy, and disposed of the condom.

As he returned from the bathroom with a warm, soapy washcloth for Tangey, she had his two-way pager in hand. Hastily, Jasiah jumped, snatched it out of her hand, and dropped the washcloth on her bare chest.

"Damn, I wasn't gonna reply on your dry-ass thread," Tangey commented as she wiped herself.

Ignoring Tangey's sarcastic comment, Jasiah read Destiny's response: *Everything is fine. Thought about u my whole way to work. Ttyl.*

"You don't have to smile so hard," Tangey threw the soiled washcloth at his face, but he caught it in mid air.

"Whatever," he tossed the washcloth over by his hamper before replying to Destiny: *Cool. I wanna c u this week.*

"Oh, my God, your dick is getting hard just by texting her," Tangey huffed as she rolled her eyes.

"I'm thinking about you sucking it," he smirked as he threw his pager on the nightstand.

"Did you wash?" Tangey inquired.

"Of course, I washed," he walked over to her with his pelvis stuck out.

"Then go ahead and put it in your boxers," she rolled over, turning her back to him. "I need a nap before heading home."

Suddenly Jasiah felt a tinge of guilt for being inconsiderate. "Hey," he interjected as he made her roll over to face him. "We cool, right?"

"Yeah, of course," Tangey smiled.

"You'd tell me if you were feeling a certain way, right?" he looked at her closely. "Right, Tangey?"

"Of course," she sat up, "You just got some good dick... and I don't want to miss out," she joked.

Jasiah just shook his head as he let out a sigh, "All I am is a piece of meat to you."

"What else are men good for?" Tangey muttered and moved to the edge of the bed. "Let me get my shit together and get home."

Jasiah didn't protest. He grabbed his pager from off his nightstand and began to text his classmate Jason to see what he missed in his last period.

"Damn, Siah... are you going to text her all day?"

"I'm texting Jason," Jasiah corrected Tangey, glancing at her but averting his eyes back to his device. "You're starting to sound a little jealous, Tangey."

"You never put anyone's picture up like you're a couple," Tangey admitted what was bothering her as her eyes sank into the picture frame on Jasiah's nightstand. "I guess it's just difficult to see."

"Thank you for being honest," Jasiah kissed her on the forehead. "I guess it's the first time I even had the opportunity."

"You've had plenty of dates to plenty of dances, balls, and galas, and you never take pictures with them."

"If you want a picture with me, just say so," he stated as he tickled her, trying to lighten the mood.

Holding back her giggles, she rolled her eyes and grabbed her pants from the floor. Jasiah watched her get half dressed before he stood and pulled Tangey over to the mirror. "Let's practice. Tell me how you want it?" He started to hug her in different positions, playfully fondling her developed hips and full breasts, as he pretended a camera man was in front of them.

"Okay, enough," she giggled as she backed away. "Oprah just said if you feel like a man is stringing you along, he probably is."

"Tangey, you broke up with me," he reminded her.

"I had to."

"I understand that," he rubbed his temple. "Let's not do this," he urged, trying to control his frustration.

"Walk me out, please," Tangey responded as she pulled on her sweater.

With a gentle smile, he did as requested. He walked her to the edge of their property and stared at her curvaceous body, slowly fading away in the distance while his consciousness drowned in thoughts of their fading relationship. Heaving out a sigh, he made a mental note to check on her later that night when he got off the phone with Destiny. While he was falling in love with Destiny, he didn't want to loss his friendship with Tangey.

Chapter 10: Y or N

A dark fog of clouds obscured the skies as lightning flashed through them; high winds raged through the streets as enormous droplets of rain splattered on the ground. Destiny watched the rain and gridlocked traffic from the entrance of her office building as she waited for Jasiah to pick her up. Lingering her gaze through the thunderous weather and the rainwater flooding the curb, she figured he would have been delayed in traffic because of the weather.

She watched her co-workers file out slowly, braving the weather. On their way out, they asked if she was alright. Slowly, the roots of impatience seized her entity as she felt like she had repeated, "Just waiting on my ride," twenty times in response. With the gush of wind swirling through the entrance every time the glass door swung open, her anxiety started to kick in as she looked at the two-way pager and read Jasiah's last message: *Pick u up @ 6.*

Lifting her gaze from the pager, she peered at the large clock on the wall – 6:20. She hoped nothing had happened to him while driving in the horrible weather.

Before she could page Jasiah to check on him, the sound of water splashing onto the sidewalk brought her attention back to the street. There was Jasiah in his Camry. She felt relieved to see him and that he had pulled close to the curb so she didn't have to jump over the overflowing water to enter the vehicle. With her small umbrella in hand, she strode out into the rain.

"God, I thought you forgot about me," Destiny admitted as she closed the door.

"Never," Jasiah whispered as he leaned closer, inhaling the mesmerizing scent of her new jasmine perfume lingering around her. They shared a brief kiss, both pulling away with smiles.

"Ya'll are so corny," a voice inserted from the backseat.

Destiny jolted back in surprise as she hadn't noticed they had company. Tilting her head back, she saw Lafayette sitting safely in the backseat with his hands tucked in his hoodie.

"Shit!" she cursed under her breath as she shuffled in her seat.

"Well, hello to you too," he replied with sarcasm as he noticed the discomfort brewing on Destiny's face.

"What's up, La?" she mumbled in annoyance as she glanced at him from the side-view mirror.

"Damn! What I do to you?" he retorted.

"It's not about you," she exclaimed, altering her tone.

"You cool?" Jasiah asked Destiny as he pulled off.

"Yeah, it's just this rain and all," she replied softly.

"Well, I'm here to tell you that it's fucked up that you didn't invite my cousin to the homecoming game on Friday," Lafayette blabbered as he leaned forward, sticking his head into the front seat area.

"What are you talking about?" Destiny retorted; her face turned sour as she sensed Lafayette's intentions. "Why would I invite him to something I didn't plan on attending?"

"I told you," Jasiah interjected, glancing at Lafayette with a smirk.

"A'ight, tell me this then. Weren't you in the parade one year?" Lafayette questioned.

"When I was Miss Junior," she admitted. "But this year, I'm barely at school. I didn't plan on missing work for it."

"Your senior year?" Lafayette questioned. "Really, Destiny?"

"I'm glad I don't have to explain myself to you," she replied curtly. Destiny averted her eyes to her blurring surroundings as rain misted the window. She didn't want to divulge her recent breakup to Jasiah in Lafayette's present. She wanted it to be a private conversation where no one would misconstrue her words.

"I want to hear this," Lafayette pushed.

"Me too," Jasiah chimed in.

Destiny looked over at Jasiah, seeing the sparkle of interest flickering in his eyes.

"So, how was your day?" she asked, attempting to deviate from the direction of the conversation.

"I want to know why you wouldn't want to go to your homecoming," Jasiah responded.

"Let's just say I did something that divided the friend group," she hinted at Jasiah as she caressed his arm with her fingertips. "For you."

Jasiah smiled as he averted his eyes toward the road. He understood what she was saying without saying it – She had broken up with Eric.

"What the fuck she do *for you*, Siah?" Lafayette exclaimed, feeling left out of the conversation, "That got you over there blushing and shit?"

"Don't worry about it," Jasiah replied as he held out his hand for Destiny to take it. She placed her hand in his palm, feeling the sturdiness of his hand. Jasiah kissed the top of her palm. "It's all good."

"Fuck that. You coming to homecoming with or without her. You gonna put this Camry back in the garage, pull out the Bubble, and y'all can see each other after the game," Lafayette declared as he slumped back in his seat.

"I think we have a standing Friday date, don't we?" Jasiah asked as he glanced over at Destiny.

"Of course, we do."

"Oh, my God," Lafayette complained, flinging his arms up in the air. "How did we get here?"

"How did we get here?" Jasiah sang out playfully.

"Nobody supposed to be here," Destiny joined in on the lyrics of Deborah Cox's song.

"I tried that love thing for the last time," they continued to sing in unison.

Irritated, Lafayette reached between the pair and turned up the radio over their voices. Both of them broke into laughter as Destiny turned the radio down.

"Naw, for real," Lafayette stated. "Friday... we can get some lunch, enjoy the parade. Destiny, you can finally hang out with the regular people and not your geeky ass friends."

"I like my geeky ass friends."

"Yeah, whatever," Lafayette muttered.

"Jasiah..." Destiny looked over at him, noticing that he was wearing his chain. A smile crept across her face as she took it as a sign that Jasiah was regaining his confidence, and she continued, "Why is he here?"

Jasiah, entertained by their banter, chuckled. "We're going to have a nice dinner together."

As his words sank in, Destiny slumped down into her seat as if she were pouting – unsatisfied with Lafayette's presence.

Jasiah drove toward the Union Station with his mind set on pizza from Unos. Jasiah and Destiny walked hand in hand through the shopping area, with Lafayette trailing behind. Initially, Destiny was nervous. She officially broke up with Eric just two days ago, and here she was with someone else. Her betrayal would be evident to anyone who sees her, just as it would be at homecoming. As they walked, swinging their hands back and forth, Destiny tried to think of a way out of homecoming besides saying she had to work.

"When are you going to wear your hair out again?" Jasiah asked as he flipped Destiny's ponytail.

Destiny peered over the railing at people bustling toward the train terminals as they tracked towards Unos and spoke out, "Sorry to inform you, I hate hair maintenance."

"What's so hard about it?" Jasiah questioned.

"Wrapping it up at night, wearing a shower cap," Destiny explained as she rolled her eyes.

"Well, I'd like to see it out again."

Equipping a weak smile on her face, Destiny nodded.

As they walked closer to the rotunda area to enter Unos, Destiny relaxed as she thought she could let her guard down. Her anxiety about being seen by Eric began to fade when suddenly, a familiar voice calling her name startled her. She stumbled and turned to see Bria standing alongside Carl, waving at her. All she thought was, *Thank God I broke up with Eric before this introduction.*

"Who is that?" Jasiah asked as he turned with Destiny, too.

"My best friend," Destiny responded as she let his hand go. "And Eric's cousin."

"Oh snap," Lafayette commented, puffing out a chuckle.

The girls met up halfway without their male counterparts.

"What are you doing up here? And who is that?" Bria interrogated quickly.

"His name is Jasiah," Destiny answered, pointing at him with her thumb over her shoulder as she stood with her back to him.

"Jasiah?" Bria looked at her. "Where did he come from?"

"Lafayette's cousin," Destiny answered.

"Lafayette? Since when you hang out with him?" Bria looked over Destiny's shoulder at the two boys glaring at her. "Girl, you know you owe me an explanation for this."

Destiny looked back at Jasiah and smiled. She decided to make light of the situation.

"You see his fine ass," she averted her eyes back to her best friend, "How much do I have to explain?"

Bria let out a hearty laugh as she peeked at Jasiah again. "Well, you have a point there."

"Wave at him so he knows he's not invisible," Destiny instructed – remembering the situation at the stadium.

"I mean, I'ma wave and smile… But you just broke up with my cousin two days ago."

"Bria, I've been trying to break up with your cousin for about two weeks," Destiny corrected her.

"Yeah, he did say y'all were on a break," Bria remembered as she waved at Jasiah. "Let me go before I miss my movie."

"A'ight," Destiny waved at Carl. "I'll call you later."

"You ain't gonna call me… But at least now I know why," Bria responded, shaking her head. "I'll see you at school."

As Destiny walked toward Jasiah, he had already turned and started walking toward the restaurant ahead of her. She knew that the acknowledgment of him being there wasn't enough. She looked up at the gilded ceiling, dreading her next conversation with Jasiah. She knew that she should have formally introduced them.

When they strolled near the entrance of the restaurant, Lafayette marched upstairs to the lofted pizzeria, and Jasiah waited for Destiny at the entrance.

"Jasiah, I told her who you were. I didn't know what she would say; that's why there was no formal introduction," Destiny explained quickly.

"I'm sure we will see them at the game on Friday. There will be plenty of time for introductions then, right?"

Destiny bit her bottom lip as she sensed Jasiah's dissatisfaction.

"In the car, I assumed you were telling me that you and Eric broke up," Jasiah diverted the conversation as he stuck his hands in his pockets.

"I was," Destiny admitted. "But it's fresh, Jasiah."

"I understand," he glanced at Destiny. "Come closer," he instructed, peering into her eyes.

Seeing the reflection of herself in Jasiah's eyes, Destiny stepped forward – with each step, her heart thumping with anxiety.

"Closer," he whispered.

She took another step, clasping her hands tightly behind her back, ending up close enough so he could lean in.

"Don't try to play me, Destiny," he murmured into her ear, sending a tingling sensation through her body.

Catching her hefty breath, she whispered back, "I've been honest with you since day one."

"So, what are we doing now?"

"We're about to kiss," she smiled at him as she brushed the side of her face against Jasiah's, trying to lighten up the mood while finding a cure for her fluttering emotions.

"You know what I'm talking about."

"We're not going to continue to have these types of conversations with onlookers," Destiny clarified, disappointed as she took a step back.

Instantly, he wrapped his arm around her waist and brought her closer to him. "I like you close to me."

"I'm here," she spoke softly, placing her hand over his heart for emphasis. "But I know your cousin is tired of waiting up there," she nodded her head toward the stairs.

"We're going to finish this conversation. He can wait," Jasiah replied, grazing his nose against hers.

Part of her consciousness was happy to avoid a relationship conversation through dinner, so she agreed and explained her breakup with Eric to Jasiah in the corridor of a historic train station. Realizing she no longer had to be reserved in her feelings, Destiny suddenly became eager to unload the weight of secrets she had been carrying since she met Jasiah.

***

"I'm over here thinking some real shit been going on in your household, and the whole time, you just found yourself another boyfriend," Bria exclaimed from the other side of the phone.

"Noooo, it didn't start out like that," Destiny protested, skimming her hand through her hair.

"Yesss, it had to."

"You want me to tell you what happened or not?" Destiny retorted.

"Okay, fine, go ahead."

Destiny began to reveal the beginning of their story – from the moment she saw Jasiah in his Bubble Caprice as she walked to the bus stop to the point that Jasiah had Lafayette track her number down because she refused to give it to him at that time.

"Goddamn," Bria muttered. "He was pressed like that?"

"He said he knows what he wants," Destiny explained before continuing to fill her best friend on their experience of getting to know one another.

Destiny went on to tell Bria about the whirlwind she has been on with Jasiah, from shopping in Georgetown boutiques for his homecoming and even about his mother, Faye's reaction toward her.

"My poor cousin didn't stand a chance," Bria recognized. "Now I know why you kept telling him to get a job. You got somebody taking you out, paying your pager bill."

"He is a really nice guy," Destiny affirmed.

"Seems that way," Bria agreed. "It's like you're damn near in a long-distance relationship, though. Bitches can't keep an eye on their man at the same school. How you gonna do it from across the city?"

"I would have to just trust him like he has to trust me," Destiny concluded.

"Oh, y'all are in a relationship."

"No one has made any commitments, and I can't start assuming."

"Didn't he introduce you as his girl to his friends?"

"I definitely wasn't his girl then," Destiny explained.

"Didn't he tell you that he belongs to you?"

"I definitely didn't belong to him when he said that either," she responded as she scratched her head – her mind soaring through the world of ifs and buts.

"So, you have this fine ass nigga *with money* in a relationship with you, and you're not in a relationship with him?" Bria laughed. "I mean, I know you can be distrusting, but I didn't think you—"

"I have to make sure he isn't saying all the right things just to get into my drawers."

A squeaky laughter erupted from Bria as she heftily said, "I'm sure he would call them panties."

"Whatever," Destiny chuckled. "And I really didn't want to break up with Eric initially. I thought he was going to be my first, maybe even my husband one day."

"He thought he was going to be your first, too," Bria mumbled. "So much for that."

"Tell me about it," Destiny sighed. "It's just like—"

"You got this brother with money on your line, and on the other hand, you got this broke ass nigga begging for your drawers…. I get it, Destiny. Whether the broke ass nigga is my cousin or not, I would have done the same thing," Bria assured her, blanketing her heart with consolation.

"It's not about the money," Destiny interjected, as she didn't want to seem like a gold digger.

"It certainly doesn't hurt," Bria pointed out.

"No, it doesn't hurt."

By the time Destiny hung up the telephone with Bria, she had agreed to flat iron Destiny's hair for homecoming. But she had also received a page on both of her pagers. Eric had paged her 911, and Jasiah had paged her on the two-way: *Will u b my gf? Y or N?*

Looking at both the pagers for a moment, Destiny replied, *'Y,'* to Jasiah. She beamed with happiness as if Jasiah had been reading her mind and ignored the other.

***

When Friday rolled around, with the sun beaming onto New Jersey Avenue, Destiny stood on the sidewalk, trying to figure out which version of Jasiah she was in a relationship with. He had transformed into the flashy boy she met at the bus stop. He was sitting in his Bubble Caprice, sporting all black, including a new black leather Avirex bomber jacket and all-black Nike Foamposites. His earrings and chain sparkled in the sunlight as she approached his car on the way to the parade route with Bria.

Jasiah's eyes gleamed as he stared at *his girlfriend* approaching him. Destiny's feminine charms elevated in the tight jeans, a black sweater, and the tall boots she wore. Her hair was out, dancing in the wind, but still covered by a baseball cap with crimson tide, the school's mascot, embroidered on it. Jasiah tried to play it cool as every fiber in him wanted to scoop her into his arms and kiss her like no one was watching.

"Bria, I want you to meet Jasiah," Destiny introduced them.

"What's up, Bria?" Jasiah greeted Destiny's best friend by shaking her hand before reaching over to clobber Destiny with a bear hug.

"You look so good, beautiful," he whispered in her ear as he gently bit her earlobe with his lips.

"You too," Destiny whispered back as she enjoyed the excitement his closeness and nibble caused.

"I'm telling you, these two need a room, man," Lafayette interjected loudly.

Destiny pulled away from Jasiah with a deep sigh and looked over towards Lafayette. "What's up, La?"

Lafayette simply nodded.

"You gonna walk with us or chill out here?" Destiny asked Jasiah, averting her eyes from Lafayette.

"We're gonna chill right here," Jasiah responded as he patted her on the butt. "I'll be here when y'all get back."

Destiny nodded and broke away from the group with Bria beside her.

"He looks even better up close," Bria commented.

"Hey, keep your eyes on Carl," Destiny warned playfully.

"I'm just saying," Bria confessed as she looked behind her. "Does he have an older brother?"

Destiny let out a chuckle. "Probably."

Mixing in with the crowd, letting the music from the marching band orchestrate their bodies, the girls danced and joked around with other classmates until they ran across Eric and his friends posted up on a wall. Destiny immediately noticed the change in his hair. He had cut his hair into a temper taper, which was a good look on him.

"Now, you know I gotta speak to my cousin," Bria mentioned as they grew closer to Destiny's ex.

"Fuck that nigga," Destiny joked.

"Dang, you are harsh," Bria laughed.

At a distance, Destiny could see Theresa lingering close to Eric, solidifying that Theresa was always waiting in the wing, if not his side chick. A tinge of contempt floated through Destiny's heart as she glanced at the girl, delving into the thoughts of comparison. Theresa had a bigger butt than her and wider hips, but she also wore her pants too small, so she always had to pull her shirt or jacket down over her muffin top. She suffered from horrible acne as well. Destiny concluded that Eric had downgraded while she had upgraded.

"I'll be right here," Destiny informed Bria and decided to hang back at a distance to avoid any awkward interaction with Eric.

"A'ight, I understand," Bria replied and walked to her cousin and his friends.

Regardless of whether Jasiah was close by, seeing Eric with Theresa, a torrent of emotions gushed through her as she aimlessly peered at the parade and waved at her teachers and others she knew in classic cars passing by. A smile crept on her face as she felt relieved to rid herself of any guilt about her quick rebound relationship with Jasiah.

"You're looking a bit different, Destiny," a boy remarked as he walked by. "What's up with you?"

Destiny looked back to see who the voice belonged to and found one of her classmates, Keith.

"I'm chilling," she shrugged bashfully.

"Okay, I see you."

Destiny looked down at her clothes. She admitted to herself that because of Jasiah, she was different- and she liked it. Thinking of her new boyfriend, Destiny took out her pager to send a message to Jasiah: *Hey, u.*

"Hey yourself," Jasiah's voice hovered from behind her ears.

Turning to the left, she saw him walking along with Lafayette's friends. A wave of relief and affection passed through her as she smiled at the sight of him. When Jasiah got close to her, he grabbed her around the waist while the boys kept walking.

"Why are you standing on the sidewalk looking so random by yourself?" he inquired.

"Waiting on Bria," she answered, looking up at the person she could call her boyfriend now. "So, you decided to walk?"

"Looking for you," Jasiah submerged his consciousness in her hazel eyes. "You were gone too long."

A smile blossomed on her face as she wrapped her arms around his waist and tilted her head. "Have you kissed me today?"

"I was tryna play it cool," he admitted as he released her from the waist and took her hand so they could walk. "I know I'ma have to hear enough from Lafayette about holding your hand when we walk…. He talked about it all the way home the other day."

"He is such a hater," she blurted out as she leaned on his arm.

"It's not stopping me. And I'm not even going to let you go with the whole block staring at us," Jasiah mentioned.

Destiny looked over in the direction of Bria and Eric, "Bria, I'ma catch you at the game!" Destiny called to her.

"I'm coming. Hold up a sec," Bria yelled back.

"That ain't the dude she was with at Union Station," Jasiah noticed.

"Carl is on the football team," Destiny informed him. "That's her cousin."

"Ohhhhh!" he laughed. "That explains the stares."

She kept her back to Bria and Eric, wanting to avoid any eye contact.

"I should tongue you down right here," Jasiah mentioned as he looked at her glowing eyes.

"Don't look at me like that," she murmured as she blushingly looked away. "Makes me feel like you're looking into my soul."

Savoring the adorableness Destiny was emitting, Jasiah kissed her on the forehead. "Why don't we skip out on the game?" he suggested.

"We will leave after the first quarter," Destiny compromised as she started to walk. "Bria is gonna have to catch up."

"I tried to get her to wait, Bria," Jasiah stated loudly.

"Why you lying?" Destiny exclaimed as she popped him. A tinge of satisfaction crawled through her as she noticed Eric looking at them.

"So, I gather Eric is the one with the curly bush and headphones," Jasiah guessed as they crossed the street.

"How did you know?"

"Because he was asking Bria who the fuck is that."

Destiny looked up at Jasiah, and a flicker of amazement shone in her eyes – feeling proud of her boyfriend.

Just as they crossed the street, the boom of gunfire pierced their ears. Screams and confusion erupted from bystanders as Destiny and Jasiah crouched down for cover.

"Come on," Destiny grabbed Jasiah's hand as she noticed a store in front of them where many were running for cover. Navigating through a terrorized crowd, they were able to get inside the store. Just as the owner was locking the door, another burst of shots rang out.

Catching his breath, Jasiah glanced at Destiny, whose chest bounced up and down. She squatted with her hands on her knees, trying to catch her breath.

"Are you okay?" Jasiah asked, hoping she didn't fall out or vomit.

"Yeah, I just hope Bria's okay."

After her heartbeat returned to normal, Destiny could hear the sirens blaring from outside. Immediately, the store owner started shouting, "If you not buying anything, leave!"

Reacting to her first instinct, Destiny grabbed two Pepsis out of the cooler. "You want something else?" Destiny asked Jasiah.

She only heard silence in reply.

"Jasiah?" Destiny looked up – his affectionate eyes shadowed with horror. Jasiah stood in his place, his eyes peering at the reflection of blue and red lights reflecting against the glass door. His chest still puffed up and down as he had not regained his composure yet.

"Jasiah, it's fine. I'm here, we're okay," she consoled him with a hug. He closed his eyes and gulped the reality that he had experienced his first shootout, Jasiah half-hugged Destiny.

"Destiny. I'm fine," he lied.

"You want something else?" Destiny asked again as she pulled away.

"Just some gum," he replied as he went closer to the door and looked out of it without opening it.

Once they were on the sidewalk again, Destiny noticed her best friend in the crowd. "Bria!" Destiny called out.

"Girl, this shit is crazy," Bria exclaimed as she had her hand over her chest. "Got me jumping over walls and shit."

"I was out here ducking low like Lil' Kim tryna dance," Destiny joked as she imitated Lil' Kim's dance moves.

The girls laughed, but as Destiny looked back at Jasiah, she recognized that he still had not moved on from the incident.

"You good?" she asked Jasiah.

"I need to check on my cousin," he responded.

"I bet it was those boys from 5th and O," Bria stated. "I saw some dudes from 7th Street around here, and I heard they still beefin'."

"This shit normal for y'all?" Jasiah questioned with a tinge of disgust in his voice.

"Unfortunately," Destiny admitted.

Jasiah shook his head.

Noticing his discomfort, Destiny took him by the hand. "Come on, let's find your cousin."

They walked quickly back to where Jasiah had left his car. Lafayette was standing there with his friends, playing Backyard Band's go-go version of "Thong Song" from his Alpine system and laughing. "See, he's okay," Destiny assured Jasiah. "Everything's cool."

"Ah, cuz, I told these fools your system cranks!" Lafayette yelled as he bobbed his head.

Heaving out a sigh of relief, Jasiah just nodded his head.

"You want to take a walk? Get your head together?" Destiny asked before they got closer to the rest of the group.

"I'm not walking around here ever again," he replied, agitated.

"I mean, the police are everywhere now... It's safe," Bria interjected.

"The police were blocking the streets off for the parade, and somebody still busted off," he rebutted, his voice squeaky as his face turned sour upon the mention of police.

From a distance, Lafayette could see the distress on his cousin's face. He walked up to them. "What you do to my cousin?" he interrogated.

Destiny rolled her eyes and told Lafayette, "Boy, shut up!"

"Look, the bitches are on you… You ain't got to put up with this," Lafayette told Jasiah as he pointed at Destiny.

"Boy, you crazy," Jasiah pulled Destiny before him and held her from behind. "This girl just saved my life because I ain't know what to do when they started shooting."

Destiny stuck her tongue out at Lafayette playfully while Bria giggled from the side.

Though still nervous about the environment he was in, Jasiah enjoyed the open affection he could show toward Destiny. He kissed her on the neck. "I was about to stop, drop, and roll like it was a damn fire."

Everyone in earshot chuckled.

Lafayette nodded. "A'ight… The game doesn't start for another hour. Let's roll to Wendy's," he suggested.

"You mean you, me, Destiny and Bria?" Jasiah asked. "We can squeeze in one more."

"We can leave these females," Lafayette exclaimed as he gestured toward Bria and Destiny.

"You gonna stop talking about me like I'm not here," Destiny interjected.

"I can handle it, baby," Jasiah assured her. "La, I just told you what it is," Jasiah added firmly.

"Girl, I like him… He doesn't play no games about you already," Bria commented from the side, elbowing Destiny.

Lafayette just shook his head and started to walk back to his friends.

"I'm worried about this nigga, and all he is talking about is the system in my car," Jasiah shook his head.

The girls stayed quiet until Bria asked, "What made you like my b-f-f so much?"

"She looked so petite and nerdy with her bookbag and shit," he described with a smile on his face. "But she is witty and clever."

Embarrassment clouded Destiny's face as she blushed.

"I think she's beautiful, but really, it's her confidence that turns me on," Jasiah continued.

"Okayyy," Bria smiled brightly to show she was happy for her friend. "Now, Destiny, what about him made you start carrying my damn cousin?"

"For the record, I didn't carry your cousin," Destiny moved away from Jasiah and looked at him. "How couldn't I give this guy a chance after I ignored him at a bus stop, and then he still tracked down my number?"

"I knew what I wanted when I saw it," Jasiah winked at her.

"Plus, he recited Shakespeare to me in the first conversation," she expressed as she placed her hand over her heart. "I mean, he did start out as my calculus tutor over the phone, too, though."

"I'm still your calculus tutor," Jasiah shook his head. "I forgot about that Hamlet line," Jasiah took Destiny's hand, pulled her to him, and kissed her, locking her lips in his emotions – feeling their tenderness.

"Oh, y'all in love," Bria recognized from the side.

Immediately, they both jumped back and yelled back in unison, "Nooooo!"

"Oh, please, everybody can see it," Bria chuckled, appreciating their happiness. "Can't stop touching each other. Protective over each other," Bria stuck her hands in her back pockets. "It's cute."

As Bria enlisted the traits of their relationship, Jasiah and Destiny gazed into each other's eyes – their consciousness wandering the same thoughts: *Is it love?*

Chapter 11: Touch

Plock! Pock!

The sound echoed through the tennis court as the tennis ball, bashed by Jasiah and Jason, swirled between the two. Jasiah served the ball, the veins of his forearm tightening as he plummeted the ball toward Jason – beads of his sweat sprinkling over the racket. As he watched the ball, Jasiah knitted his eyebrows together, waiting for a return from Jason. During the running back and forth in the court with his racket, his consciousness lingered over the moment his heart stopped when the shots rang out near the store on New Jersey Avenue.

"You're off your game, man," Jason mentioned as he bounced the tennis ball against the deco-turf court.

"I have a lot on my mind," Jasiah uttered as he got into his defensive stance-- sunlight twinkling over his sweaty forehead. "These last few weeks have definitely been an eye-opener for me."

Jason served the ball. Jasiah made the return. Hitting the ball, Jasiah derived his force from the pools of rage as he imagined himself hitting the police officer who pinned him to the ground. A faint grunt escaped from Jasiah's mouth, and the ball thwarted toward Jason. He had to duck because the ball was coming at him like a bullet aimed at his forehead.

"Time out!" Jason called as he looked back at the small dent in the fence where the ball hit.

"What? Serve the ball," Jasiah demanded, wiping the sweat off his forehead.

"Are you getting any?" Jason joked. "You're too tense, bro. That shot was a killer one."

"The question should be, am I getting any from the person I want it from," Jasiah corrected him as he pointed his racket toward Jason. "Serve the ball."

The two continued to play an intense game until it was match point. Every time Jasiah hit the ball, he poured every bit of pent-up frustration into his shots as if he was smacking away all that he had been through. One ball was Lauren; the others were police, and some were even his mother. Drenched in sweat, consumed by the fretful thoughts, his focus narrowed on the ball with no regard for the small audience that had gathered for their game, including his stepfather, Roy.

As Jasiah scored the winning point, huffing out his exhaustion, a faint wave of cheers made him avert his focus to the audience. Equipping a smile on his face, he playfully did the Dougie on his way to shake Jason's hand.

"We haven't seen you at the club in a while; what made you come out this morning?" Jason asked as they walked to the locker room.

"Talking to Destiny. I was avoiding the club after what happened with Lauren," Jasiah admitted. "But she was like, if you're innocent, Lauren should be the one ashamed, not you."

"Easier said than done," Jason retorted.

"Yeah, but it's time… When Roy said he was coming for a game of pickleball, I decided to get up this morning and come too."

"I missed hanging with you at the pool this summer for sure," Jason said as he held up his fist for a bump. "I'm glad you're back."

Jasiah lightly pounded his fist against Jason's with a smile. Once they made it to the locker room, Roy peeked his head in and said, "I'ma head over to the café."

"I'll meet you there," Jasiah replied, popping his head out of his locker.

"And you're hanging out with Roy," Jason pointed out as he nudged Jasiah. "Never seen that before."

"A lot of things are different," Jasiah shrugged. "I'ma start interning at his office over winter break."

"See if you can get me in there," Jason requested. "I know there's some fly bitches in that office."

Jasiah laughed and looked at his pager. Destiny had texted him: *GM.*

He responded: *GM – still on for 3?*

Just when he was about to put his pager back in the pocket, a beep vibrated through his hand. He didn't expect such a quick response when he read the reply from Destiny: *Y- Grosvenor Station.*

"Why you smiling so hard, Siah?" Jason inquired as he saw Jasiah's pearly white teeth revealed in excitement.

"Today should be a good day."

"You gonna get some from the person you want it from?" Jason questioned with a playful smirk on his face.

"It's a good possibility," Jasiah poured hope into his words. "We shall see."

But as Roy's car neared their house, Jasiah saw the hustle and bustle of event staff and caterers roaming around. His eyes widened in surprise. He quickly felt deflated, as he knew there was no way Destiny would let him get past second base with a house full of people.

Turning his head toward Roy, Jasiah inquired, "What's this?"

"Your mother didn't tell you?" Roy questioned sarcastically. "She's calling this a Friendsgiving."

Jasiah sat silently for a moment, agitated by the hiccup in his plans.

"What's the problem? Do you have other plans?" Roy asked, exiting his SUV.

"Destiny's coming over," Jasiah mumbled as he stared at the stack of chairs under the shade of swaying tall trees.

"Oh! You should probably inform her about the dress code then," Roy informed him before closing the door.

"Even better," Jasiah mumbled cynically as he exited the vehicle.

Once Jasiah entered his house, he noticed that the event staff had moved the normal sitting furniture of the great room somewhere else and had turned it into a large dining area for about twenty people. The table was organized lavishly, adorned with foliage and candles. He searched the table for name cards, as his mother was infamous for her seating arrangements. When he saw none placed, Jasiah headed upstairs to find his mother, hopeful that there was space for Destiny.

"Ma, why didn't you tell me you were having a party?" Jasiah yelled as he found his mother in the bathroom getting her hair done. "I have plans with Destiny."

"That girl is a leech," Faye cursed under her breath. Tilting her head toward Jasiah, she continued, "Just make sure she's wearing something appropriate...she's such a tomboy."

"We will just chill upstairs," Jasiah recommended.

"No, Chad is bringing CJ," Faye dismissed the idea. "And I want you in a collared shirt."

Understanding his mother's intentions, Jasiah frowned. His plans were ruined.

"Is there even space for Destiny at the table?" Jasiah questioned as he simultaneously tried to figure out other options to spend alone time with his girlfriend.

"Only because there was a cancellation this morning," Faye responded. "Where is your brother?"

"I assume in his room playing video games," Jasiah answered as he walked out.

"6 p.m. sharp, Jasiah!" she yelled after him.

Jasiah nervously called Destiny, hoping the event at his home wouldn't deter her from coming. There was no answer. He texted her- *call me*.

Destiny had made it clear that she wanted to avoid interactions with Faye. It took a lot for him to convince her to spend the day at his home instead of in the streets of DC. This was Destiny's first time returning to his house since they became an official couple. Pacing his bedroom floor impatiently, he decided to text her again – *Call me B4 u get on the train*.

Jasiah looked at the time – 11 a.m. He had four hours to kill. He showered, tidied up his room and bathroom, and finished up a paper for his English class. When he looked at the clock again, it was 1 p.m. – It was as if the time had slowed down as he buried his face in his palms and ran his hands repeatedly over his waves nervously. There was still no text or phone call from Destiny – he didn't want to ruin this chance. Just as he was leaving his room to see what was going on in his house, the phone rang. He leaped to answer it.

"Hey, beautiful," he answered ecstatically.

"Hey, handsome" Destiny responded. "How was your morning at the country club?"

Jasiah could hear the mockery in Destiny's pronunciation of 'country club.'

"A good workout," Jasiah replied, ignoring the sarcasm. "What did you plan on wearing today?"

"Something I can snuggle up next to you in. We are just watching movies at your house right?"

"Well, of all weekends, the Netaspends will be home this weekend with a few guests," Jasiah remarked as he referred to his family by their last name.

"So how about we just catch a movie at Pentagon City, my treat," Destiny suggested.

"I am looking forward to us having some alone time."

"But it won't be alone time," Destiny pointed out.

"I'm sure we can fit some in," Jasiah implored. "I can look in your eyes, kiss you, feel on that little booty."

As if Jasiah's lusty voice echoed in the plains of silence, Destiny gave no reply.

"Destiny."

"Jasiah."

"Isn't it better that I gave you a heads-up?"

"Yes," she responded, her voice faint as she looked over the letter she just received from Jasiah's father through her brother.

"Are you still coming?"

"If you want me to," Destiny murmured, fidgeting the letter in her hand.

"Of course, I do," Jasiah stated confidently, but he was afraid to tell Destiny it was an actual dinner party. He thought it would make what little resolve she had of coming over would vanish.

"I can pick you up if you want," he suggested as he rolled in his bed.

"No," Destiny protested. "My mother has agreed that I can drive her to UDC for some conference session, and I'll just catch the train the rest of the way... we're about to get out of here now."

"If you get to the station sooner, just text me," Jasiah stated.

"Okay."

Instantly, he hung up the phone and decided to just go to the mall and buy Destiny a casual dress. After scavenging through countless shops, he finally found a black off-the-shoulder dress at Express and stiletto black knee-high leather boots from Nine

West for her. As he gathered the receipt for the last item, Destiny texted him: *1 stop away.*

Jasiah rushed from the mall to his car, only to find Destiny standing in front of a park-n-ride sign with specks of annoyance lingering over her face. He watched her walk toward the Camry, her hair flying in the wind.

"You don't have to look so mean," Jasiah joked once she was in the car.

"I hate the cold," Destiny pointed out. "And I forgot my hat."

"You weren't waiting that long," Jasiah assumed.

She shook her head no and silently stared out of the window at the barren sidewalks of Rockville while her mind swirled around the letter she had received just before she ventured out. Jasiah rested his hand on her thigh, but seeing no reaction from Destiny, he felt like something was wrong.

When he pulled up to the house, the caterer vans were taking up most of the driveway.

"Are y'all having a party?" Destiny questioned, looking at Jasiah.

"She speaks," Jasiah pointed out as he parked.

"I've defrosted," Destiny spoke as she rolled her eyes. "But are y'all having a party?" she repeated.

"Friendsgiving is what Roy called it."

"Does your mom know I'm coming?" Destiny inquired, shadows of concern looming on her face.

"It's cool."

"Jasiah, I'm not playing a game of Guess Who's Coming to Dinner with you."

"Destiny, I don't know what that is supposed to mean, but let's just go inside."

Closing her eyes and sorting out her scrambled thoughts, Destiny reluctantly got out of the car. She had been wrestling with herself about telling Jasiah his father's whereabouts for weeks. Almost every day, she assisted Jasiah with ideas on how to find his father's location, including the latest one of contacting the Bureau of Prisons. It seemed like Jasiah always had an excuse for why he didn't follow through with phone calls.

Today, Destiny's mother told her, "Maybe he really doesn't want to know," as they drove to the University of the District of Columbia. "And confronting this head-on can have lifelong repercussions."

Pondering over her mother's analysis, Destiny felt conflicted. With mixed emotions, she felt guilty for keeping her father whereabouts a secret from Jasiah, but part of her mind leaned toward her mother's suggestion, too.

Mr. Peay told Junior about the whole ordeal with Destiny's boyfriend. According to Junior, Jasiah Sr. was surprised and overjoyed to know that his son wanted to know him. He wrote Jasiah Junior a five-page letter through Junior. Mr. Peay read it to ensure that Jasiah Sr. wasn't saying anything crazy that would traumatize the young man even more. Once he approved, he handed it over to Destiny. She then decided she would only know what was in the letter if Jasiah decided to share. She planned to reveal the information today, but she didn't want to be the blame for ruining Jasiah's mood during "Friendsgiving."

When they entered the home, Destiny noticed that the overwhelming cigarette smell that suffocated her on her last visit was now masked by the scent of spices, nutmeg, and cinnamon from the freshly baked pumpkin pies placed on the foyer table for cooling.

"I could have had my father make a sweet potato pie," Destiny mumbled as she looked at the pastry topping with a pumpkin cutout.

"Your father probably could have catered the whole thing," Jasiah responded.

Strolling through the house tangled in Jasiah's arms, Destiny marveled at the setting before her. She immediately took her Kodak disposable camera out of her purse and snapped a picture of the exquisite dining table to share with her mother. Destiny stood in front of the table for a moment, staring at it in a daze. The oversized window revealing the magnificent view of the pool and shedding elm and oak trees was the perfect backdrop to a festive table donned with candles and foliage in front of a roaring fireplace.

Destiny took off her coat with Jasiah's assistance. When he went to hang it up, Destiny went over to the fireplace to warm her hands. It was her first time in front of an open, roaring fireplace.

"Didn't Jasiah tell you no sweatsuit," Faye's annoyed voice lingered through the room as she suddenly appeared from the study.

Destiny jolted in her place as she was startled by Faye's sudden comment. Though various people were walking to and from, no one was talking.

"Oh, hello, Miss Faye," Destiny smiled at Jasiah's mother. Her eyes sparkled in that moment, admiring Faye. She was dressed in a long satin robe, and her hair was covered by a matching scarf. She reminded Destiny of a young Diane Carol from *Dynasty*.

Feeling Destiny's admiring gaze lurking over her, Faye rolled her eyes as she strolled to the side. "Hello, Destiny," she lit a cigarette. "Your little Juicy Couture sweatsuit is cute… but this is really a cocktail attire event."

"I wasn't aware that there was an event," Destiny replied as she folded her arms across her chest, "Until I saw the catering truck."

Faye puffed out a ball of smoke in frustration as she called out, "Jasiah!"

"Yeah, Ma?" Jasiah answered from the kitchen.

"Jasiah!" Both women called out at the same time.

He was startled and quickly exited the kitchen. When he joined them with a piece of ham in hand, he felt like he was facing double trouble.

"Didn't I tell you to tell Miss Destiny about the dress code?" his mother interrogated.

"I have it under control," he assured as he flashed his charming smile before stuffing his face with meat. "Come on, Destiny," he mumbled as he held out his hand while he chewed.

"Keep your door open," Faye ordered as she turned around and headed back to the study.

As soon as Jasiah took Destiny upstairs, he closed the door and turned on the television before clobbering Destiny with kisses. Guided by his uncontrollable emotions as he saw Destiny staring lustfully into his eyes, he lifted her onto the bed and playfully tickled and kissed her until she screamed, "My hair, you're messing up my hair."

Skimming his hands through her body, Jasiah stood up, took off Destiny's sneakers for her, and sent them flying. Before Jasiah could join her on the bed, Destiny moved to the edge and grabbed his cordless phone.

"Who could you be calling right now?" Jasiah questioned in a hushed tone as he took off his double-sole Timberlands and shirt. He felt like time was of the essence, and if he was going to make it to third base with Destiny, the sooner the better.

"I have to tell someone I'm safe," Destiny responded before saying, "Daddy, I'm here. Yes... yes. I know. I know," Destiny hung up the phone and turned toward Jasiah.

"I missed you," Jasiah whispered as he grazed his lips against her neck.

"I missed you too," she admitted as she hissed from the sensation of a gentle touch that sent electricity buzzing through her body.

"I'm going to tongue you down now, okay?" Jasiah foretold as he grasped one side of Destiny's face in his hand.

A smile flourished on Destiny's face as she nodded, her lips craving for Jasiah's.

Fondling her lips first, tickling her nose with his, Jasiah kissed her until he was on top of her, burying her between himself and the mattress. As their tongues danced together, he unzipped her Juicy Couture track jacket to reveal her bra. His gaze burned into her smooth skin as he kissed down her neck, making her let out faint moans as his tongue trailed her cleavage.

The heat built up inside Destiny as she delighted in Jasiah's embrace. His heart craved more as he pulled on her bra to expose her nipple. Jasiah suckled her breast while cupping and playing with the other one in his hand. Destiny moaned lightly, clasping her lips together as her heart and her soul delved into a sensation she had never felt before.

Guided by the hypnotizing scent of Destiny's skin, Jasiah kissed his way down to her navel and took a playful bite of her hip, making her jolt in surprise as she let out a muffled chuckle before making his way back to her mouth. She wrapped her arms around him, leaving barely an inch of space between them. The proximity made her grind her pelvis against his, feeling his full length against her. She closed her eyes as she felt Jasiah's firm hand skimming over her belly and making its way inside her waistband – instantly opening her eyes, she stopped him by grabbing his hand.

"H-Hold up," she stuttered in a hefty breath as she felt the intensity of the moment. "I just got here."

Jasiah took a deep breath as he tried to maintain his composure. "Just let me touch it," he whispered in her ear.

His lustful voice maneuvered her resolve as her soul craved his touch. Without saying anything, she released his hand as she buried her face in the pillow.

Removing the pillow from her face, Jasiah's eyes hovered over his girlfriend's bashful face, and they smiled at one another. Without another word, he kissed her on the lips, pulling her body into his before he slipped his hand into her waistband. A burst of excitement surged within him as his fingertips brushed past fine hair, over her clit, and then between her lips, drenching in the moisture around it. Jasiah peered at Destiny's lustful eyes as she moaned from his touch.

"You're wet as shit," he slowly slid one finger inside of her. Destiny's chest slowly lifted from the mattress as the flurry of sensations hazed her mind, only focusing on Jasiah's touch lingering over her.

She bit her bottom lip and pushed on Jasiah's shoulders lightly as if she wanted him to stop. But she truly didn't want him to. Jasiah pushed against her hands and kissed her passionately as he used his thumb to stimulate her further. Destiny felt like she was about to explode in that instant as she gasped. Her eyes met Jasiah's for a moment as she almost confessed an emotion that confused her - love. Instead, she shut her eyes and tried to determine how things had moved so quickly with him.

"Jasiah, she moaned out. "Please."

"Let it happen," he whispered to her as he slowly inserted another finger inside her.

This time, she grabbed onto his tank top, wincing at the slight pain mixed with pleasure. The feeling of her tenderness aroused Jasiah. He moaned, too, excited that he was able to touch her in such a way.

Destiny's eyes flickered open as she came close to climax, her chest heaving up and down as she flowed with the torrent of pleasure rushing inside her.

"Jasiah," Destiny moaned; her body started to tense up at the new flood of sensation.

Jasiah was silent, his movements coaxing her to ecstasy.

And right there, within thirty minutes of arrival, Destiny, intoxicated by lust, had her first orgasm. Breathing heavily, she hid her face in the crock of Jasiah's arm, embarrassed and hoping no one heard her sounds of pleasure.

"Oh, my God," she whispered as she felt her heart pounding.

Jasiah moved her face to kiss her. He removed his hand from inside her panties and pulled her close to him, gripping her hip as he felt even more excited.

"You feel that?" Jasiah lustfully mumbled as he took Destiny's hand and rubbed it over his erection.

Destiny's heart thumped ferociously as she felt Jasiah's throbbing warmth. Her mind still hazy, she bit her bottom lip and sat up, "Jasiah, you're overwhelming me."

Following Destiny, Jasiah sat up and lowered her open track jacket from her shoulders to expose her bare skin. He kissed her slender shoulder and asked, "Didn't you like it?"

Gulping her ecstatic emotions, Destiny nodded.

"Then just relax," he instructed as he brushed his hands against her body, his lips moving from her shoulders to her ear.

"Jasiah, I'm not—"

"Shhh!" he placed his finger over her lips as he turned her toward him, their hefty breaths and heartbeats in sync, dancing in the space between them. "We're not going to go that far. I just want to make you feel good."

"You've done that," Destiny pushed away as she pinched his lips gently and chuckled. "You've definitely done that," she grabbed at her jacket and started to zip it back up, gaining her composure.

"Please, Destiny," he touched her hand lightly, not forceful. "Don't cover up."

His touch sent ripples of tingling sensations through her entire body. She shuddered as she felt emotions that she had never experienced before, and she was desperately trying to hold her composure.

Seeing Destiny's reaction, Jasiah was conflicted about being persistent or not. Just seeing the glimpse of her slightly undressed body, savoring the remnants of her skin's scent lingering in his nostrils and fingertips, Jasiah was barely holding his urges in control. He caressed her with his eyes as he acknowledged her skin was smooth and flawless, and touching it, it felt like he was standing at the gates of euphoria with her, a world of pleasure that no one had entered before. He longed even more to be the first.

"Can you take the jacket off?" he pleaded as he lingered his eyes over her slender body.

"Jasiah, I just got here," Destiny stood and zipped her jacket up. "To be honest, I can't believe *that* just happened."

Jasiah fell back on the bed. He grabbed at his aching member and tried to calm down.

Destiny moved around Jasiah's room, examining her surroundings, trying to calm her urges and get herself under control. She first went over to his reading nook, sunlight scattered across the shelves as Destiny admired his personal collection. She picked up Charles Dickenson's *From Kingdom To nigger-dom: A People Lost In Translation*.

"Destiny," Jasiah moaned out from the bed as if he were having a tantrum as he stretched his hand, skimming it against the curvature of her hips.

Stepping aside, out of his range, Destiny ignored him. "Can I borrow this?"

"Take whatever you want and come back over here," he requested.

Destiny clutched the book to her chest and went over to his desk, admiring the Mac desktop before smiling at the pictures of them together at the homecoming. Then she noticed the wall of girls plastered on his oversized corkboard in the array of concert and event stubs.

"Is this your trophy wall?" Destiny asked as one girl's photos started to stick out. She was beautiful. The photos of her told a story through the years – from a little girl with braids to a developed young lady with luscious curls.

"Who is this?" Destiny took off what she assumed was the latest photo of the girl in a swimsuit at a pool.

Jasiah sat up and looked over. "Tangey," he answered.

"This your cousin or something?" she inquired.

"Neighbor," Jasiah answered as he flopped back down on the bed. "Come back over here."

"Where is your bathroom?" Destiny asked, feeling uneasy about how squishy she was between her legs.

Jasiah pointed to the door of the bathroom in his room.

Her heart still thumping from the gush of pleasure, Destiny strolled into the bathroom and cleaned herself up a bit. She leaned against the sink and thought about what she was doing there. She tapped her foot and stared at the girl in the mirror as she tried to gain her composure. She had never let Eric touch her like that. But then again, when she was wrapped in Eric's arms, she never felt the way Jasiah made her feel.

She wondered if the threat that someone might come into his room looming over her head never let her relax. Instantly, she dismissed the idea as Jasiah's house was full of people as well. Staring at herself in the mirror, she asked herself:

Why would you let him do that? You know his mother is lurking in the halls and truly doesn't want you here.

Her mind hovered from one place to another as she squeezed her thighs together, replaying the moment of ecstasy, the torrent of pleasure back in her head. Staring at herself in the mirror, skimming her hands over her body, she knew she wanted it to happen again. Jasiah had awakened something in her, which scared her but filled her heart with the sort of pleasure she had never experienced before. Now, she knew what people craved. Just as she told herself to relax and go with the flow, she heard a tap at the door.

Chapter 12: Friendsgiving

The echo of the knocks jolted Destiny out of her euphoric daze. She braced herself against the countertop and whispered aloud to herself, *"Go with the flow, Destiny."*

As she accepted the fact that Jasiah had awakened something within her that she didn't want to turn away from, she heard him ask, "Are you okay in there?" from the other side of the door.

"Y-yeah, I'm fine," she stuttered as the taste of Jasiah's lips lingered over her tongue.

"If you don't come out soon, I'ma come in," Jasiah warned as he playfully twisted the doorknob with no intention of actually pushing the door open.

Destiny silently stared at her reflection in the mirror, raking her fingers through her straight hair. From the corner of her eye caught a glimpse of the photo of Tangey, which she had left on the sink on top of the book. *'Neighbor, my ass,'* she whispered as she picked up the photo and studied it for a moment.

A rhythmic knock erupted from the door again. This time, Destiny cracked it open as the suspicions about Tangey clouded her brain.

"You can't hide in there," Jasiah jested.

"Yes, I can," Destiny retorted.

"I didn't scare you off, did I?" Jasiah inquired as he sensed grimness in her voice.

"I'm scaring myself," Destiny admitted as she peeked from the little gap in the door.

"Let's talk about it," Jasiah proposed as he stepped back from the door.

Destiny opened the door completely, and carrying the weight of her doubts, she stepped out into the room. In an instant, her eyes caressed Jasiah's shirtless body, sending her consciousness into the plains of imagination as she envisioned kissing him all over the way he did to her. Carving herself out of her trance, she averted her eyes from his toned body and focused on his face.

"What's up, Destiny? Talk to me," Jasiah mentioned, seeing her hazel eyes lost.

Destiny pondered over if she should reveal her doubts or relish in the moment. Her conflictive thoughts failed to mold into words as she just shook her head in response.

"We've fooled around a few times in the backseat of my car," Jasiah elaborated as he took her by the hand. "I thought we were on the same page with this," As he talked, he led her back to the bed. This time, pulling her onto his lap.

Feeling the warmth of Jasiah's body and his bare skin, a whirlpool of emotions birthed inside her as she bit her bottom lip to rein in her urges. Witnessing the silence on her lips as her eyes revealed the spark of the conflict in her, Jasiah understood that she wasn't saying what was on her mind.

"You know I'm extremely attracted to you," Jasiah whispered as he stroked her face lightly with the back of his index finger, looking at her affectionately.

"It just went a bit fast," she explained. "I feel like you were thinking since you have me behind closed doors, you are just going to have your way with me."

Followed by a puff of empty air, Jasiah broke into laughter. "I definitely was thinking I have you behind closed doors, and I was going to take advantage of it."

"Your mom just said don't close the door."

"You are the only person thinking about what my mother says in this relationship," he mentioned, shaking his head. "But I apologize if you feel like I rushed it."

A childish smile played on Destiny's face as she started drawing imaginary circles on Jasiah's broad shoulders in silence.

"You hear me, Destiny?" Jasiah said and began to tickle her.

"Yes, yes, stop!" Destiny giggled, shimmying in Jasiah's lap to break free from his tickling. "I just want my first time to be something special," she informed him as she grabbed his hands. Straddling Jasiah's lap, she continued, "Do you understand that?"

Jasiah lost himself in her eyes as he craved to kiss her. He started to move in closer to follow through with his instincts, but Destiny pushed him down on the bed and hovered over him. "Do you understand that?" she repeated.

"Yes, baby, I do," Jasiah answered in a soft voice as he rolled her over so that he could be on top. "But I don't want you to be closed-minded about the things we can do besides intercourse."

Destiny gulped as her eyes scrambled over Jasiah.

"I want you to trust me."

Her heart leaped against the barriers of resistance as she nodded.

Tracing his nose against her face, Jasiah made his way to her lips and kissed her deeply. Just as he unzipped her track jacket again, a loud knock on the door startled them away from each other. Destiny's heart pounded with fear of being caught as she ran her fingers through her hair and went to sit in the window nook while Jasiah slipped on his shirt and headed for the door.

"I thought I told you not to close this door," Faye lectured.

Jasiah, irritated by being interrupted, just rolled his eyes, "What's up, Ma?"

"I want you both ready by 6 o'clock sharp," she stated.

"Would you prefer it if we went over to the pool house?" Jasiah questioned.

"The furniture is in there," Faye informed her son as she turned to walk down the hall.

Seeing his mother's figure disappearing to the lower floor, Jasiah closed and locked his door again.

"Jasiah," Destiny shouted in a low tone. She couldn't believe his audacity.

"She just talking to be talking," he replied as he took his shirt off again, savoring the aftertaste of the unfulfilled emotions lingering over his tongue.

Averting her eyes from Jasiah, Destiny looked out over the backyard as she immersed her consciousness in it. He had a beautiful view of the pool and garden. Navigating through the pathways of her thoughts, Destiny thought about her own room and pondered over how she had never looked out of her singular window. Her only view was an alley shadowed by the tall adjacent buildings brimming with patchy grass and iron gates.

As she wandered her hazel eyes through the landscape revealed before her, Destiny pictured herself sitting in the window, watching the seasons change as she did her homework, relishing the peace and not having to worry about a stray bullet. She looked over at Jasiah with her eyes, her heart, and her soul filled with wishful thinking as she envied his life a little bit more.

"What are you thinking about?" Jasiah asked as he looked through his CD collection.

"Just admiring your backyard," she answered as she got up and walked over to her purse to retrieve her camera. She took a few shots of Jasiah. He looked up and smiled for a photo before returning to his search for the perfect CD to keep Destiny in the mood. She dropped her camera back in the bag and caressed his shoulders while he loaded up various CDs in the player. When he pressed play, she moved away.

"I hope you put in something we can dance to."

"Something like that."

Jasiah turned around, poked her nose, and grabbed the remote to turn off the TV. He then strode over the window and closed the curtains.

Darkness covered the room as only a streak of crimson light peeked through from the fading sun. While Janet Jackson started to sing "That's The Way Love Goes," a smile blossomed on Destiny's face-- it was a song she played every night while they were on the phone together.

Jasiah submerged himself in her smile as he embraced Destiny and started dancing with her. They moved together, with each step synchronized with the song's beat. Destiny's heart quickened as she became partially excited and somewhat frightened of Jasiah's next move.

He started in the same place he had last time – taking off her jacket. When he knelt down and kissed the top of her breast, he could feel her heart pounding wildly.

"Don't be scared," he whispered.

"Jasiah," she whispered back.

Plucking her off her feet, Jasiah carried her over to the bed and laid her down. "I promise whatever happens right now will be pleasure and not pain," he assured her.

Clasping her lips, Destiny nodded as she closed her eyes.

Jasiah hovered over her for a moment and tried to decide what he wanted to do to her as he undid the top button on his pants. Before he could decide, she slowly opened her eyes, sat up, and kissed him. Her rampant emotions were reining every atom of her body. She pushed him over and straddled him. Adding to the heat building up inside her, her mind decided to imitate Jasiah's moves earlier.

She kissed his upper body and flicked her tongue in certain areas while her hand rubbed over his length through his jeans. She could feel Jasiah pulsating through the denim, which added fuel to her flaring emotions, waking up the wild part of her soul.

Caressing his body with her lips, she reached for his ear and asked, "Can I touch it?"

Shock consumed Jasiah's mind as he gasped for breath to keep his sanity intact – his mind was bolstered by how Destiny had turned into the aggressor. Gulping while readying himself for stepping into the plains of euphoria, he eagerly agreed. He willingly helped her undo his pants. She pulled him out and was in awe at his girth and length. She moved her hand up and down like she had seen in porn. In the darkness of the room, as Destiny explored her sexuality, they made eye contact.

It was a look she wouldn't forget. The look of passion, raw emotion, and longing. She kept thinking about that moment as he helped her zip up her dress an hour later.

"I don't think this dress goes with my Jordans," Destiny mentioned.

"Oh, I got you some boots," Jasiah remembered as he strolled back to his closet for a shopping bag.

"Jasiah, you could have just told me what was going on over the phone earlier."

"I like buying you things," he smirked as he poked his head out of the closet.

Destiny blushed as she averted her focus to finding her socks and then slipped into the boots—a perfect fit. Destiny admired herself in the mirror alongside Jasiah in his khakis and open black collared shirt.

"We look good together," she admired, staring into the mirror.

"I always knew that," Jasiah acknowledged, smacking her on the butt.

She walked over to his corkboard again, looking past the "neighbor" in photos and finally landing on a little boy with his chain being held by a man. That must be his father – Destiny thought to herself. Instantly, the remembrance of the letter hit her as she contemplated tucking it under his pillow and leaving it behind. She knew that giving it to him right before Friendsgiving wouldn't be the best move. But stepping into the next phase of the relationship with this secret weighed heavy on her heart as she opted to test Jasiah's thoughts about his father.

As her eyes roamed around the room, the mess they had created together made her uncomfortable. "Let's make up the bed," she told Jasiah as she thought about how she could bring up his dad without seeming obvious. As they worked together to make his bed look like they had never fooled around in it, Destiny decided to bring up the picture first.

"Is that your dad?" Destiny asked, pointing to the photo.

Jasiah nodded as his joyful look vanished from his face.

"You look just like him," she smiled. "Dimples and all."

Jasiah stared at the photo with dull eyes in silence.

"You know you could meet him," Destiny assured him as she sensed his mood fluctuating. "If you really want to."

Embracing silence, Jasiah strode into his closet and came out with his shoes.

"You look sexy as hell in that dress," Jasiah complimented her again.

Destiny smiled, realizing that Jasiah was avoiding the subject. So, she let it go and simply responded, "Thank you, handsome."

Once they were ready for the party, Jasiah opened his bedroom door and saw his mother and Roy just arriving at the door. Manipulated by their suspicions, they both peeked inside to see Destiny sitting at Jasiah's desk, twirling in the chair. The adults breathed a sigh of relief, hoping nothing had transpired between the two. When Destiny noticed them at the door, she stopped spinning and smiled nervously.

"You need a necklace," Faye pointed out.

A confused look swarmed over Destiny's face as she grabbed at her bare neck.

"Come with me," Faye ordered as she turned on her heels. "We will meet you guys downstairs."

Destiny traced Faye's steps nervously into her bedroom while admiring the way her burnt orange silk dress clung to her hips. She had never seen her mother in a tight dress like Faye's. Once they entered the master bedroom, Destiny quickly looked around – mesmerized by the massive size of the room and the intricate details of the jewel-tone fabrics that draped the bed, the windows, and the sofa before the fireplace.

Faye went over to her vanity table and turned around gracefully with a strand of pearls. She motioned with her hands for Destiny to turn around. Complying with Faye's silent orders, Destiny shuffled her steps and held her hair up as she observed the particulars of the room. Everything was meticulously organized but reeked of cigarette and cigar smoke.

"Your hair is beautiful," Faye complimented Destiny as she put the necklace around Destiny's neck.

"Thank you," Destiny expressed as she dropped her hair and turned to look at herself in the mirror. "Freshwater pearls?" Destiny questioned.

"They are... how did you guess?" Faye confirmed as she picked up a small comb and toyed with her bangs.

Destiny shrugged as she picked up a dusty glass coaster from Faye's vanity, guessing the residue was cocaine. She blew across the glass quickly, dispersing the dust into the room as Faye watched through the mirror in horror.

"My mother has a collection. Her favorite is Tahitian pearls, though," Destiny responded as she sat the coaster down as quickly as she had picked it up. "But thank you for allowing me to borrow them for the evening."

"I think we got off on the wrong foot," Faye stated as she looked at Destiny through their reflections in the mirror. "I wrongfully judged you."

"Why the change of heart?" Destiny asked as she hooked her hair behind her ear.

For a moment, the women glared at one another through their reflection in the mirror while Faye found a response.

Averting her focus from the mirror, Faye uttered, "You're resilient... Dare I say cunning and calculated."

Hearing her poisonous remarks, Destiny moved away from Jasiah's mother. "I don't have to premediate anything in my relationship with your son," Destiny assured her. "He's just intrigued with my authenticity."

Faye chuckled mockingly. "You just continue to hold out on him," she said as she led the way out of the room. "The longer they wait, the more they value it."

Destiny could hear her mother's voice in her head as she followed Faye. In a low tone, Destiny stated, "I am the prize."

When Faye and Destiny gracefully descended the stairs, it was like they were making a grand entrance. Guests had started to arrive and were mingling by the foyer with cocktails and passed hors devours. People looked up at them, elegance dripping from each step, including Jasiah. At the bottom of the steps, a server waited with a tray of champagne.

"Take one," Faye urged her.

"No, thank you," Destiny declined as she went over to Jasiah.

"Hey, beautiful," he greeted her with a kiss on the cheek.

Destiny made a face as she immediately noticed the smell of alcohol on his breath. "Your muhva gonna get locked up for allowing underage drinking," she whispered.

"Who is going to snitch?" Jasiah asked as he took Destiny's hand and pulled her to him. "I can't stop thinking about you."

"Is that so?" Destiny pushed away. "People are watching."

"Let them watch," he dissuaded her worries as he planted a kiss on her forehead. "Let me introduce you to CJ," Jasiah stated. "It's about time you two met."

Jasiah dragged Destiny around, introducing her to various people until they got to a tall, slender boy named CJ.

Destiny immediately thought he looked like Kid from Kid N' Play.

"Nice to meet you. I'm Destiny," Destiny greeted CJ with a vibrant smile. "Have you ever seen *House Party*?" Destiny babbled.

Everyone laughed because they already knew her reference.

"I got the dance moves, too," CJ stated as he started to mimic the iconic dance sequence from *House Party*. Destiny joined in on the kick and did it flawlessly. "Oh! I like her," CJ concluded.

When Destiny stopped laughing and woke up from her nostalgic movie dance, she noticed the adults staring at them. She felt like she had messed up, as a wave of embarrassment rushed over her.

"Oh shoot," Destiny squeaked, wanting to hide.

"It's cool," Jasiah laughed as he held her hand. "Someone needs to liven this party up."

"So, how did you two meet?" CJ asked.

"She goes to school with my cousin, Lafayette," Jasiah answered. "She had me hunting her down for almost two months before she decided to be mine."

"This guy right here always gets the girl," CJ commented.

"I bet he does," Destiny looked at Jasiah questioningly.

"Don't worry, baby, I'm a retired ladies' man thanks to you."

"Sure, you are," CJ mumbled as he sipped his drink.

"CJ, you have some dirt you want to spill on your boy?" Destiny interrogated politely, eyeing Jasiah on the side, who rubbed the back of his head.

"Oh no...bro code. I believe in bro code," CJ laughed nervously.

As a waiter passed, the boys clobbered her for the crab cakes. Jasiah passed Destiny one, even though he had a napkin with five of them.

"I'ma get something to drink," Destiny stated as she walked away and toward the bar to order a soda. The view from the bar drew Destiny back to the picture window of the living room. Earlier, she could admire the pool from it, but now it was the lighting. The trees were wrapped in lights, which was something Destiny had only seen at restaurants and hotels.

"Hey, you," Jasiah came over to her. "You okay?"

"I'm fine," Destiny smiled. "Just admiring the scenery."

"We will have something better one day," Jasiah comforted her, sliding his arm around her waist as he looked over the backyard as well. Destiny didn't know whether he meant 'we' collectively or 'we' on their own in the future. Destiny figured either way, she would have a backyard where her children could see the seasons change and play freely.

"Who is going to take me home if you keep drinking?" Destiny questioned.

"I'll just have this," Jasiah answered, raising his glass.

They stood there in silence— each lost in their imagination, occasionally looking over and smiling at one another. Jasiah was about to whisper to Destiny about her tenderness when someone cleared their throat for attention behind them. They both turned to see who it was. Destiny recognized the girl as soon as she turned around.

"Heyyyy," Jasiah sang out in surprise, giving his neighbor a quick hug.

"Hey," she waved at Destiny and extended her hand. "I'm Tangey."

"Destiny," Destiny shook the hand and smiled.

"You're even prettier in person," Tangey commented.

"I was thinking the same thing," Destiny returned the compliment as she turned to Jasiah. "It seems like both of us have been in your room recently," Destiny quickly assumed.

Gulping down his drink, Jasiah nodded slowly while avoiding eye contact with both.

"So, I assume my mom invited you," Jasiah said once he came up for air and did not return Destiny's glare.

"Yeah, I assumed you knew," Tangey replied, looking at Jasiah.

"No, she forgot to mention that," Jasiah muttered as he looked around. "Can I get either of you something to drink?"

"I'm fine," Destiny told me.

"I'll walk with you to the bar," Tangey suggested.

"No," Destiny interjected, placing her hand on Jasiah's arm. "That's not an option."

"Oh," Tangey laughed as she stepped back in surprise. "Mark your territory, sis," Tangey snapped her fingers as she spoke.

"I'm not your sis," Destiny mumbled as she turned to Jasiah. "Can I talk to you in private?"

"Can we talk after dinner?" Jasiah responded, grazing Destiny's arm as his eyes hovered aimlessly through the living room.

"No, now works for me," Destiny ordered.

Just as Jasiah guided her toward the basement, Roy's voice rose through the room.

"Let's gather around the table."

"I guess it has to wait," Jasiah sighed with relief.

"This breakup can happen now or later," Destiny concluded as she gripped his hand tightly.

"Hold up," Jasiah grabbed Destiny by the arm. "I can explain this with the truth," he whispered.

Destiny stopped in her tracks.

"But let's not be rude. We need to say grace and then talk about this while people fix their plates," Jasiah urged, as he wanted to keep his decorum.

Destiny followed Jasiah to the table. She noticed there were name cards on the table, and her handwritten place card was three people away from Jasiah; however, Tangey was seated beside him. Destiny laughed to herself, knowing Faye had set her up.

She sat down uncomfortably and tried to convince herself the right thing to do was *kill them with kindness*. She turned on her biggest smile and started speaking to the older couple to her left about the lovely table setting. She refused to look Jasiah's way.

Soon, Faye was standing beside her husband, beaming like the perfect trophy wife. Destiny watched Faye's elegance as she smiled, hanging on to her husband's every word as he thanked everyone for coming. Destiny sat attentively toward the couple, though she couldn't hear anything they were saying because of her roaring thoughts.

How could you think there wasn't someone else? She repeatedly asked herself.

Looking up, she thought about Tangey's appearance versus hers. Tangey's wild, natural hair looked effortless. Her tight satin dress showed off the cleavage that Destiny would never have. Her nails were perfectly manicured, and she wore just the right amount of bronzer to highlight her high cheekbones. Destiny's insecurities crept in just as she felt a hand on her lap. She quickly turned to see Jasiah sitting beside her.

"Hey," he whispered, smiling at her. "Don't be mad," he lipped before nodding in the direction of his parents so Destiny could turn back toward them.

She felt a little relief that Jasiah had enough sense to move his own seat. She turned back to the couple just as they said, "Amen." Everyone stated the same. Destiny turned and looked at Jasiah.

"Boy, you have no poker face," Jasiah recognized. "All of your emotions been running through your face."

"Jasiah, you're lucky I'm damn near an hour away from my home because I would have walked out by now," Destiny whispered into his ear.

"Look, she was in my room after homecoming, but before we committed," Jasiah stated truthfully.

"Did y'all get the story together before you moved your seat?" Destiny poured her suspicions into her words, peering into Jasiah's eyes.

"No, I just told her I was going to tell you the truth. I'm not gonna hide it."

"How can I trust you?"

"I'm telling you the truth," Jasiah pushed as he looked around to see if he could tell who was listening. "I swear."

"And what kind of relationship do you two have?" Destiny questioned, being just as cautious of who was listening.

"I think it's our turn to get our plates," Jasiah stated, rising to his feet quickly.

"We need to talk," Destiny replied.

"Let's just make it through dinner, please." Jasiah took Destiny's hand and kissed it. "You have nothing to worry about."

They fixed their plates from the gourmet buffet set up in the dining room. They ate in silence for the most part until Faye started to talk loudly about her husband's accomplishments. She pointed out her husband's relationship with the police force, mentioning the officer seated at the table. And then Faye went down the table with a deceiving smile on her face until she got to Destiny, "And a crazier story is that Roy defended your brother, right, Destiny?"

Destiny looked at Faye, unable to comprehend the limits of the evilness of that woman. She was confused about why she wouldn't introduce Destiny as her son's girlfriend or even that Destiny's father went to high school with her husband. Destiny envisioned herself turning the table over in anger as her soul burned with fury, but instead, she cleared her throat. "Yes, that's one thing we have in common, right, Miss Faye?"

"Excuse me," Faye asked as she sipped her champagne.

"It's what we have in common. We both met Mr. Roy while he was defending a loved one."

"Well, let's move on," Faye veiled her discomfort behind her smile and pointed to the lady beside Destiny. "Mrs. Simone was the..."

Destiny had tuned Faye out. The necklace she loaned Destiny suddenly seemed to be a lasso, and Faye was holding the reigns.

"You handled that well," Jasiah recognized as he watched Destiny start to grab at the strand of pearls. "No, don't rip them off," he cautioned her. "Please," he whispered.

Jasiah quickly helped Destiny take the necklace off and placed it in his pocket.

"Is she okay?" Destiny heard someone ask.

They both looked down to see that it was Tangey.

"Everything is fine," Jasiah responded before turning his back to Tangey and averting his attention back to Destiny. "Are you okay?"

"We need to talk," Destiny stated as she played in the last of the gravy on her plate.

"Let's go to the bar for a soda," Jasiah suggested as he stood up, and Destiny followed.

"Where are you two going?" Faye asked as she smiled up at Jasiah.

"Just to the bar for a soda," Jasiah answered as he came over to his mother and bent down to tell her, "Lovely party, Ma," before dropping the pearl necklace in her lap.

Faye looked startled at the drop. But when she noticed what it was, she just threw the necklace in her water glass.

Destiny followed Jasiah, who ended up making a B line for the butler staircase and up to his bedroom.

"I told you all about Eric. You never mentioned a damn thang about Tangey," Destiny yelled as soon as the bedroom door closed. "You've been screwing your neighbor?"

"Who said that?" Jasiah said. "I said she was in my room... Like my friend. My neighbor."

"Bullshit, Jasiah," Destiny screamed as she started to get her things together.

"Hold up, Destiny," Jasiah snatched her sweatpants from her and threw them on the bed. "We can work through this."

"You can't possibly expect me to have dessert with y'all sick muthafuckahs. You, Tangey, and your goddamn mother."

Jasiah was shocked at Destiny's level of anger. "Destiny, this is not a cheating situation. I swear."

"It makes me feel really uneasy to know you have access to some pussy in the neighborhood when I'm not giving you any."

Jasiah took a deep breath, trying to figure out what to say, but his brain seized under pressure, and all he came up with was, "I need another drink."

"Can you call me a cab?" Destiny asked annoyedly.

"Call you a cab?" Jasiah laughed in surprise. "Girl, I'm tryna get you to come downstairs and eat pumpkin pie."

"Fuck pie… you see how your mom continually tries to embarrass me," Destiny blabbered on as she took off the heeled boots. "She has two other options, very valid options about introducing me. And she picks Mr. Roy was my brother's lawyer," Destiny shook her head, still in disbelief, as she started to pace the floor.

"We were having a great day. We always have a good time together. Don't start this now."

"Did I start anything?" Destiny replied. "Did I start this?"

"Destiny, you're starting not to trust me," Jasiah placed his hands together. "Please don't give in to what my mother is doing."

Destiny flopped down on the bed. Throbs of pain traveled through her head.

"I'm telling you the truth. Tangey is my neighbor. We are close."

"Where was she during the homecoming dance?"

"She's homeschooled."

"Why you never mentioned her name?" Destiny asked.

"I didn't think to."

"You thought to show her me, but I just learned about her today."

Jasiah took a deep breath. "I didn't cheat on you. I can promise you that. If you want to call a cab, the phone is right there," Jasiah yelled - turning quickly he left the room.

Destiny was shocked that the conversation ended so abruptly. She even looked out the door for him and could only see Jasiah's shirt tail swinging in the wind as he galloped down the stairs.

Destiny called a cab company, and they told her the wait was an hour. Destiny picked up a pillow and screamed into it as tears trickled down her face. She thought about snatching all the pictures off the wall and removing the framed picture of them by his bed. But then she figured, if she didn't mean enough for him to do it himself, she knew it was no use in her doing it.

After a while, Jasiah came into the room and sat there in silence with her. Because he had walked out of the conversation previously, she wasn't going to start first.

"You called a cab?" he finally asked after he noticed Destiny keep looking at the clock.

"I have forty more minutes," she answered.

Jasiah rubbed his face and tried to think of something to say so Destiny would stay. It was barely eight o'clock.

"You don't have to leave."

"I told you I wasn't welcome in your mother's house," Destiny recalled. "I don't know why you think you can make her okay with our relationship."

"I have to live my life."

"You live in her house," Destiny stated. "Your mother let me think everything was cool all afternoon. Knowing your neighborhood crush, fuck buddy, or whatever you and Tangey are, was coming for dinner."

"Destiny, I would never think—"

"I'm a seventeen-year-old with a manipulative thirty-four-year-old playing in my face," Destiny was blown away. "Tell your mother she won."

"Hold up, Destiny," Jasiah protested. "My mother doesn't get to choose who I want to be with."

"She can definitely choose who you can be without," a tear dropped from Destiny's eye out of frustration. "I'm never coming back here."

Jasiah got a tissue out of the bathroom and gave it to Destiny. "We can just see each other at your house or out and about like we been doing."

"And then you can continue to have Tangey over, too, right?" Destiny's voice broke as she wiped her eyes and knew she had to toughen up. "No, thank you."

"I don't give a fuck about Tangey," Jasiah concluded.

"There are literally twelve photos of her over there that say otherwise," Destiny pointed at the corkboard with her hand. "Twelve, Jasiah."

"Look. I had the biggest crush on Tangey since we were kids. She didn't like me back until I went through puberty. We fooled around. But then she changed on me. And we can never go back to where we were," Jasiah tried to explain without going into detail. "So yes, we occasionally got together. But you were with Eric. I have not seen Tangey since we confirmed our relationship."

Destiny didn't even care if what he was saying was true or not. She was done with the situation. From the beginning, Destiny told Jasiah that she did not want to be played for a fool. And she had been the fool all day. The phone rang, and both knew it was the cab company.

"Let me take you home. We can work this out," Jasiah suggested. "I really see a future with us."

"You talk a good game," Destiny recognized as she picked up the phone to tell the dispatch she would be right out. "Your mother said you are charming."

"I told you, you're the only one in this relationship who cares about what my mother says."

"I don't know why I ever thought something could work between us," Destiny mumbled. "Bye, Jasiah."

"This ain't bye," he yanked on Destiny's arm so that she had to be face to face with him. "We are going to work this out."

"You got enough girls on that wall you can work it out with. You don't need me," Destiny mentioned as she pulled away and hit the stairs.

Jasiah followed behind and walked her to the cab. He opened the door for her.

"Destiny, we're going to work this out," he pulled three twenty-dollar bills from his pocket and dropped them in Destiny's lap. "Call me when you get home."

Destiny cried halfway home as her heart submerged in the turmoil of emotions inside her. Moments of the evening played in her mind, from Jasiah touching her to her touching him, Faye putting the cheap pearl necklace around her neck, Tangey sitting erect and astute beside Jasiah, Faye telling her family business.

Destiny fumbled through her bag for a napkin when she came across the letter from Jasiah Sr. that she forgot to leave behind. She cursed herself because she knew she needed to see Jasiah one more time.

Chapter 13: Pick Up

The silhouette of Destiny leaving lingered in Jasiah's mind as he sat in the kitchen and nursed a rum and coke. His mind warped through the events that transpired during the dinner—he couldn't fathom what his mother's intent was by having Tangey there regardless if Destiny was coming or not.

Splinters of pain pierced through his veins. His eyes burned with regrets, and he stared into the abyss at the bottom of the glass in his hand. The sentiment of a breakup uttered by Destiny swirled through his mind. The thought of not being able to see her again was paralyzing.

His grip tightened around the glass as he bit his bottom lip. Thinking about how he had just gotten Destiny to himself, he was no longer in the shadows.

"Why are you hiding in here?" Roy's voice loomed from the side as he leaned over the wine rack and retrieved a Pinot Noir.

"My mother," Jasiah answered weakly, gulping his drink.

"What did she do now?" Roy sighed as he sat beside Jasiah and grabbed a corkscrew to open the bottle of wine.

"She invited Tangey here," Jasiah uttered as he sipped his drink. "She introduced Destiny like she was one of your pet projects... She just ruined everything."

Roy listened intently as he poured himself a glass of wine and swirled the drink in his glass.

"Why would she do that?" Jasiah blurted out, sliding his glass onto the table.

"Your mother thinks she is protecting you," Roy answered, trying to defend his wife. "But I know Destiny's a good girl. She has her head on straight."

"Did you tell her that?" Jasiah questioned.

"Faye has her mind made up. She sees a certain path for you and doesn't want Destiny getting in the way of that."

Confusion tackled Jasiah's mind as he pondered over what Roy said. He started to run down Destiny's attributes, "Destiny is a way better person to hang out with than the crowd I have in Potomac. She doesn't do drugs. She doesn't drink. She's not promiscuous. She's my study buddy and, often, my voice of reason."

"Destiny will come back," Roy concluded, patting Jasiah's shoulder. "She likes what you are offering her."

"She'll never come back here," Jasiah blurted out, "I'm sure of that."

"It might be for the best," Roy said as he shrugged. "Jasiah, order the girl some flowers. Even better, get her a little trinket or something. Girls eat that up... But for now, put on your good son face and come back inside here with the guests."

Roy's words plagued Jasiah's heart as a part of him realized he could do nothing for an immediate resolution that night. Concealing the pain in his eyes, he chugged his drink. He looked at his two-way pager, quickly scrolling through his messages with Destiny.

He texted her: *Can we talk?* After no immediate response, Jasiah straightened up his shirt and strode away to join the rest of the party.

"Your girl left, huh?" CJ asked as he met Jasiah by the fireplace.

"You saw her storm out of here," Jasiah mumbled without taking his eyes off the captivating flames.

"Tangey was listening by the door and heard you say she was nothing or something like that."

"Well, that's what she gets for eavesdropping," Jasiah shrugged, "She is the past."

"Jasiah, she said you just had her in your bed two weeks ago."

"It's been longer than that," Jasiah replied neglectfully as he checked his pager for a response, his mind orbiting around the thoughts of Destiny. There was none. "It's been over a month."

"Well, you got yourself into a fucked-up position."

"Yep," Jasiah sighed in agreement as he looked over at CJ. "Look, I'ma call it a night," Jasiah held his fist out to CJ. They dapped. "I'll check you later."

As the guests started to leave, Jasiah marched up to his room, which was still filled with Destiny's sweet scent, and found Destiny's pager on the bed.

"Fuck!" he yelled.

The pent-up emotions of anger spilled through him as he kicked the boot she left behind as well. The frustration suffocated his heart as he sat down, running his hand over his head, and called her phone. No answer.

Clenching his fists in frustration, he punched the mattress until his arm was tired. His pain swelled up in his eyes as he took a pillow, inhaled it, and screamed out his frustration into it, muffling his voice while his insides roared like thunder. He had finally found a girl who saw him for who he was and loved him and his flaws. A girl that was so tender and delicate but still had a fire within her that had him infatuated.

He picked up the phone and called her again. He let the phone ring. Again, no answer. He looked at his watch and knew she should be home by now. He hoped nothing had happened to her.

He started to pace around the floor. It had been almost two hours since she had left his house. He just wanted to make sure she was safe. Jasiah grabbed his keys, and the memory of the police officer kneeing him to the ground flashed through his mind as his keys slipped out of his hand. He picked up the phone and called her again. This time, she picked up—a sigh of relief left his mouth, washing away all his worries about her safety.

"Destiny," he exclaimed.

Silence drenched the time as seconds turned into minutes, but Destiny didn't say a word.

"I just wanted to make sure you got home safely," Jasiah announced, fragments of gloom clawing at him as her silence spoke volumes for her.

"I'm home," she responded.

"Destiny, let me pick you up tomorrow so that we can talk."

"Jasiah, what is left there to say?" she asked, her voice empty of emotions. "I've been a fool to think this could work between us."

"What?" Jasiah couldn't believe what he was hearing. "Destiny, I have no reason to lie to you."

"I feel like you continually leave out some really important shit," she stated furiously. "From the bullshit with Lauren to you having cokehead friends. And now your neighborly fuck buddy," she sighed, consuming the rage flaring inside her. "Don't let me forget to mention your conniving mother."

"I told you they aren't my friends. They are my classmates. And who the hell tries to start a relationship with someone by saying, 'Oh yeah, last spring I got accused of rape,'" Jasiah retorted as he gestured with his arms as if Destiny were standing in front of him.

Destiny was quiet. She felt like one of her fears had finally caught up to her. On the other end of the phone now was a boy she truly didn't know.

"I'm always honest with you," Jasiah maintained.

"I don't feel like you're being totally honest about Tangey."

Jasiah rubbed his temple in frustration. "You once told me the less people know, the better."

"Nigga, I was talking about associates. Not our relationship," Destiny erupted.

"Tangey tried to commit suicide when we were together," Jasiah blurted out, falling back on his bed. "I can't make her experience about me and how it made me feel because it's her shit to deal with. But that ended our relationship, not our friendship," he took a deep breath, rubbing his eyes, trying not to get emotional. "Knowing someone that you're close to is hurting that bad and you can't do anything about it is a fucked-up feeling."

"But you two remained fuck buddies," Destiny recalled after a moment of the shock of hearing Tangey's story. She gulped the rising empathy and didn't let it deter her from the facts.

"Yes. And I don't think anything is wrong with that, considering neither of us was in a relationship."

"Who knows if that's true," Destiny mumbled in a low tone, staring at herself in the mirror.

"Destiny, don't make me beg."

"You don't have to beg, Jasiah," she assured him as her insecurities about her small frame started to creep back into her mind.

"But I want you," he concluded sternly. "I only want you."

"I'm not that special," Destiny closed her eyes to restrain herself from falling into the chasm of love and hate, "You will get over me and move on."

"I don't want to get over you," Jasiah pursued.

Destiny smiled weakly as his words helped her combat her lack of confidence.

"Girl, stop acting like you don't want me as much as I want you," he proclaimed as he thought about how intimate they were in the bed. "I've never hid you from anyone. At any time. Not even when I knew you had a boyfriend."

"Jasiah, I have a headache. I need to go." She didn't want to be so easily persuaded by Jasiah.

"Destiny, don't hang up, please," Jasiah pleaded.

Sighing out her worries, she held onto the phone as she tried to weave threads of hope, trust... and love.

"We'll go to the game tomorrow," he suggested, hoping for her to agree.

"I don't want to be around your mother."

"She'll be too hungover to leave the house," he assured. "Destiny, please."

"Just call me in the morning," she instructed, attempting to hang up.

"Destiny, I love you," Jasiah blurted out. Flustered by his own words, he hung up the phone, afraid of the probable rejection.

Destiny gasped at Jasiah's sentiment as she slowly withdrew the phone from her ear. She took a deep breath and prepared herself for a sleepless night, as her mind wondered about various scenarios within her relationship with Jasiah.

Jasiah laid across his head and dreamed about his future life with Destiny like they had never broken up. The first thing Jasiah did in the morning was call Destiny. The ringing continued; each ring upped the beat of his anxiety. After moments of ringing, the call dropped. A rumbling of devastation rippled through Jasiah as he knew their paths would never coincidently cross again. He was stuck in limbo.

He sat in his room, absent-mindedly bouncing a ball off the wall, when his phone finally rang, carving him out of his trance.

"I know you have to say whatever to keep your little girlfriend, but you didn't have to carry me like that," Tangey barked into the phone.

Jasiah sighed with disappointment as he retorted, "Why wouldn't you tell me that my mother invited you?"

"She always invites me over. It's never been a problem before."

"But you know I have a girlfriend."

"What does that mean, Jasiah?" Tangey inquired. "You been claiming to have this girlfriend since October."

"Tangey, things are different this time."

"So, I'm no longer a priority in your life, huh?" she interrogated. Her voice turned squeaky as if she were holding back tears.

"Tangey, you know how I feel about you," sensing the shift in her voice, Jasiah consoled as he rubbed his temple.

"You certainly downplayed that shit to Miss Destiny," she exclaimed. "You keep acting like I'm nothing but a fuck buddy."

"I told her the truth, Tangey."

"What truth?"

"The whole truth."

"That's none of her business!" Tangey screamed.

"Calm down!" Jasiah yelled back. "If you had just acted like a neighbor, none of this would have happened."

"All I said is that she is prettier in person. I didn't have to see the photos in your room."

"She was already questioning me about all of the photos of you on my wall!" Jasiah shouted back.

"That's your fault that you've been collecting photos of me for eight fucking years."

"You know what, Tangey, you're absolutely right." Jasiah hung the phone up. Fuming with anger, he stepped over to the corkboard and started pulling photos down... Every girl he had been intimate with came off the wall- leaving only pictures of himself, Destiny, and family members. He threw the girls' photos into an envelope and stashed them at the top of his closet. As he slammed his closet door shut, he heard a tap at the door.

When Jasiah opened his bedroom door, he saw Roy standing there with his keys in his hand and a smirk on his face.

"We're headed to brunch and to handle a few things," Roy informed Jasiah. "Your brother is at his sister's house. We won't be back until after ten." Roy winked at Jasiah, which made him feel relieved. Sensing a tinge of empathy in his actions, Jasiah smiled and nodded. However, his heart still lingered over the thoughts of getting Destiny on the phone, let alone back to his house.

"Are y'all going to the game? Can I get the parking pass and tickets?" Jasiah asked as he saw Roy walking away.

"They are on my desk. Enjoy yourself," Roy replied, waving his hand as he strolled down the stairs.

"Thanks," Jasiah said.

"You can fix it, son. Just be patient," Roy yelled from the stairs.

Jasiah nodded as a gust of emotions swirled in his head. He tried calling Destiny again. Still no answer. He straightened up things in his room and went downstairs to see that the house was put back together as it was. He opened the fridge, and a wave of gratefulness passed through him as he saw the leftovers. He made himself a plate and sat in the kitchen. He called Destiny from the house phone. She answered.

"Don't ignore me," he immediately stated after her hello.

"I went to church with my mother," she informed Jasiah.

"How was it?"

"It was church," she sighed.

"So, did you think about going to the game with me?"

"I really don't feel up to it," Destiny admitted.

"But I want to see you. I need to give you your pager back and your clothes."

"I don't want them," she rejected.

"How long are you going to be mad at me?" Jasiah questioned. "This is not like us, Destiny. We always find a common ground."

"Jasiah, just give me some time."

"Time to do what? Come up with more scenarios in your head that's gonna tear us further apart?"

"Or just think logically."

"Logical thinking should have led you to understand that I am in love with you by now."

"Jasiah, don't just say things that sound good."

"I told you yesterday."

"And I thought you were saying it because it sounded good yesterday," Destiny poured her thoughts into her words.

"I'm coming to get you," Jasiah knew that if he could just see her face to face, he could make things better.

"Jasiah, stay home."

"No, tell Mr. Peay I'm coming to Sunday dinner."

"Boy, you better stay your ass up there in Potomac."

"Naw, shawty, I'm on the way," Jasiah mimicked a street accent.

Destiny laughed; the sound of her laughter blanketed Jasiah's soul in warmth as he chuckled along.

"You don't even talk like that, Jasiah," she pointed out.

"I'm still coming. Do your chores or whatever you must do to leave the house because I'm coming," he smiled to himself as he noticed Destiny being less cold than the previous conversation. "A'ight?"

"A'ight," Destiny agreed.

Jasiah faked a jump shot into the air as his sulking heart leaped at the trace of hope that things would go back to normal between them.

"I'll see you in a few," he hung up the phone before she could change her mind.

Humming in excitement, Jasiah got dressed quickly in his Redskins gear and headed for Northeast, DC. While on his way, he stopped to get Destiny flowers and decided it was a good look to get Mrs. Peay some as well. However, when he pulled up to Destiny's house, he wasn't prepared for the scene out front. There was a man sprawled out on the stoop.

For a moment, Jasiah thought he was dead. The man's open mouth revealed his various missing teeth as he lay there as if his body was already in rigor mortis. Jasiah carefully stepped around him. As he climbed the stairs, he wondered how no one had called for help. He repeatedly rang the doorbell, hoping someone would hear it over the game that was blaring from inside.

Moments later, Mr. Peay swung the door open.

"Young man," Mr. Peay greeted in surprise. "Destiny know you coming?"

"Yes, but," Jasiah said as he moved to the side, revealing the man on the ground. "I think you should call the ambulance."

Mr. Peay shook his head. "This nigga ain't dead," he opened the security gate. "Freddie Bush!" Mr. Peay yelled at the man as he kicked him lightly.

The body moved. Jasiah nearly jumped out of his skin as he moved out of Mr. Peay's way.

"Freddie Bush, get the fuck up!" Mr. Peay yelled.

"I'm up, I'm up," Freddie Bush huffed as he sat up.

"Help me get this muthafuckah inside," Mr. Peay instructed.

Jasiah stood there in shock.

"Something wrong with your hearing?" Mr. Peay asked as he grabbed one of Freddie Bush's arms.

"N-No sir," Jasiah stuttered, shaking his head. Hastily, he dropped the flowers and went to grab the other arm. A pungent smell pierced his senses as he prayed that the stench from the man wouldn't rub off on his clothing.

"Why you gotta get so fucked up?" Mr. Peay scolded the man.

"Who this nigga, Ray?" Freddie Bush questioned.

"Destiny's boyfriend."

"Don't tell her," Freddie Bush whispered to Jasiah as he climbed the steps.

Holding his breath to avoid smelling anything, Jasiah nodded in response.

"You better walk on your own in the house," Mr. Peay let Freddie Bush's arm go.

"You can let me go too," Freddie Bush instructed Jasiah with a belch. "I just needed to sleep it off a bit."

When Jasiah walked into the house, behind Freddie Bush and Mr. Peay, he was shocked at the house full of people. Everyone yelled, "Hey, Freddie Bush!"

Jasiah watched Freddie Bush wave his hand in the air as he stumbled over to a chair. Jasiah stood by the door with his hands behind his back, waiting for Destiny as a tinge of awkwardness crawled through his skin.

"Who that?" someone asked.

"Ain't that the boy that took Destiny to the game?" another guy guessed.

"Y'all going to another game?" another one asked.

"If she wants," Jasiah shrugged.

"You got it like that?" the first one asked.

"My stepfather is a ticket season holder," Jasiah responded.

"If she doesn't want to go, you can take me," Freddie Bush interjected.

Jasiah nervously stood by the door while everyone laughed. He searched for a seat but was scared just to take one without an offer from Mr. Peay.

"Jax, get your sister," Mr. Peay stated as he flopped down his lazy boy recliner. "You want something to eat, young man?"

"Sure," Jasiah answered.

"You can wash your hands in the kitchen. When Destiny gets down here, she can fix your plate."

When Jasiah saw Mrs. Peay standing in the kitchen, he felt relieved that she had greeted him with a smile. They exchanged pleasantries.

"So, I hear you had a party yesterday," Mrs. Peay stated as she handed Jasiah a paper plate.

"A Friendsgiving is what my mom called it."

"So, what do you guys do on Thanksgiving?" Mrs. Peay questioned with a puzzled look on her face.

"Have dinner at a restaurant."

"Your whole family goes to a restaurant?" Mrs. Peay sounded shocked.

"It's just four to six of us," Jasiah mumbled slightly embarrassed. He hovered his eyes over the food on the table. It was like a Thanksgiving dinner on the table. The layout of disposable aluminum trays mixed in with various Pyrex dishes reminded Jasiah of *Soul Food* the movie. He filled his plate with fried chicken, a scoop of macaroni and cheese, and some cabbage.

"Take your jacket off, and you can sit here," Mrs. Peay said, wiping her hands with a dish towel and giving him the stool from the kitchen. "Seats are hard to come by some days around here."

Shortly after, Destiny strolled down the stairs in a pair of black stretch jeans and a fitted V-neck yellow sweater. Everyone stared at her on the steps, including Jasiah. Confused by being the center of attention of the crowd, she immediately said, "What?"

Everyone's eyes moved toward Jasiah, situated in the corner of the dining room, without saying a word.

Jasiah nervously waved with his fork.

"I told you to tell your sister he was here," Mr. Peay popped his son in the chest.

"Destiny, that boy here to see you," Jax stated plainly, his eyes stuck to the TV.

Everyone laughed at Jax's laziness, but Destiny sucked her teeth and finished coming down the stairs.

"What's up?" Destiny responded, coming toward Jasiah. "I thought we were going to the game."

"I'm waiting on you," Jasiah stated with a mouth full of macaroni and cheese.

Destiny rolled her eyes, seeing Jasiah standing out awkwardly from her crowd.

"Get him something to drink, Destiny," Mrs. Peay instructed her daughter.

"You want some tea?" Destiny offered.

He nodded as he munched on his second helping of macaroni and cheese.

"You know we could just watch the game here," Jasiah suggested after he was able to wash down his food.

"No, we need to talk," Destiny dismissed the idea.

"No, we need to have some fun," Jasiah winked at her.

She stared at him aimlessly as she stuck her hands in her back pockets. Jasiah could tell that Destiny was nervous by the way she bit her bottom lip. She turned to see if anyone was paying them any attention. It seemed as soon as she turned around, everyone's heads shot toward the big screen television simultaneously. This was the first time Destiny had a male visitor while so many people were home. This made her eager to leave.

"I'ma go get my coat," she said as she walked toward the steps. As she turned around, she noticed Freddie Bush. "Did anyone feed him?"

"Nobody gave me nothing, Destiny. I been here waiting all day," Freddie Bush complained with a pouty face. "Could you fix me a plate, please?"

Destiny rolled her eyes, seeing through Freddie's manipulation tactics. "Daddy, how long he been here?"

"Me and Jesus had to pick him up from the front."

"Jesus?" Destiny looked at her father for clarity.

"Jesus, Jose... what's that young man's name?"

"Jasiah," Destiny corrected him as she shook her head. "His name is Jasiah."

"Oh!!! It's his father locked up with Junior," Jax blurted out. "That's little Jasiah!"

All eyes were back on Jasiah, which made him choke on his tea. "My what..." Jasiah questioned, but no one responded.

Destiny ran up the stairs and grabbed her purse and coat. When she got back down, Jasiah was on his two-way pager.

"You ready?" she asked.

Jasiah nodded. "Thanks, Mrs. Peay, for the plate."

"Anytime, baby."

Jasiah followed Destiny as she made her way out of the door. Suddenly, she stopped in her tracks and turned him around. "Everybody, this is Jasiah. Jasiah, that's my brother Jax, my cousin Redz, and my cousin Space, my computer geek cousin Ron." she went around introducing her family to Jasiah. "And Freddie Bush."

Jasiah waved at everyone with a smile. It was at that moment he knew that their short-lived breakup was over. When they got outside, Jasiah remembered the flowers, but they were gone. Only a single red rose bud was in the grass. He picked it up and presented it to Destiny.

"I bought you and your mom flowers, but it seems like someone stole them," Jasiah told Destiny.

Destiny took the single flower and thanked him.

"By the way, Freddie Bush needs to be in somebody's rehab center," Jasiah mumbled.

"My father is helping him with his veteran services," Destiny informed Jasiah as she followed him to the car.

"I thought the man died on your stoop," Jasiah recalled as they walked to the car.

Destiny just laughed, but Jasiah didn't find any humor in what he was saying.

Nevertheless, he smiled to himself, thinking everything would be okay between them as he watched her slide into his front seat, still giggling. Once he was behind the driver's side, Jasiah looked at himself in the visor mirror. Looking at his treasured heirloom diamond pendant, he recalled the off-handed comment Jax had made.

"So, my father is in the same prison as your brother?" Jasiah questioned, closing the visor, and starting the car.

"About that," Destiny bit her bottom lip.

"How long have you known that?" Jasiah continued as he pulled out of the parking space.

"I was working on something," Destiny admitted. "But this is not the opening conversation I thought we would have."

"We don't need to keep talking about Tangey," Jasiah stated.

"Why not?"

"Because I'm not questioning you about Eric."

"It's not the same thing, Jasiah."

"Why not?"

"Eric is my ex-boyfriend who I never fucked. Who I told you about from day one. Who I broke up with to be with you," Destiny explained.

"You broke up with him to be with me or because he was disrespecting you?" Jasiah questioned.

"Both," Destiny shook her head. "But you're not going to turn this on me. I've been honest with you."

"Destiny, I've been honest with you too."

"Jasiah, I left your house feeling deceived."

Jasiah pulled the car over at the gas station on Florida Avenue so he could look at Destiny.

"Are you getting gas?" she asked.

"No, I want to look at you in your eyes when I say this to you," he said as he turned to face Destiny. "You have nothing to worry about when it comes to Tangey or anybody else. Do you understand me?"

Destiny just looked at him, losing herself in his eyes.

"Destiny, I'm serious," Jasiah affirmed.

"Okay," she slumped down in her seat.

"I don't want to fight with you because of shit my mother does either," he added.

"Well, I must take that out on you. I can't disrespect her."

"Just go easy on me… A game of tennis could be a good stress reliever for you too," Jasiah joked.

"We need to move," Destiny uttered. "I'm not tryna get carjacked sitting here like this."

"Broad daylight on a Sunday?" Jasiah placed his car in drive mode. "So where to? And when the hell were you going to tell me you knew where my father was?"

"Jasiah, I was going to tell you yesterday. That's why I was a little off when you initially picked me up from the train station."

"How the hell did y'all figure it out?" Jasiah wondered aloud.

"Wasn't that hard… my dad mentioned it to my brother on a phone call. Like Destiny got this friend… Junior was like the nigga in here with me, and it went from there."

"So, my father knows about me?"

"Jasiah, let's go somewhere, park the car where it's *safe*, and talk about this," Destiny suggested.

"Destiny, how long have you known?" Jasiah pulled into the Wendy's parking lot on New York Avenue. "We gonna get carjacked here too?" he asked sarcastically, seeing Destiny peeking out of the passenger side window to inspect her surroundings.

Destiny reached into her purse and pulled out the letter. "Long enough for me to get this for you."

"What's that?" Jasiah tried to snatch it.

Destiny pulled the letter back quickly. "You need to relax," Destiny said as she looked at him. "I know you are anxious, but I don't want you to get upset reading this in Wendy's parking lot."

He took a deep breath and looked at his girlfriend.

"Jasiah, I'm serious. I know how I felt in the car last night trying to process shit. It was a long ride home."

"Destiny, just tell me what you know," Jasiah urged.

"Your father is at Morgantown in West Virginia. He has a few months left before he goes before the parole board again," Destiny answered. "He will add you to his visitor list if your muhva approves."

"I'm eighteen. I don't need her approval," Jasiah concluded.

"You still live under your muhva's roof," Destiny reminded Jasiah. "You gotta stop going against your muhva… no matter how deceitful and manipulative she is when it comes to this."

"Why are you defending her?"

"I'm not defending her. I'm concerned about you," Destiny explained, shaking her head. "You don't know how many homeless kids I go to school with. Sleeping on people's couches or staying with people they don't want to because they can't get along with their muhva," Destiny sighed as she stared empathetically into Jasiah's eyes. "This shit could tip your muhva over the edge."

Jasiah sulked in his seat for a moment. His head was spinning as he processed everything. "Fuck her."

"Jasiah, that's my line. That's what I say," Destiny laughed out of surprise. Caressing his thigh, she tried to soothe his anxiousness. "You gotta play it cool."

"I'm always cool," Jasiah sighed and looked at Destiny. "I do appreciate you, shawty," he placed his hand over hers. "You definitely figured this shit out for me."

"Cause you green," Destiny winked at him with a smile playing on her lips. "And where did you pick up this *shawty* shit from?"

Jasiah aimed a mischievous smile at her as she heaved out a defeated sigh. "Now, can I get the letter?"

"No," Destiny retorted. "You owe me a nice day out for that bullshit I went through yesterday," she stuck the letter back in her purse. "Where are you taking me?"

Jasiah could hear Roy telling him to buy her something nice. "Tysons."

"Tysons it is," Destiny sat back.

After they spent a cheerful afternoon together, Destiny gave Jasiah the letter, making him promise not to open it until he got home. Swallowing his anxiousness, Jasiah agreed. However, once he was alone in his room, he was hesitant to open the crinkled envelope.

But once he did, tears trickled from his eyes when he read his father's words,

"I love you, son. There isn't a day that goes by that I don't pray to Allah for your safety."

In the letter, his father told him the names of family members and what neighborhoods they lived in. He apologized for not being present in his life.

Jasiah read the letter over five times, and each time, the expressions on his face changed—happiness, sadness, peace, and conflict. He clung on to every word his father scribbled on the paper—each word spiraling a storm of emotions in him. He memorized some lines. He mimicked some of the slang.

The only time he mentioned Faye was to say:

"I'm thankful your mother figured out a way to give you the life that you deserve, son. Lady Faye always lands on her feet."

The only time he heard "Lady Faye" was when his mother had too much to drink and started to refer to herself in the third person. Jasiah started to wonder how his mother became Lady Faye, but he was more engulfed in the knowledge of his Sheffield family that he never knew existed.

Once Jasiah finally put the letter down, he picked up paper and pen and started to write back to his father. But after writing the date on the upper right-hand corner of the notebook paper, Jasiah hit writer's block. He knocked the paper off his desk and threw his pen against the door in frustration as he realized he didn't even know how to address Jasiah Sr. in a letter.

Chapter 14: Family

On the evening before Thanksgiving, Destiny anticipated continuing with the tradition of her playing sous chef and dishwasher to her father as he prepped various dishes for the holiday. She usually looked forward to her mother coming downstairs after her nephews were in bed to mix the aroma of collard greens cooking with the sounds of her "oldie but goodie" music. With a smile, Mrs. Peay would beckon someone to join her in the area between the dining room and the living room, which served as a dance floor some days and arguing space on others.

Before Junior went to prison, he would come over and show off his hand-dancing moves. But after his imprisonment, the family would gather on the dance floor and mimic his dance moves, breathing life into the shadow of the joy he had left.

However, this Thanksgiving Eve was a bit different. Destiny couldn't imagine behaving that way in front of Jasiah. While he was eager to help in the kitchen as Mr. Peay's new apprentice, Destiny was ashamed about how they had to maneuver around the small galley kitchen. She felt embarrassed at their cracked floor tiles and lack of counter space as she compared their humble home to Jasiah's lavish accommodations. But she couldn't turn him down as he insisted on coming over to learn the recipe of macaroni and cheese he had tasted the previous Sunday at her home.

"Well, I didn't know you grated the cheese by hand," Jasiah mumbled as he held a brick of sharp cheddar against the grater. "Why doesn't he just buy the shredded?"

Destiny shrugged as she peeled the potatoes for the potato salad. "Just the way he does it," she said while her eyes remained fixated on the potato.

"I've never seen a chunk of cheese this big," Jasiah whispered as he held up the cheese in the air.

Destiny giggled as she shunned him with her elbow, glancing at her dad. "It will go faster if you stop talking about it," she lectured, pinching him on the side.

"O-ow!," Jasiah screeched at the sharp pain she caused. "And I thought people cooked like this *on* Thanksgiving," Jasiah added as he rubbed his side.

"I suppose. But we eat early," Destiny explained as she ran the peeler through the length of the potato. "I have dinner and sit around with my family making jokes, and still get to Bria's house before they even break bread," Destiny continued as a smile crept on her face, feeling prideful at her tradition. "I usually go over there and get to eat stuff we don't serve, like fried shrimp."

"Not this year," Jasiah stated with a smile as he winked at her.

"Nope, not this year," Destiny affirmed with a sigh, tilting her head to the side as she thought about having to sit at a dinner table with Jasiah's mother. Her mind couldn't fathom what they would talk about.

"You not finished with that cheese yet? I'm about to take the noodles off now," Mr. Peay yelled from the kitchen.

"Oh, shoot!" Jasiah squealed as he started to grate feverishly.

Peering at Jasiah's twitched face, Destiny laughed.

"Go in there and learn that part, cooling the noodles, and start your roux. I'll deal with this," Destiny spoke through her laugh as she stood up to take Jasiah's place.

"You're the best!" Jasiah exclaimed as he quickly pecked her on the temple before heading into the kitchen.

While Destiny grated the cheese, her eyes hovered over Jasiah and her father. The flecks of embarrassment still mingled through her veins as she compared her house to Jasiah's, but seeing Jasiah comfortable, she felt like he wasn't judging her.

And Destiny's father surprised her as well. Mr. Peay barely used to look at Eric, let alone show him how to do anything.

Navigating through her thoughts, Destiny brought the shredded cheese into the kitchen and chimed in, "Daddy, don't let him mess it up. I'll never hear the end of it."

"He got it," Mr. Peay looked impressed.

"You hear that? I'm a natural," Jasiah bragged with a smirk carved on his face as he whisked the roux for the cheese sauce.

Destiny simply went back to peeling potatoes. Soon, Mrs. Peay joined them downstairs, and her eyes widened in surprise when she saw Jasiah and Mr. Peay cooking together. Averting her eyes toward Destiny, with a witty smile on her face, she winked at her daughter and turned on the radio.

"It's after ten, and that boy still here?" she whispered to Destiny. "Your daddy getting soft."

Destiny giggled, her heart brimming with joy upon seeing Jasiah and Mr. Peay bonding as she watched her mother pour a glass of Hennessy.

"Mr. Peay, how much more are you doing tonight?" Mrs. Peay inquired playfully as she dipped her hips to Tina Turner singing "What's Love Got to Do With It." Grooving with the beat of the music, she snapped her fingers and bopped her head to the song.

"I'ma finish up prepping this mac and cheese. Then, get these potatoes on for the potato salad. And I'm done," Mr. Peay rambled.

Mrs. Peay rolled her eyes as she sighed. "Hurry up and peel those potatoes, Destiny," Mrs. Peay joked as she took a seat at the table.

"You better get in there and do those dishes," Destiny replied mockingly.

Mrs. Peay looked in the kitchen at the stack of mounting dishes and flicked her hand, dismissing the idea of her touching them. Turning to her daughter, she stated, "That's your job," before sipping her Cognac.

"Naw, Ma…. You gotta help do something," Destiny complained, shaking her head.

"I'm the DJ," Mrs. Peay announced as she shot back over to the radio with her glass in her hand and played a CD – Smokie Robinson's Greatest Hits. She effortlessly moved her body to the rhythm as she lip-synced the words "Cruisin'."

Destiny laughed at her mother's antics as she finished with the last potato. Wiping her hands clean with the hand towel, she left her station and joined her mother in the center of the room. With the beat of the song roaring through the house, they bopped to the song and danced around each other, relishing the joyousness of Thanksgiving in their style. As the pair crooned to the music and moved about rhythmically, Jasiah peeked out of the kitchen to watch them dance until Mr. Peay's voice resounded from the kitchen, "Come on, you're almost finished. Just gotta put the cheese on top."

Jasiah felt like he had accomplished something as he sprinkled paprika on top of the macaroni and cheese. As he savored the aromas within the kitchen, Destiny and Mrs. Peay's smiling faces flashed through his eyes as a part of his soul envied Destiny for having the true feeling of a holiday in her home. While the spice settled on top of the cheese, Jasiah imagined having a dad to teach him anything.

The sound of Destiny's giggles brought Jasiah out of his trance as she came into the kitchen, stumbling over her own feet.

"Daddy, I'll start the potatoes. Go on out there with Ma," she coaxed.

Mr. Peay wiped his hands on a dish towel and went to join his wife's hand dancing to Rick James and Smokie Robinson crooning "Ebony Eyes." Jasiah watched them dance, imagining him and Destiny dancing just that way in the future. When he turned to her, she was washing dishes.

"Hey, girl," Jasiah called as he came up to her and rubbed her butt.

"Boy, don't get put out," Destiny squeaked as she elbowed Jasiah.

"Well, I'ma go dance with your momma," Jasiah joked as he retreated back to the archway to watch her parents at a distance.

"Cover up that mac and cheese with some foil," Destiny instructed.

"Where the camera?" Jasiah questioned. "I need to take a picture of this."

"Boy, please," Destiny rolled her eyes.

Jasiah went back to watching the Peays dance. Soon, he imitated Mr. Peay's steps in the kitchen doorway.

"You don't know what you're doing," Destiny stated as she grabbed one of Jasiah's hands. "You need a partner to really hand dance."

Clasping her hands in his grasp, Jasiah winked at her and playfully spun her around on his fingertips. Destiny blushed as she caught how Jasiah was looking at her. She could see the love in his eyes. At that moment, she realized that she was in love with him. But she didn't want her parents to catch a whiff of their enchantment.

"It's getting pretty late," Destiny told Jasiah as she let his hand go and went back to the sink.

"I still gotta learn how to make this potato salad," Jasiah announced.

"You will learn that another day," Mr. Peay interjected. "We want to make sure you get home safely."

Jasiah's happiness quickly deflated. He didn't want to leave.

"I'll walk you out," Destiny said as she dried her hands with a hand towel.

"Dang, y'all put a brother out fast," Jasiah joked as he looked at the pot of boiling water.

Mr. Peay laughed and asked, "We will see you tomorrow, right?"

"Yes, sir," Jasiah answered as he followed Destiny out of the kitchen.

Basking in the joyous ambiance of the Peay's home, Jasiah watched the Peay's dance before making eye contact with Mrs. Peay.

"Thanks for having me," Jasiah told Mrs. Peay as he lightly bowed before her.

"Oh, baby, thanks for keeping Destiny company. I'm glad I didn't have to peel those potatoes while she grated the cheese," Mrs. Peay smiled. "Next time, we have to teach you how to step," she grabbed Jasiah's hands and started to sway from side to side with him.

Destiny noticed Jasiah's excitement oozing out as he tried to follow her mother's steps. She laughed at how hard he was smiling.

"A'ight, a'ight," Destiny broke it up playfully.

"Don't be jealous." Mrs. Peay laughed.

Rolling her eyes, Destiny pulled Jasiah toward the door.

"Your parents are so cool," Jasiah complimented Destiny once they were alone together on the front steps.

"They a'ight," Destiny smiled as she wrapped her arms around Jasiah's neck. "I'm glad you came," she admitted as a sudden feeling of relief came over her.

"I'm glad I came too," Jasiah whispered, wrapping his arms around Destiny, instilling warmth against the cold night air. "I don't know why you were so nervous. I should be the nervous one."

"It's just that you live in all that space, and our home is so small."

"I would love to have what you have in there any day," Jasiah stated honestly.

"Boy, I have to share one bathroom with four other people, and you have your own in your room," Destiny reminded him, "I'd take that any day."

"I'd take you any day," Jasiah said as he tilted her face back to him until their eyes met.

A surge of emotions gushed through Destiny, swarming her face as she blushed. Under the shade of the stars, basking in the moonlight, Destiny felt like she could tell Jasiah how she felt about him.

Once they shared a kiss, the tingling sensation within her wanted to go with him. She truly didn't want him to leave, but she knew she had to let him go. "You better go before my parents get nosey," Destiny whispered to him as she unlocked her lips, skimming the skin of Jasiah's lips with her own as she talked.

"When can you start spending the night out?" Jasiah asked, holding on to her.

"I never asked," Destiny confessed. "But I can promise it would have to be after graduation."

"I was thinking of getting a hotel room for my winter formal," Jasiah whispered to Destiny in a lustful tone.

"Get out of here, boy," Destiny shook her head as she pulled away from him, ignoring Jasiah's statement. "Get in the car," Destiny turned him around, patting his back as she looked around to ensure no one would attempt to walk up on him.

"A'ight, I'm going," Jasiah affirmed as he turned back around and pulled Destiny close for another kiss.

"Go, Jasiah. It's cold," Destiny instructed; she relished in his touch. "And just pull off."

"I can't let my shit warm up?" Jasiah quizzed as he stepped off the stoop and unlocked his car door.

"Boy, bye," Destiny yelled as she turned her back, waving her hand, hoping that would make Jasiah leave. She looked back once she was on the other side of their security gate to watch Jasiah pulling out of the space.

He honked the horn as he sped down their street to the stop sign. Destiny went inside to see her parents swooning to Smokey Robinson's "Being with You." Reflecting a lighthearted smile towards them, Destiny bypassed them and went into the kitchen to finish the dishes. Humming along to the music blasting in the living room, she cut down the fire on the potatoes as she left the kitchen and decided it was time for some more upbeat music to play.

"No, no, no," Mrs. Peay protested as she watched her daughter going through their stack of CDs. "Smokey has the mic all night," she informed her daughter before Mr. Peay turned his wife with ease.

Destiny sighed and left for her room, awaiting Jasiah to call so that they could talk until they were delirious into the night. She closed her door, and her eyes hovered over the cream sweater dress Jasiah wanted her to wear hanging in the closet. Thanksgiving was always a casual affair for the Peay family, but now, Destiny's evening would be spent at the Four Seasons in Georgetown.

***

Tearing through the cold night air, Jasiah made his way back to his home—the anticipation of the day to come swirled within him. His excitement was evident as he entered through the side door to the kitchen, singing the tunes of "Cruisin'."

"Boy, you don't know nothing about that," Faye told her son when she overheard his singing.

The essence of the joy he experienced at Destiny's home still pumped in his veins as Jasiah grabbed his mother by the hand and playfully tried to dance with her as he sang, "Cruise with me, baby."

"Stop now," Faye protested, popping her son's hand. "Where have you been?"

"With Destiny," he responded. "I went over there last Sunday and had the best mac and cheese I ever tasted. Mr. Peay taught me how to make it."

"You shouldn't be in the city like that. Something could happen to you," Faye schooled her son. "And especially not around those Peays."

"What's wrong with them?" Jasiah inquired as he stopped dancing. "Seems like a normal family to me."

"Looks can be deceiving," Faye mentioned as she lit a cigarette. "I'm telling you for your own good."

"Her father is a federal police officer, and her mother works at Children's Hospital," Jasiah explained as he looked on at his mother for an explanation. "They aren't drug dealers."

"You don't know what they are into," Faye declared.

"Stop being judgmental," Jasiah demanded, sticking his hands in his pockets. "You don't know them."

"*You* don't know them," she corrected him.

"What are you judging them based on?" Jasiah inquired, specks of frustration lingering in his voice. "What Roy told you?" he assumed.

"Personal experience," Faye hinted as she puffed out a smoke ring into the air. "Mr. Peay might be on the straight and narrow now. But don't let him fool you."

Coughing from the drifting smoke, Jasiah muttered, "You'd say anything to make me stay away from Destiny."

"Jasiah, I just don't want you to get in over your head with her. You have a bright future ahead of you. And I'm too young to be a grandmother."

"Ma," Jasiah laughed. "I always strap up."

"Yeah, 'til you don't," Faye assumed as she averted her eyes to her nails. "Those Peays are like roaches. They everywhere, they multiply."

Jasiah broke into laughter.

"I'm telling you," Faye continued, keeping a stern look on her face. "I'm serious, Jasiah."

"Tell me how you know the Peays?" Jasiah demanded. "Don't keep beating around the bush, Ma."

In the heat of the moment, Faye thought about telling Jasiah about her interactions as a young girl with the Peay family. But holding back her truth, she reminded herself that she didn't want her son to know that side of her.

"That's what I thought," Jasiah shook his head. "Is the way you judge Destiny the way you think people would judge you if they knew my father was in prison instead of dead?"

"I don't have to worry about that because everyone pities the woman whose first husband died a tragic death, leaving her to raise a young boy all alone," Faye batted her eyes as if she were a damsel.

"That's not the truth," Jasiah reminded his mother.

"It's the truth as far as I'm concerned, and all of Potomac," she looked at her son. "And it better stay that way, for both of our sakes."

Jasiah shook his head in disgust. But he knew there was nothing that he could say to make his mother see the error in his ways, so he decided to focus on something he needed.

"If you can't be nice to Destiny at dinner tomorrow, I'll just stay at the Peay's instead of meeting you at the restaurant," he informed her.

"Don't be silly," Faye dismissed the idea. "It's our tradition. Plus, Roy's daughters are coming," Faye mentioned plainly.

"Robin and Rachel?" Jasiah questioned as he was shocked.

Faye nodded. "Since RJ has been spending weekends with Robin, they are feeling more connected to the family."

"One big happy family," Jasiah stated sarcastically as he continued to his room.

Laying on his bed, Jasiah relived through the memory of being in Destiny's home—the excitement, the joy, the friendliness... the feeling of being at home. His heart craved that homely feeling for ages, and he found it in her home, not his. He scanned the walls of his bedroom, adorned with built-ins filled with memorabilia and framed awards. When his eyes landed on the photo of him and Destiny, he picked up his cordless phone and dialed her to recount the evening's events with her and feel the joy of the evening all over again.

***

The next day, Jasiah could not imagine the atmosphere of the Peay household as they celebrated Thanksgiving. He was slightly overwhelmed at the number of people Mrs. Peay introduced him to, including Jax's wife, various cousins, a couple of uncles, and an aunt, before he could even lay eyes on Destiny.

"Hey, beautiful," Jasiah whispered in Destiny's ear once he made it to the kitchen, where she was working diligently to help her father get various dishes onto the table.

"Hey, handsome," Destiny smiled back at him.

"Tell me how I can help," Jasiah offered as his eyes feasted on the array of food that covered the stove and kitchen countertops.

"Everything is done. We will say grace as soon as I get these rolls out of the oven," Destiny informed her boyfriend as she brushed against him intentionally.

"Hey, y'all too close," Destiny's brother, Jax, interrupted as he entered the cramped kitchen. "Give me three feet."

Jasiah jumped at Destiny's brother's words, but Destiny rolled her eyes as she continued to move around the kitchen and cram various dishes on the limited countertop space.

Seeing a tinge of embarrassment on Jasiah's face, Jax laughed. "I'm just messing with you, Siah... It's okay if I call you Siah?"

Jasiah nodded as he relaxed his tensed shoulders and said, "It's what my family calls me."

"Cool," Jax stood by the entryway awkwardly for a moment.

"Can I help you with something?" Destiny asked as she opened the oven, launching a new sweet scent into the atmosphere. Everyone looked at the perfectly browned dinner rolls.

"I'ma help you with the rolls so I can say I did something," Jax volunteered as he grabbed an oven mitt.

Destiny turned to find an empty bowl large enough to house the rolls. "Get the butter," she instructed Jasiah.

Jasiah relished being a part of the little task that others may have considered mundane. He soaked up the little details that the Peays did effortlessly. From cherries and pineapples adorning the ham to the extra slather of butter Jax placed on top of the rolls. Everything to them was effortless, but to him. It was like little droplets of love he had never received.

Soon, everyone was standing around the table, hands interlocked as Mr. Peay said grace. Jasiah had never experienced such camaraderie within a family. Nervousness crawled through him when everyone started going around the table, saying what they were thankful for. It was a new sentiment to him as his family had never done this. Many people were grateful for their health, family, and their jobs. Jasiah's heart was racing as his turn came closer and closer.

He heard Destiny say, "I'm thankful for my family, friendships, and common sense." Anxiety shackled his heart as his turn came, and he nervously said, "What she said." Everyone stared at him for a minute, their eyes waiting for something more to come out. Those seconds felt like hours to Jasiah as silence killed his nerves, and suddenly, everyone broke into hearty laughter. Destiny elbowed him, hinting at him to say more. "I-I'm thankful for my life," he stuttered his second response when the laughter died down.

"You should be," Destiny whispered as she looked over at him.

"I wanted to say I'm thankful for you," he whispered back as his nervousness subsided.

Destiny blushed as she averted her eyes toward the food. Jasiah felt like this Thanksgiving topped anything depicted in Black film. The aroma of freshly cooked Southern-style cuisine and the smiles on every family member's face brought forth a strange but serene feeling in his heart. He laughed at the stories he overheard. He helped clean up messes that children created. He watched football. He studied the game of spades being played and even the way Destiny's cousins stood up to smack cards on the table. Jasiah felt like he was receiving a life lesson while Destiny was joking with family members.

He admired how she moved around with ease, being able to joke with anyone. Her interactions with certain people made more sense when she whispered backstories of her family members to him occasionally. As much as Jasiah was in awe of their family dynamic, the family was in awe that he went to Sidwell Friends and lived in Potomac. Jasiah expected more people to question him about his father, but they were interested in him going to school with "white folks". He wanted someone to bring up his father so he could also ask questions. There were moments when Jasiah would find himself beside Jax, wanting to ask if he knew Jasiah Sheffield Sr. He wanted to ask Mr. Peay if he remembered anything about his mother years ago. Jasiah's mind shuffled through so many questions that he was afraid to ask.

"How the hell did you meet Destiny?" one cousin asked once the crowd had thinned out to what seemed like the regulars and a few extra children.

"Chance encounter," Destiny answered for Jasiah as she magically appeared on the steps. "Jasiah, I'm about to change for dinner. We should be leaving, right?" Destiny added.

"Leaving? Where the hell you going?" Mr. Peay's voice rose from his recliner.

"To dinner with his parents, remember?" Destiny reminded her father as he ascended the stairs.

Anxiety slithered through Jasiah's heart as he started to get nervous about any more questions being thrown his way with Destiny gone.

"Y'all eat late," Jax recognized as he turned his attention toward Jasiah. "Who just finished cooking?"

"And who needs to go anywhere with all this food here," another person chimed in.

"We go out to eat on Thanksgiving," Jasiah answered as he tried to avoid saying where. For the first time, he felt ashamed admitting his family didn't cook dinner at home, and his mind tensed as he sensed that even more questions would arise.

"What's open on Thanksgiving?" Mr. Peay inquired.

"The Four Seasons," Jasiah responded shyly.

"Damnnnnn," a bunch of people responded.

Jasiah could feel sweat beads forming on his forehead as he prayed Destiny would hurry up. He looked at his watch and then focused his eyes on the television even though he couldn't hear it because of all the chatter around him.

"Four Seasons, my ass, where are you taking my sister?" Jax questioned.

Jax's question made people laugh.

"I'm serious," Jasiah answered.

"Y'all not slick," Jax continued. "Daddy, you letting Destiny leave the house?"

Jasiah nervously looked at his watch again to avoid eye contact with anyone. Though they had plenty of time to make it to Georgetown, Jasiah wished Destiny wouldn't take much longer to prepare.

"Leave the young man alone," Mr. Peay intervened without removing his eyes from the television.

"Daddy, look at her…. She not dressed for Thanksgiving," Jax joked as Destiny descended the stairs.

Everyone, including Jasiah, looked up at Destiny coming down the stairs. Her hair was loosely pinned up, with tresses framing her face. Jasiah admired his girlfriend, thinking the tight ivory sweater dress was a great change from the jeans and T-shirt she had been sporting all day.

"Jax, leave your sister alone," Mrs. Peay scolded as she came out of the kitchen, drying a pot. "She looks perfect."

"Thank you, Ma," Destiny smiled.

All evening, Jasiah was dreading leaving the Peays, but now, he wished they could get out the door faster.

"Daddy, what's going on here?" Jax questioned, trying to agitate his father.

Mr. Peay ignored his son.

"Why she dress like this and he got on a T-shirt?" Jax continued.

"My sweater is in the car," Jasiah interjected as he stood up and met Destiny at the bottom of the steps to take her hand.

"Don't explain yourself to him," Destiny stated calmly.

"They are so cute," Jax's wife, Chanel, exclaimed. "Leave them alone, baby."

Jasiah looked at Destiny in the eyes. Her aura was enchanting to him. It was as if he was in a spell until they were alone in the car together. Then, a new wave of nervousness settled in both of their hearts. Jasiah was worried about unveiling the hostile dynamic between his stepsisters and his mother. Unbeknownst to Destiny, it had been at least five years since they sat down and had a meal together.

Jasiah thought about how everyone at Destiny's house was friendly, and any arguments were resolved quickly with jokes and laughter. That wasn't the case with the Netaspends. They held age-old grudges. Jasiah started to think of scenarios where Destiny would be a punching bag for his mother to take out her frustrations. He cringed, thinking that he had made a mistake by inviting her.

Destiny, on the other hand, was worried about fitting in for such an occasion. Everything with the Netaspends was always pretentious. Nevertheless, Destiny still longed to fit into Jasiah's world while Jasiah was trying so hard to get out.

As they grew closer to their destination, Destiny wondered if this was worth being humiliated for. She took a deep breath as they rode through the stranded streets toward their destination. She could hear her mother telling her, "You can handle anything."

"Maybe this was a bad idea," Destiny and Jasiah stated in unison as they entered the Georgetown area.

They looked at one another in surprise.

"We had such a great day together; maybe we should have just parted ways at my house," Destiny explained her hesitancy.

"I was thinking the same thing," Jasiah affirmed as he pulled over on a side street.

Silence lingered between them as Jasiah found a parking space on a residential street.

"You can take me back home," Destiny resolved as she searched through her purse for a piece of gum, "Or I can catch a cab from in front of the hotel."

Jasiah threw the car in park and turned off his headlights before responding. "I was thinking more like we both shouldn't go," Jasiah stated as he opened his car door.

"What are you doing?" Destiny inquired as she hoped he wasn't feeling sick to the stomach.

"I have to change."

Jasiah went into the trunk and came back to the backseat instead of the front seat with a pair of khakis and a Coogi sweater. Letting her urges control her mind, Destiny positioned the rear-view mirror so that she could watch Jasiah undress. When he was down to his boxers, he looked up, and Destiny looked away.

"Come back here," Jasiah suggested with a smirk on his face.

Destiny played with her hair as she bit her bottom lip, acting like she didn't hear him.

Leaning forward, he touched her shoulder. "Come here," he instructed lustfully.

With her emotions blazing inside her, flamed by Jasiah's lusty voice, Destiny unzipped her boots and took off her coat before climbing into the backseat with him.

"I've been waiting for a moment alone with you all day," Jasiah whispered as he touched her on the hip to bring her closer. Destiny threw her legs over his bare thighs.

They kissed a long, sloppy, wet kiss. Jasiah skimmed his hand under Destiny's dress, making his way to her thigh. Feeling no resistance from Destiny, with their lips locked, he kept going. Just as he made it to the waistband of her panty, he could feel her warm hand inside of his boxers. He gasped as he felt her stroking his erection.

"Destiny," he moaned out her name as he gripped her panty so tight, he felt like he could rip them off her.

In the midst of their erotic breaths, they were so close that Destiny felt like she could feel his heartbeat against her chest.

Driven by the heat, she didn't stop stroking and traced Jasiah's neck with her tongue down to his collarbone, where she bit him lightly. Savoring the warmth of her hand and the tenderness of her lips, Jasiah moaned again and gripped her thigh ferociously that she felt as though his prints would be left behind.

High on ecstasy, Destiny continued as Jasiah's touch flared her emotions even more. The excitement of getting seen or caught in the car aroused them. Destiny's tongue made its way to Jasiah's ear, and she whispered. "You want me?"

Her statement, mixed with the atmosphere, made Jasiah's head spin. He exploded and shuddered as he reached for Destiny's breast with his other hand.

"This is like a wicked game of twister," Destiny joked as she looked at how they were entangled in one another's arms. "Right hand, left breast, left hand, right thigh," she continued to joke as she wiped her hand on Jasiah's shirt.

Jasiah laughed as he slid his hand from under her dress. He laid his head back on the seat and waited for his heartbeat to return to normal.

A spark of emotions burned ferociously inside Destiny as she craved for more, but she put a lid on it—not driving herself into something she might regret later. "So, back to me going home," she stated as she climbed back into the front seat.

"Girl, if anything, I would be getting us a room right now," Jasiah mentioned as he pulled on his khakis but kept his fly open, attempting to air dry.

Destiny giggled.

"You think you ready for this?" Jasiah joked as he grabbed his crotch.

Taking a peek at it, Destiny shrugged as she weakly said, "Only time will tell."

Jasiah stayed in the backseat after he was dressed and stared out of the window for a moment. The street was so still. He rubbed the condensation off the back window to peer in the windows of the row homes around him. He could plainly see people enjoying the holiday through their bare windows as a tinge of sadness swirled in his eyes. Destiny looked back at him.

"Are you okay?"

"We should have just stayed at your house," he confessed with a sigh.

"We can go back," Destiny encouraged.

"No," Jasiah said, shaking his head in disagreement.

Despite his conflicted feelings about his mother, he knew he didn't want to disappoint or enrage her by not showing up. He looked at his watch and recognized they were already ten minutes late. He laced up his Timberland boots and got back into the front seat.

"We will figure this out with my mother," Jasiah told Destiny as he turned on his headlights.

"Jasiah, I'm not going to let her humiliate me in a restaurant," Destiny concluded as they drove down the street.

Jasiah didn't know how to respond to that. Part of him agreed with Destiny, but embracing hope, he wished his mother would respect what he said last night. He stayed quiet until they pulled up to the valet at the Four Seasons.

"I should definitely wash my hands," Destiny whispered as they entered the hotel.

Jasiah chuckled to himself on the inside but agreed that they both should use the restroom before finding his family at the table. Destiny had tunnel vision on her way to the restroom. She washed her hands and checked herself out in the mirror. She repositioned a few bobby pins as a set of women entered the restroom.

"You see how that bitch just sits there," one woman stated.

"I don't know why Daddy can't see that she is only there to spend his money," another one concluded.

Destiny looked at the women through the mirror before they both disappeared into stalls. She wondered if they were Roy's twins. She slowly fumbled through her purse for her lip gloss, hoping they would continue to talk.

"You call tell that she doesn't spend any time with RJ," one complained from behind the stall. "That boy can barely hold a decent conversation unless you're talking to him about a video game."

Destiny's eyes widened as she recognized them as Roy's twins at the mention of Jasiah's younger brother, RJ.

"Why did we agree to come again?"

"I don't know about you, but I need my car fixed."

Hastily, Destiny left the bathroom not wanting to be still at the sink once they exited the stalls.

"I was wondering if you fell in," Jasiah joked.

"You didn't see your stepsisters walk in there?"

With surprise in his eyes, he shook his head. "How did you know it was them?"

"I overheard them mention RJ," Destiny explained as she started to walk with Jasiah through the intricately decorated hotel lobby. "But they were in the stalls, so of course I said nothing."

Jasiah nodded as he held out his elbow so Destiny could take his arm. "We will see them at the table."

They walked to coat check first before the hostess walked them to a large round table in the center of the dimly lit restaurant. Roy stood to greet them.

"We were afraid for a moment that you two got lost," Roy joked as he greeted Destiny with a hug.

Destiny smiled as she explained, "No, we were having such a good time at my house; it was hard to leave."

Faye coughed and mumbled, "I bet."

"Hello, Miss Faye," Destiny spoke as she tried to take a seat across the white linen-clothed table but noticed purses were already in the chairs.

"I saved you two a seat right next to mine," Faye mentioned as she mustered up a fake smile.

Jasiah took the seat beside his mother.

"Does your dad serve a specialty on this day?" Faye tried to make small talk.

"Everything is special there, Ma," Jasiah answered. "I should have brought you some of my mac and cheese. It was like that!"

Hearing Jasiah's honest remarks, Destiny giggled. "My dad takes pride in his sweet potato pies," Destiny answered.

"You two should not be hungry then," Faye responded.

"We ate at two," Jasiah answered as he picked up the menu. "I'm going to eat again."

Before Jasiah could open the menu, the twins returned to the table. Jasiah got up to give them hugs and introduce them to his girlfriend.

"Oh, Destiny... you're from DC, right?"

Destiny nodded. "Originally from Northwest until my parents bought a home in the Gallaudet area."

"Oh, cool," Robin stated. She was the thicker twin. "I am in real estate, so if they are looking to sell, I'm your girl."

"You might have a deal when I'm ready to purchase, but they aren't moving."

Soft giggles went through the table. And then, a deafening silence took over as everyone drowned in their menu while RJ was busy with his Gameboy. Destiny brushed against Jasiah's thigh playfully with the back of her hand. He leaned over to whisper in her ear, but his mother elbowed him before he could get a word out. Awkwardness blanketed Destiny's mind as she looked around the table, trying to figure out what they were staring at after she read that it was a prix fixe menu. Witnessing the other side of the spectrum, Destiny felt strange among the Netaspends as her family always chatted about something over dinner. They spent so much time talking that often the waitress had to come back two or three times before people really paid attention to the menu to order. The silence grew more uncomfortable for Destiny after drink orders were taken. She shuffled in her seat, hovering her gaze through everyone, hoping for someone to speak up before looking at Jasiah, who was typing on his two-way pager. She was wondering who he was texting until her pager started to vibrate. Destiny reached into her purse to read the message under the table: *These mfas are so whack.*

Destiny texted back: *Can u talk, pls?*

Jasiah responded: *No.*

Destiny rolled her eyes as her heart shrunk under pressure and sipped her water. "So, who is the oldest?" Destiny decided to ask the twins, breaking the dome of silence.

"I am," Rachel responded. "By how much, Daddy?"

Roy looked up from his Blackberry and carelessly spoke, "One minute forty seconds."

"I have twin nephews... Two minutes apart, and the way they act, you would think there's at least a year's difference," Destiny replied as she hoped the conversation would not die quickly.

"That's how Rachel acts," Robin commented, rolling her eyes.

"The oldest is the oldest," Rachel affirmed. "Right, Daddy?"

Roy just nodded.

With Destiny's spark, the conversation started at the table. Jasiah noticed that everyone chimed in except for his mother—a ripple of sadness waved through his heart as the liveliness of Destiny's family resonated within his mind.

"Jasiah always has his door closed," RJ commented. "Talking on the phone with Destttinyy." The way he sang out Destiny's name made everyone laugh.

"Don't worry, son, when you get Jasiah's age, you will be on the phone too," Roy spoke out in a comic tone. "At least you kids have your own line. I had to deal with my momma yelling from another phone, 'I need to call the prayer line,'" Roy made everyone laugh by mimicking a woman's voice.

"Is your mother still with us?" Destiny inquired.

Roy nodded. "Same house on 1st Street."

"I bet she's proud," Destiny interjected.

Roy continued to nod, lowering his gaze.

"Daddy followed in his father's footsteps," Rachel acknowledged. "My grandfather was a public defender until he died in 1990."

"Nice," Destiny nodded, admiring their family's accomplishments.

"What does your father do?" Robin asked.

"A federal police officer at the Pentagon," Destiny answered.

Faye almost choked on her drink. Everyone's attention jolted to her as she wiped off the droplets of the drink leaking from the corner of her lips. With a slight shake of hand, she waved everyone's attention away.

"No one followed in his footsteps," Destiny added as she sat back in her seat.

"Well, Jasiah is the only one with hopes to be a lawyer one day," Faye interjected. "Out of this quartet."

"Well, at least he doesn't want to be like his father," Rachel whispered to Robin, but Destiny heard her.

Destiny looked at Jasiah for a reaction, but there was none. She assumed he didn't hear the snide comment or didn't want to acknowledge it.

"Some of our biggest influences in our lives aren't even our parents," Destiny commented, looking at the pair of twins. "I'm sure you two can relate."

"Oh, most definitely," Robin affirmed as she nudged her sister to stop with the side commentary.

Time passed until they talked their way through dinner about personal experiences and childhood memories. As the table was cleared, Destiny was surprised to realize that she had a good time without any discouraging incidents with Faye. When they all stood to leave, Roy decided that Destiny should go home by car service with his girls while Jasiah could drive them back to Potomac.

"If I knew this is where we were parting ways, I would have met you by the bathroom," Jasiah joked at coat check.

Destiny rolled her eyes and replied, "I had a good time."

"Because my mother was silent," Jasiah assumed.

"A win is a win, right?" Destiny chuckled as she hugged Jasiah.

"Definitely," he kissed her on the lips. "You gonna come hang out with me at my house tomorrow?"

"We'll see," Destiny replied, wishing they didn't have to part.

Chapter 15: First

"You stood me up for some crappy meal at the Four Seasons," Bria complained as she rode the train with Destiny to Pentagon City.

"Best thing they had was the mashed potatoes because I was not eating roasted pumpkin or Brussels sprouts," Destiny rambled on. "The stuffing was weird with some kind of mushy nuts in it. I was like, where is the sausage?"

"You know you like that bougie shit," Bria commented with laughter in her voice.

"I do," Destiny admitted as she smiled. "I really do."

The girls laughed.

"At least you had a good time," Bria concluded as she looked out of the Metro train's window at the tunnel's passing lights.

"Shockingly," Destiny shook her head. "I keep forgetting to ask my brothers about Faye. I want to know if they know somebody who can tell me why she has a stick so far up her ass."

"You'll probably be her 2.0 version," Bria stated sarcastically. "Forget all about your days on the train when Jasiah put you in that Benzo."

"Whatever," Destiny shook her head in disagreement because she didn't want to fill her head with dreams of togetherness when she knew they were preparing to be even further apart.

"Jasiah will forget all about me in college."

"Why aren't y'all applying to the same schools?"

"I want to go to whatever HBCU offers me in scholarship, and his mom wants him to go to Harvard."

"What does he want?"

"I don't know what he wants, to be honest," Destiny recognized. "I know he does want to be a lawyer. But as far as school goes, I think he's content with the idea of Harvard."

"You should apply for Harvard, too," Bria suggested.

"Harvard doesn't want a Black girl like me. I don't play a sport. I'm sure they will waitlist me."

"Your GPA and SAT scores are top-notch. Destiny, don't play yourself."

"I just want to be realistic. Even if I get in, who is paying for it?"

"You've been applying for scholarships... If it's meant for you, it's meant for you," Bria coaxed her. "First one to graduate from college in your family and a Harvard graduate. Girl, you could tell Miss Faye kiss your entire ass."

Destiny quietly thought about applying.

"Destiny, don't sell yourself short," Bria nudged her. "If they accept application fee waivers, we will both apply."

"You know you want to go to Spelman."

"I said I would apply, not attend."

"Okay, I'll apply if I can get an application fee waiver," Destiny confirmed.

"That's what I'm talking about," Bria smiled. "Don't let one of those snow bunnies at Harvard steal your good Black man."

Destiny had not thought about what would become of their relationship past August 2000. She jokingly responded. "That's if the world doesn't stop, right?"

"Those NASA-type scientists will figure out everything before the clock strikes twelve on January 1st," Bria replied.

Once their train was above ground, Destiny pulled out her pager. She paged Jasiah: *Wyd.*

She didn't expect such a quick return message. *Thinkin of u n the car last nite.*

Destiny smiled to herself.

"What are you cheesing for?" Bria asked as she snatched Destiny's pager and read the message. "What you do in the car last night?" she whispered.

Destiny motioned her hand in a jerking motion.

Bria laughed.

"Theresa might be pregnant," Bria blurted out.

"If she might be pregnant already, that means they were fooling around before Eric and I actually broke up," Destiny recognized quickly. "It has barely been five weeks."

"You did that math fast," Bria zipped her jacket as they approached their stop.

"Well, whatever the case. It is… what …it is," Destiny concluded.

Though Destiny acted like she didn't care, the thought of Eric cheating on her bothered her. She dismissed her own dishonesties and thought about Eric's pleas for their relationship to work; however, he was sliding into something else the whole time. Destiny's fist tightened as she thought of Eric being more deceiving than her. She started to play back scenarios to see if she had missed an inkling of the game they were playing behind her back.

"How far along is she?" Destiny questioned.

"I'm not sure. But I do know Eric's ass is grass with my aunt and uncle."

"If it got to them, she's far enough along. Why didn't you tell me, Bria?" she started to feel betrayed by her best friend.

"You continuously told me you were on a break from him when I knew anything was happening," Bria held her hands up. "I'm just saying."

Destiny didn't accept the answer but didn't want to take out her frustrations on her best friend for the mess she created in her previous relationship. It was Eric and Eric alone who owed her any type of explanation.

Why didn't he just break it off with me? Destiny wondered.

As the girls walked into the mall, Destiny started to question how long it would be before Jasiah's patience also gave out. They had grown close and intimate so quickly that she began to fear if she kept turning him down, he would lie and cheat on her as well. He had plenty of space and opportunity to do it.

"Don't get into your head about it," Bria broke the silence between them. "Trust me – you definitely won in this game of rebound love."

Destiny rolled her eyes and texted Jasiah: *5 p.m.? Dinner?*

He responded: *Later. Movies?*

Even though Destiny told Jasiah she would spend her Friday afternoon out of school and off work with her friend, she wondered what plans he had made for the early afternoon.

She replied: *Wyd?* After she realized he never really answered her the first time she asked.

"So, you want to try Macy's for a dress first?" Bria asked.

"Yeah, that's probably my best bet," Destiny replied as she twirled her pager, awaiting a response.

"I asked for a cell phone for Christmas," Bria stated.

"So did I," Destiny smiled. "My father cut off my pager after he found out I had this."

"Maybe Jasiah will get you one," Bria suggested.

"Doubt it," Destiny uttered. "If he got me something like that on his stepdad's bill, I would have to look at myself differently."

"I wouldn't care how Carl got it," Bria admitted. "It could be prepaid for all I care."

The girls giggled.

"But since this shit with Eric is going on, my mother is on me extra hard. I had an appointment to get birth control this morning," Bria confided to her friend.

"Don't take the condom off," Destiny warned. "I'm telling you, even with the pill."

"The way I'm moving these hips, he better be faithful," Bria playfully rotated her hips like she was using a hula hoop.

"I'm just saying. You see what Eric was doing behind my back."

"While you were on a break," Bria added.

Destiny nodded as they finally got to the formal gowns.

"Don't even touch that silver dress. You know you're going in black," Bria stated.

"I feel like I need to get out of my comfort zone," Destiny stated. "And keep 'em guessing."

"You would keep 'em guessing if you hit a Charli Baltimore," Bria suggested.

"I'm not ready for red hair," Destiny admitted.

Bria picked up a short red velvet dress. "At least do the red dress."

"I'll try it on," Destiny took the dress from her friend. "And the silver one."

"Tell yourself every color is your friend," Bria also picked up a light blue dress.

While Destiny was in the dressing room, she looked at her pager and saw no response. She debated on whether she should text him again. Destiny started thinking that Tangey was in his bed since she decided to spend the daylight hours with her best friend instead of him.

Destiny tried to distract herself, but as she looked at herself in the silver satin dress, she toyed with her gifted Tiffany bracelet for a moment. She felt like she had turned into all the girls she saw her brothers dating before marriage – someone who could be pacified with trinkets instead of facing the truth. She took a deep breath as she stepped out to show Bria.

"I guess you don't like this one," Bria stated.

Destiny shook her head no.

"Come on, let's see the next," Bria urged.

Destiny went back in and thought that she was getting ahead of herself by shopping for a dress so soon. They might not even make it to the winter formal in mid-December.

"What's taking you so long?" Bria yelled.

"Just tryna put some lotion on these knees before I come out in a short dress," Destiny reached into her purse.

Destiny thought she heard two people giggle for a moment, but maybe someone else had overheard her nearby.

When she came out of the dressing room, she was shocked to see Jasiah leaning against the wall with Bria. She narrowed her eyes at him.

"Hey, beautiful," he winked at her.

"Did you tell this nigga it was our time this afternoon?" Bria asked.

"I did," Destiny hunched as a smile crept across her lips, and she felt relieved.

"She already missed Thanksgiving at my house because of you," Bria rolled her eyes.

Destiny took a sigh of relief and came over to Jasiah for a hug.

"Nigga, if I knew we were coming to tree box on your girl, I could have stayed around the way," Lafayette made his presence known while he leaned on a nearby rack.

"You look good in red," Jasiah told her as he twirled her around for a full 360 view. "This is it."

"I think so too," Bria seconded his opinion.

Destiny made a face. "I don't know. Red reminds me of his muhva."

"Aunt Faye's favorite color," Lafayette uttered.

"His muhva can't own the color of the season," Bria commented. "Girl, wear that dress."

Destiny looked at herself in the mirror.

"Definitely pick that dress, so we can move on," Lafayette also chimed in.

Destiny looked at Jasiah through the reflection in the mirror. She told herself that she had to stop doubting him. He winked at her.

"Jasiah, can you help me with the zipper?" Destiny asked as she walked back to her dressing room.

"Oh! I will be over by the dresses to see if I spot anything else," Bria caught on quickly. "Come on, Lafayette. Help me."

"I don't want to look at dresses," Lafayette protested.

"Boy, bring your ass on," Bria stated through clenched teeth as she walked away.

Despite the hustle and bustle of people in Macy's trying to find a Black Friday deal, Jasiah nonchalantly followed Destiny into the dressing room.

"Why didn't you text me back?" Destiny asked Jasiah in hushed tones as he helped unzip her dress.

"Just wanted to keep you guessing," Jasiah responded in a whisper as he slipped one strap off her shoulder and kissed Destiny's bare skin.

"Not cool," Destiny looked at Jasiah through the reflection of the mirror in the dressing room.

"You have nothing to worry about," Jasiah whispered as he kissed her on the neck.

Destiny closed her eyes as his lips brushed against her earlobe. She leaned against Jasiah, enjoying how his hands roamed her body as the dress fell to the floor. Jasiah watched his hands run across the front of Destiny's panties through the reflection of the mirror.

Destiny grabbed hold of the edge of Jasiah's jeans as she felt his fingertips touch her love button.

"I want you," Jasiah whispered.

Destiny's eyes shot open. She locked eyes with Jasiah through the mirror. She could see the insatiable lust in his eyes, and no matter how much she enjoyed his touch, she didn't know whether she was ready to satisfy it.

Destiny pulled away. "You can wait for me out there while I get dressed," Destiny stated as she grabbed her jeans.

Jasiah pointed at his noticeable erection with both hands.

Destiny rolled her eyes as she quickly slipped into her jeans and grabbed the dress off the floor. Jasiah watched her get dressed in silence. He wondered what he did to offend her. He noticed that she wouldn't even look his way as she dressed.

"Are you okay?" Jasiah asked after she sat down to put on her Nikes.

"I don't know," Destiny admitted. "I got all in my head when you didn't answer my text messages."

"But I'm here," he held his hands up.

She looked at him. "Leave out first."

"Destiny, what is going on?"

She didn't know what was going on with herself. She liked the way he touched her. But his words made her feel pressured suddenly.

"Jasiah, I just don't want to feel so anxious."

"You know I love you, right?"

Destiny looked down at her bracelet. She rubbed it with her thumb. Before she knew it, Jasiah had pulled her into his chest. "Destiny, what's up?"

Destiny felt like she was melting under his stare... "I love you too," she assured him.

"You have nothing to worry about," he kissed her lightly on the lips and squeezed her butt with both hands.

"I'm glad you're here," she admitted.

"Me too," Jasiah kissed her again.

There was a tap at the door. They both looked down to see large feet in front of the dressing room.

"Shit," they whispered to one another and giggled.

"Men aren't allowed in this dressing room area," someone stated with authority from the other side of the door.

Jasiah turned and opened the door. Before Destiny knew it, he had been turned into a character. "You saying I can't be in here with my good-good girlfriend," he asked as he smacked his lips and rolled his eyes with a neck roll.

Destiny burst into laughter.

"Come on, girl, they tripping," Jasiah snapped his fingers in front of the security guard's face and walked past him.

Destiny tried to hold in her laughter as she followed Jasiah's sashay to a cash register.

"I don't know what you are laughing at," Jasiah rolled his eyes and held his hand on his hip until the security guard left the area. Then he laughed as well.

"I mean, you sure changed up character fast," Destiny stated, tilting her head. "Should I be concerned?"

"You can thank Men on Film from *In Living Color* for that one," Jasiah started to talk in his normal voice.

Whenever Destiny thought about how Jasiah started acting feminine without warning, she giggled at herself until they were alone at his house three hours later.

"I thought you said we were going to the movies," she reminded him as they pulled into his driveway.

"In the theater room in my basement," he responded.

Destiny rolled her eyes. "Is your mom home?"

"They went shopping in New York for the weekend. It's just me."

Destiny's neck snapped.

"Well, Lafayette is supposed to spend the night, but he said he would get a ride out here."

"They gonna have to use MapQuest to get here," Destiny mumbled as she grabbed her purse.

As the pair entered the home, the smell of Faye's Virginia Slim hit Destiny like a ton of bricks. She let out a fake cough. "I still can't believe your mother smokes in the house," Destiny mentioned. "I want to open a window so bad."

"I'm used to it," Jasiah shrugged. "I'ma light a candle in my room."

"I thought we were going in the theater room for a movie," Destiny looked at Jasiah.

"I lied," he smiled as he led the way up to his room.

Destiny rolled her eyes as she followed. Her stomach started to do flips as she climbed the steps. Things didn't ended well the last time she was in the house. She held her breath as she entered Jasiah's room. She was prepared to be greeted by his trophy wall. Instead, she was pleasantly surprised that all the photos were removed except hers and a few of him alone. She took off her coat and hung it over the desk chair before taking a seat and watching Jasiah get comfortable.

When he got down to just his jeans, she bit her bottom lip, looking at the ripples in his abdomen.

"You can take your shoes off," Jasiah stated.

Destiny kicked off her Nikes.

Jasiah turned on the radio. Destiny noticed the lotion on his nightstand instead of on his dresser. She giggled.

"What you laughing at?" he asked as he went through his CDs.

"What were you doing with that lotion over there?" she inquired.

He started to blush. "Whatever, man," he went back to flipping through the large vinyl CD case. "What do you feel like listening to?"

"I know y'all got HBO; let's see what's on tonight," Destiny got up and grabbed the remote. She turned on the television and noticed that Jasiah had been looking at a DVD. She pressed play. Moans could be heard immediately as a couple appeared on the screen.

"This what you needed the lotion for?" Destiny inquired as she watched the woman bend over the back of a chair for the man to enter her.

Jasiah didn't say anything. He tried to grab the remote from her hand.

"Noooo, let me see what you're into," Destiny ran away, holding the remote out of his reach. "I already see it's white girls."

"You want to watch it?" Jasiah asked- ignoring her comment.

Destiny nodded as she went back to her seat at the desk.

"Why you staying over there?" Jasiah sat on the bed. "Come over here," he coaxed.

"I'ma sit on the floor," Destiny stated. "I'm not gonna be rolling around in your bed with you every time I come over here."

Jasiah fell back on the bed. "I don't know why you keep fighting this."

Destiny took her soda and Snickers candy bar from Jasiah's bag on his desk and sat on the carpeted floor. She leaned against the bed and tuned into the sexual activities on the screen.

"You're really gonna watch this?" Jasiah quizzed as he slid down to the floor beside her.

Destiny shrugged, being bashful about her intrigue.

Jasiah grabbed a pillow from his bed and placed it in her lap. They watched the couple have sex all over the house. Both of them made jokes about the actors' faces or the sounds they were making. When the next scene came on at a woman touching herself to tease a man, Jasiah asked, "Do you ever do that?"

"No," Destiny answered.

"Why not?" Jasiah inquired.

Destiny sighed. "Afraid, I guess."

Just thinking of how innocent Destiny was started to excite Jasiah. Destiny felt like she had been too honest. A rush of warmness flowed over Destiny as she thought about Jasiah watching her please herself.

"I have to go to the bathroom," Destiny stated, moving Jasiah's head to the floor. She quickly went into his bathroom, closing the door behind her.

"Should I pause it?" Jasiah yelled from inside the room.

"No," Destiny took a deep breath and looked at herself in the mirror. Wondering how long it would be before Jasiah cheated on her if she didn't give it up to him soon. They had not been together that long, she thought. But at the same time, Destiny couldn't deny their attraction to one another. She took a deep breath and figured she would just let it happen. Even though she pictured her first time being some romantic evening in a hotel bedroom, she thought she could settle for making love for the first time in his empty mansion.

When she came back into the room, Jasiah was still on the floor, but he had turned the lights off. His dark bedroom eyes were fixated on Destiny as she moved closer to him.

She lay on top of him, and they kissed. Jasiah's hands eagerly roamed Destiny's body until he had enough courage to unhook her bra strap. As soon as it popped, Destiny started to retreat. She pushed on Jasiah's shoulders to sit up.

"No, no, no," Jasiah whispered as he tried to keep her close.

"I'm fine," Destiny told him as she slipped the bra off through a sleeve. "Let's just turn on some music," she suggested, trying to buy herself some time. She grabbed her soda and took a long swallow.

Jasiah took a deep breath and got up from the floor. He played Usher's "Nice & Slow." By the time he came back, Destiny was lying on her back, resting her head on the pillow. Jasiah lay between her legs, and they shared a long kiss. He rubbed himself against her until he couldn't resist touching her. She flinched a bit when he went to unbutton her jeans but didn't stop him.

"I want you so bad," Jasiah whispered in her ear as he tried to slide his hand into her waistband, but her jeans were too tight.

He kissed his way down to her waist as he started to pull off her jeans. He playfully bit her on the hip as he pulled the jeans from her waist. Destiny hissed as she lightly ran her nails up his back. The sensation made him shiver before he sat up to pull her jeans and socks all the way off. He held out his hand for her to sit up. He then pulled off her shirt, and as he ran his hand over her arms, he could feel the goosebumps.

"Jasiah," Destiny moaned out when he took her nipple in his mouth and slid his hand into her underwear. Her knees buckled as his fingers rubbed between her wet lips. She pulled away and shielded her body as she moved off the floor to the edge of the bed. "What if someone comes home?"

Jasiah went over to his door and locked it without saying a word. As he walked back over to Destiny, he unbuttoned his jeans. He grabbed the remote from the floor and turned the television off. In the room's darkness, he laid Destiny back on the bed. They kissed again, but Destiny shivered under him.

"Want to get under the covers?" Jasiah asked as he stood to take his jeans off.

Destiny slid under the covers, taking off her underwear in the process. Once Jasiah lay on top of her again, he could feel how fast her heart was beating. He figured he better slow down before she stopped him altogether.

"You okay?" he asked as his hand ran over her thigh.

She nodded.

He kissed her and hugged her body instead of trying to touch her intimately with his hands.

"Destiny, please," Jasiah begged as she kissed him on the neck. "Please let me have you."

"Jasiah, I want to," she kissed him. "I just don't want things to change between us."

"Don't you know that I love you," he gripped her hip, thrusting himself against her so that she could feel how aroused he was.

He kissed her deeply. "Don't you know that?" he questioned as he touched her.

She gasped as she hooked her arm around his neck. "Jasiah, please," she moaned out as she braced herself.

"Destiny, please," he asked again as he felt like he would explode if she touched him in the least bit.

He listened to her moan as their body heat started to rise between the sheets. Destiny tried to touch him, but he moved her hand.

"Jasiah, let me," she requested.

"I want to be inside of you," he responded as he stopped touching her.

All of the heat she had been feeling all over her body started dissipating. Their heavy panting slowed to deep breaths as their heart rates slowed.

"Do you really love me?" Destiny asked.

"I've been telling you that I'm yours since our first date, Destiny," he rolled over on his back.

"I just don't feel that special," Destiny stated honestly as she stayed on her back.

"But you are," Jasiah promised her as they both lay there looking into the darkness.

Destiny reached over and touched Jasiah's hand. He intertwined his fingers with hers, fighting against his urges to devour her.

Destiny laid on her back, fighting the urge to be devoured. The voices that were usually telling her to make him wait were silent. Her body was saying *do it*.

"Are you going to sleep over there?" Destiny asked playfully as she turned on her side to look at Jasiah.

"Just thinking about you," Jasiah turned on his side to face her.

Destiny snuggled under Jasiah and kissed his chest. He kissed her on the top of the head and held her.

"I'm just scared either way," Destiny admitted.

"What do you mean?" Jasiah quizzed.

"If I don't do it, you'll cheat. If I do it, I don't want things to change between us."

"I won't cheat," he stated as he caressed the curves of her body with the back of his hand. "If I gotta wait, I gotta wait... we just have to put our clothes back on."

Destiny couldn't believe he said it. "Really?" she sat up in the bed.

"What you got is worth waiting for," he answered as he sat up just enough to plant a kiss on her breast gently. Destiny bit her bottom lip as she watched his gentle kiss turn into a suckle of her right breast and then her left. When he noticed that she wasn't resisting but enjoying what he was doing, he laid her back and touched her again. He came up and tried to kiss her as she moaned out his name.

"Destiny, tell me you love me," he instructed as he could feel her about to reach climax.

"I love you," she nearly shouted as she dissolved under him.

It was like music to Jasiah's ears. And the pulsating on his fingertips urged him to try again.

"Don't you want to feel me?" he asked as he positioned himself on top of her. He rubbed his hardness against her as he stroked himself. A slight nod was all he needed from her.

Destiny squirmed under him. He held her in position by gripping her thigh with one hand. He bit his bottom lip as he tried to touch his tip to her entrance.

She hissed slightly and squirmed again.

"Please, baby, I'll get a condom," he continued to beg but didn't get a response right away. A silence fell over them. Destiny was not squirming away from him anymore; she wasn't saying anything either, but her hazel eyes were as expressive as the first time he stared deeply into them.

He took her silence as compliance instead of indecisiveness. He reached over to his nightstand and grabbed a condom. He ripped open the packaging with his teeth and slid on the condom while Destiny watched his movements in the darkness of the room. He could feel her legs begin to tremble. He leaned down and kissed her reassuringly.

"Jasiah, I'm scared," Destiny whispered softly.

With his free arm, he scooped her petite frame into his grasp and said, "Don't be."

He kissed her, and he continued to kiss her until her body started to relax in his arm. Then, he moved slowly to position himself. She tensed up again and grabbed at his shoulders. Her iron grip stopped Jasiah for a moment. He waited for her to push him away or say something, but she didn't.

He pressed his weight against her gently and whispered, "Destiny, relax," as he got the tip in. She jumped and started to scoot back, but Jasiah's heavy frame had her trapped.

She looked up at him with watery eyes, pleading silently for him not to continue. He met her gaze as he slid both arms around her and playfully blew on her neck.

Destiny giggled like an innocent child.

"You trust me…. Don't you?" Jasiah asked as he stroked her hair.

Destiny lightly whispered, "Yes."

"Trust me with this," Jasiah pleaded as he lightly touched Destiny in a way that made her moan.

"Jasiah," Destiny hissed.

"Trust me," Jasiah repeated as he kissed Destiny on the neck. He caressed her body, overwhelming her senses. The euphoria of pleasure filled every vein in Destiny's body while being wheeled by Jasiah's hands.

"I trust you," Destiny confessed when her body started to ache for more. The fear in her eyes had transformed into desire. "But I'm scared," she whispered faintly.

"What are you afraid of?" he asked as he started kissing her breast. "You afraid you gonna like it?"

Destiny exhaled and enjoyed the sensation of his kisses as she felt his erection sitting between them.

He kissed her on the mouth passionately and smiled when he felt her hands roaming up and down his back. He took his chance and positioned himself to enter her again.

Destiny's mouth fell wide open as she gasped from the ripping sensation between her legs. She held onto Jasiah's back tightly, making him feel like he was surrounded by her love as he dove in deeper.

"Baby," he moaned out as he felt her insides grip him tightly.

Destiny took a deep breath as it settled in that she was losing her virginity. She closed her eyes as she embraced the pain that came with being slowly ripped open by Jasiah.

"Oh, Destiny," Jasiah moaned out again as he kissed her. She could barely kiss him back as her focus was on riding the wave of pain and finding the pleasure growing within her.

"You okay?" Jasiah asked as he tried to stroke as slowly as possible, allowing himself to relish in her tenderness.

Destiny nodded as she bit her bottom lip.

Jasiah leaned in and held her body close, securing Destiny in his love.

Destiny held him back as she felt like they couldn't get any closer. She closed her eyes, hiding her face in the crock of his neck, hoping he would finish soon. She felt his lips tenderly kiss her shoulder while pleasure started to overcome her.

The CD stopped, and there was nothing but the sound of them breathing and the bed rocking.

As Jasiah felt her body relax, he grabbed her hands and quickened his pace, making Destiny moan out. He let go of her hands and cupped her face to passionately kiss her again. She could feel him start to pulsate inside of her, which aroused her. They released simultaneous deep moans while their lips faintly touched.

Jasiah shuddered, hoping he would make Destiny feel as good as she had made him.

"Oh, my God!" Jasiah almost yelled as he lay there, going limp still inside of her.

Destiny froze, not knowing what to do. Jasiah kissed her on the forehead and raised up slowly, feeling like he was peeling himself away from her. He sat on the edge of the bed and noticed the blood on the top of the ripped condom. He got up to flush it down the toilet and started the shower. Dismissing that Destiny could get pregnant the first time they had sex. He came back into the room with a towel wrapped around his waist.

"I'ma find you a shower cap," Jasiah stated.

Destiny nodded as she sat up, squeezing her thighs together. She felt raw and tender between her legs. She brought her knees up to her chest, rested her head there, and tried to convince herself that she had not made a mistake.

Chapter 16: Decisions

Jasiah stood in line at the post office to mail a handful of packages that could change his life forever. They all would send his mother through the roof if she came to know about them. The number one thing that would anger Faye would be his letter to his father. He finally mustered up enough gumption to write Jasiah Sr. back, detailing the turmoil he felt as a fatherless child and that he would like to visit him after graduating high school.

Jasiah attempted to give the letter to the cashier first. Feeling apprehensive as he handed over the large envelope stuffed with his raw feelings and photos of himself, his fingertips wouldn't leave the edge.

"You sure you want to mail this, son?" the woman asked as she noticed him holding on to the tip of the envelope.

"Yes," Jasiah answered as he released the paper and confidently laid the rest of his outgoing mail on the counter.

North Carolina A&T, Xavier University of Louisiana, and Duke University were colleges he discussed with his guidance counselor, and they both agreed that it would be a great backup plan for Harvard. Jasiah's heart pumped faster as he paid for the postage, realizing he couldn't reverse his decision now. Even if it were just applying, his mother would question his motives when the acceptance or rejection letters rolled in.

Sitting in the car, he looked through his CDs before heading to his first day back at *Netaspend, McMillian & Associates* since he worked there over the summer. Though Jasiah usually drove in silence to ponder his decisions, he decided to play the Marvin Gaye CD *"What's Going On"* this time. As he rubbed fingerprints from the CD to make sure it didn't skip, his pager went off. It was from Destiny: *Break a leg.* Jasiah smiled, thinking that's what he told her when she had an interview.

He was humming the tune of *"Distant Lover"* as he entered the office building on Connecticut Avenue. He felt nervous for the first time. Even though he has been coming to the office for what felt like his entire life—he felt the weight of this internship. This was the first time he had to juggle between his classwork and work. As he opened the large, frosted glass door to the office suite, he remembered his instructions from Roy, *"Ask for the Hiring Manager, not him."*

"You here for Mr. Netaspend?" the receptionist, Megan, inquired as soon as Jasiah stood before her.

"Mrs. Gossan, please," Jasiah informed her of his intent as he grabbed a mint from the bowl on her desk.

"Oh, one moment," Megan looked surprised.

Jasiah looked around at the Christmas décor as he waited. The large red and white poinsettias and oversized Christmas tree were extremely similar to the décor in his home.

"Mr. Sheffield, you're right on time," a voice erupted from behind him.

Jasiah turned around and smiled at the hiring manager. She had called him 'Mr. Sheffield' since he was a little boy playing around her desk on afternoons when he came to the office with his mother. They hugged briefly.

"I was surprised when Mr. Netaspend told me you would intern with us during the school year. I didn't know you were seriously interested in this career path."

Jasiah nodded as he followed her. "More corporate law than criminal, but I'm definitely interested."

"We need more Black lawyers in any focus," she responded as they entered her office.

She gave Jasiah a packet of paperwork to complete before handing him a Blackberry and showing him his cubical among the paralegals. He would start assisting them with research. He went through the afternoon in training and never saw Roy or Chad. By the end of the day, Roy was coming through the door, and Jasiah was exiting.

"Getting settled in?" Roy asked his stepson, never looking up from his Blackberry.

Jasiah nodded, "Yep."

"Great."

They continued on their way to separate destinations. Jasiah looked at his watch and texted Destiny while he waited for the elevator: *OMW*.

He figured he could pick Destiny up from work at least twice a week since he was already in the downtown area.

"So, how was your first day?" Destiny inquired after she greeted Jasiah with a kiss on the cheek.

"It was mostly paperwork and learning how to work a new damn copier," he responded.

"I hate entering those billable codes," she recognized.

"Exactly," Jasiah rested his hand on Destiny's leg as he drove. "So, can we get a quick bite to eat, or do you have to get home?"

"I'm sure we have enough for you at home," Destiny answered. "I have to make sure my nephews did their homework, and I could definitely use your help with this Calculus homework."

Jasiah nodded. "Now you know I'm looking forward to some alone time with you," he looked over at Destiny. It had been over a week since they had sex for the first time. He didn't want another weekend to go by with her avoiding him. "Can you fit me into your schedule this weekend?"

Destiny bit her bottom lip as she nodded. "I just got an invitation to the holiday party at my job. It's going to be in Old Town Alexandria. A black-tie affair," she informed Jasiah so that he wouldn't start an uncomfortable conversation about sex with her.

"Do I get to be your plus one?"

"Of course," Destiny smiled. "I know you have a suit."

"Girl, I'll get a tux if you ask me to," Jasiah playfully squeezed her thigh.

Destiny smiled. "What do you want for Christmas?" Destiny inquired.

"You," Jasiah answered without hesitation.

Destiny rolled her eyes.

"Whatever you get me is fine," Jasiah shrugged. "And I have an idea of what I want you to have. I want to see how well I know you."

Destiny smiled. She felt like she was smiling all evening as her father asked Jasiah if he was hungry instead of asking Destiny, "What is this little nigga doing here?" like he would have mumbled with Eric. She changed her clothes before they ate, and Jasiah completed Destiny's homework while she helped her nephews with theirs. He also watched the first quarter of Monday night football while Destiny cleaned the kitchen. She could hear her phone ringing upstairs and admired Jasiah and her father talking as she went to answer it.

"What are you doing?" Bria asked on the other line.

"Cleaning the kitchen," Destiny answered as she started downstairs with the cordless phone stuck to her ear. This time, when she passed the living room, she giggled at Jasiah yelling at the television, thinking her family had rubbed off on him.

"Your brother over there for the game?" Bria inquired.

"Girl, that's Jasiah."

"He over there like that?" Bria sounded shocked.

"Yeah... him and my father are watching the game... what's up?"

"I was calling to ask your opinion on something, but never mind," Bria sighed.

"Okay," Destiny quickly responded. "I'll call you after he leaves. Cool?"

"Yeah, that's cool," Bria accepted before hanging up.

All of the anxiety she felt months earlier was a distant memory as Destiny listened to Jasiah and her father discuss player stats during commercial breaks. But once she finished cleaning the kitchen, she slipped on her Timberlands by the door, handed Jasiah a wrapped plate of leftovers, and told him it was time to go before he could overstay his welcome.

"I'm coming every day," Jasiah stated as he sat his plate on the car and pulled Destiny into his chest to shield her from the cold.

"Mr. Peay gonna start asking for money on the food bill," Destiny joked.

"He can have it," Jasiah kissed her on the lips, "as long as I can have you."

"Jasiah, get home safely," she pulled away. "Call me when you get settled in the house."

"A'ight," Jasiah opened his car door. He sat his plate inside. He turned around to see why he could still feel Destiny next to him. Generally, she would rush back into the house and wave at him from the door. He thought she wanted another kiss, a reason for them to connect. But instead of her waiting in longing, he found a masked gunman who had a gun to Destiny's head. Jasiah knew that she and he had the same bewildered looks on their faces.

"Give me those keys, muthafuckah," the guy yelled, now pointing the barrel of the gun at Jasiah.

Jasiah quickly threw the keys at him, yelling, "Here!" as he reached for Destiny. He was ready to pull Destiny with him out of the way and let the assailant have one of his prized possessions.

But before the masked man could enter the car, a brick hit him in the head.

Jasiah and Destiny turned to see Freddie Bush standing there, heaving over the gunman, who was trying to scramble on the ground. Freddie Bush placed his huge foot on the masked gunman's armed hand, making the gun fall to the ground.

"Get your father!" he yelled.

Destiny instantaneously lifted her foot and stomped the gunman in the face. Jasiah ran into the house to tell Mr. Peay what was going on outside. When he looked back, he could see Destiny still enraged, repeatedly kicking the gunman wherever her Timberland landed while Freddie Bush stood watch. Jasiah had never seen such rage in Destiny's eyes.

"What the fuck, Destiny?" Mr. Peay stated as he pulled her away from the assailant and kicked the gun farther away.

"Call the police," Destiny responded as she backed away, gasping for air. She sat on the stoop to catch her breath and gain her composure. "Call the police!" she screamed as tears streamed down her face.

"Oh God," Mr. Peay stated as he pulled Destiny by the arm. "Get your ass in the house!"

"Jasiah," Destiny called his name. He was frozen in place with fear. "Jasiah!" Destiny screamed, hoping her voice would bring him out of the trance as her father dragged her into the house, away from the scene as people started coming out of their homes.

Jasiah turned to Freddie Bush, the man he once saw sprawled on the ground, now standing tall like a guard. "Get your car keys and go in the house," Freddie Bush urged as he closed the car door and leaned on it before taking a pint of Velicoff Vodka from his back pocket and gulping the contents.

Jasiah picked up his keys, just inches from the gunman that lay unconscious at Freddie Bush's feet. He made his way into the house as the sound of police sirens grew near. Inside the house, Destiny was pacing the floor, and her father was on the phone.

When she looked up at Jasiah, she grabbed him, and they held one another tightly. Destiny whispered, "We're okay… we're okay," into Jasiah's chest; both of their heartbeats attempted to normalize.

"Aunt Dee, you have paint on your boots," one of the twins yelled.

Both Destiny and Jasiah looked down to see the blood on her right Timberland.

Then Destiny noticed the trail of bloody boot prints she had left on the floor.

"Shit!" Destiny cursed.

"Watch your mouth," Mr. Peay told his daughter casually as he headed back out the door. "Jasiah, I called Roy. He is on his way."

Jasiah sat down, nervously awaiting Destiny to clean up the floor. He wanted to hold her again and hoped that he could find some words to describe how he felt.

"Go to your room," Destiny finally told her nephews.

Jasiah watched the boys run up the stairs.

"Destiny, are you okay?" he finally figured out something to say.

"I'm fine," she shrugged. "I just need some new boots," She tried to joke, but Jasiah couldn't laugh. She sighed. "I can't believe someone tried to carjack you in front of my house," she added as she looked at Jasiah. "Are you okay?"

He felt compelled to lie, "I'm fine… I'm just glad Freddie Bush figured out how to stand on his own two feet today."

They both laughed. "This is the most sober I've ever seen him," Destiny added. "I haven't seen him stand up this straight in years..." Destiny stretched as her mind started to wander.

Jasiah was quiet because he didn't know what to do next.

"I'm sure we'll have to give a statement," Destiny continued as she headed toward the door.

Jasiah followed her. When they reached the doorway, the mask was off the gunman, and the two of them were unprepared for what they saw.

It was Eric. Bloodied, bruised, and handcuffed while an officer read him his Miranda rights.

Destiny gasped as she watched her neighbor's prying eyes. She moved her neck around to loosen some of the tension that was building up in her.

"I'm supposed to be able to protect you," Jasiah whispered as he wrapped his arms around Destiny, "But I didn't think it would have to be from your ex."

"I'm sorry," Destiny apologized as she watched the police talk to her father.

Jasiah hugged Destiny tightly and whispered. "I would have given him anything to make sure you were safe."

Jasiah's words felt genuine and reassuring to Destiny as she leaned into him for a brief moment. She took a deep breath, but as she inhaled and looked at Eric from a distance, her entire body started to fill with rage.

"I told you he wasn't nothing but a lil' nigga," Mr. Peay hollered at his daughter once he noticed her standing in the doorway. "See what the fuck I'm talking about? You see what lack of motivation and desperation looks like?!"

"Why would you do that?" Rage spilled into Destiny's words as she left Jasiah's side. It was like her father's words were, "On your mark... ready...set... go!" sending Destiny out the house and descending the stairs to approach Eric. "What is wrong with you?"

Eric mustered up the remnants of his strength to yell, "Fuck you! Fuck you and him!"

Before anyone knew it, Destiny cocked back and hit Eric in the jaw with a left-handed hook.

A loud cracking noise traversed through the block. Everyone watching yelled in unison, "Whoa!"

"Hey, hey, hey," the police quickly turned Eric away from Destiny as blood spewed from his mouth while another attempted to grab her.

"I got her… I got her!" Mr. Peay yelled firmly as he came closer to his daughter, blocking her from the police's touch. "I can control her. Her emotions are just running a bit high right now."

"So, you two know one another?" the police officer asked.

"*Eric Jackson* of 1314 E Street Northeast," Destiny responded.

***

Those words echoed in Jasiah's mind once he finally got home that night. *Eric Jackson of 1314 E Street Northeast.*

He tossed and turned, thinking of how his evening with Destiny started out so great and ended so ugly because of *Eric Jackson of 1314 E Street Northeast*. Jasiah didn't know when he finally drifted off to sleep after the umpteenth time remembering Destiny's fury. He had never witnessed a woman behave like she did at the threat of danger. He couldn't imagine her turning so violent. His mind was foggy as he started to ponder if his mother was right about staying away from the Peays.

However, in the morning, he was awakened by Destiny's calling. Jasiah regretted not closing his curtains last night as he felt blinded by the bright sunlight in his room.

"How are you, handsome?" she asked in the sweet tone she always used.

"I don't know," Jasiah answered, not wanting to admit how traumatized he was by last night's ordeal.

A long pause sat on the phone with them as they both tried to figure out what to say next to one another.

"What did your mom say when you got home last night?" Destiny inquired, as she felt a little hurt that he didn't ask how she was doing. "She wouldn't even get out of the car."

"She said a lot," Jasiah admitted as he stretched and wiped the goop out of his eye. "I couldn't sleep last night."

"Me either," Destiny acknowledged. "I can't believe Eric did that."

"How did he know I was there?" Jasiah questioned. "Was he stalking you?"

"Bria called while I was washing the dishes, and I told her I would call her back once you left," Destiny recalled. "But I would never guess that—"

"Destiny, if she set me up… that's messed up," Jasiah sighed.

Another silence fell over them. Destiny stared at the ceiling of her bedroom and Jasiah was doing the same in his own bedroom.

"Jasiah, I hope you're not blaming me." Destiny broke the silence. "I had no idea that—"

"Destiny, I believe you had no idea. I know you wouldn't do that to me, to us… But my mother isn't convinced."

Destiny cursed under her breath.

"She kept asking me last night if you were worth it…. If being with you was worth my life… If I could—"

"Are you breaking up with me?" Destiny interjected as she felt like he was taking the air out of her lungs as he spoke.

"Destiny, I love you... It's just—" Jasiah didn't want to say that maybe his mother was right all along. She knew something bad would happen, and he knew he couldn't stick around to see if the violence surrounding Destiny would get worse.

At that moment, as he lay in his bed, he started to acknowledge that the chasm between their lives was wider than they could ever imagine.

"It's just what, Jasiah?" Destiny wanted him to finish his statement as she curled up under her covers.

She winced at the memory of the cold steel firmly pressed against her head when she closed her eyes and prepared herself for Jasiah to tell her they didn't belong together. Both moments that she never thought she would experience in life.

Jasiah exhaled while Destiny waited with bated breath. He looked over at the photo of them on his nightstand. Running his thumb over her photo, he knew he wasn't prepared to break his own heart. Even with all that transpired the night before, he was still intoxicated with Destiny, her eyes, her tenderness, her resolve.

"We just need to figure out how we will see one another again," Jasiah concluded.

Destiny didn't realize she was holding her breath until she took her next breath, filled with relief.

"I love you, Jasiah," she whispered.

"I love you too, Shawty," he affirmed as her words made him smile. "I want to see you," he added.

To Be Continued...

Epilogue

Laws of Life Scholarship Essay Contest

Destiny Peay

12th grade – Dunbar High School

ESSAY PROMPT: *Discuss recent laws that are shaping your community.*

The Nation's Capital is experiencing a rise in crime under the tutelage of Mayor Anthony A. Williams. While he has focused his administration on gentrifying the District, he has cut one thousand DC Jobs, leaving many civilians destitute under the guise of "management reform savings."

The loss of employment has had a trickle effect on our society as a whole. The Chocolate City is riddled with violence, leaving young African American residents as the target. Statistics show that 1 out of 300 residents have a chance of being victims of a violent crime. However, my question is, does this statistic include violence at the hands of those who took an oath to protect and serve?

Recent reports by The Washington Post have claimed that the Metropolitan Police Department shot and killed more DC residents in the 1990s than any other prominent American city police force. These statistics make Washington, DC, the perfect place to rally and protest not only because it is the Nation's Capital but also because it is the epicenter of the police brutality rampage.

Many would say that the increase in police-related shootings is in direct relationship to the current War on Drugs. With many neighborhoods being plagued by the crack epidemic, reports show that not only has the murder rate of young Black males doubled, but it has also created a movement of mass incarceration. Since the creation of the 1994 Crime Bill, the country has had a 300% increase in the number of people in prisons and jails.

Washington, DC, has contributed to those statistics, leading to new burdens on families and its own social services. The prison incarceration rate tripled that of the jail incarceration rate in the District from 1990-1997. Due to the National Capital Revitalization Self-Government Improvement Act of 1997, felons from the District of Columbia were scattered around the country to various federal faculties because the prison, which was 20 miles from the city, was closed. This action further broke up connections in Black families due to distance and diminished the mental health of offenders.

So now I ask, across the country, is this violence caused by those who took an oath to uphold the civil liberties for all?